The Oath

The Oath

Henry Cantleberry

Dedication

For Leah and Olivia, I could not have written a word without your love and support.

Contents

Contents

Chapter I
The Raid

They came in the night. A rampant black fog preceded the raid, enveloping every shrub, tree, and hut in the Crestwood. The hidden stampede was thunderous and unmistakable. The shrieking of raiders, stamping hooves, and the clanging of swords echoed throughout the valley.

Cal woke in confusion and fear as a torch crashed through his window and rolled across the floorboards. He leapt from his bed and stamped it out, but more landed with a thud onto his roof. He could do nothing about them.

As the vandals screeched outside his window, his attention was drawn to them. *Who were these raiders, and why had they come?* He tiptoed to the window and peered out. The black fog obscured almost everything except one raider, illuminated by his burning home.

The creature was nothing like anything Cal had ever seen or heard of. Cal was drawn to its deep green eyes that were wreathed in flames; they were the only clear thing among the black fog. As he looked further, he found a silhouette of a two-headed horned beast plodding on four cloven feet in front of his home. The creature carried a sword in one hand and a glowing staff in the other. Cal's breath froze.

He peeked out further to better understand what he was seeing, but three arrows suddenly flew through the window, narrowly missing him as he barreled onto the floor.

His palms and elbows chafed against the wooden floor; the sting ignited his anger. "Gods damn you all!" Cal spat.

Curled on the floor, he protected his face from the heat of the smoldering rafters above. As cool air blew between the floorboards, a realization struck him.

"The crawlspace!" It was his only means to escape.

All he had to do was remove two, maybe three, floorboards, crawl to the back of the farmhouse, and escape into the woods. This was his only hope.

He grabbed his knife from his trousers and jammed it between the floor panels as glowing red embers rained around the cabin. He pried with all his strength to lift just one board as the cabin filled with smoke and left him gasping for air. The board lifted, but there was scarcely enough space to get even his smallest finger through. He thrashed the blade back and forth until, finally, the gap opened. The cool air from below whooshed through the gap and filled his lungs.

With one last effort, he dug both hands underneath the board and yanked it free. He was almost clear and it was just in time.

As air rushed into the room, the fire sprang to life, igniting the curtains, his bed, and every splintered wood. With his remaining strength, he forwent the knife and urgently tugged the next board, snapping it in his hands. He had broken through and dove into the cool underbelly of the crawlspace as the burning rafters came crashing down.

His escape was far from complete. Even among the dirt, he could breathe again as the air rushed over him and was sucked into the flames. He crawled as quickly as possible, finally reaching the panel to his rear yard, and gently cracked it open. The flames gave enough light to see much of the rear yard through the black fog. It looked clear, but the panel obscured much of his view. He held his breath and listened for them, but he heard neither raiders nor horses behind his home.

"Now is as good a time as any," Cal muttered, wiping his brow. He kept a firm grasp of his pants with one hand, his knife with the other, took three deep breaths, and broke open the panel.

He bolted through the dark yard and into the woods. The night air whipped past as he frantically ran from his home. The farther he distanced himself from the raid, the clearer the night appeared before him, as if the black fog dissipated behind him.

After dodging several trees and bushes, he found a large mound to hide behind. He listened for approaching hoofbeats among the dense forest but nothing came. He saw only the black night and heard only his heart pounding in his chest. He exhaled a deep breath of relief, knowing he had escaped the immediate danger.

In the distance, he saw the blaze roaring in the dark. *Who were they? Why had they come? Why'd they burn him out?* Curiosity gnawed at him as the faint sound of the raiders echoed through the forest. Their shields and spears rattled endlessly as they shouted into the night, but no sound revealed their identity and the black fog obscured everything.

They reminded him of the tall tales folk told at the tavern. Most were just stories, but the churning in Cal's stomach told him some of them might be true enough. As far as he could tell, the black fog and their glowing eyes were unprecedented, real, and it terrified him. If he was going to find out who they were, he'd have to quietly sneak back.

He removed his boots, put on his trousers, and began a slow stooping crawl, doing his best to avoid the brush. He picked up his pace as the sound of the flames drowned out each step he took. As he crept closer, the night sky once again became visible and the great void of blackness trailed farther into the valley; the marauders moved with the fog.

Still shaking, Cal hid himself on the edge of the woods, crawling along the ground in the tall weeds. The firelight flickered all around, reflecting off every leaf; his home was fully engulfed. The heat kept him warm and vigilant throughout the night. It dawned on him that his neighbors might see his home like a beacon and come to his aid. As he sat with hope in his heart, he gazed down into the valley and knew his neighbors would not come. Their homes, too, were burning.

For the rest of the night, his eyes were fixed upon the road, awaiting the return of the raiders, but they did not come. When dawn passed, he emerged from the brush and gazed around the husk that was his cabin. What was left was still smoldering, and the air was filled with ash and smoke. Cal clenched his fists in frustration. All he wanted was a coat before trudging into town to warn the elders.

He glanced over at his makeshift stable and was pleased to find it had not burned down, but his mare, Alice, was nowhere in sight. That was poor luck as well. The walk to town would take him at least until late afternoon without his horse.

Upon closer inspection, Cal found no sign of blood, but her door was broken open from the inside; that was a fortune he welcomed. Alice knew all the trails around the farm, but he suspected she might be hiding around the field. Before he left to find her, he picked a horse blanket off the ground, shook it, and threw it over his shoulders.

Cal silently crept toward his modest corn field. Although he was confident no raiders remained, he strove to be hidden. The field was untouched by the raid and the hair on Cal's neck raised. *Why weren't the fields burnt? Did they come to just kill me?* As the plumes of smoke rose in the valley, he remembered this attack was about more than him. Someone had attacked many Crestfolk, and he'd feel much better if he found himself reunited with other survivors. However, his first step was to find Alice.

Cal searched the wood and the field in hopes of finding her. After a few moments, he decided to chance a whistle and blew. Silence followed for some time, but after a long minute, a palomino trotted between the rows. Although her blonde coat was dusted with the ashes, she happily trotted toward him. Cal couldn't help but smile as she fell right into his arms.

"We're gonna be okay, girl," Cal said, patting and looking her over from her head to her hooves. After a thorough review, she nuzzled right into his chest, forcing him back. She was fine. He didn't take any more time and hopped onto her back. He felt her coarse hair through his fingers, and her heartbeat quickened. They were both ready to get away from all the ash and dust. He gave one squeeze, and they were off.

Cal headed to the Fork, the northernmost village in the Crestwood. Nestled at the base of a serrated mountain range, it was one of three crossings over the treacherous River White. The jagged mountain range strung together over three hundred leagues around the wood in the shape of a great crescent. Folks called the realm "the Crest" for short. This was his home.

By midday, Cal arrived at the Fork. At first sight, Cal felt as if someone had punched him in the gut. All the village was burnt down, and nearly every structure was destroyed. The stone walls were blackened, and several chimneys toppled over onto the streets. The brave few folks who survived the fires were found scattered outside their homes lying over patches of dry blood where the raiders cut them down. There was no one left.

Cal stopped his horse and gazed at the town. The elders, his friends, everyone he knew had been killed and he didn't know why. He all but dropped his reins in despair when finally, someone caught his eye… someone alive.

Bill stood in the middle of what used to be his store with a broom in his hand. He was a slightly pudgy, older, and pale man who had settled at the Fork many years ago. He had a short white beard that merged into his horseshoe bald patterned head. He once owned a well sought-out shop among the Fork and he always prided himself on having all the necessary items for the weary traveler. He'd often say to any passing through the Fork, 'he traded in trade.'

At the moment, Bill looked adrift. His shelves were broken, his stores were burnt, and there was no one else around to share a friendly nod. As Cal looked on, Bill began sweeping and clearing a path from one end of the shop to the other. Cal grinned at his friend; Bill had it right.

They had been partners for a few years. When the last of Cal's family died, Bill took it upon himself to better befriend and mentor him. If he hadn't, the town elders would have likely whipped Cal for any number of offenses by now.

Cal was twenty and ambitious. He always looked for other opportunities once his mother had gone and Bill always liked that about him. Cal had the trim figure, and enough muscle to move any supply crate Bill had ever asked of him. His hair was short, shaggy brown, and his face was young enough to pass for a misguided youth, but his chin bore sufficient hairs to say otherwise. Once their partnership had formed, the pair often found themselves discreetly trading one item or another about the Fork and then around the Crestwood.

Cal rode toward him grinning from ear to ear. When Bill looked up and found the familiar young man riding bareback into the village, he was shocked.

"Gods be damned! It's good to see ya, lad!" Bill called, dropping the broom to the ground and jogging over to him.

"Are you hurt, Bill?" Cal asked, dismounting Alice and greeting Bill with a hearty hug.

"I'm fine," Bill replied, slapping Cal's back as his eyes glossed over.

Of all the folk, Cal was relieved his friend survived.

"It's good to see ya, lad, but there's noth'n left!" Bill lamented, waving his hand across the town. "They didn't stand a chance."

Many of the dead were scattered throughout the streets; everyone else had burned up inside their homes and shops. The town was charred, hollow, and crumbling. A good fall wind would eventually blow the remaining buildings over and the forest would reclaim what was left. It would be like there had never been a village.

Bill grimaced. "We can't leave 'em to the crows or worse."

Cal let out a long sigh. He hoped to find help among the Fork, but there was none to be found. Everything fell on their shoulders.

"No, I suppose you're right. I think all we can do is collect those along the road for the pyre. We have to move on... the raiders will return."

"We need to stay put till morn'n," Bill insisted, waving Cal aside. "We won't travel but a few leagues until the night comes and they'll be after us, mark my words."

Cal looked over the ruins of his village bewildered. There was no shelter left. "Whereabouts, Bill? It's all gone."

"The cellar again. I've gathered what food an' supplies we need," Bill reassured, pointing to the cellar door.

Cal reluctantly looked over the scorched hatch face. It was blackened and charred like every other surface. He was a little more comforted, realizing they could be concealed. Yet also, to Bill's point, it was getting late and he didn't want to be out in the open wood at night. Cal let out a long sigh and agreed to stay.

They first gathered the remaining goods that had survived the flames and brought them into the cellar. They collected the sacks of potatoes, turnips, and grains. There, Bill kept a variety of wines untouched from the raids aside from the two recently emptied bottles. Cal wagered Bill depleted them the evening prior.

Cal also found almost all the furs and clothes had gone up in the fire, but luckily he found a green tunic that fit him. They also found several knives and bows survived unscathed behind the counter. Bill was by no means any good at hunting but Cal had a knack for the bow. He could hit a squirrel on the worst day and the Crestwood was bountiful, if you only applied yourself.

Once the cellar was stocked, they spent the rest of the afternoon gathering the dead. They placed them near a home where embers from the previous night still glowed. At sunset, the pyre was stoked with fresh fuel, but neither man wished to stay long. They lingered until the last light of the day and the silence spoke as loud as any last words they could have given.

Bill wept for a moment, and Cal felt it too. Everyone they knew had been erased. Cal clenched his fists in anger. He didn't know who these raiders were or why they had come, but there was nothing more they could do that day. Before the sun sank, they gave their neighbors the only fitting end they could.

Bill raised his head enough to nod at Cal. It was time. He led Alice just inside the woods and tied her up. It was risky leaving her exposed, but there was no other choice. He lightly tied her to a tree in hopes she would have sense enough to make herself scarce again if they were to return. At this point, all Cal could really do was hope. Just as the last light vanished from the treetops, he gave her a pat, returned to the burned-down store, and descended into the cellar.

The cellar was cold, but it was dry. Cal layered himself with what spare hides remained, and Bill spent a moment fastening the hatch on the inside. He tied off a rope to the stairs, to the hatch, and back to the stairs.

"That ought to do yer," Bill muttered, knotting the rope thoroughly.

They were both exhausted. This day had been fire and death, and it felt good to embrace the cool cellar at the end of the trying day.

"Drink deep," Cal said, handing a wineskin over to Bill. It was quickly emptied; the wine helped with the courage.

The cold crept in. Each man bundled himself in layers of burlap and drank to keep them warm. They sampled a variety of vintages that evening as they rested by a solitary flickering candle while lying in bedding made of the remaining furs that reeked of smoke and sweat.

"If we don't make it, think of the poor soul who might find us among the taters and turnips," Cal jested, wrapping his legs in burlap. Both men hemmed and hawed back and forth, urging the other to quiet himself among the echoes.

"We'll be found out if we don't stop," Bill laughed, tears falling from the corner of his eyes.

As Cal wiped his cheeks, he was taken aback with the small joy he felt at the end of an awful day. It was almost over but they needed to look past it. "I think we're of the same mind on where to go... the Mid?" Cal asked.

Middletown, or the Mid as everyone called it, was seventy-three leagues south. The city had walls, supplies, and the soldiers at hand to confront the raids. That's where they would find aid.

"Aye," Bill replied, wiping his mouth. "We'll take what rations we're need'n for a weeks' travel an' make through the country south. As long as we're keep'n off the main road an' the White on the right, we can't miss."

Cal nodded and settled in for a long night. His smile faded with every passing moment. There was little to do except quietly drink and stare at the hatch the raiders might enter.

"Do you think they might see the light?" he asked, hiding his trembling voice.

"I reckon not with everything else smoke'n an' crackl'n up there," Bill said. "Fret not, we'll make it through the nights, an' to the Mid without notice."

Cal took some comfort in what the old man said but not his eyes. Bill averted his gaze fighting against the same fear of what unknown creature might be prowling among the woods.

Cal removed his dagger from its sheath and placed it close to his side. Should any beast make trouble this evening, he swore he would not go out without a fight. As the evening passed and the candle slowly dimmed, Cal kept his eyes firmly fixed on the hatch that led outside.

Chapter II
The Council

Sir Kenneth stared out of the Mid's keep as a flood of refugees poured in from across the north. Dregs, he called them. Whatever had routed them from the north was no concern of his, but as the Commander of the Midguard, the influx of refugees had become his personal daily headache.

It was chaos. He was charged with keeping the peace, yet there was none to be found. The inns and taverns were filled to the brim with Crestfolk and their troubles. Why Lord Malcolm allowed them to infest the city was beyond him. There was nothing to do except use a firm hand to keep everyone in line.

Sir Kenneth had been summoned to a high council meeting with the Lord of the Mid while the local Merchant's Guild stood around the chamber hanging on every word. As far as he was concerned, most of the councilmen were misguided lordlings, and they, no doubt, wanted to discuss the rumors of mysterious demons plaguing the realm. Sir Kenneth knew otherwise.

The rumors surrounding the raiders were codswallop and hearsay. This attack was caused by no more than brigands and lowly marauders. Day after day, the situation deteriorated and bile rose in the back of his throat.

Sir Kenneth waded through dozens of merchantmen who filled the outer hall of the council chamber. Men with feathered hats, velvet coats, and greedy hands. How deeply they could fill their pockets was always their first concern. They were not without their uses. The Mid's position among the realms was a direct result of the continuous trade from east to west.

The Mid rose steadily for hundreds of years into a major trade city. The merchants here fared better than the Masters of the Twin Harbors, and by leaps and bounds better than the Masters of the Fork. At the Harbors, the boatmen made their coin ferrying men and supplies, but it was a slow crossing.

The larger caravans preferred the Mid where the river was narrow, the bridges were high, and the merchants bought their way into the council chamber. In Sir Kenneth's opinion, the council should be governed solely by noblemen. If it were, his lordship would not be tethered down by the thoughts of lesser men.

Yet, they were not the worst offenders in the hall. Lord Malcolm welcomed Darwishmen, Elvians, and nomads as much as their trade. He didn't have to break up the day-to-day disputes. Sir Kenneth did, and he had little patience left for any of it.

While he waited for his lordship to receive them, Master Gregory waddled over to speak with him. Gregory was a merchantman of the family Kearn who could trace their heritage to the settling of the Mid. His family were among the wealthy few who prospered from the trade monopoly and kept their hold on power for hundreds of years. He was among the greediest and most conniving council members.

"Good day, Master Gregory," Sir Kenneth said dryly. "How goes the trade?"

"As well as can be expected, Constable," Gregory sighed.

Sir Kenneth gritted his teeth. He never liked being referred to as a "Constable." It was an old and antiquated name for his position that had long since been elevated. After all, he commanded seventeen hundred Men-at-Arms who kept the peace of tens of thousands of folk. His men referred to him as Commander, but the small folk would not let the name tradition die.

"Just last week, I received fine silks and wines from the northeast," Gregory remarked. "You know, the Elvian dry red. And this week, the carts trickle in with little or nothing at all. Some markets have stopped entirely. Every day, more Crestfolk crowd our streets looking for a harbor among the storms of the north, I tell you. We'll be overrun in a few days!"

"I assure you, Master Gregory, we will have order and the trade will flow. There's nothing out there but brigands and ruffians. I have half a mind to rid the city of all the Crestfolk, but our lord will have none of it."

"I am sure the situation could be resolved in several ways. I know you've heard your share of the rumors from the north. Perhaps we may be able to convince the good lord that action should be taken to resolve this influx of folk," Gregory whispered.

Sir Kenneth raised his eyebrows in surprise. *Did Gregory have the necessary support from the other council members to force such evictions?* It was the surest way in the Knight's mind to restore the peace among the city, but before he inquired further, the older councilman surveyed the hall and motioned the Knight to come closer.

"We must hastily return order to our city and secure our trade routes! Of course, if we can, it would be beneficial to temporarily aid these people in some fashion. I'd wager you can be counted on to support such an end?" he whispered.

"Of course! The guard is working tirelessly to quell the unrest and keep the peace. But I am convinced we would do well to move these people along," Sir Kenneth said without hesitation.

"Then we must, as a unified council, demand action from our good Lord Malcolm. I have no doubt he will accept our position," Gregory declared.

"What request will you make of him?" Sir Kenneth questioned as he eyed the merchantman warily.

"Leave your concerns to me, sir. We shall see your ranks swell with good men to combat this plague, and the city will soon return to us. However, first, I have a few more members to seek out and I will see you in the great hall," Master Gregory concluded. He nodded to Sir Kenneth and then made his way around the great hall.

Additional troops were appealing, but Sir Kenneth didn't know where Gregory would find such folk. He would need at least double or triple the number of men to swiftly round up the Crestfolk and steer them in a southerly direction. After all, Sir Kenneth wasn't a cruel man. He would not turn folks back north toward whatever their problems were, but priorities demand he close the borders and set outposts beyond the city.

"Commander?"

Sir Kenneth turned to find his young red-haired captain briskly moving toward him. Willem wore the burgundy tunic of the city watch and the emblem of the Mid over his heart: a blue bridge spanning a white river. He stood out among his captains as young, eager, and sometimes naive.

"Sir, I have just received another report confirming the northern Crestwood homes are afire," he exclaimed as Sir Kenneth quickly pulled the young man aside.

"How did you come by this?" he whispered.

"The skinners and pelt traders are reporting the frontier homes can be seen smoking from one valley to the next. Robyn Carrol said he turned his mule around as soon as he saw it, sir."

"That means very little," Kenneth insisted. "For all we know, he saw their chimneys!"

"I don't think so, sir," Willem stammered. "Robyn said the smoke was as thick and black as tar. It filled up the sky with more than just chimney smoke, sir."

"Damn!" Sir Kenneth exclaimed, planting his hands on his hips. He had hoped not to confirm the news to the council, but more than likely he wasn't the first person to hear it.

"Keep me informed of any other reports," he snapped.

"Yes, sir. One more thing, the Par'sha have arrived and have been received by Lord Malcolm as we speak, sir," Willem continued.

The blood rushed to Sir Kenneth's temples. The Par'sha were a hardy nomadic people with hundreds of sparring factions. Their territory was east of the Crescent realm and spanned a thousand leagues. They roamed through a vast sea of grasses and bluffs and followed herds of antelope and bison as the seasons changed.

They notoriously kept to themselves. When the Par'sha did engage with the Western peoples, they were known to shed blood in defense of their rights and territories. They were distinguished fighters and riders of strange and exotic animals like mammoths and giant bear-sloths. They would surround the caravan trains with all manner of mounted giants and would hurl long darts by the hundreds. Sir Kenneth sighed and rubbed his temple as he considered this development.

"Who came, and what did they say?" Sir Kenneth asked.

"Sir, Su'ca claims to be the daughter of a great Par'sha chief named Craa'su. She said she speaks on behalf of all the nomads, and she would only speak to the lord of the city, sir. So, the guard brought them here and his lordship received them first thing, sir. Damndest thing!"

Sir Kenneth had heard of very few clan leaders from the nomad folk. Craa'su was the exception and his reputation was fiercely renowned. If the Par'sha ambassador was his daughter, then Sir Kenneth imagined she would be an ardent negotiator.

"You did well, Willem. Ensure they are escorted, without incident, and returned outside the city once they have concluded their business!" Sir Kenneth commanded.

"Will they not stay for an evening, commander?"

"Not likely. They do not dwell in the cities for long. However, if I am wrong, I will find out," Sir Kenneth replied. He dismissed Willem to continue his duties and immediately made his way toward the main hall. Sir Kenneth fervently tried to stay outside of the politics between the Mid and any other peoples, but the morning had presented him with too many quandaries and coincidences for him not to act. He needed to know the intentions of the Par'sha because the defense of the city would likely depend on it.

The main doors to the great hall stood as tall as the height of three men. They were made of rich dark-red mahogany and the history of the Mid and the families who built her was carved into every groove. Sir Kenneth's own family, Gyle, was privileged enough to be mentioned among the founders.

The guards opened the doors without hesitation for their commander. As he passed through the doorway, his name and title were announced and reverberated through the hall. The Par'sha party turned to examine the new arrival as he approached the Lord's high table, and all eyes in the hall met him.

The Par'sha were made up of five members. All were garbed in weathered animal leathers, and their own complexions were as dark as their animal skins if not darker. Their jewelry was fashioned of bone, gold, copper, bright white and orange feathers, and blue glass beads. Su'ca was centered among her people but appeared far more decorated than her peers. She had more exotic paints upon her skin, her wrists and neck were adorned with precious beads and metals, and her shoulders were covered by the hide of a great brown bear.

Lord Malcolm sat at the center of a long, semi-oval wooden table. Seated beside him were his most trusted advisors, his wife Lady Alma and his senior advisor, Master Hector. Malcolm's family was one of the oldest and noblest families of the Mid and they had long been the stewards of the city.

"Please continue, my lady," Lord Malcolm said diplomatically. Su'ca returned to her conversation, and the interruption and silence ended.

"It was agreed our territory would not be trespassed," Su'ca coldly continued.

"And we have not broken that agreement," Lord Malcolm calmly retorted.

"Then who has set aflame the great grass-sea? Who has plagued our land and slaughtered the great herds? Who has broken the agreement?" she demanded.

"That was not my people and, to my knowledge, no peoples of the west."

"We know the west is where the attackers have come from. The Par'sha will not be intimidated!" she maintained.

Lord Malcolm gazed back at Su'ca, unmoved. "You are not wrong, Su'ca, daughter of the great Chief Craa'su."

"My Lord?" Master Hector questioned, tilting his head to one side. The lord held up a hand, and silence gripped the advisor. The lord turned from his advisor; his gaze met Sir Kenneth's.

"Have you confirmed the rumors, Commander?" Lord Malcolm inquired.

All eyes fell to him. This was not how Sir Kenneth wanted to break the news. Not in public view of the hall and certainly not among the nomads. If Sir Kenneth had his way, he would privately confer with his lord, the council, and brace them for the truth of it. He would make his opinion known that even if a hundred trappers had reported the burning of the Crestwood, all other reports of these raids were exaggerated. However, his lord forced him to divulge the most recent news in front of the Par'sha, half the court, and the gods! He grimly nodded to his lord.

Lord Malcolm took a deep breath and understood. The attacks were true. They spanned the breadth of the mountains and deep into the northern Crestwood, where no lord laid claim.

"Someone has wronged you," Lord Malcolm repeated, returning his attention to Su'ca. "But the west is vast. There are many realms and many kinds of folk. My city is flooded with many folk from the Crestwood, which lies north of us. They too have been wronged.

They too have abandoned their homes in vast numbers because someone has set fire to their homes and driven them from their lands. They too are angry and have questions. Would you bring my words to your father?" he asked.

Sir Kenneth could see on the face of Su'ca she was taken aback by the grace of Lord Malcolm and his honest words. Sir Kenneth found his lordship often commanded the respect not only from his people but from all diplomats who came before him.

"I will bring your words to my father," she agreed.

"Please tell him this city is concerned by these crimes as well and we will investigate. However, we cannot and will not be held accountable for an offense we have not committed. Above all, tell him we endeavor to have peace between our peoples."

"I will tell him these words," reassured Su'ca. "… but know that the Par'sha too will 'investigate.' We will find these Westerners and drive them from our lands. If they choose to fight, blood will flow like a river."

"I understand, my lady. Will you stay and rest from your weary travel?" he said, rising to his feet.

"We will not, great lord. My people will return to the great grass-sea soon. First, we will eat, but we are eager to return."

"Very well. My hospitality is yours. I offer you food and water from my table, and should you change your mind, shelter. My house will see to them both," he replied. The lord then motioned the Par'sha to the main doors, "May your steeds be swift and your travels safe."

Su'ca nodded low, turned, and her party exited the hall.

Lord Malcolm exhaled in relief as the Par'sha left. He waited only a moment and beckoned Sir Kenneth to approach. Sir Kenneth ascended the steps to the table and bowed.

"My Lord?"

"Assemble the council," Lord Malcolm commanded.

"As you command, my lord. Assemble the Council!" Sir Kenneth shouted into the great hall. The great red doors opened, and a gaggle of councilmen stepped through, all vying for placement at the lord's table. Sir Kenneth purposefully found a seat at the extreme left of the table. Unlike the other gentlemen, he had no great ambition to compete for the Lord's grace. He was the Commander of the Midguard, whose place was assured. Once every seat was claimed and the hall was filled with the Merchants' Guild, the council sat as one body.

Lord Malcolm stood before everyone. "Gentlemen, it is apparent an enemy is raiding throughout the Crestwood; now we have heard that raiding has reached the eastern grass-sea beyond the Hook."

The council murmured as they grasped the ominous situation. The raiding spanned the Crescent Mountains from the eastern tail end where the mountain curved like a fishhook to the western hills where Darwishmen settled.

Lord Malcolm raised a hand, silencing the clamor, "Gentlemen! The Par'sha will muster their forces along the border and suppress the raiders. This, I have no doubt."

"We need to counter them at once," Master Wendall interrupted. "You have heard the rumors as well as I. The black fog precedes them; fire and death are left in their wake. If what you say is true, the raiders have pillaged at least eighty leagues in every northerly direction and further to the east. A force that can cover such a distance along the whole damned mountain range must be a vast host, and they are approaching our borders with haste! We must meet them in the field before they lay waste to the whole realm!"

"And what of our own defenses and city, Master Wendall?" Lady Alma interjected, tapping on the table. "You may be correct, and this is a significant force, but how are we to fight the black fog? These rumors have all the feel of dark tidings! The common folk speak of wild creatures in the night."

The council grew restless at this notion. Many had heard a variety of tales and of horned creatures and all involved the mention of a perverted darkness.

Master Gregory stood and pressed his fingertips together. "We do not know what dark affiliations they possibly keep. However detailed the rumors, I do not believe in magic gnomes and nymphs. Nor do I believe in evil grims or goblins. That being said, Lady Alma makes a fine point. We should not leave the city defenseless and risk open war with an unknown and dangerous foe. What we do know is that there is an enemy upon our doorstep and there is spectacle about them. No more! We cannot and should not assume the worst."

"If we do nothing, these marauders will continue throughout the Crest, burn the grain of the Mid, and a thousand homes. Does that put us in a better or worse position, Master Gregory? My lady? We may be behind high walls, but we are already overrun, and our stores are already being depleted. We mustn't hide!" urged Master Wendall.

"What of the Par'sha?" Sir Kenneth interjected. "They will be victorious on the battlefield and push these raiders back to the west. Yes?" Around the table, all council members met his question with agreement and nodding.

"I agree. That horde will fight savagely. If we decide to take the fight to these raiders, the enemy will be facing two fronts instead of one and they will be routed thoroughly," Sir Kenneth said confidently as the council met his point favorably.

"Would you leave the city undefended?" asked Lady Alma. The clamor silenced quickly at Lady Alma's solemnity.

"I would not, my lady. However, the Midguard is not equipped to wage war, defend the city, and maintain order among the masses. I do not have enough men," Sir Kenneth admitted. He looked around as the council again broke into squabble and disarray. His eyes met with Master Gregory across the table, where he found the councilman nodding in approval.

"Gentlemen!" called Lord Malcolm. "What is to be done?"

"Hear me, friends," said Master Gregory as he stood once again. "We have the men here and now. Let us enlist the small folk. You, I, and the commander have seen plenty of good fighting men who are eager to return home. Let us form them into soldiers of the Mid! Let us shield them and arm them with spears! They will gladly fight in defense of their homes and ours."

Sir Kenneth now understood Master Gregory's motives. He meant to arm the citizenry. It was a bold move and would serve the purpose. However, Sir Kenneth was skeptical. Arming the country folk did not make them soldiers.

Upon hearing his words, the rest of the council slapped the table in approval.

"And who will pay these men to defend the Mid and the Crest, Master Gregory?" asked Master Liam.

"I will gladly lend in my share of the coffers to ensure the security of the Mid. Would you do the same, Master Liam? Master Rhoades? Master Wendall?" Master Gregory countered.

"I will assist you in this burden," Master Hector chimed.

One by one, Sir Kenneth watched as every merchantman of the council fell in line and offered their coin. Master Gregory had just outmaneuvered the entirety of the council and Sir Kenneth was going to have thousands more under his command.

"It will take time to train these folk," said Sir Kenneth.

"Time we may not have," agreed Lady Alma.

"Gentlemen, I have heard you," said Lord Malcolm. "First, we must gather more information. We are acting on speculation and grasping with too many unknowns. We will assemble four hundred men to ride north and ascertain the truth behind these raiders. However, I will not send untrained men to death."

"My lord, I fear we will greatly weaken the guard," responded Sir Kenneth.

"I understand your concerns. Prepare three hundred riders from the guard and enlist another hundred adept riders from the Crestfolk!" Lord Malcolm commanded. "We should be able to find a sufficient number of folk who can ride, fight, and serve as your auxiliary."

"My auxiliary?" Sir Kenneth questioned, shock on his face. The hall fell silent, and every important figure in the realm laid their eyes on him.

"You are correct, Commander. I trust you to seek out this unknown enemy and, if able, drive them back," Lord Malcolm confirmed.

"My lord! My place is here defending this city."

"You are an invaluable commander of men who can and will lead the vanguard of the Mid. Furthermore, I know you will judge the situation accordingly and send a thorough report back here. This is why I have chosen you for this difficult and important task. Master Wendall, I wish you to accompany Sir Kenneth as his second. You will serve him well and assist him in this task. Uncover these villains, gentlemen. We need answers."

Sir Kenneth hesitated to reply. His place was in the Mid; his duty was overseeing the order of their city. To leave it amidst the chaos was irresponsible. However, his fealty was sworn always to his lord and to follow his commands. "Aye, my lord. We will leave once we have all the necessary provisions, my lord," he replied, while Master Wendall reluctantly nodded.

Lord Malcolm gave a curt nod. "Master Gregory, see them well supplied," he said, turning to the councilman.

"As you command, my lord," nodded Master Gregory.

"Master Hector and our Master-at-Arms, Sir Pavel, will prepare the defense of the city in Sir Kenneth's absence. Master Gregory, with the assistance of all leading members on this council, will encourage the enlistment and reinforcement of our garrison. We are not yet at the point of conscription, but if this enemy reaches our doors, we will do so. Sir Pavel and his men will also be responsible for their training. Once we receive word from Sir Kenneth and Master Wendall, we will revisit our stratagem. As of now, I intend to join Sir Kenneth upon the field with enough of our forces to combat this threat," Lord Malcolm declared.

"My lord, your place is here in the Mid," begged Lady Alma.

"I know what you would say, my dear. Council, I feel this threat is very real and will require all our combined efforts. I intend to fight, to defend the Mid, and I believe we will fare better if we bring the fight to them," he exclaimed.

"I fear we will subject our city to theft and lawlessness if you leave us undefended, my lord," urged Master Liam.

"I will not abandon my city. There will be sufficient guards here to protect our people and defend our city. We must also encourage our citizenry and many other folks who do not join our forces to continue south toward the Harbors. There is still safety in that direction," Lord Malcolm replied as he stood to give the final word throughout the hall.

"Pass the word throughout the city... raise arms in the defense of the Crest!"

The great hall erupted in cheers and applause. The guards behind the Lord began a rousing song of the Mid, and many who knew it joined as it rang throughout the hall.

"Commander?" yelled Lord Malcolm. He motioned for the knight to approach him. Sir Kenneth barely heard his lord through the commotion. He approached and took to a knee beside his lord.

"I have a task for you, sir," he said. "I need you to quickly find the Par'sha and speak to Su'ca before she departs. Tell her I have one final message to deliver to her father. Tell her the Mid will ride against these raiders and attack from the south! We are allies in this fight! This is vital for her ears, my friend. Do you hear me, sir?"

Sir Kenneth nodded in understanding and exited the hall. As he made his way through the keep, the folk he passed were in an uproar of anticipation and eagerness as the word had passed from one post to the next. As the echoes rang throughout the hall, his own enthusiasm rose; he was about to lead men into the fray.

"To war!"

"To war!"

"To war!"

Chapter III
The Vagrant

Cal and Bill survived the long night. As soon as they woke, Cal untethered the latch, pushed up the cellar door, and emerged. The Fork lay silent and calm; its embers doused by the morning dew. It was a good sign. Cal was eager to leave the scorched village behind them. He found Alice where she had been hitched the night before and was thoroughly relieved to find her unharmed. The raiders had not returned. Cal grinned with a glimmer of hope.

Bill prepared an ample breakfast of cheeses, bread, and apples. It was better to overindulge because they had far more stores than they could pack. They ate slowly, taking one last look over the Fork. The town was a husk of its former self, but in the quiet hours of the morning among the chill forest and chirping birds perched along the debris, there was a peace. Cal took comfort in that. With their stomachs full, supplies packed, and spirits raised, they quietly departed.

Their journey to the Mid was an uncomfortable trek. They marched from dawn until dusk, never lit a fire, kept watch over one another, and moved along the white road that wound alongside the river. The indirect route extended their journey by nine days, but it also afforded them further concealment among the dense forest.

Bill hoped they would be received by one of the many fishing villages along the white shores, but to their dismay, no one was to be found. A thousand villagers deserted their huts in the wake of the raiders. It was a bad omen for the realm. However, as gloomy as their journey was, it was also uneventful. All their precautions proved successful.

Their spirits rose when they entered the Mid only to be dashed at the border. They were nearly among civilization again and they could seek out the help the Crestfolk needed. Yet even among the Mid's countryside, there was no one. The folks had gathered what precious belongings they could carry and abandoned their homes here as well. The last five evenings, Cal and Bill helped themselves to what food remained and they slept soundly indoors.

Cal knew the Mid was on the horizon when the realm transformed from a large forest into cultivated farmlands that rose and sank with the hills. As the woodland cleared into open plain with rolling hills that stretched to meet the sky in the distance, Cal was in awe. Even among his travels with Bill, he had never left the Crestwood before. It was his home and everything that he always needed; it offered shelter and food, and it provided him with the companionship he needed to stave off his loneliness from losing his family. However, here, Cal saw the horizon for the first time and the vastness of the space was overwhelming.

Then he saw the city. They arrived on the outskirts of the Mid just after midday. Cal did not know men could build such grand objects. His imagination of the cities of the world did him little justice as the walls and towers grew beyond measure and size as they approached the Mid. In a single morning, the world had grown beyond his dreams.

They hadn't crossed the first field before six patrolling cavalrymen thundered toward them from over the rolling hills. Each man wore a rust-colored tunic over worn leather armor and carried a spear. By the emblem on their tunics, Cal knew they were Midguardmen. They charged toward Cal and Bill so fiercely, Cal briefly thought to gallop away. After all, the patrolmen didn't know them, and they looked ready to fight. Had it not been for Bill, Cal would have spurred Alice hard and hoped for the best.

"Hold there!" The lead horseman shouted as he came to a halt. "What business have you got in the Mid?"

"We're looking for shelter," Cal replied.

"You and everyone else. No room for you lot. We're crammed full on the east and west bank. Most freeloading folk are heading south now... those who can't fight that is," the horseman snapped. The last thing Cal wanted was an altercation with the Midguard.

"I understand, sir. Do you know of any place outside the city where we might stay? Perhaps, a farmhouse, we might rest for a night. We're weary from the long road and could use a good meal."

"I told you, we're full up of freeloaders. We'll take you round the east gate, where you can join the old and young folk who are heading south. That is unless you'd join the fight. The lord calls up all men who are able, and you look able enough, son."

"Oh, I bet it's a fine rabble!" Bill spat. "By the manners of yer ilk, they found yer folk growing like weeds about the dung heap. Oh sure, ya sprouted up some, but shit is shit!"

Cal glared at Bill. It was evident they had different thoughts on how they'd conduct the exchange and Bill was clearly going to have none of the guard's rudeness. When Cal turned back to the patrolman, to his surprise, the guard grinned wide at the comment.

"You're a bit mangy, grandfather. That'll get you in trouble one day. Men like me won't be around to protect ya from them ghosts in the dark."

"I'm not need'n protection from no boys play'n at war!" Bill rebuked. "So, if you've finished showing us what a kinda man ya think ya are, we'll find our own way."

"Alright then, grandfather, you've got stones. But I can't leave you unescorted. Charly, be a good lad and accompany these men to the east gate," said the Sergeant, smirking wide as he picked up to a trot and the other horsemen followed him.

"Don't mind him. He's just as pleasant with all kinds of folk," Charly reassured them. "Come on then. I'll see you safely round to the gates."

"Thank you," Cal nodded. He let Charly take the lead and gave him some distance. The cavalryman led them to the east side of the city. They could see the north gate was shut from a distance and noted several men were patrolling atop the wall. As they approached the city, the fields cleared, and they could see a steady line of refugees exiting the east gate to the south. Had they been unescorted, Cal and Bill would have found the gate easily. The departing folk were numerous and made of all kinds of people, but all had the look of mountain and woodland folk. They were young, old, men, women, Elvian, and Darwish. Cal could tell these were folk of the Crestwood.

Charly halted his steed as they gazed upon the lines of folk. "Well then, this is where I leave you. These folk are heading toward the Harbors. Plenty of villages along the way. Quite safe. If you are thinking of joining the fight, you should seek out the recruiters just inside the gate. Look for any guard wearing the sigil of the Mid, and he'll show you where to go. Don't mind the sergeant none. You two would do well. If we raise enough men, we'll rout those buggers, eh?"

Cal nodded and thanked the cavalryman as he rode north. Cal waited to speak with Bill until Charly was well out of earshot.

"Why in the hell did you provoke the sergeant?" Cal demanded.

"What? He n'sulted us! He n'sulted 'em!" Bill maintained as scores of different folk trudged through the gates. "Listen to me, Cal. Yer a good lad, but we're not home no more. Some folk will take advantage of ya and look down at ya here. Don't let 'em! We're decent folk an' deserve more than an upturned nose."

"I just think we could have gone about it a different way, is all."

"I know ya did, but he was an ass. Some folk will push ya in this world. You've got to stand your ground an' push back. This here..." Bill gestured to the gates and walls of the Mid. "... is one of those places. We've got to look out for ourselves."

He was right. The Mid was the first city Cal had ever seen and there were more people streaming out of it than he had ever met either. It was a different world than his small village. "I see your point, Bill," Cal conceded. "What are your thoughts on joining them? They clearly know of the raids and are doing something about it. It might be worthwhile to check it out."

"I'm not sure I'd join some damn-fool Midguard! Why not make our way south with these folk? There's trade to be had south.

And where there's decent trade, there's peace," Bill countered. The line of folk stretched for beyond sight. They were Crestfolk, his folk, who had been driven from their homes, and it didn't sit well with Cal.

They hadn't talked about the raids, or at all, during their journey. Keeping silent kept them hidden. Now, as their journey ended, Cal wanted to make his thoughts known. "What about standing your ground and pushing back?" Cal replied. "I've been thinking about those raiding bastards every moment for a week now. All our neighbors are likely gone and turned to ash because someone cut them down when they weren't looking. Who's gonna stand for them?"

Bill was taken aback as his words were thrown back at him as he thought a moment and sighed. "You're right, son. You're the kind of man I'd like to fight 'long side if a fight was need'n to happen," Bill said. "Cause you're a good man, Cal. Ya join because stand'n's the right thing to do. But don't go join'n a cause for revenge, son. That's not me an' I know it's not you. So, I won't stop you from join'n if that's what ya want, and I may consider join'n m'self. I just think there's no shame in lett'n the Midguard do the bulk of the labor is all."

Cal smirked at the old man and considered his words. "I want to know what the Mid is doing about this," Cal exhaled.

Bill reluctantly nodded. "Alright, lad. Let's see what force these Midfolk have collected," Bill relented.

"Tell you what, Bill. We'll hear the men out. I'm not looking to sign up for some army venture for years to come, either. I just want to beat these demons back and rebuild, is all," Cal assured him.

"I know, lad," Bill assured, patting him on the shoulder.

The gate of the Mid was just as imposing as the size of the city. The massive oak doors stood as high as five men with black iron straps bolted to the wood as reinforcement. Above the gate, two towers stood, with several more along the walls. The wall spanned the entire city and ran along the banks of the river. It was as if two walled cities were narrowly separated and yet connected by bridges.

Few were entering the city. Upon passing through the massive gates, they found no less than seven guards who were directing the crowds and encouraging all fighters to join the cause.

"Follow the roads to the Harbor!" One guard yelled. "You will be safe! The Mid will protect you! There are camps along the roads! The realm could use an arm like yours, young fellow. To the square, m'boy!"

"With all these people vacating, I think we'll be able to find somewhere to rest our heads," Cal shouted through the crowded gate.

"I'm go'n to speak with one of them guards. I want to see what they're offer'n," Bill replied.

Cal led Alice off to the side of the main street and kept an eye out. The crowds were full of folk, but he did notice a lack of young men and women. "Perhaps, the ranks of volunteers had already swelled," Cal thought as Bill returned promptly.

"They're say'n there's a square straight ahead an' we can't miss it. Just head due west, and we'll find it," Bill relayed.

They journeyed further into the Mid. As vast as it looked from the outside, it was nothing compared to what it held. There were inns, taverns, and brothels where a traveler could find respite. Commerce boomed with silks and spices from far across the continent. The taverns shelved Darwish ales and Elvian wines of every variety. The markets stored fresh fruits, grains, vegetables, and a great deal of fish. Folk toiled at the forges crafting shields and spears. The Mid appeared to be the center for all trade and culture.

Once they reached the square, they found something else entirely. Here was the stage for great debate and discussion. The square was surrounded by fifty marble pillars, and each was connected by a beam. The square was roofless but at its center, a raised marble stage stood where orators were encouraging all folk to 'Defend the Mid!' Hundreds of spectators were listening to every word and most were in support, but not all. As they entered the square, Cal listened as an elderly man questioned a portly speaker.

"… Hear me, I beg you," cried the elderly man. He looked homely and worn as if hardship was a traveling companion. His beard was scraggly, and his brown robes were tattered, yet his eyes that shone from his underfed face were sharp and piercing. He paced back and forth across the stage, and his words were rapid and to the point as he engaged the speaker.

"What of the fog?" he asked as the crowd fell silent. "What of this black terror and the smoke from which the raiders came? It is no coincidence that their arrival coincides with this foul mist. This has all the makings of dark magic! There are men, not unlike myself, who may be of use and could counteract this darkness. However, we must not blindly run into the danger."

The speaker examined the old man with one eyebrow raised. He had faced numerous opponents upon the stage recently, and one by one, they had all lost the debate against him. Master Gregory was accustomed to verbal duels with men from all ranks of society. This vagabond was no different from the rest.

"I confess there are elaborate rumors spreading through the city, but there are many tales of wonder throughout the world, sir. The reports speak of mysterious two-headed horn demons shrouded in the blackness, but have you ever seen such a thing? I have not and so, I must conclude this report is exaggerated!" Master Gregory scoffed at the claim, waving the vagrant aside.

"What is real, my friends, is someone has raided our neighbors to the north, and they are heading south! We can assuredly say *that* is real. My friends, if there are horsemen, then we can ride out and dispose of them. And, in the unlikely circumstance these raiders are assisted by some kind of magic, I promise they still can be killed like any other man!" The crowd roared its approval in Master Gregory's favor.

"Yes, many folk and fouler things can be killed. Even those who can manipulate magic can die, but we speak of a host who is aided by dark sorcery!" The old man pressed. "If we send our young folk into the void without a thorough understanding, bold though they may be, we will surely be sending those men to death. So, I ask you, is the lord of this city and you, sir, denying the darkness..."

"... Good people! I know it is hard to conceive." Master Gregory interrupted with arms outstretched, tired of the debate. "There are foul things in this world, but it is evident that good men can and should fight this darkness. We are well aware of the risks. So, let me reiterate the facts. The Crest is under attack. We do not know who attacks, but it is evident they raid along upon every village in the wood. Your lordship is confident these are just raiders and thugs!" The crowd raised their fists and cheered on Master Gregory.

The elderly man reiterated something in reply, but Master Gregory continued without giving his opponent the floor.

"My friends, will you stand aside as your neighbor's homes and fields are destroyed? Would you watch as our friends are butchered, raped, pillaged, and plundered?" Gregory shouted.

"No!" The crowd cried.

"Then stand, sirs! We are in need of capable men, my friends. Will you not answer our lord's call?"

"Yeah!" The crowd cried into a fevered pitch.

"Then join us! We need fighters. We need riders. The constable is still in need of surplus riding men. You sir? Will you join us?" Master Gregory directed his question to a young man near the edge of the stage. As it happened, the councilman pointed to Cal.

The attention startled him. In truth, he was afraid to battle these creatures; they were real enough and they frightened him. However, it was his folk among the crowd, swept up with the same vigor that he felt, and all of them were ready to take up the call.

"I would fight..." Cal replied, but the crowd erupted in cheers before he could finish. As soon as he agreed, dozens of nearby men approached him and began shaking his hand and patting him on the back. He nodded, said his thanks, and the next man stepped in to congratulate him. Had they not been riled, Cal might have finished what he planned to say, but the crowd was too agitated to listen to much of anything else. The debate was over. Folk were convinced to fight back.

As folk began to leave the square, Master Gregory called out above them. "My friends, remember, the archers are to be organized just outside the Trout Tavern. If you wish to join the spearmen, you will need to assemble by Helga's Trading Post just north of us, and all horsemen are encouraged to sign up at my own establishment, Elena's Inn and Tavern. The Mid thanks you!"

The elderly gentleman left abruptly once he had lost the debate and made his way through the crowded square. "Damn fool! Out of my way!" he cried.

Cal heard him as he brushed by him and Bill as well.

"How else should we fight, sir?" Cal genuinely asked before the old man departed.

"What?" he asked confounded.

"How should we fight them, sir? Moreover, how would *you* have us fight them?"

The old man stroked his beard and paced around as he eyed Cal from head to toe.

"I would not commit such a force just yet. Too soon. We should seek out the enemy of darkness cautiously. A small group, maybe twenty. We need to know of their power, and we do not. Once we know who and what we are dealing with, then the lord of this city can make plans for their war. Not before! Any attempt to fight the darker magics of the world without a clear understanding of them is courting our own death," the old man reiterated.

Cal considered his words. Although he looked like a disheveled madman, he made some sense.

"There may not be time for any reconnaissance. I cannot speak for the other folk, but they pillaged throughout our valley in an evening, and I suspect they followed us as we traveled south toward the borders of the Crest. In fact, they could be around the Mid as we speak. I'm no soldier, but standing up to them before they scorch the whole realm may prove the best course."

"Aye," Bill interjected.

"Perhaps?" the old man answered inquisitively.

"What road did you take?"

Cal hesitated to answer. "My companion Bill and I traveled the White Road south."

Without pause, the older man quickly followed with another question, "From where, my boy... where?" The old man insisted as he stopped pacing if he could not conduct his next move without Cal's answer.

Cal looked at Bill, and he appeared just as trepidatious.

After a pause, Cal whispered, "We come from the Fork."

The old man's eyes widened as if Cal confirmed his suspicions. "Did you see them? Answer me true!"

"I saw a glimpse through my window before three arrows almost took my life."

He gripped Cal's arm, "You must come with me!"

"Sir?"

"What are your names, my friends?"

Cal answered after another hesitation. "Cal and this is my friend, Bill," Cal motioned.

"Cal, I mean you no harm, but I must hear what story you and your friend have to tell. And I wish there not to be prying eyes and active ears. So, allow me to offer you a drink and respite from your travels and, in return, all I ask is that you share with me what you know of these creatures," the old man said.

Cal's first inclination was to decline, but the old man spoke with an odd sincerity; he was desperate to know more about the raiders and Cal felt a small obligation to share his story. Resting, even for a moment, was also tempting. So, Cal nodded.

"Good! Follow me," The elderly man exclaimed as he led them through the crowded streets.

The city was abuzz with anticipation of war. All kinds of folk were celebrating, trading for weapons, drinking ales, and visiting their favorite brothels for more private matters. In fact, the old man led Cal and Bill to an establishment called Nightingales. This appeared to be a bordello, much like several others, but it also served as a tavern. The older man briskly entered and greeted the bartender.

"The booth in the corner, Nigel, three meads, and privacy!"

Nigel nodded, almost expressionless, as if the elderly man's demands were routine.

Nightingales looked like the inside of an illustrious privateer's sea cabin. Dark walnut columns carved with sea creatures and bare mermaids lined the room and the beams were draped with red silk cushions. It was harsh, yet elegant in its own way.

The old man sat in the corner, away from the other patrons, and lit a lantern in the center of the table. Cal imagined many back-alley agreements had happened at this very booth in which they sat.

The folks in the establishment were few and kept company with the courtesans at hand, but all looked rough in one form or another. Before the silence broke, the wench brought three meads full to the brim to the table, and the old man smiled at the young woman as he passed her a few silver coins.

"To our health, my friends; we'll be in need of it," the old man toasted. He raised his cup, drank heartily, and nearly downed the entire drink.

"My name is Alec. I've often been called the wanderer, the user, the inebriated, and an all-around degenerate by most civilized communities," he said bluntly. "I confess my best qualities lie outside my rugged appearance, and often I have been disregarded as you saw today by my opponent on the stage. However, that does not mean I am wrong in my concerns or positions. Furthermore, it does not mean I am without quality."

He tugged at his sleeve, and with a twist of his hand and snap of his fingers, a small blue flame sprang from nothing between his forefinger and thumb.

Cal's eyes widened. He checked the man's hand thoroughly, but Alec held no candle or wick within his fist. A single flame arose from his finger and burned in the evening and not a single patron noticed or raised their voice. Everyone had heard of tales of magic, but no one had seen such things. Yet, here it was like the glow of the spring sun after a harsh winter. Alec was a conjurer.

Bill was equally mesmerized and speechless until a quizzical look came over his face. Cal didn't need to read his mind to understand his thoughts. *Were they just not seeing some trick? Was this real magic?* Bill squinted his eyes and scratched his beard as he attempted to touch the flame.

"Damn!" he yelped.

"A wonder, is it not?" Alec smirked at Bill. "Yes, it is real and a wondrous thing. I grant it is not much, but it demonstrates my abilities." Alec opened his hand, stretched his fingers, and the flame vanished. As the light faded, the booth dimmed, grew colder, and less joyous.

Cal wondered if all magic was so immersive.

"Have some more mead, and the chill will lessen," Alec said, almost as if he could read Cal's thoughts.

"Regardless of my faults, I am a conjurer, a practitioner of magic, some would say a wizard, but ultimately, I am a man with gifts who desires to do the most good I can," he continued. "For some time in my life, I cannot say my path was the noblest pursuit. I am a man, after all. My gifts have been dulled and lackluster, especially in my waning years, but recently I can feel the flow again! I can feel the waves of rejuvenation and power course through my veins. This started, maybe a few moons past, and continued to increase dramatically when the most recent events around the mountains unfolded. Then, when all manner of folk started migrating south, I felt as if a great and dark predator was hunting us all. The darkness is coming, my friends. I have heard many variations of this from many folks, but I can feel the magic inside me grow for some purpose. Magic begets magic, even if it's dark."

Cal and Bill looked at each other, overwhelmed by the scope of what Alec had told them, and each drank more of their mead.

"I know dark magic comes with them, my friends. And I will not stand idly by because I have seen it destroy countless things in my life. I will fight it somehow, and I believe you may be able to assist me. Of all the folk who have departed the Crest, none have come from as north as either of you and, to my knowledge, few have seen them. That is except for you."

Cal's heart plummeted, and he wished he hadn't mentioned where he came from. He wished he was back home safely in his cabin smoking meats and harvesting the crop. That was the life he wanted, but it already felt like a distant memory. Furthermore, he was not accustomed to talking with wizards about dark and ominous tidings over a flagon of mead, and in a questionable establishment. He must have looked concerned because Bill clasped his forearm and patted him.

"It's alright, lad, tell him what you know," Bill reassured. Cal was relieved to know his friend was beside him. So, he took a drink and wondered where to begin.

Chapter IV
The Conspiracy

Master Gregory waded through all the small folk he had patience for that day. He greeted, smiled, and shook more hands in the last week than he ever intended his whole life. Hundreds of commoners happily darted through the crowds to meet him. After all, it was he who roused the city. Master Liam didn't have the heart for it. Master Hector was far too busy organizing the new volunteers for the Midguard. Master Wendall was of some help, parading himself about the city in his new armor like a peacock. No, the task of rallying the Crestfolk rested in Gregory's capable hands and he relished it.

Orchestrating the passions of men came as easily to him as the trout came to the fishmongers among the Mid. He would cast a net of encouragement and ideals around them, and the small folk would become ensnared by the hundreds. In the end, all followed him and signed up for the Midguard.

However, it was tiring work. He spent a few days traveling by cart outside the gates in the hopes of engaging young folk to turn back to defend the honor of the Mid. He fared well in those avenues, but he was meant for the square. The square was his stage and the commoners gathered there day after day. It was *the* place for the great debates along with the games of strategy and chance. Gregory argued more than most and he considered a debate a thrill. So, it was no wonder why he excelled at the forum because he practiced his art at every opportunity.

His family was fortunate to be blessed with wealth. And where wealth could be had, education followed. His family collected a sizable fortune and was able to afford their children a comprehensive education. Gregory took advantage of it. With a thorough understanding of commerce, laws, art, and philosophy, he developed strategies to corner his family's markets. He diversified his trade beyond his father's and those ventures bore fruit. He became one of the wealthiest men in the realm and then he was invited to climb the political landscape. His years spent honing his skills of negotiation in the marketplace prepared him well in the council chamber. His future was bright.

He left the forum in the early afternoon after he bested another misanthrope and wanderer. This particular commoner frequented the square and voiced criticisms of the constable and sought to corrupt the youth with strange tales of far-off places and of beings who can do the unbelievable. Master Gregory had already spoken many times that day and grew tired in the sun. When it came to the plebeian, he decided to rout him thoroughly and move on with his day.

Once finished at the square, he departed swiftly. The road to the tavern was well known to him; he inspected his properties one after the other along his path. He reviewed ledgers among the grocers and butchers. He perused the finer silks for his more affluent clients, but in all honesty, he often kept them for himself. He always counted the barrels of ales, wines, and spirits to verify a cask hadn't wandered off, and lastly, he would end his assessment at Elena's.

The tavern was a polished jewel among the rocks. When he entered, he summed up the common folk present. He was happy with the progress. Many folk found their way into his establishment and signed into service. When they completed their declarations, a bar could be found within an arm's length for libations and cheers. This was not the overall goal, but a welcome byproduct of his labors. If he were tasked by the Lord of the Mid, he always wished to be paid for his service. In this case, the common people would supply the down payment.

With politics well attended, there was one remaining task to conduct. He ascended the adorned staircase to the second floor of the inn and tavern. He kept an office here where tabulations were calculated and noted. Many of his managers would find him here, verifying the revenue of his establishments and the day's tally needed to be assessed.

He expected to see earnings in a fair number of markets. War, by nature, was increasingly more profitable than peace and he was calculating the cost and profits of the venture. He would see initial gains in raw metals, leathers, drinks, and whores. The past week was lucrative in all those categories. The city had also purchased vast quantities of grains, vegetables, and meats. Lord Malcolm asked him to supply the venture and he enthusiastically did so. Overall, his stores were not completely depleted, but they were seriously diminished.

After reviewing the day's total, he compared it against the expenses. The largest cost by far was the coin he gave to the Mid to hire and supply fresh troops. However, this cost had been offered for two purposes. The first was to convince or to guilt other council members into matching his efforts. He cared not which reason they had chosen to fund as long as they committed. The second reason was to invest in this endeavor. *If one is to acquire coins, one must spend coins.* He gambled, paid, and every rich merchant on the council followed him. Now, most of those coins were returning to his lavishly laced pockets.

He was pleased to find his earnings had continued to increase today. They had steadily climbed after the initial call to arms and were likely to continue for a few more days, or at least until the quota of men that agreed to serve was filled. Master Gregory had every intention of motivating the small folk to do so and see the Mid well-armed, fed, and supplied.

He finished marking the numbers, tabulating the totals in each column and closed the ledger. He reached for his decanter, poured a helping of aged Darwish brandy, swirled the glass, and smiled. For all his profits and overflowing chests, they held little interest in the grand scheme. His plans had been propelled into action, and he relished the thought of their achievement.

He had not urged so many councilmen for the sole purpose of his own gains. Although he also saw the use of it and took advantage, he had far greater ambitions. His wealth amassed, and it allowed him to wield authority and power on the council. He relished his new political powers and basked in the debates, savoring the influence he held over the realm. To shape the Mid's political landscape was a euphoric wallow for Gregory. He had enjoyed the play for years and was eager to see another act unfold. Then, a day not too long ago, the plot developed further, and another council member proposed such a change that would possibly alter the entire political landscape.

He reclined in his chair, recalling the memory, when a knock rapped at his door, and a cloaked man entered. Gregory turned to find the very same council member entering his private quarters.

The man removed his hood and snuffed out the candles one by one. Master Wendall seldom visited. They were not friends, but neither were they enemies. However, if he visited him, his colleague typically had a purpose.

Little more than a week ago, Master Wendall approached him outside the council. The attacks were fresh on the minds of the people and were little more than campfire stories. No one could have ascertained the authenticity at that time. When Wendall approached him, he requested Gregory's help in convincing the council to counter the attackers in force. This request seemed odd to Gregory, and it aroused his suspicion of Wendall. In Gregory's opinion, Wendall was an astute merchant, but not a man entirely shrewd at politics. Simply put, Wendall was a man who understood the worth of a commodity but not how to sway people to purchase the item. At the time, his proposal was entirely too blunt, without real merit, and altogether premature. And yet, Wendall believed it to be sound. So Gregory requested time to consider the proposal.

Gregory pondered his request for many days; there had to be an alternative reason for the maneuver. First, he asked himself why Wendall could be so confident in the validity of the rumor. *Had he seen the attacks firsthand?* It was possible he had seen them, and he might corroborate that, but to Gregory's knowledge, Master Wendall had not left the city; he liked to be aware of his rivals' whereabouts.

Then the next question came to mind. *Was Wendall himself involved in the raids?* Gregory considered the notion but doubted the possibility. No man was beyond corruption and it was mildly entertaining to conceive Wendall's affiliation with the raids beyond the borders. Ultimately, Gregory did not know the depths of Wendall's involvement. If Wendall was affiliated and the purposes of the raids were to disrupt or kill his competitors, then why call for aid to stop them? He would not. On the other hand, he may have coordinated or requested an attack, and his relationship with the raiders had dissolved. If that were the case, he might desperately desire to silence his disreputable affiliates before their tongues went wagging. The conception was not impossible, but overall, Wendall was too rigid to be associated with either venture.

Then, another consideration came to mind. *What would happen if the Mid led an expedition into the Crest?* Many armed men and women would leave the city. Important noblemen would surely lead the efforts if convinced. At the time, Gregory wondered who might leave the Mid, and now he reassured himself in that thinking.

Lord Malcolm, Sir Kenneth, Master Hector, and Master Wendall were all readying themselves for war. Several other council members may depart as well. If so, did that free Master Wendall to take some action? Master Gregory scoffed at the notion. How could

Master Wendall have known he would be tasked to take up the vanguard and join Sir Kenneth? It perplexed Gregory.

After earnest consideration, Gregory consented to Wendall's proposal. Three main reasons convinced him to do so. First, there was profit to be made in the venture. For Master Gregory, this was satisfying, but not ultimately why he would agree. Secondly, he agreed to the proposal because he did not understand Wendall's request. He wanted more information to ascertain why Wendall so desperately desired this course of action, and Gregory needed more time to undo his old friend's plans if he so desired. So, Gregory would consent.

The third reason was the most compelling. If the Mid projected itself outside their borders, their interference would send waves to the other realms. It could mean greater influence or possibly even greater war. This reason alone burned in the deepest recesses of Gregory's heart. The Mid could develop into a more powerful city with the whole of the Crest under its guard. Gregory saw every reason to see that outcome and beyond it. So much, that Gregory wondered if Wendall did as well.

However, he dared not discuss it with any political ally. The idea was so fragile that a whisper could wither it away before it had an opportunity to grow. He pondered about those reasons as the wheels were in motion and the caravan departed. As soon as Sir

Kenneth stepped in the Crestwood with a host, the Lord of the Mid might as well declare to the Harbors, the Kingdoms of the West, the high Elvian cities, the Darwish halls, and the various western peoples that the whole of the Crest was under his protection. He may even place a crown on his brow. Oh, the world had changed in a moment, and no one had even noticed.

He rose and filled an additional goblet for Wendall. The room had dimmed substantially, and they took to the balcony where night was forming on the horizon. The green landscape met a sky of darkening reds, oranges, and purples, all fading to black. The night air was redolent with the sounds and smells of commerce carrying into the evening. The smiths were working late crafting and the clanging of steel being formed could be heard from his veranda. Every able-bodied man and woman had visited metal workers and tanners for refits. He grinned, knowing the coins were flowing.

"The task is well underway, I should say. They will not stop beating the hammers and stitching the leathers for some time; I believe many are profiting," Master Gregory teased. "You among them, I should think."

"I am faring well, but I'm positive you shame us all. I was told you had created a factory out of a stable where a commoner enters through one door, exits from another dressed as a soldier, and you personally choreographed the entire production. I had to see it for myself and, even now, it runs smoothly. The spearmen are forming in record numbers. I should think Lord Malcolm will be en route faster than anticipated. Well done," Master Wendall replied.

"You are too modest, sir. You, too, have been hard at manufacturing. You have fashioned more bows and spears than the city has ever seen. I see the old men whittling away good yew and stringing them with hemp and linen. So much so, that the city is in short supply of both, and we've begun shearing the long manes of our horses for the strings. I was beside myself when I came upon a pair of bald steeds." The two laughed heartily for a moment.

Gregory kept his eye on his opponent as the man chortled.

Wendall's beard was narrow and came to a fine point. His mustache was wide but tilted upward as he laughed. Underneath his cloak, he had removed his new armor, but the unsullied silks he wore marked him as a man of a higher station. He looked like the ubiquitous well-groomed merchantman who was attempting to conceal his station. Gregory thought him foolish to try.

"I must say, you look dreadfully nefarious and theatrical. Are you here to undo me, as they say?"

"I am not," Wendall sniggered as he removed his hands from underneath his cloak, where he carried a small bag and placed it on a table. "On the contrary, I bring you gifts, but it was difficult to think of a gift fitting for a man of your status. I'm told you have everything.

Then it dawned on me how you favor some jewels over others, and I thought I might review my gems and select a few choice items of note. I believe you will be pleased."

"How thoughtful, my old friend! I can't imagine what I've possibly done to warrant such a lovely gift. You are far too generous," Gregory grinned. He sipped from his goblet, wondering how the game would unfold tonight. So far, a reward had been dealt for his support and Gregory was eager for the next request.

"I imagine you are not visiting in that ridiculous disguise to offer me trinkets. Come now, how may I be of service?" Gregory asked.

Wendall leered at him and then warily glanced around the room. "I admit I am not altogether comfortable in this attire. There are many cloaked men in the city, and as I made my way toward your establishment, I watched them and tried to move as they move. I feel I am lacking in a shadowy grace."

"Do not be too hard on yourself. With time, I'm sure you will master the art of subterfuge."

"I fear I will not have the opportunity. I believe Sir Kenneth means to leave immediately. And as to your question, I have two requests." Wendall braced himself and stroked his pointed beard. It appeared he had spent moments crafting the proper words for the requests, and now, when pressed to reveal it, he had to reform his thoughts.

"First, I am grateful for your trust and support in the council. You must have your reasons for endorsing the war effort, and I am sure you are profiting extremely well from those reasons," Wendall began.

Gregory scoffed under his breath at the last remark. He anticipated such a comment and smiled. "It is true, I see profit in many endeavors, but it was not my only reason," he teased. "Come now, you were saying?"

"I must admit, when you spoke at the previous council meeting, I briefly thought you might oppose the motion and side with Lady Alma," Wendall retorted.

"Ah well, she made a valid point, and I've found her to be quite lovely, don't you think? A woman's intuition in matters of state can be quite invaluable. Additionally, I sometimes think that men can be convinced if all points are heard, and then led to the conclusion one desires. I try to enhance the points men favor, and if they are not mine, I diminish them. Men can be led in a variety of ways. Additionally, if I were to have consented from the commencement of the council, other members may have been suspicious of me."

"I had wondered why you opposed me at first. You do have a way of broaching the middle ground."

"Is that why you enlisted my help?" Gregory inquired. He hoped for more clarification and Wendall appeared to make an opening for him.

"Partially. You can be extremely persuasive where I am not," Wendall flattered as Gregory enjoyed his candor. "I requested your aid for a similar reason, as to why I am here this evening. You see, I am in great need of your influence and power. However, I cannot be affiliated with you."

"Oh, come now…" Gregory delighted. "I am sure I am not so untrustworthy among my peers."

"Master Gregory, you misunderstand. You are clever, greedy, and deceitful when you desire but it is not always about you. No, I was speaking of myself. You see I am being watched."

Solemnity had taken Gregory. He may have been too caught up in the playful banter. First, it dawned on him that Wendall had a well perceived understanding of himself, and he may need to rethink many conclusions he had made about his colleague.

"Are you in danger, my friend? May I provide you with safe passage or some such?"

"Yes, and no. At this time, I cannot be seen, shall we say, colluding with other council members. I have some affiliations who might not agree with us merely speaking, and if seen, it may endanger my life and yours. I suppose you could say I am edging a dangerous line. And so, I must wander the streets at night and seek out help where I can."

"Previously, you came to me where I might help convince others to go to war. Have these contacts changed their minds? Are they in favor of the raids? Have you placed yourself in a dangerous position, my old friend?" Gregory asked hoping to delve into his deeper query.

"Now, now, Gregory! You assume too much. I assure you, my previous request was genuine and I very much desire the Mid to take to the field." Wendall's tone tried to reassure. "No, the associates I speak of have entirely different and complicated reasons to want me, as they say, bereft of life. In fact, I do not know if it is wise to implicate you with these matters." His morbid tone did not dissuade Gregory.

In fact, Gregory was even more so invested in such a scandal. Who would ever want Master Wendall dead and for what purpose?

"Master Wendall, you have already implicated me. Your presence, although poorly masked, implicates me. Come now, what troubles you?" Gregory pressed as Master Wendall averted his eyes.

"Tell me, will you join the conquest?" Wendall asked. It was a bewildering question.

Martial arts had never been appealing to Gregory nor applicable to his skill set. Other men were better fitted for such an exhausting activity. His passions were commerce, trade, wealth, and power. So, he became somewhat gluttonous and fat in his pursuits, and he had no intention of joining the fray. He also assumed most thought this of him.

"I confess, I will not be joining the campaign. I feel I would make a poor warrior," Gregory replied.

"Yes, but I can imagine no one else who would suffice as our logician." Wendall smiled. "I am pleased you are staying in the Mid, because the first reason I am here tonight is to ask you to note which council members stay in reserve as we depart the city. I wish you to observe their activities in my absence. Additionally, I wish for you to take note of their more suspicious activities and possibly interfere as you see fit."

Gregory's puzzle grew increasingly complex. It was not uncommon for politicians to be corrupt in one form or another, but he wondered who and what affair vexed his peer.

"This is most alarming. Is there someone specific you wish me to observe?"

"No, I believe if you uncover, shall we say, traitorous behavior among them, then we might be able to corroborate each other's examination if questioned. And so, in the end, you might be able to exonerate myself."

Gregory's pulse quickened at the concept of a traitor within their midst. The plot thickened once again and Master Gregory reveled at the idea of driving the political landscape with such an opportunity. He considered the ramifications again. *What actions could another council member have possibly conducted, which would be considered traitorous? Also, how was Wendall affiliated and did he partake himself? Could they have truly orchestrated these far-off raids for their lucrative gains?*

"Interesting! Would you be able to elaborate on the treacherous nature?" Gregory asked.

Wendall gazed at Gregory. "Recently, I found a place where a whispered word carries swiftly across a hall. I overheard a pair who have partnered together in a plot against the Mid. They mentioned a plan if we succeed or if we fail in our efforts on the battlefield. They intend to undermine the very foundation of the Mid, my friend."

Gregory took a deep breath as he contemplated the claim. It was no small thing to accuse anyone of conspiracy and treason.

"Unfortunately, I was forced to retreat before I could uncover both culprits. My retreat was not graceful, but it was successful. However, I have felt a second shadow follow my every move since the meeting and I am confident I am suspected of being an eavesdropper. I fear I may be in great danger, but I fear for our city more." Wendall said.

"Indeed," Gregory seriously ruminated. "Wendall, you must bring this issue before his lordship and let him dispense justice!"

"I cannot. I heard them say a great many things, but I can only identify one of them. It is a dangerous game to accuse someone without evidence other than your word. Once the accusations fly, I wish them to firmly land on the appropriate party. So, that is why I wish you to conduct a separate investigation. If so, I am confident you will uncover the treason I speak of, and you can verify my story. Of course, if you'd rather not support me and I were to be found on the other end of the accusations, you would be rid of another rival on the council." Wendall was blunt and seemingly earnest.

Gregory understood his thoughts. Although, he did not know if he were to believe them.

"There are many council members I would need to watch. Indeed, I would need to hire... oh, say, five capable and trustworthy men trained for such work."

"There are talented men who can be found in the depths of the Mid if you know where to look. Perhaps I can assist in narrowing your search. On Sunday around noon, I wish you or your man to investigate the south tower of the keep. A meeting is known to happen then. If not, I would take note of who might be in the vicinity."

Gregory nodded in understanding and reviewed what Wendall had revealed to him. A pair of conspirators, at least one councilman, is prepared to commit treason against the Mid and weaken the war effort. They are also planning for multiple outcomes and holding a meeting in the keep. These were dangerous circumstances, and a man would lose his head if a wrong accusation were to fall. Gregory understood Wendall's concern for the situation.

Wendall drew his hood and moved toward the exit. He finished his drink in delight. "You know, this is quite good. I must remember to pack some for the journey."

"I will have a case delivered to you. Is there anything else you would ask of me?"

"Oh yes, I nearly overlooked the second reason I sought you out. I am setting aside lumber and stones in order to reinforce the weak point in our walls should the time arise. I would request you do the same. And if someone should discover our meeting, I advise you to divulge this as our topic of discussion this evening."

"Very well. I will also have the walls thoroughly investigated by our stonemasons," Gregory replied. "I do wish you a safe journey and may you return swiftly and victoriously."

"You might be the only one, I'm afraid," Wendall teased.

Their departure was interrupted by men shouting from the main hall. Gregory furrowed his brows in anger. Elena's was an establishment known for the environment and décor, but it was not a bawdy tavern.

Wendall moved to the door, cracked it, and peered through. "It appears our constable is upset at his selection of volunteers. That man is without tact," he noted.

"He can be a foul commander, I grant you, and he is often cross with the productive and the more progressive motions we often propose in the council. Perhaps he is the traitor I am looking for," Gregory jested.

Wendall smirked remarkably wide at the remark. "I fear we all would be doomed if it were him," he laughed. "At least I can watch for him closely as his second, and no one would suspect me."

They both chuckled at the absurdity of it. The argument had begun to boil as Sir Kenneth shouted vulgarities at what appeared to be a homeless man. The tavern came to a halt, and the festivities ceased altogether.

"Oh well, forgive my hospitality, but I must attend to him," Gregory said dryly. "… before he frightens away the whole operation. I must admit he makes for a wonderful distraction. Instead of exiting through the front, may I offer you an alternative route? Exit the room and descend the staircase to the left while the crowd is engaged with our dear constable. It will lead you to the back entrance. I wish you well."

Gregory watched as Wendall left the room. He darted through the corridor and made it to the staircase, as suggested, without an eye laid upon him.

Once Wendall vanished out of sight, Gregory leapt with anticipation, quickly crossed over to the balcony, and opened the mysterious bag of gems. The conversation had been most engaging, full of half-truths, and altogether satisfying. The last thing to do was to review the gift Wendall had left for him. The bag was filled with blood-red rubies that sparkled in the candlelight.

"My word, Master Wendall! Your payment is well received, but what exactly are you purchasing? My service? My time? Or my loyalty?"

Chapter V
The Oath

"The beginning is a reasonable starting point," Alec said with a grin.

Cal returned the smile, but he was not reassured. Cal and Bill kept quiet on the matter during their journey south, as they knew what each other went through. Cal took a deep breath and drank from his flagon to settle his nerves. Any story worth telling went down better with ale, some folks would say.

"I was sleeping. I cannot tell you the hour, but I heard the thunder of rattling armor, swords beating across shields, and the stampede of hooves underfoot," Cal recalled.

"I have questions, my young friend. First, what did you see of them?" Alec interrupted.

"Just after they came, they threw a torch through my window. Once I put it out, I crept to the window to see them. They were almost formless amidst the fog, but the firelight gave one of them shape. He had curled horns on both heads; his eyes burned with a green fire! He had six limbs; he stood on four hooves and waved a sword above his head, screeching toward the sky. His other hand carried a staff pulsating with the same strange green hue his eyes had shown…"

Alec held his hand up, and Cal paused. The old man drank again and stared through the candlelight in confusion and terror.

"Many have described such things, but none have mentioned a staff!" Alec soberly admitted.

"Is that significant? I mean… well, what does it mean?" Bill interjected.

Alec shut his eyes to reflect; he sifted through his deep knowledge of magic only to return to the present without a firm answer. When he returned, he looked even more distressed than before.

"I won't lie to you. It confirms to me that dark magic does aid them. If you are correct, then you may have seen a practitioner of such a magic."

Cal felt the chill flood over him like a frigid wind in the depths of winter. He had escaped something much more terrible than he could fathom, and he had been closer to death than he ever cared to be.

"What could be done then? If we find 'em, can we kill 'em?" Bill, ever the optimist, asked.

"You could, but most likely at a terrible cost to our newly enlisted soldiers. These… people are aided by a magic that, I believe, consumes their very essence. Are they charmed? Possessed? Enhanced? I cannot say which, but it terrifies me," Alec warned, staring a moment longer into the candle.

Nothing sounded optimistic, but what struck Cal were the old man's own words. "What do you mean by *people*?" he asked.

"There are many unique creatures of this world, but the one that you speak of and has been rumored by so many others is quite unusual. I know of no beast with as many heads and limbs. And what of this darkness? Why does it mask them so?"

Cal had no answer to give, and Bill was just as confounded.

"What else could they be?" Bill asked. Alec again focused on the puzzle at hand.

"Let me ask you this. What did they sound like?" Alec challenged.

Cal closed his eyes and reflected on the night. "There must have been dozens of them, maybe hundreds. The rumble of their hooves was deafening." Cal hunched forward as the recollection came to his mind.

"Good," Alec complimented as if Cal were a student who had recited a song without error. "But let me ask you this... think carefully now! What did they sound like? Did you hear the whinny of a horse?" Alec emphasized.

"No. I don't remember hearing any neighing," Cal answered after scratching his chin and reflecting for a time.

Alec appeared disappointed with his response.

"The beasts chuffed and snorted," Cal recalled.

That wasn't the answer Alec was prepared for. He stroked his scraggly beard and continued to ponder what he had just heard.

"That is very strange, my young friend!" Alec exclaimed. "If not a horse, then what did they ride upon?" The old man mused as Cal's curiosity piqued.

"What do you mean?" Cal asked.

"I think they were men riding beasts, but perhaps they were not horses. Something with hooves, yes. But I am beginning to doubt it was upon the horse!" Alec mused.

"What other beast could carry men so swiftly?" Cal countered.

"It is not unheard of. The nomadic tribes of the east ride upon exotic beasts like bear-sloths and mammoths. There are realms of the west where men have been known to ride upon birds of terror, and other island peoples ride upon water dragons!"

Cal let out a laugh. He knew of the nomads, but... dragons and mounted birds? Those were stories for children.

"I can't speak of dragons, but I know the stomping of hooves when I hear it," Cal stated confidently as Alec smiled back.

"Assuredly, time will show us what is true, my friends," Alec replied.

"Well, it doesn't matter if they're a creature or men riding something else! How are we s'posed to fight 'em with all this darkness and this magic?" Bill demanded.

Only then, as Bill's persistence continued, did Alec stumble over an elegant and brilliant thought as the candle flicked on their table, and he stared through it.

"Magic is sometimes simple, I've found. Where there is darkness, shed light. Where fire is rampant, douse it with water."

"That's not amus'n," Bill huffed.

"... And it's also confusing," Cal interjected.

"These are confusing times, I'm afraid," Alec said, grinning to himself.

Bill's frown grew with puzzlement and frustration. "Shall we carry torches an' pails of water? Tell us how to fight 'em or all you're do'in is wast'in our time!" Bill spat.

Alec smirked at him. "Fret not, Master Bill. My purpose is not to annoy you. Before I can be sure of what I should do, tell me what happened after you saw them, Cal?"

Cal hadn't realized his story wasn't finished. Both Bill and he were distracted by Alec's eccentricities and trivial questions.

"Once I poked my head out to better look at the creature, three arrows flew past me. They nearly found the mark. Following that, I broke open my floorboards, crawled under my home, and fled into the woods. I escaped them, but I snuck back to uncover who had attacked me. I found my house ablaze and the raiders had ridden off. I only snatched the quickest of glances at them through my broken window."

Alec nodded in understanding and appeared to mull over everything that Cal had said.

"Have you anything to add about them?" Alec asked.

Bill grew flustered and shifted in his seat. He shared no details of his night with the raiders in the Fork, but Cal could imagine. Their neighbors were slaughtered right outside his store. Cal wouldn't have shared it either.

"Truth be told, I heard a fair commotion m'self an' leapt to the window. It was dark, 'cept the road just out my window. The blackness breezed through the streets an' I knew the worst would follow. So, I hid in the cellar," he shamefully admitted as he avoided his eyes.

Cal realized the real reason why Bill hadn't discussed the raid.

"I didn't see 'em at all, but I heard 'em. Just as he said," Bill motioned to Cal as he kept his head firmly down. "They trampled, burned, and killed 'em all." He said no more as he dashed his tears into his sleeve and drank deeply into his flagon.

"There, there, my friend," Alec consoled, producing a worn handkerchief. Bill took it and proceeded to blow his nose and wipe the tears he was trying to conceal from them.

"Gentlemen, you have trusted me with your story and with that, I have become enlightened. If you would grant me one final question… I think I may have a proposal for you. What are your intentions now?" Alec asked.

Cal had considered what his intentions were going to be ever since a torch flew through his window, but when Bill spoke, he all but decided. Those were their friends and neighbors. And despite everything they didn't know about the raiders, he wanted to fight back and, for that matter, he could help. He'd been more than a decent rider since he was a young boy, and he could shoot an arrow through a rabbit's eye if given the chance. He could also track as well as most woodsmen, but he was far from the best.

"I'd like to join the fight," Cal announced. "I know you have mixed feelings, Bill, but I don't think I'd be right to leave without fighting for our homes. So, I won't continue south. I intend to sign up with the cavalry if they'll have me. I know the Crestwood, and I think I could be of use there."

Bill furrowed his brow and sighed. His face said it all. Bill had hoped to venture the southern road with the other Crestfolk and Cal to accompany him. Maybe because he was afraid. Maybe because he was ashamed. He took a long gulp from his flagon and wiped his chin with his sleeve.

"Well then, I'd have hoped to at least have slept on it, but I see your mind is made. Ya sure, lad?" Bill asked.

Cal knew Bill might ask once more, but he was sure. Someone needed to stand for the Crestfolk, and Cal wanted to be the one to stand for them.

"I am."

"Well then, I'll be there beside ya an' watch'n after ya. I was never much of a horseman m'self, but I reckon I could manage. Although, I'm short a mare," Bill mustered.

"Bill, you don't have to come with me," Cal insisted, but Bill waved him off.

"I'll not be moved, lad. If ya go, then I'll go too. We've got to stick together now!" Bill declared as Alec nodded in agreement.

"Good. I believe we can help each other," Alec responded. "May I propose a pact? Let me accompany you and share in your quest. Help me uncover this mystery and defeat this dark magic. I, too, will shield your backs and guard you as you sleep. I ask you would do the same for me."

Cal didn't need a moment to think it over. The man before him was flawed in many ways but spoke with a queer elegance and truth. There was trust and resilience to be found in him. He raised his flagon to Alec and Bill and looked at both men.

"Done," he said as they toasted.

Cal finished his drink, and for the first time in over a week, he was at ease. He had found a welcoming companion among the Mid, and they had a semblance of a plan that didn't involve fleeing or hiding for their lives. Even if their proposal meant they would purposefully join the war effort, it was exciting and new. Cal was even enthusiastic about having the eccentric Alec with them to combat these foes. He didn't know what Alec might do, but the prospect was optimistic.

The waitress appeared again as the glasses emptied. "Another, my friends?" she inquired, "… or perhaps something else?" She brushed her hand gently across Cal's face. It was warm, soft, and welcoming to him, but his blushing cheeks betrayed his youth.

"Oh my, so young!" she laughed.

"Naomi, my love, I'm afraid we have more pressing issues," Alec interceded.

He climbed onto the table, reached for an old bastard sword, and removed it from an elk rack on the wall. He had almost no control as the dull blade came whooshing down off the wall. As the commotion unfolded, no outcry came from the patrons.

Cal wondered again about the exact nature of the relationship Alec had with the curious tavern. Perhaps the old man lived here, but he did not know.

"Tell Amelia I will miss her dearly, but I'm afraid we too will answer the call of our Lord Malcolm," Alec continued.

"Shame. We had thought to set aside a place for you and your friends this evening," Naomi gushed. She winked at Cal and continued to caress his face as if to dissuade at least him.

"Perhaps another time," Alec insisted. "We must away. Be a good dear and have Nigel fetch my staff."

Naomi frowned and went to the bar to deliver Alec's message.

Cal stood to follow Alec to the exit, with Bill behind him. He had considered making the argument to linger a little longer, but Alec was determined to be on their way.

The group made their way through the tables, and just before departing, Alec was handed a long wooden staff with a heavy head and a pocket atop it. Alec shoved the sword in his belt loop and took the staff from Nigel. "We may need accommodations this evening, but I am unsure. If not, I wish you well. Oh, and feed the cat," Alec directed.

Nigel continued drying the glass in hand and nodded. As they departed, Cal seriously suspected Alec was the proprietor of *Nightingales.*

***

Evening had fallen upon the city, but the tempo did not slow or falter. Lanterns glowed from every establishment, and the walkways were frequented by many groups of folks parading and celebrating. Calls and shouts echoed from the markets to taverns. All were encouraged to join the war effort. The Midguardmen had little control, and some even joined in with the libations. The mood was high.

Cal, Bill, and their new friend Alec had passed many inns, taverns, and shops on their way to the elegant Elena's Tavern. The outer walls were painted in a variety of blues and turquoises. The windows were elaborately colored with each panel displaying one great scenic visage after the other. The pictures in the windows glimmered numerous far-off places. Many onlookers stopped and gazed at the wonders the windows displayed.

The inside of the tavern was bright with autumnal colors, the walls were filled with tapestries and art, the banister was ornately carved, and it smelled pleasant. The tavern itself was bustling with company. There were fighters, gamblers, Men-at-Arms, rich merchants, Crestfolk, and Midfolk.

Along the far wall was a long table where folk gathered and were volunteering for the cavalry. Seven men of the Midguard sat at the table. At the center, an older, heavy-chested, and slightly plump man was seated. He wore a deep burgundy tunic outside his chain mail with the city's crest embossed over his heart. He grew egregiously long, light-colored sideburns to overcome the signs of balding atop his head. He overlooked several men to his left and right, as they signed folk into service.

Cal recognized the man had an air of command as Alec led the party to the table where a stocky Darwishman, a few years older than Cal, was volunteering.

The Darwish were a short, hardy, and often bearded people, but the tales exaggerated them; they were no different than other men. That was another fable conjured by intolerant men who didn't favor them, because the Darwish preferred living in the earth than above it. Some often called them dwarves as an insult to them and the name of their people. The Darwish did not find it amusing.

The Darwishman standing in the tavern had a friendly smile; his deep brown beard was carefully manicured, and his mustache curled up at the ends. He carried a halberd that stood a foot over his head with his comparatively small shield slung around his heavy red leather outer coat.

"It's a common misconception that the Darwish do not ride upon horses," said the Darwishman. "How else are we to travel the long road with these short legs?"

The young Captain attending to the Darwishman considered his comments with great puzzlement as if the thought had not occurred to him. After a moment of internal debate, he began to mark his name when the older heavy man stopped him.

"We haven't the time to outfit a proper saddle to your... stature, nor do we have time to train the horse," sneered Sir Kenneth.

The Darwishman didn't seem bothered by the comment; he replied with a broad smile. "Aye. Well, lucky for me I brought a wee filly with me who is accustomed to my... stature shall we say. So, if that is your concern, fear not."

"We are in immediate need of skilled riders, Master Darwishman. We mean to outfit, supply, and be moving within a day or two. No more! The infantry is accepting perfectly..."

"Forgive me, sir," the Darwishman interrupted holding up a hand. "I'm a skilled rider and, I'll wager, better than most of your men of the Mid. I've seen my share of skirmishes around the western hills, and like I told your young companion, you should not believe everything you hear. You're likely to make a fool of yourself in front of your men. At least, more of a fool than you already are."

Sir Kenneth smiled insincerely and stared back at the Darwishman. "Oh, I see, a funny dwarf! Another misconception, I'm sure. We can be funny as well in the Mid. I'll have Captain Willem take your name down. Tomorrow, we'll assemble at the city stables. And Master Gregory has set aside rooms for all in the auxiliary or, in your case… um, a cupboard." Sir Kenneth hissed as the men at the table sniggered.

The Darwishman grasped his axe with two hands and sneered as each Midguardmen at the table stopped their laughter and prepared themselves for a halberd appearing in the vicinity of Sir Kenneth's head. The tension grew at the table when an unfamiliar hand was gently laid on the Darwishman's shoulder and stood beside him in consolidation.

"Gentlemen, are we not allies in this fight? Shall we dispense with the insults?" Alec demanded.

As the old man intervened, Cal grew uncertain of his new companion. What sense compelled the old man to interfere in another's affair, he did not know.

"Ah… Alec, the user!" Sir Kenneth spat. He rose, and his men followed. As they stood, each man placed a hand on his sword or dagger hilt. All in the tavern noticed the disturbance, and silence quickly followed. "You're looking unusually sober. Have you exhausted the customary concoctions to smoke, drink, and dull the senses? I wonder, do you know where you are?"

Alec smiled. He was accustomed to Sir Kenneth's quips and jabs. His remarks were without much impact like autumn leaves falling to the ground.

"I feel quite right, as a matter of fact. Thank you for your concern, and as it were, I am standing on the east side in Elena's Inn and Tavern. You know, the establishment owned by Master Gregory."

"Ah! I am delighted to hear you are unencumbered at the moment. When I arrest you, the defenders will be unable to claim inebriation, and you will not be exonerated from your crimes."

"And may I ask what crimes have I committed this evening?"

"Vagrancy and obstruction!" Sir Kenneth replied coldly.

"Forgive me, constable, but the law states I must be unwanted in the establishment to be a vagrant," Alec insisted.

"YOU'RE ALWAYS FUCKING UNWANTED!" Sir Kenneth yelled.

Everyone within the tavern became still.

"How can I be unwanted if Lord Malcolm requested my assistance, Constable?"

Sir Kenneth ceased the visceral hatred and replaced it with confusion. "What in all the Gods are you talking about?"

"I am here to answer the call, Constable," Alec declared.

Sir Kenneth broke out in a long howl. Once he did, his men and the entire tavern hemmed and hawed.

Although the tension had broken and Alec looked amused at their response, he appeared quite determined.

"In fact…" Alec held up a hand to silence the crowd. "I have brought men to aid you and scout for you."

Sir Kenneth wiped the tears from his eyes and reached for his goblet. He swirled his wine, drank, and wiped his chin. "You're mad! Why should I allow this farce?"

"Why wouldn't you? Our lord calls for men to defend the Mid. I volunteer myself. Would you defy your lord?"

"Gods! We need men of worth. Fighting men!" Sir Kenneth snarled. "Men who can kill. Men who can take orders. You would be a hindrance to our campaign and his lordship. If I were to let you gallivant about with our colors, we would be the laughingstock among the realms."

Alec grinned at the notion of himself garbed in the Mid's colors. "I think you judged me too harshly, Constable. Yes, I've disagreed with you on an occasion, but I'm not without the ability to follow commands. Are you and Lord Malcolm so rich in allies that you would turn away fighting men? I'm sure I, too, could be of use to the cause."

"Hah! And what use could you possibly be?" Sir Kenneth snickered.

"Oh, you don't know. I have many characteristics you find lacking, I am sure. However, I have always possessed a critical eye. No doubt, even you could say otherwise. And my eye has found you a pair of superb scouts. You have many men no doubt from the Crest, but these men know every backroad and hill from the western territory to the hook." Alec embellished the details, but he did it well.

Cal gave Bill a side-eye glance and a nod in hopes Bill understood the need to corroborate the story.

Even the old knight fell silent; he was interested in the prospect. However, he remained skeptical.

"You!" Sir Kenneth pointed at Bill. "What's your trade, and where are you from?"

Bill hesitated only a moment. He was never in favor of being addressed in public. "I'm a trader. Bill's me name. Some say Sweet Bill, an' others just Bill. I owned a trade post up the Fork. Many came through there an' I would see 'em well stocked."

The room fell silent. No one had seen or heard from anyone as far north as the Fork since before the raids.

Alec had said as much earlier, and when Bill mentioned it, you could hear a pin drop.

"This is a partner o' mine, Cal," Bill continued. "He's a good lad. He farms land an' I help sell his crop. Now an' then, he helps me trade about the Crest."

Most folks peered at the pair like a pale shadow. But then a rather large man descended the staircase and approached the pair. His clothes were made of fine silks of purples and reds. His wrists jingled with chains and cuffs and his rings were lavishly decorated. He was the richest man Cal had ever seen.

"Excuse me, sir? Master Bill of the Fork? Mercantile and alike? Forgive me, I forget your surname," Master Gregory interrupted.

"That's correct, sir. Roaker's me family name, sir," Bill replied.

"Gods be good! I have known this man for years, albeit through postscript, but we have shared good stock many times," he comforted. "Welcome, my friends, to Elena's. I am Master Gregory the proprietor of this establishment."

"I know ya well, sir," Bill responded as they shook hands.

"I had not seen you this evening, Master Gregory," Sir Kenneth interrupted, eyeing Master Gregory.

Master Gregory shifted his attention to the old knight. It was apparent he did not want the merchant to interfere with his affair. "No, I was upstairs attending to business, you know, and you were to task in my hall. No doubt conducting the Lord's business. Of course, I took note when the shouting began. Elena's, as you know, is not that kind of uncivilized place," Master Gregory replied coldly.

"I am tasked to recruit rough men," Sir Kenneth rebuffed. "Additionally, it was requested that those rough men assemble in this very establishment. I'm sure you can understand if a misunderstanding occurs."

"Oh, what I understand clearly, among other things, the Commander of the Midguard is to maintain the peace. Surely that is understandable," Master Gregory implied.

Sir Kenneth narrowed his eyes and folded his arms, but the councilman turned away from him to address the other party in the squabble.

"What do we have here? My opponent from earlier this afternoon. Come, Alec, what is it you ask of the Commander?"

"My companions and I wish to join and scout for the cavalry, Master Gregory," Alec responded.

Gregory smirked in surprise. "My goodness! Opposition in the afternoon and enlistment in the evening. I have never known you to alter your mind so quickly. What could possibly have convinced you?"

"My new companions are well versed in the Crest, as I have said, and they would be misused as mere soldiers. They will be able to scout, and well, if given the opportunity. And if I assist them, I may be afforded answers to my questions surrounding this darkness. So yes, I will serve," Alec responded.

"Indeed. I must find some means to thank these two men," replied Master Gregory. He ran his eyes over the pair and remained unimpressed. "You understand that his lordship is uninterested in temporary service. The Mid requires you until the enemy is vanquished."

"I will sign that agreement," Cal insisted.

All eyes around the table and the tavern fell on the young man. Cal hardly believed he'd interrupted, but he wanted to be heard. He stepped forward so that the table could see him.

"You had asked me earlier in the square if I would join and I hold to what I said, sir. I would fight them and drive them back, but that is not enough. I am not one to let these raiders murder the folk of my home. I have seen what they have done, and raiding is far from it. They burned out our folk, and the ones who didn't burn, they murdered. I saw nothing of them plundering and we cannot afford to distribute justice lightly to this kind of evil. When evil folk threaten death upon your people... you end them. I would also like to add that we haven't the luxury of rejecting good fighting folk. I care not where they come from. I will fight with the Master Darwishman if he'd like to fight with me."

Cal's words lingered among the silent tavern like a hymn. Then the patrons rose and toasted. Only Sir Kenneth remained unmoved.

"Agreed. I'll fight on those terms," the Darwishman nodded. He offered his hand to Cal, and they shook.

"Indeed," replied Master Gregory. "And well said!"

"May I draft such an oath for my companions and I to sign?" Alec asked. Master Gregory seemed pleased at the outcome. He turned to Sir Kenneth, who nodded with disdain.

Alec sat at the table in front of Willem. He was handed a parchment and quill; he began to pen.

"I hereby swear and affirm to submit myself in the service of Lord Malcolm, in defense of the Mid and the Crest against a foul and unknown enemy. And I swear to assist in the defeat of this enemy, so that they may never return, and reinstate peace in the realm. And I will follow the orders of my commander to the best of my ability. I offer my fealty, my sword, and my honor. This is my oath."

Alec finished writing, handed the document to Willem, and addressed the crowd, "I wish to extend an offer for good folk to join our party and the cause." Cal, Bill, and the Darwishman followed him in signing the oath, and then a few more folks formed a line.

Chapter VI
The Nomads

Su'ca and her party returned to their country seven days after meeting the Lord of the Mid. They covered more than a hundred leagues through abandoned farmlands of the Mid, the southern Crestwood, and the eastern range of the Crescent Mountains.

Past the mountains, the land transformed into an immense rolling grassland cut with bluffs and canyons; the only shade available was found among the few oases and only the great herds and the Par'sha knew where each oasis was located. The clans traveled all their lives from one hunting ground to the next, finding rest at the few sanctuaries the country offered.

Su'ca knew the land. Her clan had roamed the northern grasses for generations and she could lead her party blindfolded to the clans. A foreign traveler, however, would not survive alone in this country.

That was the difference between the western realms and the Par'sha. The realms always spoke of ingenuity and that the nomads would live better if they adapted to the ways of the cities, but Su'ca never understood this. Civilization made those peoples weaker, not stronger. They could never appreciate the beauty of the lands, the majesty of the herds, the simplicity of their lives, the toughness of their people, or their freedom to roam the land. They could never survive the great grass-sea.

The territory was avoided by the civilized realms for a thousand years. Yet, cities developed on both sides of the territory urging commerce to inevitably follow. Several hundred years ago, a southern route was mapped out, connecting the farthest eastern coastal cities to the western realms. Over time, the city peoples learned to negotiate and eventually pay various Par'sha clans for the permission to travel through the great grassland.

Some clans grew rich with silks, spices, wines, and coins to do with what they pleased. However, if the clans were not satisfied with their payment, caravans were known to vanish from the realm.

Once the trade routes were established, the western peoples left the Par'sha to their nomadic ways. Their trade was the only influence over the clans and it was precious to them. The realms would not challenge the Par'sha to a conflict or risk their profits. The country was too vast, the Par'sha were too many, and war would be too costly. That was why the most recent attacks had been so unexpected.

Had the western people finally decided to challenge the strength of the horde? Su'ca repeated this question to herself when she had departed for the Mid. Upon her return to her land, she did not have an answer.

From the edge of the territory, it took the party another three days before they caught up with the clans. Craa'su collected the various clans who bordered the northwestern territories and began moving them southeast. The priority was to move them out of harm's way; then he would return west with all the mounted warriors available. Su'ca knew as much but did not know if her father had begun his journey until she came upon their trail.

Every clan along the border had amassed into one mighty roving tribe. The grounds were trampled, the grasses crushed, and the clans moved slowly but surely. When they came across the trail, it was as though a highway had formed overnight. Her people were close.

As they approached the horde, they found several pods of bear-sloths with mounted warriors covering the rear of the column as the horde traveled east. The massive beasts were slower than the horses and the mammoths, but they were fearsome to behold.

When threatened, the bear-sloths stood on their hind legs and used their arms and claws to swat at any attacker; this protected the rider. When on all fours, a Par'sha rider would launch darts to keep any enemy from approaching. A single dart was larger than an arrow, struck deeper, and could kill with a single blow. Defeating a single bear-sloth and rider could be done, but surviving a pod of them was unlikely.

Su'ca and her warriors approached openly and in clear view behind the horde with the blunt end of their short-spears raised above them. As they neared the end of the column, the giant sloths turned to meet them and made a low bellow to warn the horde ahead of an unexpected approach. The beasts rose one by one, ready to strike, and without warning, a string of horses parted the long grasses on her flanks. They were well prepared to defend the horde.

"Your father will be pleased you have returned," called a familiar long-haired warrior.

Tahop'ka was one of her father's most trusted warriors and a friend. He assisted Craa'su in gathering the tribes after Su'ca departed. He wore black fur around his shoulders just like Su'ca. The bravest, most reliable, and tested warriors had a unique pelt bestowed around their shoulders by their clan's chief. From that point, the warrior would be known as a Crato'sha; the clan's protector.

Not every warrior was ordained in power, and those who were proudly displayed their pelt. A Crato'sha's shoulder pelt originated from the most fearsome beasts and had single plates interwoven beneath the skin. In battle, the Crato'sha could be struck many times and not fall. Some were famed to be invincible.

Tahop'ka waved off several riders and they did so without question. When a Crato'sha gave a command, it was followed as if the chief had spoken. The warriors turned their horses and returned to their positions. Some rode into the long grasses and a few rode to the sloth-riders who stood down and returned to following the horde.

"When will my father depart with our warriors?" Su'ca asked.

"Not before the young and the old are safely delivered to the next water. We should arrive before the sun sets," Tahop'ka replied.

"How many clans have we gathered?"

"Twenty-three survived the fires," he mourned.

Su'ca pulled on her reins, hands trembling, and gaped at him in disbelief. A clan consisted of at least a few hundred people to as many as a few thousand, and a small few had more than that. Thirty clans bordered the northwestern territories and never had so many of her people been killed or lost in an instant.

"The other clans could have traveled another trail," she suggested, grasping at some hope.

"They are no more!" Tahop'ka interrupted coldly. "I saw the great grass mountains burn and trap thousands. No one has seen the Mee'kanos, the Pra'kanas, or the Teha'kanos. When I sought out my sister's camp, I found only ash. Craa'su has gathered all who remain."

A glossy film formed over her eyes, but she buried the grief deep within her heart. She was a Crato'sha of her people. Her clan would look to their warriors like herself for inspiration among these dark times and the time for bravery was now. As the endless grasses fluttered in the wind, she decided to withhold her grief until those who were responsible had met their death at the hands of the Par'sha.

"I am sorry for your kin," she said, pushing aside the tears.

"I am sorry for all our kin," he lamented as he left her to join his warriors. Tahop'ka would turn his grief into anger, and when they came upon the enemy, he would be first to redden his spear.

When Su'ca had been sent to the west, she had not known the extent of what her people had suffered. Another clan sought her father out for assistance, followed by another. All the envoys spoke of an attack in the night, and great fires surrounding their clans. In response, Craa'su sent out riders to gather every clan, and he sent his most trusted warrior to the Mid; it was the first place to seek answers. Now that she returned, she did not think she had found those responsible.

Once she entered the realm of the Crest, she discovered abandoned villages and an empty country until she reached the city of the Mid. Only then had she begun to question her suspicion of at least the people of the Mid. Now, as Tahop'ka informed her of the death toll, for the first time, she worried about her people.

The last few hours of the march were without incident or surprise. The horde trudged forward and converged into the lush oasis where they set up their camp. They erected thousands of hide shelters and lit fires for cooking and warmth.

Su'ca found her clan in the heart of the haven. Their position among the clans had its advantages as they rested near the cool and refreshing waters. When her party arrived, she gave leave to her brethren warriors so they could rejoin their families. Her clan had greeted her and her companions warmly, gently nuzzling their foreheads together in an embrace. The clan was whole once more.

After her welcome, she found a familiar hut at the center of her clan. Her father's tent was larger and adorned with more vibrant colors and skins. It was the mark of the chieftain. The entrance was parted open to anyone, especially the Par'sha elders, to consult and visit him. A visitor would come bearing gifts for his assistance and sit upon a rug before him. The people often brought him food, hides, weapons, and gems. For their loyalty and contributions, he offered them protection and vision.

She entered the tent and found Craa'su entertaining two allied chiefs. Craa'su wore a white hide from an albino long-tooth cat on his shoulders with long golden chains draped across his pelt like those of the western lords. His chest was bare apart from the dark paints that told the story of his many victories as a young warrior and as a chief.

His gauntlets were heavy leather with gold and blue jewels woven into them. He was still fit for a man who had lived sixty summers. He had a strong jaw, a trimmed beard bearing white streaks, and his hair braided to one side; the other side was shaved.

When he rose to become the chief of his clan, Su'ca was not yet born, and now he had held the title longer than most. He had overcome two rivals; however, the right to challenge was still available to a clan member. Yet, no one was admired or respected more than Craa'su.

He did not greet her as his daughter. He sent her on a task as a trusted Crato'sha, and he expected her to report back as such. He held up his hands to his guests and they held silent.

"Forgive me, riders have returned from the west, and I must speak to them. Tell your warriors we will ride tomorrow and fear not. The clans will be protected," Craa'su reassured. The elders stood and bowed. Each turned and nodded to Su'ca as they left.

Su'ca took to the center of the tent and kneeled before him. She tilted her head in respect, and he returned the gesture.

"Tell me of the westmen," Craa'su directed.

For the entirety of her return journey, she had thought about how she might answer this question. She had not found the culprits, but she at least spoke to Lord Malcolm of the Mid. He was not a friend like another clan would be but he appeared not to be their enemy. She wondered throughout her journey if Craa'su would see that.

"I did not find the attackers in the west," she answered.

"I did not ask if you found the attackers. Tell me of the westmen!" he repeated, gazing through her.

She stared back at him. She was no longer a child to be scolded. She was a warrior of the Par'sha and had long since learned to control her fear of her father and everything else this world had to offer. She began again.

"We rode into the Mid and found their villages abandoned; there was no sign of resistance or the attackers. We kept riding and found their city full of the westmen; that is where the people retreated. Once we arrived, Lord Malcolm of the Mid treated with us..."

"Were you not halted by their soldiers?" He interrupted.

"We were questioned by their soldiers when we arrived. I told them I wished to speak to their Lord about the Par'sha, and I was brought before him. They welcomed us."

Craa'su stroked his beard and considered her actions. "That was foolish. You did not know if they were your enemy."

She could only smirk at this. They would have been fools to ambush them. "We met no one outside the Mid except the many peoples who were leaving to head south. They drove them like oxen.

These western peoples were not fighting; they were fleeing. You asked me to find the westmen who attacked our people. These were not them, and I knew there was no reason to fear them."

Craa'su nodded in understanding, drinking from a waterskin, and motioned her to continue.

"Lord Malcolm received us as I am received by you. He first asked why we had come. When he said this and did not first speak of the many peoples fleeing or the attacks, I knew I would have to speak many words with him to find the truth."

"They do not speak straight as you or I," Craa'su said, moving his hand between Su'ca and himself.

"I know, father, but I did not want to speak many words with him. I wanted to speak straight as you have taught me. So, I thought of what I had seen. I saw many people from their country who had abandoned their homes. Many men were seeking refuge and a chance to speak with their Lord in his home. They were a troubled people, but he would not acknowledge it. So, I pressed him. I asked him why his lands were empty, why the villages in his country had been attacked, and why he had done nothing. When I said this, I struck true to his heart. That is when he finally spoke the truth to me," Su'ca said, holding her hand over her heart.

"What did he say?" Craa'su eagerly asked.

"He told me many people had been attacked in the north, and they fled south. He protects them now. He asked again why we had sought him out. I told him of the fires of the great grasses and our people had been scattered. I stared into his eyes when I told him this attack was from the west. He stared back and told me the Mid did not attack our people."

Craa'su clasped his hands together, thinking of all Su'ca had told him. "It gives me great pause to believe a man who must be pried open. Yet, many westmen are like this. Do you think his words were straight and true?" he asked.

Su'ca had thought long about this. He had said many things to her but, overall, she believed Lord Malcolm was honest when he spoke.

"I do, father. His words were strong, and he was adamant; it was not the Mid who did this. Before we left their hall, he offered us food from his table and offered care for our horses. As we ate, men began to shout for war and blood like warriors often do before battle. I was approached by his man and he said the Mid would ride north against the attackers. He said we are allies in this fight."

Craa'su sat for a long time, weighing everything he had heard. It was much to consider given the history between the peoples of the cities and the Par'sha. "I do not know if I trust any westman. I have seen many western peoples pass through our land and most trade words as if they mean nothing. They will say one thing, but then not keep what they have promised. I do not know this Lord Malcolm, but I know the reputation of many of his merchants that come before us seeking passage. If you trust this Lord Malcolm and his words, then I will trust his words," Craa'su remarked, challenging his daughter's assessment.

Su'ca knew of what her father meant. Every dealing with the merchants was a tireless negotiation. Yet, what she had seen of the Mid, the fleeing people, and what Lord Malcolm had shared, nothing gave her further doubt. "I do, father," she confirmed without hesitation.

His deep green eyes reflected the flickering candles of his tent as he stared at her in silence, before nodding and turning his attention to the candles. He may have been the chief of her clan, but she knew her father and he accepted her conclusion. Only a small doubt remained as a furrowed brow crossed his face.

"What is your mind, father?" she pressed.

He turned his attention back to her. "I believe the Mid did not attack us, but I am still of a mind that some westmen have. You say this Lord will ride against these attackers, but I question his heart. Will he truly fight them or speak words with them? The westmen are a weaker people like this. They sometimes talk of peace before their spears have seen blood. What if he is of this kind?" Craa'su explained.

Su'ca gritted her teeth; she had not considered this. Lord Malcolm had treated with the Par'sha, and their audience was received expeditiously. Even she found this surprising at the time. *If Lord Malcolm was this diplomatic, could he be open to talks with these attackers as well?* It was concerning.

"I do not know," she admitted, looking away from Craa'su. "All the city cried for war when we left. I believe with all my heart this is what they meant."

"What of the man who said they will ride north and that we and the Mid are allies? Who was this man and why did these words of war not come from Lord Malcolm's lips?" Craa'su insisted.

Su'ca had not thought of the knight since they had last spoken. He was short with her like westmen can be. If she had been elsewhere with him, she would have considered punishing him for his rudeness.

"He was Lord Malcolm's man, a knight. They discussed their war once we left their hall. When they finished, the knight found me. He spoke the words of his Lord. I have no reason to doubt him," she decided.

Craa'su narrowed his eyes. He did not appear to like her answer. "Then we will see if they mean what words they have said," he responded. "I will be cautious if we meet them in the west."

"The west?" she replied, her heart racing with anticipation to face their enemy head-on, and to clutch her spear, ready to strike.

"Yes. Hear my words and spread them to our people. The horde will ride out when the day breaks. We must travel far and strike our enemy fiercely. We will push them from our lands and then further into the west. I will find these westmen, and we will strike at their homes; then no westman will ever come to the east again."

Su'ca smiled at the declaration.

"If the Mid joins us…," Craa'su continued, "… they will be welcomed, but they will not hinder us from this. We will unleash the horde and the western realms will be reminded of our fury…"

Chapter VII

The Party

Cal and his companions received orders to assemble at the city stables just after first light the following morning. Once their business with the constable concluded, the libations and celebrations continued. The tavern smelled of ales as the bards played songs of the Mid amid the cheering and toasting. Men congratulated the party, and Cal received many commendations for his speech. It was the second time he had been applauded for his commitment that day. He wondered if his speech was truly impressive or if the city's enthusiasm for the volunteers had simply reached a fever pitch. It was likely the latter.

Cal was particularly delighted that the young Darwishman, Halden, son of Halfa, joined their party, and the Darwishman seemed happy to be received by other Crestfolk. Cal thought him fearless to stand in front of more than half a dozen men ready to fight for the opportunity to wage war with the real enemy. Now more than ever, the realm needed folk like him, and the constable was too prejudiced to see it. If Alec had not intervened, the argument would have escalated into a brawl, and folk would likely have been killed. The deaths would have been needless, and their sword-arms would have been missed.

Before Cal knew it, he was handed a goblet of sweet wine and cheered by an elderly chap. The wine was light, sweet, and tasted of peaches. Cal enjoyed the ease of its consumption and promptly had another goblet filled, followed by another. Drinks were bought, passed, and shared until a feverish euphoria came over him, and he wore an infectious grin.

Sometime after Cal's fourth glass, Alec suggested returning to Nightingales. It wasn't as lavish as Elena's, but the old tavern had proven to be far more welcoming that day than the constable had been at Elena's. Perhaps Alec felt the same after his confrontation, although Cal did not know.

Regardless, Cal was interested in the girl with the golden curly hair who had given him so much attention at the tavern, and he agreed wholeheartedly to the proposition. The four men stumbled through the streets, like so many others that evening, seeking out warmth, shelter, festivities, and additional company.

They found Nightingales as they had left it, and yet all had risen in spirits and were now friendly in salutations. The old tavern had a warm glow about her as the hearths came alive in the evening. The silk-red cushions glinted from the firelight and old men sang unfamiliar shanties. Nightingales transformed into a delightful tavern where the toughest-looking customers were as merry as the next; perhaps this is why Alec called it home. The only person who appeared the same was Nigel, who stood vigilant at the bar as before, almost as if the same glass required hours of cleaning. Cal felt happy for the first time since before the raids.

They found a private sitting room with a warm hearth surrounded by several empty chairs. The party sat by the fire, exchanged introductions, and raised glasses to their company. As the evening continued, Cal found himself comforted by a cushioned chair, a warm fire, and a few more glasses; his eyelids grew heavy until he could not keep them open any further.

***

Cal woke to a knock at the door in a room he had no recollection of entering. His head throbbed and the sunlight through the glass window seared his eyes, but overall, he was in good condition. He rose to his feet and opened the door. His heart fluttered at the lovely smile of the girl he'd hoped to find the prior evening. She wore a white blouse with a deep neckline and a blue apron that hugged her lower curves.

"Your companions are breaking fast down the hall, Master um...?" Naomi asked.

Cal caught himself hesitating from her extraordinary beauty, but he finally managed to finish her sentence. "Cal! My name is Cal," he greeted.

She giggled at his pause.

"Master Alec tells me your party has chosen to join the Midguardmen, and you're to scout for the cavalry."

"I have. I mean… we have," Cal sheepishly corrected. "We should depart for the stables soon if we are to be on time. I hope not to risk a poor first impression of us."

"Your first impression of the day is not so poor," she teased.

"Naomi, the platters!" yelled Nigel down the corridors. The business of morning breakfast could be heard down the hall, and both looked in the direction of the call. Plates were being filled, and mutters of the morning could be heard quietly.

"I have to go," she sighed. She turned to meet his eyes and smiled. "… but perhaps we will be lucky enough to see each other some other time."

Suddenly, his head did not throb, nor did his body ache.

"I would very much like that. Although, I do not know what the guard will require of me. Still, I hope the day will bring me back to the inn," he said, grinning.

"Good. I will look for you this evening, then," she said, smirking as she turned from him.

His eyes followed her curves down the corridor as she left him and he let out a long breath. *May the gods bless me with a fortunate return!*

"Cal, let's get going!" Bill shouted from down the hall.

Cal pulled himself from his thoughts, closed the door, and splashed himself with water from a bowl on the nightstand. Bill was right; he needed to get going and they all had somewhere to be. He quickly dressed and left his room.

His companions had already found their way to the tables. Each man received a serving of eggs, sausages, and bread. Bill shoved a plate into his hands as he entered the room.

"We can't lollygag this morn'n, boy! Make quick work of it!" Bill remarked.

Cal devoured his meal and poured the contents of his mug down his gullet. He recoiled at the sour, residual taste of a kind of tomato juice while the others laughed at him.

"That'll clear ya head for the day!" Bill chided and patted his shoulder.

Bill was right; the concoction woke him.

They departed the tavern in haste and recovered the two horses they had between them. Halden's horse was a chestnut-colored bay filly whose mane was braided, her coat was neatly brushed, and her saddle was well-polished. Any passerby who saw the lovely horse would know that she was well kept.

"Halden, out of curiosity…" Cal began.

"… How do I heave myself onto my lovely Ginette here?" Halden finished and scratched beneath her chin.

Cal immediately regretted asking. Even he was susceptible to the legends of Halden's people, and he always thought the Darwish disliked heights.

"It's alright, my friend. No offense is given. First, she must be taught young, like this one here. She's three summers along now, and I've trained her since she was a foal. Her saddle is fitted, not unlike any other man of the realm, only smaller. She knows when I want to attend to her and comes right over. At Darwish stables, we have raised platforms purposed to assist us."

"Huh! A Darwish stable?" Cal repeated.

"It's not as uncommon as most people will have you believe. All folks train with horses; we're no different. Although I'll admit, we like to work with the smaller horses and ponies. We keep them in a comfortable pen just inside the iron mine my family keeps in the western valleys. It's no great Darwish hall but comfortable enough and well-hidden. That is…" he stammered. "… until the darkness came." He fought against the tears that were clearly collecting.

The heavy words lingered like rolling clouds on a stormy day; the grief was too near for most Crestfolk.

"I'm sorry, Halden," Cal apologized.

"No need, Cal," he reassured. "It's hard not to think of them. I'm sure you do as well."

Cal's chest tightened. Where most had begun to grieve, he somehow felt shame. He had lost before, but his family, Bill, was strolling in front of him and had been looking after him for years now. Not that he really needed it. He had known his grief for some time and had learned to live with it. He was one of the fortunate ones in that regard, if there were any.

"Fear not. Many folks have gathered now, and we'll show them how the realm fights!" Halden grinned and wiped away the tears.

Cal's spirit rose to see his new companion determined to do something.

"Although, I think you'll need more than the bow. Have you no good sword or spear?" Halden asked.

"No. I thought we might be armed sooner or later."

"Ugh! Sure, they'll hand you a piece of steel that's just been forged, but there's no guarantee of its quality. Some of these smiths are good, but most are rushing along. I've seen some of the foot soldiers as well. Some of their blades are shit! Let me seek out my kin by the forges. There we will find a quality Darwish smithing at work folding good steel. Those legends are not without merit. For your party's hospitality, I will purchase you a blade worthy of the Darwish warrior!"

"You are too generous, Halden. I confess I am not a practiced swordsman or spearman," Cal admitted.

"I'll find time to school you on the subject. I'm not a swordsman either, but I can show you how to defend yourself. How are you with the bow?"

"Better than most, I should think. I've hunted most of my life and I can place an arrow in a rabbit or squirrel most times."

"If that's the case, then you shouldn't be modest. Keep them at a distance for now, and you will be fine. At least until I've measured your ability to wield a blade and instructed you further," Halden insisted.

"I'm grateful for any instruction, but that will have to wait," Cal replied. "I can see a good number of folk gathered up ahead; it looks like we've arrived."

Hundreds of Crestfolk were assembled outside the stables. They were hunters, woodsmen, and the women consisted mostly of Elvians. They were garbed in green blouses and tan trousers and covered in chestnut brown cloaks. They looked as if they blended with the woodlands. They also wore light and flexible red leather armor around their torsos, shins, and forearms. They looked better prepared than most. Most of the menfolk had bows and darker cloaks, but few had leather guards to protect them. Regardless, all were kin of the realm in Cal's eyes.

"Tie off your ponies to the fence and form a line. You're to be fitted today. We have bracers, greaves, and pauldrons for those who need them. If you have your own, that's alright, but everyone will be issued a chest piece and a gorget with the Mid's crest. You will need a spear, a shield, and a sword. If you've got one, that's alright too. Lastly, units will be assembled after you've been issued gear. Come on then, move along!" Captain Willem shouted as folk approached the stables.

All manner of folks hurried into the stable. Once inside, Cal saw the full scale of the operation and the numerous stations along the long corridor. First, the party approached tailors who measured each volunteer and handed out surcoats of the Mid.

Halden was the only one whose tunic had to be altered. The party began to look like real soldiers once they donned their new burgundy coats. Once Halden's coat was trimmed, they were fitted with leather braces, greaves, and chest armor. Some preferred studded leathers, and others wore leather plates. Some wore helmets crafted by Midfolk, and others wore Darwish helms. It was clear all craftsmen who could fabricate leather armor had been summoned to do so for the realm. The entire company of folk would have the look of the many peoples of the Crest.

The party was then herded further down the corridor, where smiths had forged fresh weapons for the riders. The city had amassed a large cache of shields, spears, swords, bows, and arrows. The weapons were leaning against the walls of several empty animal pens. Cal was handed a shield and a quiver to sling over his shoulder by the Sergeant-at-Arms.

Before he was handed his spear, Halden interjected, grabbed the weapon, and inspected it. He removed his glove and shaved the back of his hand with the blade of the spear. "That'll do, lad. Keep it sharp, and it'll serve you well," he commented. He nodded in approval and proceeded to inspect Bill's and Alec's weapons. He returned a sword and a shield on behalf of Bill to the Sergeant-at-Arms for better ones. Halden himself accepted no weapons. He brought his own halberd, wore a shield on his back, and carried an ax on his hip.

Cal emerged from the stable, looking fit and feeling overwhelmingly invincible. His companions, too, had a soldierly appearance about them.

Bill walked taller for an older man, and Halden, although only adding a surcoat, was pleased with his new emblem. Even Alec looked inspiring despite the rags he wore underneath the fresh clothes he was given.

"Alright then, men! Riders to me!" a gray-haired man in gleaming chainmail and a fresh surcoat commanded. "My name is Master Wendall, and I am Sir Kenneth's second. I will be assisting him in our mission. We are the first to venture north and judge the enemy. It goes without saying that our report is vital to the Lord of the Mid. We must uncover the enemy, whatever the cost. Some of you brought your own horses and others are without. See Captain Willem, and he will sort you out. Everyone else, retrieve your ponies and we are to ride outside the west city gate. I aim to gauge whether you good folk are as skilled as you claim you are. So, let us be off!"

Folk retrieved their horses upon Master Wendall's command. "I s'pose we're off to Captain Willem," Bill said aloud.

"… And quickly before the best horses are taken," Alec agreed.

"We'll retrieve our mounts while you acquire yours. We will only be a moment," Cal interjected.

Alec nodded, and the party divided. The walk around to the front of the stables was not far, but Cal began to understand the weight of his new gear. The leather bracers and greaves slightly slowed his stride, the leather of his chest armor rubbed around his neck, and his helm felt tight around his forehead as the nose guard rubbed back and forth across the bridge of his nose. All these minor inconveniences required him to awkwardly muscle himself forward. He would need a few days to accustom himself. However, in the meantime, he would make time in the evening to adjust some of his new gear.

They reached their horses, and Cal mounted promptly. He glanced at Halden just in time to witness his incredible acrobatic acumen as he nimbly ascended to the top of the fence and balanced himself with his halberd. Ginette swiftly brought herself alongside Halden, and he hopped on her.

"A capable rider indeed!" Cal grinned as he was eager to see what other skills the Darwishman offered.

"We'll see for sure who can ride," Halden laughed. They trotted back around the stables to find their companions mounted and joined by five other riders.

"And here we all are," Master Wendall commented as Cal and Halden approached.

"May I introduce Master Cal of the Fork and Master Halden of the Western Valleys," Alec introduced.

"Good day, gentlemen," Master Wendall said, inspecting them as they arrived.

Cal nodded at the folk in front of him and realized he had seen them at Elena's the prior evening, signing their oaths after he had. His eyes met two androgynous Elvians, identical in height, slender in frame, and with dark blonde hair who each shaved a side of their head. They had only added new tunics to their already fitting wardrobes.

The Elvian legends were equally as embellished as the Darwishmen. They were called elves in the stories and were rumored to be fantastically gifted. Their folk were tall, gaunt, and they moved with a grace reminiscent of dancers on the stage. They were also rumored to be snobbish toward other men of the realm, but Cal found these two had friendly faces and kind smiles.

The only difference he could find between them was one shaved on the right side and the other on the left. One carried a long slender bow, a quiver overflowing with arrows, and a single curved bastard sword at their hip. The other carried an Elvian spear with an elongated curved blade, a small shield on their left arm, and several long daggers at their waist.

Cal couldn't help himself but closely examine their ears for a distinguished point; to his amusement, he found a slight angle.

To their left, atop a white and brown horse, rode a black-haired, scrawny man whose sun-touched skin marked him as a man of the far eastern cities. His hair was in a knot atop his head and he had a light beard around his jawline. He decided to forgo a helm and wore his dingy gray leather cloak on top of his other new attire. He carried a wooden shield and a short sword at his waist.

The next rider was a behemoth of a man who rode the largest horse Cal had ever laid his eyes upon, but that was the least interesting detail about him. He was covered from his helm, which masked his face, to his boots. He wore a unique set of plated leather gauntlets, a hood over his mask, and he sported so many hides that Cal wondered if he had visited a tanner rather than a tailor.

To complete his ensemble, he accepted only the tunic of the Mid. He slung a war hammer over his shoulder, and he carried a large, unorthodox, and yet simple blade at his hip. The strange blade looked so heavy that Cal doubted he could even lift it with both hands. The giant looked forged for violence.

"I'm told you and Bill are well versed in the roads and country around the Fork and northern Crestwood?" commented Master Wendall.

Cal glanced at Alec and hoped his embellishment had not gotten out of hand. Cal had spent some time on the road with Bill but altogether thought the expectations were surpassing his actual knowledge.

"I am, sir," Cal replied. "Bill and I can manage navigating around many of the most northern roads."

"Good! And you, Master Darwish, I'm told you have knowledge of the western ranges near the borders?"

"I could navigate us from Galton's peak all the way to the High Slopes if you should like, and we could take paths hidden from sight if needed," Halden responded.

"Very well. I shall let you know if we require your insight," Master Wendall acknowledged. "This unit is made of the various peoples of the Crest. May I introduce Eris and Yslanna of the Elvian folk? These young women are both capable trackers and woodsmen from the eastern hills."

Both women nodded sequentially as their names were called. Eris, with the right-shaven head and the bow, and Yslanna with the left-shaven head and the long spear. Cal made a note to remind himself.

"The gentleman in the tattered leather coat is Jacoby, who comes from the great coastal cities of the east. He is a man of many skills and trades. He has spent many years abroad, here, and within the borders of the Crest. He is also a capable man on the field. He shall aid us as well."

"Pleasure, mates," Jacoby chimed.

"Lastly, the large gentleman is Clydes. He is mute and his penmanship is limited at best. However, he managed to communicate with a map that he hails near the Slopes somewhere. He has been assigned to this reconnaissance unit as well. He may prove useful and, if nothing else, intimidating to the enemy."

Clydes clearly understood his name, and he nodded at the comments made about him.

"Together, you have been assembled to scout for the Mid. Your collective knowledge should be sufficient to assist the vanguard, track, and find the enemy. Much is dependent on your assessment of the situation, and it goes without saying, the commander is relying on your reports and the reports from the other scouting parties."

"Will no Midfolk ride with us?" Alec asked.

"The Midfolk make up the other scouts," Master Wendall answered.

"Will the Commander shun us for the entirety of the expedition, or will we be allowed some courtesy to join the venture?" Alec interjected.

Cal considered his point. If the other scouts were solely Midfolk, then he had singled out their unit to all Crestfolk before anyone had been reviewed.

"I will not tolerate your contempt, Master Alec!" Master Wendall rebutted. "As long as you don the Mid's colors and have sworn your oaths, then you are expected to comply as commanded. Is that understood?"

Alec shifted in his saddle, restraining the impulse to question the new hierarchy of things. "I only wish for our success, Master Wendall. And we will fare better if we are incorporated," Alec stated.

"We all have gambled upon this venture, Master Alec, and perhaps you should invest more faith in it. Not that it's your concern, but I have personally vouched for this unit. So, you may direct your misguided anger at myself if you so choose. I may be a simple merchant, but I understand the value of knowledge, and this party knows the roads. For this reason, each of you should prove invaluable to the vanguard. Furthermore, I expect our unit to succeed, and I dare say, our unit's service shall be far more useful than any other's. Are there any other questions?"

Alec refrained from retorting.

"When and where might we be off?" asked Eris.

"We will likely depart tomorrow, and I can assure you that you will be at the forefront of the effort. We will locate the enemy and, if necessary, delay them. Any other questions?"

The party replied to Master Wendall with silence. "Very well, off with you to the training grounds."

The party made their way with the other riders through the city, beyond the western gate, and to the open ground along the west bank of the River White. The fields had been cleared away for the assembled army. Rows of tents were erected for the guard and the newly acquired infantry. Many folk were strewn around the camps, gathering, marching, and admiring themselves in their new garb.

The cavalry trotted to an open field, where they broke out into a run. They passed by the Lord of the Mid as he reviewed the troops. The company covered at least three leagues, circling the entire camp while the Captains led the gallop. Many folks kept up with the pace, and others fell squarely behind. Once they had concluded the gallop, each unit ran through a newly constructed obstacle course of barrels and straw men.

Cal was pleased his new companions showed immense skill among them. The Elvians were graceful with their chosen weapons; Eris landed arrows on every target and Yslanna was elegant and powerful with her spear. No dummy was left unscathed by them.

Halden wielded his halberd with deadly precision as he managed to impale one and followed that by removing the limbs of two other dummies. All manner of folks were impressed by the riding Darwishman. Jacoby and Cal both landed several arrows on targets, but not as many as Eris. Clydes barreled through the dummies and cut several in half. The next obstacle-course runner had little to show following the giant.

Alec and Bill showed far less skill. Bill himself lacked horsemanship, but managed to ride for the entirety of the day. When he ran through the course, he succeeded in impaling one dummy and received a passing nod from the reviewing Captains. Alec abandoned the spear altogether and ran through the course with a sword and shield. He wasn't without skill, but his mastery of the horse and sword simultaneously was wanting.

Altogether, the party was approved by all reviewers. Even the vanguard commander, Sir Kenneth, who sat alongside Lord Malcolm, gave a meager approval of many riders, including the scouting party. The day saw many folk marching, galloping, and training. Most of them were able enough, but others were replaced, reassigned, or removed altogether.

The day of riding, evaluations, and training ended sometime after midday. The cavalry was led to supply wagons where tents, cookware, and rations were distributed. Meanwhile, the new infantrymen took the field, ran through formations, and learned to lock themselves together to form a valiant shield wall.

The party gathered what supplies they needed and found a spot among the thousands of folks. Bill assigned himself as the cook for the party, and Eris made herself his assistant. The pair had cleared brush, set the pot with fresh river water, and then started cooking fish from the river. The River White had teemed with fish since before the Mid was settled, and it was one of the chief reasons stores had not been completely emptied by the saturation of folk. Many new soldiers would eat heartily in the basket of the Mid that evening.

As the party set up camp, Halden and Alec returned to the city for last-minute supplies. Alec reasoned it might be the last night near the Mid, and it would be good to gather a few items prior to their long and unknown journey. Halden had business with the Darwish forges.

They had ridden hard from the rising sun to the mid-afternoon, and Cal's body ached. His new tunic was damp with sweat, his hunger was overwhelming, and some parts were tender and rubbed raw. Once camp was set up and the late afternoon was underway, he set his weapons aside and removed his new armor. He sat in front of the low campfire and tended to it as he enjoyed the setting sun.

The evening sky enveloped the countryside while hundreds of fires covered the landscape and thousands of volunteers surrounded their campfires. His party was no different after each had disarmed and disrobed.

When the evening came, Alec and Halden returned with assorted items and a Darwish sword for Cal. It was a single-handed broadsword, and it flowed through the air as he swung it. Cal was overjoyed with such a generous gift.

As the evening continued, the twin Elvians sang songs of their people, Jacoby regaled tales of the other causes he had previously worked, and Bill kept everyone fed.

Clydes was the only one who sat apart; he kept armed and clothed for war the whole evening. Occasionally, he tapped his feet when the songs began, but he primarily stood a vigilant watch. No one asked, but no one minded either.

The same spirit and vigor were held by all cavalrymen throughout the encampment on the bank of the River White. That was until the bells rang out into the dark night.

Chapter VIII
The Darkness

Gregory rose from his bed in confusion and crossed over to the balcony as the alarm sounded from one tower to the next. The night guards hastily ran through the streets toward the eastern walls and ascended the towers. Someone had arrived.

He threw on the nearest garments and descended the stairs of his luxurious villa, where some of his servants had already succumbed to panic and fear. The rumors of the enemy had spread through the city, and the smallfolk imagined the worst kind of creatures associated with darkness. It was no doubt part of their stratagem, but Gregory could not, and would not, come to any conclusions until he saw what inspired such a spectacle from the parapets on the high walls.

"Ronald, summon my carriage. Once I've departed, lock the gates and gather everyone in the cellars. No one is to leave until I return!" Gregory commanded.

"It is too dangerous, my Master. The demons come for us all," Ronald protested.

"I have no time to argue! Do as I say!" Gregory scolded.

Ronald lowered his head in retreat and proceeded as Master Gregory instructed. The carriage was brought forth without further delay and all household members assembled as instructed.

His destination was the northeast wall. He yearned to unfold the grand mystery of the enemy and, finally, put his eyes on the culprits. Once their identities were known, many doubts would be put to rest. He would also have another clue to the conspiracy that clung to the forefront of his mind surrounding supposed traitors to the Mid.

All the city stirred in the early morning. Citizens occupied the streets in confusion and terror while Midguardmen assembled at their posts along the city walls. Outside the city, the new recruits of infantry and cavalry had been startled awake on the western bank of the river, and it was only fate the river separated them from the enemy. They simply needed to cross over the bridges through the city and to be of use on the eastern side.

Gregory swiftly made his way to the northeast tower. As he neared his destination, he heard the sizable cavalry begin to move through the city toward the eastern gate. The vanguard rose immediately to the call, and Sir Kenneth was now leading them to the front. If anyone had slept through the bells, the thunderous hooves upon the cobblestones surely stirred them awake.

When the council set out to raise a mounted cavalry, they aimed to enlist a few hundred able bodies at the very least. As a result of good recruitment, they had instead raised two thousand. The volunteers overwhelmed all expectations among the cavalry and the infantry. As they rumbled through the streets, Gregory began to fully appreciate the force before him, and it gave him hope.

Gregory arrived at the northeast tower and ascended the staircase. Anticipation seized him as he rushed to peer over the wall. The moon gleamed over a cloudless sky and the luminescent night brought everything into view. A heavy fog bank stretched across the horizon as hills and the tree line vanished behind a vast black screen; only the moonlight gave it shape. As he gazed out, the wind gushed around him as if running from the black storm. Gregory's chest seized.

"What devilry could've conjured this?" he said aloud.

"Master Gregory," a faint voice stuttered behind him. Gregory turned and found Master Tammany, the most ancient of the council members, behind him. As he appeared before Gregory, he was shaken beyond his usual frailty. His hands and knees trembled as he reached out to steady himself and, nearly collapsing, Gregory stepped in to brace the old man.

The bowmen rushed wildly past both council members to assume positions along the parapet; each one filled the space between the embrasures. Soldiers hurried to distribute arrows, javelins, large rocks, and oil above the gates.

"Master Tammany, this is no place for the meek or foolish! The guard will trample you down!"

The defenses were prepared in recent days due to Sir Pavel's insight. However, no one believed the enemy was so close to the city. Now that they were before them, Gregory was relieved the old knight had made such preparations.

"I could not resist. I had to witness them with my own eyes," Tammany said. Gregory understood the feeling well. However, as intimidating as the power was before them, he was skeptical. *Was this more than an illusion? How did they intend to challenge the city? Did the enemy occupy the whole dark mass?* It was a chilling thought. The Mid needed to be prepared to counter any action and Gregory saw no one of position commanding atop the wall.

"Whoa there!" Gregory shouted as he stopped the next guard, who ran past them. A young woman stopped and turned to Master Gregory. She was startled by the councilmen.

"Who raised the alarm?" Gregory demanded.

The young soldier gaped for a moment. "I do not know, sir. I've only just arrived!" she replied.

"Then go! Find the captain on watch and tell him the city's masters await him here at the northeast tower. Away now!"

"Right away, sir!" she said, bolting along the walkway.

Tammany gave Gregory an inquisitive look. "If you peacock as his lordship, they will assume you've taken the command, Gregory," Tammany grumbled.

"I see no other masters along the wall, and it is imperative we know exactly what has happened," Gregory retorted. "I have no doubt Lord Malcolm and Master Hector will be along at any moment. In the meantime, you and I will do."

Tammany withdrew almost immediately; it had been a long time since he had shown opposition and longer still since he had been verbally chastised. Only a few moments passed until the captain arrived.

"Master Gregory, Master Tammany, I came at once. What do you require, sirs?" the captain of the guard called.

"What is the situation? How many and from where?" Gregory inquired.

"Much is still unknown, sir. The whole countryside became enveloped under a black fog just like the rumors had described. It was as if a heavy black sea swallowed the horizon, and now, it's as it looks. We are an island among nothingness. If you follow me, sir. If the moon wasn't out, we might not have seen any odd shape at all, but there…" the captain pointed. "… see how it forms in the distance."

Gregory stared at the elongated black mass stretching across the landscape and creeping closer to the city walls. "I grant you, this is an odd and unknown phenomenon, and I cannot deny what vision has befallen my eyes, but this doesn't rule out unusual ill-weather or some such event," Gregory replied.

"Those are my very thoughts," Lord Malcolm agreed. He entered the northeast tower swiftly and his entourage consisted of Master Hector, Master Liam, and Sir Pavel in the rear followed from behind.

"Although I must say, it is the most peculiar fog I have ever seen," he continued.

"Ah, my lord, I thought you might not be long. I was just speaking with Captain… What was your name, lad?" Gregory asked.

"Neville, sir."

"Ah yes, Captain Neville was just speaking of the black fog; the rumors are without disappointment."

"Indeed," Lord Malcolm replied, looking over the parapet. "Captain, what else happened before the alarm rang?"

"One of our sentries spotted a few riders up north at some distance just outside the darkness. Then they vanished with the rest of it. Very strange, my lord. Nothing else has been seen in the distance. Once they vanished, it was as if the darkness was venturing closer. I swear, my lord. The blackness swallows everything like the sea. One moment, you can see a clumping of trees and the next moment they're gone; it chilled me to the bone. I considered all the signs, and that is when I had them sound the alarms."

Lord Malcolm, Master Gregory, and the entire entourage gazed over the wall once the young Captain had finished; last remark concerned them all. The air stung in the silence as Gregory and the other council members verified the captain's claim. The distance between the walls and the blackness diminished as the earth vanished beneath a black smokey veil.

"How long ago?" Lord Malcolm asked.

"Just a few minutes before the bells, my lord."

Gregory calculated the time from the first sighting to now. He was not pleased with the results and how much ground the darkness had gained.

"Nothing else?"

"No, my lord."

"Very good. Off with you to your post. No one is to engage without my order."

"As you command, my lord." The captain bowed and was off. He began bellowing orders along the walls.

The remaining council members huddled around the Lord of the Mid as all peered into the abyss.

"I do not know what may come once the darkness reaches the wall. I do not know what force awaits beyond it, if anything, and we are clearly running out of time, gentlemen. Does anyone have any suggestions?" Lord Malcolm asked.

No one spoke. Gregory took the moment to collect himself. He cast the dread from his mind and began to grasp the scene in front of him. "I believe this darkness must be an illusion. If that is the case, there is some kind of force conjuring it, and no force can take our city without breaching our walls. Illusion or not, we still have the advantage of height and protection. Let them come." Gregory reasoned aloud. It was not a brilliant military strategy, but the reality of the situation needed to be reinforced to all the advisors. And so, each councilman was awakened from the grips of fear.

"Master Gregory is correct, I should think," Sir Pavel confidently agreed. "They will require some form of siege weapon to take this city. Surely, there would be some sign of that. They would also need to see us as well if they were to accurately destroy our gates or even a small section of wall."

"If you mean to wait idly while they move closer and strike at us from behind this blackness, then I disagree entirely!" Hector urged, waving Sir Pavel aside. "How are we to know what lies beyond that blackness? How are we to know of any such weapon until it is too late? If we wait, they may destroy half of our city if they have even *adequate* siege weapons. They wouldn't even need to see, much less aim. Master Gregory and Sir Pavel assume they've come here to conquer. They may have merely come to wipe us out. If that dark cloud comes too near and we do nothing, they could rain fire and death upon us. We cannot wait!"

Gregory's brow furrowed with frustration. He wanted to refuse him, but Hector made several valid points.

"They couldn't roll siege weapons onto the field without our knowledge," Sir Pavel countered.

"Look upon the field!" Hector spat, pointing to the black fog. "This darkness surrounds everything in front of your eyes, and you question how the enemy can be hidden! This dark apparatus could allow them to see us perfectly. Have you considered that? Then, they could simply barrage us at their leisure. We mustn't wait a moment!"

Sir Pavel had no answer and Lord Malcolm carefully weighed each man's argument.

"I concede our position is slightly disadvantaged should they decide to bombard us by some means, but surely, we are not so weakened behind our walls. We can surely return a volley and counter their attack," Gregory retorted.

"We have little time for either course; the darkness closes in on us and we have but a half-hour to choose to hide behind these walls or take the fight to them. I, for one, believe it is foolhardy to hide. We must throw them off balance and meet them in the field!" Hector insisted.

Gregory ruminated on Hector's comments. Their decision would possibly decide the fate of all the folk under the Mid's protection that night.

"Your thoughts are sound, Master Hector. Sir Pavel, ready the bowmen to loosen a volley upon the darkness once in range. Standby for my word," Lord Malcolm commanded.

"My lord, they haven't anything to aim at," Sir Pavel said.

"The darkness will suffice for now."

"And if they have siege weapons, my lord?" Master Hector asked.

Lord Malcolm did not answer right away. Without further information, any course of action was a gamble. After moments, he furrowed his brow, and he curled his left hand into an iron fist.

"Begin the evacuation of all inhabitants on the eastern half of the city and set aside a reserve division to assist. All folk on the eastern bank are to cross the bridges immediately. If the time comes, prepare to evacuate the rest. I want the rest of the infantrymen promptly formed into the city and positioned behind the walls as soon as possible," Lord Malcolm ordered.

"They are already en route, my lord," Master Liam interjected.

"Good. Lastly, prepare to release the vanguard and sweep them on their left," Lord Malcolm continued.

An icy knot formed in Gregory's stomach; the die had been cast.

"My lord, we may be sacrificing the core of our cavalry to an unknown enemy..." Sir Pavel protested.

"Enough!" Lord Malcolm exclaimed, holding up a hand. "We cannot let our fear govern our actions! Let us find out what lies beyond the darkness. I'll wager someone does, and I mean to know the make of their mettle this very morning. Besides Sir Pavel, Hector is right. They will not expect such a move. We will occupy their attention with arrows and then send in the cavalry upon their left flank. The river bars them on their right; they must stand their ground or retreat northward." Lord Malcolm had learned to command and defend his home over the course of thirty years and all the council present agreed. It was a sound plan.

Sir Pavel swelled with pride. His lordship gave him a firmer hope than he had possessed that night.

"It will be done, my lord," Sir Pavel assured. He turned and began passing orders to each Captain along the wall.

"Master Hector, make your way immediately to the eastern gate and relay my orders to Sir Kenneth. He hasn't been released through the gate yet and I wish for him to be unleashed at the preferred moment. His signal will be a flaming arrow loosed over the gate."

"As you command, my lord. If we succeed, should I prepare the infantry to meet them in the field?" Master Hector pressed.

"Although I am confident in this decision, this maneuver may prove too bold. Time will tell. The new infantry shall stand in reserve along the walls as I have commanded. Master Gregory is accurate in his assessment as well; I am not ready to abandon our defenses just yet. Our walls are strong, and no one has ever breached them. So, we will shield the attack and prepare to defend the city."

"As you say, my lord," Master Hector nodded and left for the east gate.

Master Gregory stood beside his lord as the other advisors hurried off to pass the commands. Gregory mildly grinned as he found himself within earshot of the Mid's seat of power advising a tactical course in the early hours of the morning.

When tasked with the logistics and preparation of the troops, he felt suited for the appointment. He poured over the few manuscripts of war the library had to offer for valuable insights into producing the materials, food, and armor for the war effort. However, he considered it unlikely he'd actually apply his newfound military knowledge upon the battlefield.

As the half-hour passed, the tower received reports all along the walls and from all the companies. Bowmen nocked their arrows along the ramparts, beside them stood a thousand spearmen, and the cavalry assembled just inside the eastern gate. Sir Pavel and Master Hector returned to the tower after all preparations and commands were given. All were ready to engage.

The dark cloud steadily crept over the few remaining leagues between them. As it edged closer, the darkness crossed into range of the archers and Lord Malcolm patiently waited to give the command. The tension coiled like a snake among the councilmen. Lord Malcolm remained steady. Once satisfied, he gave Sir Pavel a nod.

Eagerly, Sir Pavel turned to his Captains and relayed the message. "Draw!" Sir Pavel yelled.

In unison, every archer drew his bow and aimed high.

"Loose!" he shouted.

At once, arrows flew from all along the walls and vanished within the black void. All in the tower watched and fell silent as they patiently listened for the strikes of the falling arrows. The reward arrived when hundreds of arrows struck within the darkness, and the screeches of creatures and mounts alike echoed across the fields. Cheers rang out along the walls from the ramparts to the grounds below. And as quickly as the shouts rose, they all fell silent once they saw the response. The black cloud emitted spots of oranges and yellows; then hundreds of fire-arrows burst into the sky.

"There's definitely a force!" Master Gregory blurted as he took cover within the tower.

"Shields!" Lord Malcolm called out into the night.

At once, shields were raised along the ramparts. Those without protection ducked beneath anything that provided shelter, and all others hid tight along the walls. Most of the men came through unscathed by the fire-arrows, with few exceptions. The Midguard loosed another volley in return.

"We will seize the victory yet," Sir Pavel remarked with vigor. "I will send ten thousand arrows over the walls before they wound a tenth of my men."

Gregory appreciated the potency of the old knight, but another matter caught his attention. The fire-arrows had not flown into the night without hitting their marks. The roofs of a few connected homes had caught fire. The companies of men below propelled themselves into action, gathering water from troughs, and battling the blaze. However, the fire-arrows continued to fall, putting their men at risk and causing further fire to spread. Dozens of roofs burned within the city.

"I'm afraid we may lose a significant section of the city before you are able!" Gregory exclaimed, clenching his fist. "Master Hector's prediction was not without merit."

At once, the councilmen abandoned the view of the dark cloud and turned to the city; it was chaos below. The hundreds of silhouettes desperately rushed below carrying buckets from the river.

"There are fires along the whole northern wall!" Master Liam stated.

Lord Malcolm nodded in agreement when another volley of fire arrows fell from the sky.

"How can they reach us so?" Master Liam queried.

Sir Pavel launched another wave of arrows to counter theirs.

"It matters not. We have their attention here and now. I want every man below who can be spared to put out every fire in the city," Lord Malcolm commanded. "We must act before the enemy damages too much of us. Sir Pavel, unleash the vanguard!"

Without hesitation, Sir Pavel ordered the closest group of bowmen to loosen a grouping of lit arrows over the eastern gate. They were already prepared for such a task, lit the arrows that had been tipped in oil, and released. They sailed through the air away from the engagement and landed outside the eastern gates. In an instant, the great oak doors swung open, and the vanguard sprang from the city like ravenous wolves for a winter meal.

Thunder shook the walls of the tower as Sir Kenneth barreled toward the blackness. The column of horses swept along the walls with spears and torches in hand. Gregory thought that they had the look of a blazing serpent slithering into the night.

Upon their thunderous arrival, the darkness divided in two and collapsed. The smaller of the dark masses immediately retreated to the northeast and swept over the field just ahead of the cavalry. Gregory admired the view as the larger fog bank and the force within blindly maintained their assault. The vanguard erupted from around the eastern wall and onto the field. Once the cavalry turned, the enemy faced a wall of mounted men charging toward them like a door sweeping open over the northern fields. Only then did the enemy realize the peril as the larger dark bank retreated north along the river; eerily whooshing over the grounds just out of reach.

Gregory could not believe the speed of the evaporating dark fog. As the cavalry covered the field, the great dark cloud glided over the grounds as if being forced by the fall winds. All the men atop the walls roared in high spirits, and Gregory smiled at the absurd sight.

"Sir Kenneth must be related to the weather gods!" Master Gregory snickered. Sir Pavel and Master Liam haughtily chortled, yet Master Tammany sneered at the comment.

"You brazenly mock the gods?!" Tammany exclaimed.

Sir Pavel patted the elderly gentleman on the shoulders and embraced him. "Rejoice, my old friend, and forgive Master Gregory! He does not blaspheme without thought. He celebrates Sir Kenneth as you should now!" Sir Pavel howled.

Master Tammany shook off the old knight.

The councilmen returned their attention to the field before them. The predawn light broke as the sky brightened in the farthest eastern horizon. The dark cloud continued a swift retreat just ahead of the vanguard. Gregory turned his attention to the field below to what remained of the host who perished under a barrage of arrows. A few remained scattered around the field, but that mattered little to Gregory. He cared only to uncover their identities. He squinted at the figures to try to discover who they were but could not resolve the mystery at such a distance in the predawn hour.

"I had not expected such an outcome this morning, but now that the enemy is retreating, what is our course of action?" Sir Pavel asked.

Gregory returned his thoughts to the present moment. "Shall we join Sir Kenneth upon the field?" he asked.

"Agreed. We must deploy at once and continue to drive them out of our borders and further still," Hector chimed.

Lord Malcolm grinned at the suggestions. "I agree we must deploy, but they are swiftly riding well ahead of our cavalry. I will not abandon Sir Kenneth to this task alone. However, we mustn't leave these walls without tending to the minor damages done to the city and properly outfitting the men before we depart. It is clear to me that the enemy has a vast mounted force," Lord Malcolm replied.

"My lord, how could you know this?" asked Master Hector.

"My proof lies before us on the field, and I am certain that is why Sir Kenneth could not overtake them," replied Lord Malcolm.

The dawn began to cover the field with sunlight, and Gregory saw what his lordship had implied. The scattered remains of the enemies and their mounts were strewn about the field.

"An even better suggestion, my lord. We will pass orders immediately to ready our forces for travel," Sir Pavel remarked.

"That is well, gentlemen, but first see what remains of the fires," Lord Malcolm commanded.

"My lord, I would feel remiss if we did not inspect the fallen enemy below! It is imperative to know who we are facing," Gregory insisted.

Lord Malcolm paused and surveyed the field. "I do not deny I am also curious. Sir Pavel and Master Hector shall see to the fires immediately. Master Gregory, Master Liam, and I will form a company to inspect the dead. Once finished, I want all efforts to be focused on seeing our forces ready for departure. Master Tammany, you are also welcome to join us should you desire."

All the councilors agreed. Gregory reviewed the city landscape and knew the fires were well managed. Several homes had succumbed to the blaze, but scores of men threw themselves at the fires. It would not take long for Sir Pavel and Master Hector to come to the same conclusion. With the fire under control, Gregory turned his attention to the dead upon the field in giddy anticipation.

Chapter IX
The Pursuit

All the disheveled cavalry madly rushed to arm and armor themselves once the bells rang out. They stormed through the city, and when the time came, they burst through the gates without waver or fear and forged ahead like a skiff breaking through the storm. Cal was sure many folk were eager and trepidatious, but when the gate opened, not a single cavalryman hesitated. The great wooden doors rose, and every rider kicked hard; he, too, was caught in the exhilaration of the charge, leaving all his concerns behind.

Sir Kenneth charged straight at the enemy as he led the valiant cavalry. For a moment, Cal's first ill impression of the man faded, and a glimmer of the kind of knight that folks told in tales of legend shone. The commander rode like a man who understood the duty expected of him and pushed directly toward the great dark bank of rolling black clouds.

The darkness moved from the ground like a churning black sea, and as the cavalry approached the towering, formless dark, Cal almost gave in to the fear of it. However, unexpectedly the blackness divided in two, creating a vast chasm. As the smaller division of darkness faded into the nearby eastern wood, Sir Kenneth and the vanguard darted toward the larger portion of darkness from around the eastern walls. Cal hoped to catch and fight the enemy after seeing the darkness flee from them. The larger dark bank of fog retreated almost immediately, and the cavalry gave eager chase. First, they followed for a league and then another. Then they followed until the Mid was no longer in sight, and they followed it further still. A half-hour passed before Cal realized the enemy was pulling away, but Sir Kenneth and the cavalry refused to cease the chase. It was an hour when the horses slowed to a trot. It was midday before they stopped completely. The enemy had escaped them.

They reached a creek that divided the farmland and scattered woods; the Crestwood was near. All the cavalry stopped, watered, and recovered for a time. Even the stoutest fighters were tired from the morning's ride. It had truly been a challenging morning with few results.

Once Alice finished drinking from the creek, Cal led her toward the edges of the crowded cavalry. He found bread from his saddlebags and shared it with his new companions. It was the first meal of the day, and although it was meager, all were grateful. In their haste in the early morning, the tents, food, and almost all the supplies for the trek north had been left at the encampment. Most of the cavalry had forgotten greaves or helms in their excitement.

The meal did little to curb his hunger. As he gazed into the dense Crestwood and his stomach ached for further sustenance, it dawned on him. *Surely their vexing enemy had been hungry and tired as well.* They rode just as determined during the grueling pursuit and had handily kept out of reach. In addition to where they might be and their state of condition, his thoughts turned to the mysterious darkness that followed them. It had dissipated early in the chase, and he did not know why.

"I haven't seen the darkness for hours," Cal commented. "Once we galloped into the woodlands, I think it vanished, but that was closer to dawn. Even then, the only thing I saw of the enemy was the dust kicked up from the ground."

Alec grunted as he stood and nodded in agreement. The old man was worn from the ride, and his face was flushed. Cal noticed he had all but finished his waterskin, and he would need to replenish it before they departed.

Bill was perhaps worse than Alec. He continued to stretch his back in all manner of ways to relieve the pain that surged through him.

"Yes, I thought it too coincidental that the darkness vanished near the dawning of the day. The woodlands, I think, also slowed us," Alec said, leaning on his staff. "The daylight is our ally in this, I believe, and we are blessed still." He rummaged through his pocket, retrieved one stone, and paired it with another in his hand. One was light, frail, and wet. The other was a shade darker than the first, hard and sharp.

"This is a sunstone, and the other is a moonstone. I happened to store the moonstone in my saddle before we left, and I had just found the sunstone in this very creek. The gods, damn them all, favor us and our cause," Alec exclaimed.

"I'm not sure what good these stones are to us... and what grievance have the gods done to you?" Cal asked.

Alec continued to beam as he reverently wiped the mud and dirt away from each stone. "The magic speaks to us, my boy! The daylight is too powerful for their conjuring. I dare say the torches may have unknowingly saved us from certain death last evening. With these stones, I will store some sunlight, and it may prove useful when the night comes. And to your second inquiry, I have never approved of the gods myself. They are petty, their love fleeting, and they care extraordinarily little for the happenings of us mortals. I have no doubt of their existence, but I question their qualifications."

"I know truly little of the gods, and perhaps they know little of me. Of what I know, they are demanding and can be fickle. But, if they've blessed you with a sunstone in your time of need, then perhaps they're more involved than you know," Cal countered.

"I am confident they have blessed this cause more than myself. We have quarreled for some time, and I would think it was a begrudging gesture, if anything. Yet, I am not without a grateful heart, unlike them. I will be, and am, thankful."

Cal wasn't sure of the logic of the old man, but he trusted the old fellow would use his gift to the utmost of his ability. Alec arranged the two stones onto the head of his staff. He paced across a meadow as he muttered to himself, raised the staff to the sky with one hand, and palmed the head of his staff with his other hand.

Amused, Cal continued to watch the old man, and Bill joined him.

"I'll admit this only to you, when he's fix'n to conjure his magic, I can't help m'self an' I'm filled with wonder!" Bill whispered.

Cal looked behind him and grinned at his old friend. Bill was as mesmerized here as he was at the tavern the other day. Alec was only muttering to himself as far as Cal could see, but he understood what Bill meant. To witness real magic was unheard of, and to see even a flicker of it twice in less than a week was as if the stars had aligned.

Cal wondered if the old conjurer would create that glint of magic in the next moment. Then perhaps all the folk present would believe in the old man's abilities, and they too would be able to enjoy the extraordinary spectacle. As Cal relished with Bill in a moment of wonder, a familiar official trotted up to them.

"The Commander calls for all the scouts to make their way to the head of the column. Let us make haste and do our duties," Master Wendall called. Reality immediately set back in for Cal.

"I will muster our party at once," Cal replied. Master Wendall nodded and trotted back toward the head of the column.

Cal sent a whistle that was well received. The unusual scouting party assembled toward him, apart from Alec, who was in a deep trance. Cal walked over to the old man and gently laid a hand on his shoulder.

Alec finished his low utterance. He turned, and his eyes pierced Cal.

"I'm sorry, my friend, but we've been called to action," Cal soothed as Alec eased his gaze and relaxed himself.

"Of course," Alec said. "Then let us away to the commander." The old man chuckled to himself.

It was only a short trot. When they arrived, they found four other small scouting units huddled around Sir Kenneth. The difference between the groups was immediately apparent; the other scouting parties had solely been made up of Midguardmen. It was clear Sir Kenneth trusted little of the Crestfolk, if at all.

The party rode up into the last open space available, where Cal sat in the center between Alec and Jacoby. The remaining party members followed behind them in pairs.

"As you know, we were unable to catch the enemy," Sir Kenneth began. "I have no doubt some black magic has aided them in their speed. Regardless of their assistance, they are still vulnerable in numerous ways. As you saw throughout the morning, they can be pierced with arrows, killed, and they can be pursued across the country. So, contrary to rumors, these creatures are mortal. This ride has taken a toll on them just as much as us."

"Perhaps," Alec whispered in a low tone.

Cal glanced at the old man, finding a defiant grin, but he believed it was a reasonable assumption. Fatigue was etched across all the cavalry's faces.

"We have taken a moment here to recover, but I intend to continue this pursuit. I have no doubt they are resting now while the chase has ceased. So, we will continue and measure the stamina of them. Once they have been caught, there will be little resistance. I want parties ahead to the north and the east. You are to locate and report the position of the enemy. Should they turn on you, give them chase and lead them to me."

"Constable?" Alec interjected.

Sir Kenneth peered at the old man with a loathsome gaze as all other eyes shifted to Alec. Master Wendall was beside himself with shock as his mouth gaped openly like a freshly caught trout.

"Perhaps your eyes have deteriorated from your long years," Kenneth spat. "I will not tolerate your impudence, you old fool! You will refer to me as commander! Any further insolence will be met with severe punishment. So, choose your words carefully, soldier!"

"Forgive me, Commander, my eyes are weary from travel, and I consider myself corrected," Alec said.

Sir Kenneth smirked. He was pleased Alec was beginning to form obedience.

"However, I do have a question," Alec continued.

Sir Kenneth's arrogant smile vanished in an instant as he snorted. "Pray tell, you old fool. I wonder what question you would risk a lash upon your back?"

"Merely this," Alec started. "If we continue to drive them as we have, we will exhaust ourselves. Is that the wisest course of action?" Alec's point made little impression upon Sir Kenneth as the knight stared back at him in contempt. However, the other riders shifted in their saddles, exchanged wary glances, and furrowed their brows.

"There is enough vigor among the men to see the task through. If you and your party find yourselves too weary, then perhaps the rear is the best position for you."

"We are not yet worn, commander," Cal interjected. "... And Alec makes a vital point."

"Does he now?" Kenneth said. "I have more than enough trained fighting men. The enemy is well on the run, and we could have the whole inconvenient mess cleaned by late evening. So, should an old fool's concerns discourage us?"

Cal shifted under the weight of the callous man but then shook off his stubborn gaze. "I wouldn't have us deterred, sir. I am committed to this cause and our success; so is my friend. If he has a good point, I would want to hear it just as I heard yours. I think your appraisal of the enemy is accurate. They must be worn from keeping just out of our grasp. Perhaps so much that they could not defend themselves if we came upon them. On the other hand, it has been a tiring pursuit. If I might add, few of us have brought enough provisions. We will be well-worn and hungry if we keep up this pace. We should consider that."

The commander looked Cal up and down, and his grin returned to his face. "You are astute, boy. And you've assessed us true. However, you keep questionable company. Do you know the old man that counsels you?"

Cal seized his breath. He did not really know Alec but felt as if he knew him. In the two days that he'd known him, the old man had been odd and rambunctious, but he had also been honest and welcoming. He cautiously showed the pair of them the slightest ounce of magic. It was a glimmer of joy that warmed him, whereas, oppositely, the darkness filled him with fear. That was enough for Cal, and he was resolute and somewhat relieved when Alec asked to join them.

"I know enough," Cal responded.

"Enough?" Sir Kenneth asked, tilting his head. "You've acquired a vagrant who has plagued the city streets with his corruption. He takes to the square daily and madly lectures on for hours on end. Of course, this is only after he overindulges in substances that warp his mind. Once he finishes rambling and misinforming our youth, he staggers to that filth of an establishment, where he ends his day in a drunken stupor. Did he tell you of this?"

Alec lowered his head and sat shamed in his saddle; all men present fell silent. He had not mentioned every detail of his habits when they met, but he had been upfront with his reputation and the conditions that afflicted him. That meant something.

"I do not know of all of Alec's trespasses, and I'm not interested in the past of the man. I am interested in our common cause. We signed an oath together. So, I am bound to him, and he is to me."

Sir Kenneth sneered back at Cal with delight. "So be it. You will be responsible for him then, and you will be responsible for the successes and failures of your entire scouting party. You are hereby promoted to this unit's sergeant," Sir Kenneth declared.

A lump formed in Cal's throat. He had come to fight for his home, but he knew little about leading folk, much less so his new companions, whose lives were just put right in his hands. His palms went clammy.

"You are to take your party to that east ridge and follow just behind the cavalry. My orders stand, Sergeant. Should you come across the enemy, lead them to me. However, if you or your companions fall behind, fail to meet the conditions of your oath or my command, then you will be charged with desertion and treason," Sir Kenneth continued.

Cal was reeling from the position he had just been put in, but there was nothing to be done. As he glanced behind at his party, it became clear; these folk were his responsibility now.

He turned back to Sir Kenneth. "Yes, sir," Cal replied.

Sir Kenneth passed orders to the remaining scouts. All the units dispersed and formed around the north and east of the main body of the cavalry. The trot to the ridge was silent for Cal as he pondered the unusual circumstances he found himself in. He was unsure if the sudden promotion was a blessing or a curse. Perhaps the gods that Alec despised played a part and knew the truth.

"That was unexpected," Alec reflected.

Cal turned to him in disbelief as the party trotted further from the vanguard.

"Yeah, if I'd have known a promotion was available, I would've spoken up m'self," Jacoby chided.

Cal broke from his thoughts to see a few chuckles among his new friends.

"Then again, I'm not familiar with you personally, but I have heard of your reputation," Jacoby commented to Alec.

"Everything you've heard has undoubtedly been exaggerated. Have I striven to question our local policies? Yes. Have I been a disturbance? Only to the commander. I'll have you know many welcome my inquisitive mind," Alec replied.

Jacoby let out a chortle.

"Have you let substances warp your mind?" Cal asked.

Alec averted his eyes and turned from him; a chord was struck. There was a truth there, and it needed to be asked. *What if he was still controlled by those substances? What if he could not conjure when they needed him?* A sliver of a doubt crept in Cal's mind.

Alec shed the shame from his face and replaced it with a determination. "I have spent my life dedicated to the knowledge of magic. I have been successful at times, I have failed, and I am as you see me now. Perhaps more worn, but nevertheless, wiser. There was a time I believed certain herbs would increase my understanding of the deep magic. Soon after, it was hard to distinguish whether I wanted to expand my knowledge or the herbs called me. That was long ago.

Folks don't often understand the reasons behind a man's actions, and they seldom forget his faults. So, to answer your question, let me make assurances. I am no longer that man."

As Cal listened to Alec, he was reminded of the reasons he joined the company with the odd fellow. He spoke honestly to a fault. Here, at the beginning of their journey, honesty among their small party was a necessity, and they would need to trust each other regardless of their past transgressions. It was then all lingering doubts faded because Cal trusted Alec.

"I know," Cal replied. All fell silent for the remainder of the trot.

They arrived on the ridge just as the vanguard mounted and resumed the chase. The enemy was easy to track in the early morning due to their stampeding retreat. However, the farther they traveled north in the afternoon, the tracks dispersed wildly into the forest.

The scouting party carefully observed everything within the woodlands but saw no sign of the enemy. The tree cover continued to worsen as they traveled farther into the Crestwood, and the woods continued to slow their pace. After the first few hours, they lost sight altogether.

"Does anyone see the cavalry?" he asked. The party stopped and looked through the Crestwood.

The day's ride had worn on them all. Even the mighty Clydes looked weary as he heavily perspired beneath his leathers and rested the weight of his war hammer on his burly steed.

"I cannot see them, but I can still hear them," Eris replied. "The overgrowth weakens my sight, and the ride covers the sound. They are somewhere through the brush and over that hill."

Cal considered himself lucky to have a pair of Elvians among them. Few Elvian traders passed through the Fork, and as far as their skills were concerned, Cal found that the Elvians practiced great discipline. They took time honing their skills, mastering their trades, and were a people of patience.

At present, Eris had the look of a woodland hunter who had mastered the art of tracking over years of practice.

Cal knew he could count on her judgment and her ears if he needed to.

"Good. I'd only been hoping we hadn't lost them. Keep an ear out as best you can," Cal responded.

"We have not fallen behind if that is your concern. The cavalry tire as well. I can hear the horses waning," Yslanna commented.

Cal didn't like the sound of that. It meant Alec's warning had come to pass and all the folk had pushed themselves to the brink. If a confrontation came about, then they would not be as fit to fight.

"We need to keep riding if they do. They might need our aid before the night ends. Let's continue into the wood. Keep a sharp eye out for anything," Cal replied.

"I can ride closer to keep an eye on 'em," Halden remarked.

Cal considered it. "No, I think we should stick together within eyesight. I don't want us to split and become separate. If the enemy is close, I fear a single rider would make an easy target. We stay in pairs at minimum. Eris can ride ahead with someone if it eases her hearing at all. I'll keep to the rear and look out if someone would like to join me," Cal commented.

All nodded and spread apart in pairs. Eris and Yslanna rode slightly ahead, Halden and Jacoby paired next, Clydes and Bill followed them, and Alec and Cal brought up the rear.

The time vanished as the dusk drew near. With the evening approaching, a horrendous hunger came upon Cal. He finished the last of his dried meat and continued to drink from his pouch to ease his appetite, but he found little relief. The hunger distracted his mind more than the task at hand, and he often failed to keep his eyes peeled on the road ahead or behind him.

Alec, with heavy eyelids, was clearly unable to stay vigilant, much like the rest of the party. Cal took it upon himself to carry out the task, but he, too, was on the cusp of exhaustion.

He didn't notice at first when the darkness reformed. The day's waning light faded from sight, and the forest grew darker in front and behind him. However, the darkness crept among the dense forest like a light fog. He snapped back as if waking from a dream and grabbed Alec's arm.

The old man gasped in a moment of fear, which turned into a quick anger at the young man. However, his anger subsided as he turned from Cal to the forest, and his pulse rapidly quickened.

"I think it's time we rejoin Sir Kenneth," Cal muttered.

"I think you may be correct, my boy," Alec replied.

In an instant, Cal lashed the reins and kicked Alice. Although she had been drained throughout the day, she responded to Cal without hesitation and broke out into a fierce gallop.

"Go!" Cal shouted into the night.

All the party jolted awake and launched themselves ahead. They rushed through the forest like wild boars, and the darkness enclosed around them. Arrows flew from beyond the darkness and skimmed over their heads.

The party became surrounded by a churning blackness in the forest, and Cal grew afraid that he might never see the sun again. And then, without warning, a wave of light burst into the night and shredded through the black mist.

Chapter X
The Warrior

Su'ca and the Par'sha separated the next day with eleven thousand of the clan's best warriors and headed toward the mountains. Craa'su could have continued deeper into their territory and convinced other Par'sha clans to join him; the horde might have swelled to thirty thousand. That would have been a welcome addition, but Su'ca's father understood the need for action.

The clans looked to him for his leadership, guidance, and decisiveness. Seeking out the other clans would have taken too long; the fervor for bloodshed may have died over the journey. It was an unnecessary risk. In any case, a horde of eleven thousand was still a very respectable size. It may not have been the hordes of old that numbered a force of one hundred thousand men and beasts strong, but their force was made of lean warriors, fast horses, and powerful bear-sloths. No forces of the west could match his people's spirit, and the horde was eager for retribution.

Meanwhile, the remaining clans continued east on top of the backs of their mighty mammoths; they were safe. As was tradition, a few seasoned warriors were selected to stay behind to protect the clan. They were asked to forgo the bloodletting and uphold another duty altogether; raise the next generation of warriors that one day would take their revenge on behalf of all the Par'sha if the horde should fail. It was among the highest honors that could be bestowed.

Only a few times in the long memory of the clans had the Par'sha banded together. When they had formed the horde in the past, their victory was assured.

They traveled steadily by day and rested by night. The bear-sloths slowed the pace of the horde, but this mattered little. Craa'su was in no hurry. The vulnerable were far removed from danger, and the enemy would soon enter their next life under the spears of the clans.

First, the enemy had to be found. Su'ca watched her father prepare the clans. Like his forefathers, he planned to utilize the speed of his horses to surround his enemy while his powerful bear-sloths kept their attention. He had every direction around him scouted as the thunderous horde approached and patiently waited for the scouts to return with the whereabouts of the enemy. When the time came, they would be fresh and poised for battle.

The scouts struck out for several days before her arrival and returned with little agreement of the whereabouts of the elusive enemy. This was an unusual conclusion. They had initially sought out the enemy where the attacks began. The remnants of the encampments were scoured for the enemy, but they were nowhere to be found. All evidence suggested the enemy were no longer in Par'sha lands.

After all the failed reports, Craa'su steered the horde straight past the remnants of their former encampments. Some warriors disliked being led so close to places of death, but those who raised these concerns were either superstitious or ashamed. Ultimately, few had given outcry.

Some considered her father cold; Su'ca knew her father was a shrewd chieftain. He had purposefully driven the horde directly over the grounds of the dead. The horde traveled steadily every day, and the eagerness for bloodshed burned at the warrior's heart like a fire. However, fires die if they are not fed. Some of the horde had already grown frustrated with the elusiveness of their enemy; Craa'su knew how to stoke the fire within them. He rode them through the burned encampments, knowing every warrior would witness firsthand the destruction of their kin. Their blood would once again come to a boil, and when the time came, they would howl to be unleashed. Only then would he release them.

They reached the last encampment on the third day of their journey. The fires purged the land of the grasses and the remnants of what used to be one of the clan's hunting grounds. The fires had burned for leagues but ultimately suffocated at the bluffs to the east. All that was left were the trampled grounds of the enemy.

So, Craa'su drove the horde further, and Su'ca smiled as they continued westward. This trampled ground, like the highways of the west, would lead them directly to the ones responsible.

The horde rested on the border of the Crescent realm. The lower eastern peaks of the Crescent Mountains stood tall on the horizon's edge, and the great forest waved in the wind almost like a friend beckoning Su'ca and the horde to come. They dismounted and let all the beasts graze what grasses could be found. They built great fires along the last ridge that lay before the Crestwood. Every fire was surrounded by a dozen warriors who prepared in their own way for what was to come. Some ate and recovered from their ride, while others grew restless and wrestled one another. One warrior would sing a great story, and at the next fire, another warrior would pick up where the last song left off. They brought drums, wooden flutes, and stringed boxes. The warriors' song reverberated over the open field and the clans danced. Once the sun sank over the farthest western mountain, all that could be seen was the Par'sha people swaying to the throat songs with the playful firelight of the ridge.

Su'ca was no different. She ate, drank deeply, and danced to the songs of her people. She loved the deep rumble of the throat songs, but that night, the sounds were interrupted. It was a small difference and had been unnoticed by most. However, Su'ca was a student of the songs; she could tell when the key had been missed. The difference in the songs that night came not from the horde but from the fields below. It was a strange void of blackness that let no light through. When she gazed into it, no horse or bear-sloth was seen, but she could hear them whinny and roar in the blackness.

The beasts were frightened in the dark, and shortly after, she saw them stampede around them. The animals charged in every direction. Some ran away farther into the black, and the rest ran through the encampment like mad dogs. The songs stopped altogether at the stampede and the Par'sha leapt into action to quell the uneasiness of the animals. However, once the songs stopped, the horde heard a whistling that could never be mistaken for anything else. Arrows burst from within the deep black fog surrounding the clans.

She stood and let them fall where they might. Su'ca knew there was no hiding and no cover to be had. Once the first volley fell, and she found herself with no harm done, she let out a blood-curdling cry. The warriors at her fire followed her example and howled with her. The spirit grew throughout the horde as they cried as one people. Her patience was rewarded. The horde would fight today.

After the first volley, she retrieved her hide-shield and held it above her head to protect her further. There was only one response for the cowards in the dark. She gathered a few darts and shifted them to the shield hand and then poised her launcher in the other ready to sling her first dart. In a single motion, she set, drew her arm back, and launched one dart after the other into the darkness.

The Par'sha dart was as long as a full-grown man, and the pairing of the dart and launcher made for a deadly weapon. It was swift and light; the dart could be hurled supremely farther than a spear, and a single strike could impale an enemy from which they would not recover. She launched one dart followed by another in the direction the arrows had come from until she had no more to send.

After the darts were sent, she unsheathed her short-spear. The blade was the length of a man's arm, the handle was half the blade's length, and the width at its base was as wide as a man's hand. The Par'sha were known to drive their blades with deadly accuracy deep into their foes. Some say the last thing heard from their victims was the unique sound of the short-spears entering and exiting the body. It was designed to deal a single death blow; she had nothing else in mind.

With a single whistle from Su'ca, a dozen mounts reappeared from within the darkness. She mounted the steed in a swift jump and charged straight into the void. Those who had survived the initial volley continued to follow their Crato'sha's example. Without hesitation, her party of warriors leapt directly into the blackness outside the light of the fires. As she barreled through the night, she found herself in a fine fog that obscured her vision only to the space of a large tent. Yet, the light from the encampment somehow broke through the all-consuming haze; the horde was not completely blind. Any remaining fear had left her in an instant, and she continued to gallop headlong with her warriors into the unknown.

As Su'ca rode through the fog, arrows flew around her and she directed her warriors straight at the source. The enemy suddenly appeared within the blackness and they were even stranger than expected. The enemy were mounted upon massive giant rams with curled horns, and their eyes burned with a green hue. The rams chortled and bucked at the approach of the Par'sha warriors, which unsettled the beast's rider. The enemy who rode the rams had the same green eyes that blazed into the night. They covered their bodies with dirty-white bones as if armored, and their helms featured horns akin to the rams they rode. They bore the look of horned skeleton demons in the dark.

The first warrior Su'ca faced continued to draw upon his bow and loosen another arrow, but he became hurried as Su'ca ferociously charged at him. With a swing of her spear, she struck at him once and again, but his bone armor deflected each slashing blow. She immediately changed tactics, shifting her swing into a thrust, and she drove her spear deep into his chest. She found her mark as he let out a long howl, and the green hue vanished from his eyes. She let out a warrior's cry as the first of her foes collapsed and fell from his mount.

As he hit the ground, his helm rolled from his head, and a man's head came into view. His visible skin was covered in black char from his narrow face to his torso, but even under the dim light, she could see the pink hue beneath it. His head was hairless except for the stubble on his chin. This was a man of the west and Su'ca knew It. Her rage built like magma within the earth; she was determined more than ever to pillage all the western cities for their arrogance.

As the revelations came to her, more arrows came from beyond the darkness. One warrior fell and then another. There was no time to make more assessments, and she charged at them again and again. She drove her warriors from one group of enemies to the next. The ground quaked beneath her as they trampled and speared every man as quickly as possible. During the ferocious battle, she found other warriors and rallied dozens of Par'sha to her. They joined her as they mounted any creature panicking in the open field. Those without mounts continued to fight near the base of the firelight. The rest of the horde amassed like the great herds of the grass-sea and wheeled around the encampment. Even a few warriors managed to mount the giant sloths and huddled back-to-back with each other. Although their pods were small, they were still formidable and drew the attention of the enemy. And as the horde fiercely fought and their spears reddened, the fog suddenly dissipated around them, and the grounds cleared.

Once again, Su'ca and all the warriors of the Par'sha were able to see each other clearly across the battlefield under the night sky. As the fog cleared, the enemy could be seen appearing from behind the veil of smoke, cowering toward the mountains of the Crest like thieves caught in the night.

Su'ca was taken aback by the sorcery of it. *How could the enemy conjure this illusion, and why did they reappear?* This question burned in her mind.

She turned her attention from those questions to the field. Even at the end of the battle, the warriors pursued. She called out to them to discontinue the chase.

"Let them run," she yelled. The battle had been won, and the horde had won it. She let out a victorious cry, and the horde followed suit. She reveled in the victory and thought of the songs they would create. Before the night's end, the warriors would etch the beginning of a valiant story that would echo through generations and all the city peoples would know what happened on the doorstep of the Crescent Mountain.

Su'ca returned to the fires with her remaining warriors. The difference between the living and dead was substantial. The grounds around the camps were littered with many dead clansmen. Hundreds had been struck down in the enemy's initial assault. Yet, her warriors took more from the enemy.

Had their foes come across a weaker opponent, they might have succeeded, but the Par'sha would not be snuffed so easily like a candle in the dark! Each warrior burned in their heart with the rage of an agitated wildebeest, and the wind cannot so easily extinguish that fire.

Like all her warriors, she helped collect the dead. There were a few heavy hearts. It was a blessing from the gods to meet the afterlife in battle. Most of the warriors rejoiced in the good fortune of their brothers and sisters as, one by one, they were prepared for the glorious pyre. The dead were gathered and laid side by side so they could be seen one more time by their warrior brethren. Their blood was wiped away, and some of their most valuable possessions were placed in their arms to assist them in the afterlife.

Su'ca prepared those she knew and wished them well into the next life until Tahop'ka came.

"Follow me," he beckoned.

She followed him to a distant fire where many warriors gathered around the dead. Beside each fallen warrior, four of the enemy lay beside them. Each fallen Par'sha at the fire bore half a dozen cuts. Those gathered had ruthlessly fought each other at close range with spear and shield. As she looked at the faces of the dead, she understood why she had been brought. She knew the man laid down alongside all the others; everyone knew him. Her father had been pierced by many arrows and cut many times, but it was the single arrow in his chest that had taken his life.

She kept herself from weeping. He would not want a Crato'sha of the Par'sha to weep for the dead.

Tonight, he would join the elders on the eternal plains; he would hunt like a young man and spear a bison for all the clan to enjoy. She brushed his coarse braids from his face, wiped the dirt from his cheek, and removed the arrows one by one. When she had finished, she folded his arms and placed the five arrows to take with him to the afterlife. A few tears escaped her as she prepared him for the journey.

She finished and passed word for every warrior to gather tinder for the great pyre. The warriors who gathered complied immediately and dispersed. All except Tahop'ka. He stayed with her a moment longer.

"Did you see him?" she asked, finally standing from her preparations.

"I did," he replied.

"And did he leave this world a warrior?"

He put his hand on her shoulder and smiled. "When the enemy came in the night and struck without honor, your father was pierced by two arrows, but he did not fall. He took his spear, his shield, and stood his ground like a mighty bear-sloth. His warriors assembled around him and shielded him. They sent more arrows, but all the warriors stood as one and protected each other. They were united under shield and spear and would not be moved. So, the enemy came themselves; they were fools to do so. They appeared from within the fog and came from all directions. There were many, but your father did not cower. The enemy struck with the ferocity of the wolfpack, but none could sink their teeth. Your father stood mighty and swatted one down and then another. All the warriors fought just as courageously, and they killed many. Eventually, a few warriors fell on the swords of the enemy. Those warriors who remained drove them back into the obscurity, where they retreated like cowards, but that was not the end. When they could no longer fight spear to spear with the Par'sha, they retreated, and again, they loosened their arrows from beyond the fog. Those arrows fell on the last of the warriors, and your father was one of them. None could have stood as boldly as he did."

Su'ca could no longer contain the tears from behind her eyes. They flowed beyond her control, but it was not all sorrow. Her father had lived like a warrior, fought like a warrior, led like a warrior, and died like a warrior. His song would be sung for generations.

"I am glad he left this world as a warrior does, but I'm sad his life has ended. I wish I could have done more for my clan and my father in their time of need," she lamented.

Tahop'ka squared himself in front of her, raised her chin, and looked deep into her eyes. "No one could have done more," he insisted.

Su'ca had not realized he was struggling with her father's death as well, but his eyes said differently.

"I fought with all the strength of the long-toothed cat. I pierced many enemies across the foggy haze to get to your father, but more came from beyond the fog. I could no more help your father than you could have. And when death almost came for me as well, you gathered the clans and drove them like the hunter. You speared the enemy as if they were antelopes upon the great grass-sea. You broke through them and surrounded them as the Par'sha have always done. You saved the horde when no one else could. Your father would have been proud of you."

She smiled for the first time since the last song was sung and placed her forehead to his.

She stood for a time and wondered what direction the horde would take beyond the dawn. Vengeance was inherently necessary for the Par'sha. They had struck all their clans, which was unforgivable, and now the enemy had the audacity to strike at the horde. They had suffered dearly for the second mistake, but it would not be enough. She swore to herself then that she would replenish the great grass-sea with the blood of the enemy well before the deep rains at the end of the summer. However, before vengeance could be taken, someone would have to be selected to lead the Par'sha.

Every clan was led by a Chief Crato'sha. It was only fitting that those selected to lead the clan were from those already chosen to lead its warriors. And among the clans, only one Crato'sha would be chosen to become the head of all the clans; the Partho'sha. The position was not always necessary. Often, the clans lived in peace, and there was no need for a Partho'sha. However, once a horde had been assembled, the war had begun, and a leader must be chosen to see them down the path. Her father was that leader, and now another would take his place.

"We will need a new Partho'sha all the clans will follow," she commented.

Tahop'ka nodded in approval.

"First, our clan will need to select a new first among the Crato'sha, and then we should choose a Partho'sha," he replied.

"No. We must have a leader of the clans now. Decisions must be made for the horde. If the sun rises tomorrow and no leader is chosen, we will be without direction. A dart should always be aimed before it is thrown," she countered.

Tahop'ka looked unmoved by her words. "You are right to seek out a leader and continue our war. We are all right to want vengeance for the clans, but there is nothing more we can do today and there is nothing more to fear this night. The sky is clear, and we will watch for any changes to it. The dawn will rise from over the horizon, and we will not have lost the war. All our plans can wait until the morning has come and the choosing has happened. And I will wait a little further until our clan has chosen your name so that we might count it among the others."

She did not disregard the comment; it was clear Tahop'ka wanted this outcome. She would lead her clan if they chose her to lead them.

However, there were other Crato'sha whose clans were powerful and wanting of position and there were Crato'sha who had led for numerous years and had earned the respect of all the clans. Even before her father's death, some would talk of the next Partho'sha in the shadows where none could hear.

"It matters very little if my name is chosen among the clans," she began. "There are others who believe it is their time to lead. If my name rivals another's, the horde could be split in two and war among the clans could follow. I would not have that be the outcome. I wish for only one thing, and that is the death of our enemies of the west."

Tahop'ka thought long about this, but none of her words seemed to deter him. "There are some who think they should lead, and the Crato'sha will weigh them next to others. I wish your name to be among them. You are a Crato'sha as well. Your name holds as much weight as the next one. You will be spoken of with great favor after today. These other Crato'sha did not fight the enemy as you did, and they did not lead as you did. I think it is fitting that you should take the place of your father. I do not think there will be war among the clans. Our war with these westmen has only just begun, and this battle has only made our people more resolved. So, I am content to wait for a leader worthy to lead us in it."

She had no more words to counter him. If they called her name, then she would answer them. "Then tomorrow, when the sun rises, our clan will decide who will lead us," she concluded.

"Then the clans will decide who leads us all," he finished. Perhaps others were as adamant to hear her name among the other Chief Crato'sha. The horde decided who would lead and which wind they would follow; this is how it had always been done.

All that remained was to mourn and rejoice at the pyre. They toiled late into the night and found enough kindling to cover every warrior. When they lit the pyre, the blaze towered so high that the flames rivaled the tallest structures of the western cities.

Su'ca basked in the warm glow blazing into the night like a beacon. The enemy would see them unafraid of their darkness. Instead, it would be the enemy who would cower before the Par'sha in the dark and wonder when the horde would come.

Chapter XI
The Skirmish

The magic pierced through the dark forest like a bolt of lightning blitzing across a stormy summer night. The mysterious aura surged through the air, overwhelming Cal's senses. All other concerns ebbed from his mind as if washed away by a spring rain; his fears were disregarded, his hunger satiated, and the exhaustion that consumed his body subsided. He sat with a clear mind, poised for battle, and ready to unleash his own fury.

When he opened his eyes, he found the blinding light emanating from the head of Alec's staff streaming into the forest. He covered his eyes with his hands, but it did little good; he was forced to turn away.

As he looked upon the forest, he found everything in sight revealed; the dark fog immediately disintegrated before him. The edges between the light and the dark formed a great round dome as if they were in an ancient cathedral of the gods. Under the light's radiance, the immediate forest was illuminated and the enemy was exposed, blind, and cowering in every direction. They wore a mixture of furs and a kind of bone armor, and they were mounted on beastly creatures. Like Cal, they attempted to cover their eyes with their hands, shields, and swords. However, they failed at the attempt, and all succumbed to the intensity of the glow.

With Cal's back turned to the light and the startled creatures before him, he found himself free and able to strike back at their pursuers. As the magic coursed through his limbs and his nerves settled, he retrieved an arrow from his quiver and drew back on his bow. With his mind clear and his body rejuvenated, he released. The arrow sailed through the air, without any attempt at deflection from the enemy and hit his target square in the chest. The flaming green hue of the creatures' eyes faded as he fell from a gargantuan ram. Once the body collapsed, the mount retreated into the deep forest and it dawned on him: they were mortal after all. They were made of flesh and blood beyond the dark veil, and they could be killed if given the opportunity. Cal turned to his companions, but no command needed to be issued for the remaining party members to join the fray; the initiative had left the enemy, and it was squarely in their hands.

Eris joined him and began raining one arrow after another on the enemy. Her skill alone kept the entire swarm of creatures ahead of the party solely occupied on her. Four of them fell to the ground before any other foe even reacted.

Yslanna and Clydes each saw the opportunity to strike, as they charged into the forest and swept the enemy around the party. Yslanna fluidly glided her spear from one side to the next like a skilled dancer. As her long Elvian blade ebbed and flowed, each precise slash found the weak points in their armor. She opened the belly of one and the neck of another easily landing strikes underneath their raised arms.

Conversely, Clydes swung his hammer violently like a rabid animal and with such purposeful force that the steel helm on each enemy cracked under his powerful strike.

Not to be outdone, Jacoby and Halden swung around the other side of the party and leapt into the forest as well. Their battle prowess was equally impressive as Jacoby began hacking and thrusting at the first pair of opponents that he crossed, and Halden shrewdly thrust his halberd into one foe and slashed the head of another.

Only a few moments passed before any of the enemy regained their senses from the initial blindness. Those with swords and spears were primarily occupied with the chaos of Yslanna, Clydes, Halden, and Jacoby charging from every direction around the center of the light. Those who had bows drew them, and loosened arrows at anything that moved.

Eventually, a few clever creatures retaliated, loosed arrows at the blinding light, and Alec became a sought-after target. Bill courageously brought his horse in front of Alec, drew his sword, and held his shield high to deflect the few incoming arrows that flew in their direction. He was so preoccupied with the arrows flying past, he almost didn't see the lurking foe who charged Alec from behind on his giant snorting ram. Alec drew his sword and reined his horse away from his attacker, but Bill arrived with his sword outstretched and ready to strike. He drove his horse between them and, at the last moment, deflected the oncoming blow of the enemy's sword. With a swift slash of his sword, Bill struck the poor creature as a few more arrows flew past all of them. The creature fell to the ground, and the enemy archers succumbed to Yslanna's blade as she flanked them.

The fight lasted only a few moments before the darkness retreated and the enemy with it. They had fought bravely, but the momentum could not be overturned. Once the arrows had begun to fly and the brawlers were unleashed, the enemy had little chance to recover from the onslaught. In moments, almost two dozen became mortally wounded and were strewn around the grounds. All the other wounded creatures leapt back into the darkness, and the skirmish was won.

The light diminished significantly and softened into a warm glow from the staff and the meager night sky peered from beyond the forest canopy. They were back again under the cover of the night and the waning moonlight.

As the light shrank, Cal felt the rejuvenating power cease as if he stepped out of the sunshine. He looked to Alec, and the old man slumped his arm, collapsed into his saddle, and panted heavily as if the weight of the staff could no longer be held. Everyone had rushed to the old man's side.

"Are you alright?" Cal asked.

Alec struggled to raise his head and meet eyes with the young man.

Cal brushed the disorderly gray strands from the old man's face, and a wrinkled smirk emerged.

"That took a toll on me," Alec exclaimed.

Alec's spirit was still intact, but his appearance told another story. All his robes were damp with sweat, and his face was flushed. Cal speculated how the magic worked and what it exacted from the old man. Where Cal found himself jubilant for a time from the magic, he wondered if Alec succumbed to a reverse effect.

"Alec, we are alright for the moment. You can cease the light if you wish. We will manage until we rejoin Sir Kenneth."

Alec wiped his brow, rested the base of the staff on his stirrup, and picked himself up from his slump.

"No. This magic may be the only defense keeping us from being set upon again, and I intend to muster what strength I can to save our commander, the great oaf. For now, I will reserve my strength and the light for the fight to come. You will all need your own lights to help guide you through the dark forest, and if we're lucky, we may yet survive this night."

Cal nodded and knew what must be done. "Quickly, we must have torches!" Cal ordered.

All began hacking at suitable dead branches, all but Bill. The color had all but left his face and he was showing the same signs of weariness as Alec. Cal wondered if Bill's proximity to the magic affected him adversely or was it another reason altogether.

"Could we rest a moment, lad? I'm all but spent an' I'm afraid I'll collapse if I travel much further," Bill asked.

Cal mulled over the request. The day had been extremely long, and, by the grace of Alec's magic, they found victory. However, the clash of steel carried on the wind. If they did not muster all their strength and rejoin Sir Kenneth, the whole cavalry could fall that very evening. Cal would not have it.

"Bill, take a moment and bask in the light," Alec suggested. He held his staff over Bill's head. The glow covered him like a halo and Bill breathed a little easier.

"I can feel it wash over me body," Bill reassured him. "But only just. It's like something else drains me."

"Just take the moment and breathe. Once we have the torches lit, we must ride. They need us now, and we could use a good man like you beside us," Cal encouraged.

It was all Bill needed to hear. He inhaled deeply and brought his sword and shield to his chest. The light reflected the slightest red streak from Bill's sword.

Behind Bill's horse, one of the creatures lay dead. Under all the mystery, they were only wild men in the night. Bill had protected him as he fired arrows from a distance, and Cal beamed with pride at the old shopkeeper.

The torches were hastily fashioned together by Jacoby and, after producing flint, they were lit and passed along.

Alec postured himself upright in his saddle once again and braced all his energy for the upcoming fight. "I will assist your flames, and they will burn the brighter. However, I warn you now, this feat is consuming my energy rapidly. If I should fall, you will have to carry on without me. Muster your courage, my friends," Alec cautioned.

"We must turn the tide before that happens! We shall ride abroad of each other and charge at them from behind. Clydes and Yslanna are to lead us at the center, Halden and Jacoby to their left, Eris and I will guard their right and I want Alec and Bill to fall behind us. We must relieve Sir Kenneth and muster the rest of the cavalry," Cal added.

"I imagine we will make quite a sensation," Yslanna commented.

"Augh, yeah!" Halden smiled. "When the day concludes, we'll have singlehandedly won the war, and I'll accept thanks from that blowhard commander personally."

Yslanna grinned at the short fellow.

No one disagreed with the direction. Clydes expressed his excitement with the hoisting of his massive war hammer and torch above his head, grunted faintly, and charged through the trees along the trail. The party followed behind the great black horse the giant rode upon, and they thundered through the forest. If this were any other occasion, Cal would have considered a nightly gallop through the Crestwood reckless, but their flames were indeed made brighter somehow, and the forest grew clearer in the light.

As they hurdled through the thick overgrowth of trees, they came upon the darkness once again. Clydes did not hesitate upon approaching the wall of churning blackness and he charged headlong at the fog. All the party followed him and just as they were about to enter the darkness, the light again burst from the head of Alec's staff. The blackness was eviscerated before them, and a grassy field appeared. The party swiftly maneuvered and spread themselves out on either side of the charging giant like a pack of wolves. As the dark fog evaporated and the clear dome reformed, the enemy again appeared before them on the ground, all drawing their bows and loosening their arrows in the cavalry's direction. Like before, the light startled and blinded the enemy.

Clydes led the charge as he struck the first blow on the unsuspecting enemy, and his massive horse trampled over the next. He charged through like a raging bull, purposefully swinging his hammer in one hand, and his torch in the other. Once the enemy recognized the danger, they scattered thoughtlessly in any open direction. The party members eagerly hacked and speared as they trampled every foe they came across. The plan was working.

As they charged the enemy from behind, the first signs of the cavalry appeared, and a deadly engagement was well in hand. By the look of the cavalry's poor condition, it was clear the vanguard was on the brink of collapse and on the verge of losing the battle. The enemy had infiltrated, surprised, and attacked from all sides. Each force had interwoven into a tapestry of steel and blood, and all were fiercely fighting one another hand to hand. More than half of the cavalrymen were unhorsed and scattered throughout the field; the vanguard itself was disorganized and leaderless. All the fresh, pristine tunics and new leather armors were now caked in sweat, grime, and blood.

Here in the heart of the Crestwood, the Midguard and Crestfolk alike were fighting purely for their lives.

There was little time to lose. The party encircled the outskirts of the two forces and continued to assault the rear of the enemy at lightning speeds. Halden, Jacoby, Clydes, and Yslanna took the brunt of the charge while Eris and Cal continued to loosen arrows until none remained. As they attacked, Alec followed behind shedding a penetrating light onto the field that pierced through the haze and dissipated the darkness. The light beamed on the soldiers as if the fresh morning sun on a cold winter's day. It was a welcome spectacle. With the fog clearing and their sights restored, all the Midguard and the Crestfolk began finding their targets as they swung their swords and thrust their spears. Conversely, the enemy cowered and paused in the light, and as such, they suffered under the sudden rain of steel that came upon their heads.

The party kept up their momentum, but as they charged around the perimeter relieving the vanguard, another area fell to the chaos as the black fog swallowed the ground behind them. Their efforts weren't enough; they had to risk themselves even further.

"To the center!" Cal called. "To the center!" He struck Alice with the reins and fiercely kicked as he pulled her to the left. And as he turned inward, he drove Eris, Clydes, Yslanna, Jacoby, and Halden to the center of the battlefield. They pierced through until they were well into the midst of the fighting, but the light shone outward and onto the faces of the enemy, blinding them. The vanguard pushed back and the momentum swung like a pendulum. The battle continued for a half-hour. The vanguard hacked, pierced, and loosened arrows at the enemy and valiantly rallied in the end.

The darkness, and the enemy with it, retreated into the forest. The starry sky returned into view, prominently casting moonlight over the Crestwood. The battle had concluded with the sound of the remaining enemy vanishing in every direction into the dark depths of the forest.

As Cal pondered his next action, the light that beamed into the night and helped the cavalry in their hour of need, vanished. Like many, Cal turned to see the disturbance. Alec, slumped over his mount, keeled over and collapsed onto the ground. He immediately dismounted and ran to aid the man where a small huddle of Crestfolk formed.

A few stepped aside for Cal and his torchlight. He planted his torch in the ground, knelt beside Alec, and placed him in his arms.

Alec looked like any frail old man would, and yet strikingly unfamiliar. The man that Cal knew was cantankerous and full of life. However, the man in his arms had lost all the color from his face, his wrinkles accelerated as if he had aged another ten years, he shivered to the touch, and his pulse was weak. Whatever magic he had conjured, it had coursed through him and left him hollow.

"Stay with us, you old fool! Who will rub this victory in the commander's face if not you?" Cal shouted.

The old man's eyes shifted to the young man. He panted, trembled, and nodded. With all his remaining strength, he beckoned Cal to come close.

Cal obliged him and shifted his ear directly in front of the old man.

"I feel… life… grasping," Alec whispered. The old man's eyes were darting back and forth as he clenched Cal's arm.

"Cal!" Halden yelled. "Move aside, ya great oaf!" Halden appeared from behind a flaming-red-haired woman whose shield sported a hundred fresh dents and cuts.

"Halden, it's Alec. I'm not sure what should be done. He's frozen to the touch. Perhaps, the Elvians know of something that can help him," Cal replied.

Halden came alongside and put his hand on his shoulder. "Cal, I'm afraid the toll is even larger. Bill's hurt. He's got an arrow broken off between his ribs. It's not good, my friend." Halden replied.

The night air froze and Cal's chest seized mid-breath. He held one injured friend in his hands, and his dearest friend, his last family member, was hurt among strangers and also needed his aid. Cal felt ashamed he could not run to Bill's aid, but Alec could not be abandoned. The old vagabond who had been disregarded by most had just saved the cavalry with his magic and laid motionless in his arms; it would be cruel to leave him now. The tears formed in his eyes as he avoided looking at Halden. He didn't know what he should do or if he could even do anything at all. As he looked past Halden, he met the eyes of the red-haired warrior behind him and found a kind face behind the grime and blood; she understood. All the Crestfolk had understood the hardship that vexed his soul.

"What should I do?" Cal asked, like a boy without direction. Just as he asked, the slightest tug of his arm pulled him back. Alec still had life in him, and he was dearly grasping onto it.

"Fires... light fires!" Alec whispered. His head slumped, his arms dropped to his side, and his eyes closed.

"What?" Cal shouted. He shifted Alec in his arms to hear him better, but he was unresponsive. If it weren't for the old man's faint pulse, he would've assumed him dead. "Damn you! What do you mean?" Cal repeated. There was no reply except his faint breath and even that felt frozen. And with that thought, an epiphany struck Cal and he understood.

Halden patted his back and attempted to soothe him. "We've got to rest now, Cal. The fire can wait," Halden pleaded. Cal ignored him now that he understood.

Alec needed the fire to warm him and breathe life back into him. Bill needed the fire to sear the wound after they removed the arrow. They all needed the light to keep the darkness at bay. The old man seemed to always have a reason for the madness and there was no time to lose.

"We need fires. We need kindling. We need them around everyone," Cal ordered.

Halden sighed and knelt beside him, but his hesitation said otherwise.

"Cal, I know you're hurting. Alec is in our hands, and Bill is in good hands with Eris. That's what they need. If we light fires, they may come for us again. I don't know if we can risk it," Halden urged.

"You don't understand, Halden. The fires will help us. All of us. Alec and Bill need the fire tonight to survive. We have scores of injured men who need it now. If we do nothing, we may lose far more. And if they should come back, we will not have the magic. Alec can't help us. It will just be us. He told me once 'Magic can be simple.' Warmth can fight the cold. Fire can fight the dark and seal the wounds of our injured. We can use the fire!" Cal appealed as Halden thought silently for a few moments.

"Alright. I'll see it done," Halden relented, turned to the few folk huddled, and reiterated the command. Word spread among the vanguard and those able quickly gathered wood from the forest. A cord was gathered, followed by another as they began lighting a perimeter of fires around the remaining vanguard. All the folk who had survived assembled around the flames. Those who were injured were brought beside the fires and their wounds were cleaned and sealed with the scourge of heated steel; many cried out in the night. Others vigilantly stood watch as they fed the flames just to reassure themselves that the dark fog had not reformed.

Once Halden returned and a fire was lit, Cal and the Darwishman carried the old man closer to the flames.

Cal sat with Alec for a time and let the waves of heat radiate and brush over his face. As he held Alec, the old man's shivers lessened over time until they were gone altogether. He looked better under the soft glow of the flame, and although his eyes remained shut, his breathing calmed, and the color had returned to his face; Cal knew he would live. All the men who had been injured would now likely live to see the next day. At least Cal hoped more than anything.

Cal turned to Halden, "Where's Bill?"

"Just over the knoll," Halden motioned.

Cal looked Alec over once more and reminded himself that he had done all he could. "Would you look after him?"

"Of course. I've got the watch here," Halden reassured.

Cal quickly strode through huddles of folk to get to his friend. His heart pounded in his chest as he searched frantically between the fires of the encampment only to find that Eris and Yslanna were kneeling an arm's length away. He was relieved to find his companions were so close but disregarded the feeling altogether when his eyes found Bill.

Bill was pale as a ghost, and as he lay in Yslanna's lap, she gently wiped a damp rag across his forehead. He was bare-chested save for the dark tunic that was torn into long strips and wrapped around his torso. Bill appeared to gain some relief from the cool rag, but it was clear he had lost a great deal of blood, and his dark bandages were, in fact, soaked through.

Cal knelt beside him and held his hand, hoping to provide him with comfort that his friend was here. It shamed him not to have been here earlier to comfort him. Cal wiped away the tears that formed in the corner of his eye when Eris placed her hand on his shoulder.

"We've removed the arrow and sealed the wound, but I'm afraid he's been losing blood for some time. He was struck at the earlier skirmish," Eris explained, eyes glossy and red.

Cal was in shock. *Where was Bill struck, and why didn't he say anything?* Cal realized he had.

Bill asked them to rest, and he told Bill they had to keep moving forward. Cal grew with frustration and anger. At the time, he didn't question whether Bill was unwell or injured. He assumed the magic had drained him like Alec, but he was wrong. Now, his oldest friend was on the brink of death, and the blame perched on his shoulders.

Cal clenched his hands in anger only to abate the feeling when a weak hand squeezed back. Cal looked at his old friend and found his eyes open and looking back at him. Bill even managed to smile at the young man.

"What's this now? Griev'n are ya? We can't have that, m'boy. If I'm not long for this world, I would rather have a story. I loved the old songs m'self. How about one of 'em instead?" Bill asked.

Cal laughed as Bill knew he would. Bill had always known how to comfort Cal during his darkest days. He had cared for him when his mother died, he had taught him a trade to make a living, they had broken a rule or two along the way, and now they had fought together. Bill knew him better than anyone.

"I'm sorry, Bill," Cal wept. "I didn't see you were hurt earlier and I should have," Cal said, through a tear.

Bill grasped his hand even harder and patted him with his other hand. "Now, my lad, you've done noth'n wrong! Look at me, boy!" Bill insisted.

Cal stopped and wiped his tears with his sleeve.

"You're not to blame here. No one is to blame," Bill continued.

"They're to blame!" Cal shouted as he pointed at the enemy lying on the ground around them.

"No, lad," Bill retorted calmly. "I hold no ill will toward 'em who did this either. I chose to come here. I chose to fight alongside ya. This is my doing an' I don't want you blam'n yourself and I don't want no revenge in my name. Do ya hear me, lad?"

Cal nodded. He took a moment to think about what Bill said. He had always been like that as long as Cal knew him. He was never one to hold a grudge, even against those who wronged him.

"Right, then. I'm go'n to shut my eyes an' rest for a while. I've been wait'n a while to see ya an' I'm a bit tired. You look after these folk here. They need someone to look after 'em an' I reckon you're the man for the job," Bill said with an admiring tone. He shut his eyes and fell into a deep sleep.

He breathed his last sometime in the night.

Chapter XII
The Loss

Sir Kenneth dreamt of the battle. The vivid and relentless images flooded his mind. The dream began peacefully with him upon his horse galloping along the northern road. Then, just after dusk, the fog descended upon the vanguard from every side of the Crestwood like a tsunami. At the very moment the darkness surrounded them, hundreds, if not thousands, of fearsome warriors upon frightening beasts charged with spears drawn. The cavalry engaged in a brutal battle.

Even under the circumstances of the initial attack, Sir Kenneth was an experienced and trained soldier who understood the situation before him. He steadied his nerves and drew his sword when the darkness came. When the enemy emerged, he courageously led the cavalry and swatted away one attacker, followed by another. He had fought valiantly and his sword found the mark on many foes. In the end, however, the vanguard was overwhelmed by their ferocity.

Most of the cavalry had been unhorsed, and they were struggling to repel the attackers on foot. Before Sir Kenneth could countermand any movement of the enemy, a heavy blow struck him and everything turned black. Sir Kenneth feared little but as his sight vanished, his heart flooded with dread. The dream soured, and there was little to do but lie there beaten, consumed with regret, and feel his life slowly slip away from his grasp. When the moment had all but consumed him, a glimmer of sight returned for the briefest moment, and a piercing blue light blazed among the battle. It darted in the heavens like a comet, and life sprang from all around him in a blanket of hope and wonder. All thoughts of dread were removed.

The dream ended, and the sunlight seared his eyes as he fought to open them. He rubbed his eyes, but his sight remained blurred. As he rolled over to cradle himself away from the sunlight, an unbearable soreness plagued him from head to toe. His sword arm throbbed uncontrollably, and when he attempted to push himself up from the ground, he found his left shoulder bruised and weak. Sir Kenneth heaved with his remaining strength, and at last, he stood. The blood rushed to his head, throbbing uncontrollably. This distracted him from all the other pains.

He reached around his head and found a bandage tightly wrapped. At first, he grew concerned that he may have received a terrible wound, but after some light prodding, he found himself relieved. The rag wrapped around his head held little blood, and all of it was dried. His wound was little more than a tender lump above his left ear. The helmet took the brunt of the strike which rendered him unconscious and the blow deflected onto his shoulder. He could have been in much worse shape.

When the blurriness subsided and the fuzzy forms of men took shape underneath the midmorning sun, he gauged the situation around him and his remaining force. The losses were substantial.

He tried to recall the battle to make sense of the field before him, but the memory was woven together with the vivid dream that was fixed in his mind; he was not sure where the truth lay. He remembered they were set upon by a vast host, and the enemy's numbers, their quality, and the rumors surrounding them were vastly underestimated.

The bulk of the memory consisted of flashes of a heated battle and then nothing except a light among the darkness. However the battle unfolded, the result led to hundreds of wounded soldiers clinging to their very lives. Their wounds were wrapped and, more likely than not, they would sit out the remainder of this conflict; some of them would be crippled for life.

They were lucky compared to the number of cavalry who covered the ground alongside the enemy; he was aghast at the heaps of corpses. The vanguard, or what was left of them, were assembling the dead. It had been a costly evening. Overall, all of the newly assembled cavalry had joined in the long pursuit and it was very possible the bulk of those men were lost in the night.

As he perused the busy soldiers along the gap, he found why the dead men were piling: they were to be burned. The vultures would have only feasted a little this morning, because the pyres had been formed for the fallen Midfolk and Crestfolk. *Did Master Wendall order the action?* Sir Kenneth thought it foolish to forgo the traditional burials. However, he did not know who was commanding in his absence. Master Wendall may be among the dead, and one of his Captains could have taken command. Whoever was giving the orders, the decision seemed hasty to Sir Kenneth. The soldiers had fought hard, won at a significant cost, and deserved to be carted back home toward the Mid or wherever they had come. As he looked on, he found not only had the fallen soldiers been robbed of a burial by their families, but they were to be joined with the slain enemy.

All the dead were being heaved onto the fires without prejudice. The act disgusted him. Soldiers should be honored for their sacrifices and not desecrated.

Sir Kenneth turned from the pyres and found those who were not actively burning the dead were preparing their horses and the injured for departure. They had left Mid in such a haste that he had forgotten no carts were available for the injured to rest. During the pursuit, he drove them deep into the Crestwood, and all were far removed from assistance. Briefly, he regretted pushing the cavalry.

Sir Kenneth began calculating the manpower required to undertake such a journey. *How many men had been set aside for transporting the wounded? What was left of the enemy?* They may have been scattered to the wind, but he would not know without reports and the only way to get answers was to find the one in command.

"You there? Soldier?" Sir Kenneth called.

A young man whose chin hair was barely more than fuzz turned to meet Sir Kenneth's eyes. He had been tending to the wounded folk, filling their water, and checking bandages. His armor was scratched, muddied, and sported black soot from the battle. Despite his youth, he looked as grizzled as any soldier would after a fight.

"What?" The soldier snapped, wiping his brow under the midmorning sun.

Sir Kenneth's jaw tightened. Perhaps the lad was still a boy in many ways, and he had much to learn about discipline. Sir Kenneth knew this was one of the many issues among the untrained common folk with which he would have to contend.

"Do you know who I am, boy?" Sir Kenneth queried frustratingly.

The soldier shook his head.

"You're speaking to the commander of this cavalry," he continued.

"I thought he was dead, sir."

"Clearly, I am still among the living."

"You don't look like no commander, sir."

Sir Kenneth met the young man's response with perplexity only to realize half a moment later his own armor had been removed. He became exasperated with the irritating young man.

"Enough. Who has ordered these bodies to be put to fire?"

The soldier shrugged, glancing toward the rest of the cavalry. "Couldn't say, sir. I was just following the crowd, really. My sergeant's long dead, and when someone started giving orders, everyone just followed along. Not sure if it was any of the headmen," the young man replied.

Sir Kenneth was unsure how to proceed. *Were all his Captains dead? Had Master Wendall fallen as well?* He tried to recall the event again, but the images remained as elusive as before. However confounded he was, there was still some semblance of organization, and someone had control of the situation; that gave him some relief. His head pounded, and his legs buckled. Sir Kenneth collapsed to his knees and clutched at his bandage.

"You need a healer, sir!" The soldier exclaimed as he rushed over to the old knight with a damp rag in hand.

Sir Kenneth took a few moments to recover himself. He was more injured than he realized. The inquiries and the morning sun left him lightheaded and warm to the touch.

"Are you not one?"

"No, sir! I was told to look after them that's been injured. Keep them in the shade and make sure they've got water and such. But I can get you the healer, sir. She's around here somewhere."

"Fine, call the healer to me. Once you've accomplished that, you will seek out whoever is giving the orders and summon them to me at once. It's urgent!" Sir Kenneth demanded.

"Yes, sir," the young man acknowledged and departed.

Sir Kenneth crawled beneath a large tree where the other injured soldiers were gathered. Their wounds had been wrapped and the color had returned to their cheeks. They would live. He spotted a waterskin lying beside an unconscious woman, took it, and he drank. The water quenched his thirst, but his stomach merely reminded him that he had been without food for well over a day. He was weak. As he looked among the injured, a small doubt formed in his mind. *Could he continue as charged? Could the cavalry?* He reserved his remaining strength for that conversation.

It was a few moments before a group of new soldiers approached. Sir Kenneth pushed himself upright to receive them, but he found disappointment as there were no Midguardmen nor trusted

Captains among them. As the soldier leading the group neared, he recognized the young man.

He was the sergeant whom Sir Kenneth promoted the previous day. He wasn't without a good mind and he had advised caution in the pursuit. To the young man's credit, he may have been right, but that could not be ascertained now. Sir Kenneth needed reasonable folk who could lead, even if they were common woodsmen. Behind the sergeant was a familiar Darwishman to his right, an unfamiliar Elvian to his left, a man of the eastern cities, and not one soldier he knew.

"Gods, what has become of us?" Sir Kenneth exclaimed.

"I see you've awoken..." Cal replied.

"... and your spirit has returned," Halden remarked.

Sir Kenneth wasn't amused and he had all he could take of witticisms and disorderly soldiers.

"That's enough! Who is in command here?"

"You're lucky. Most of the folk haven't been as fortunate to see today's sun," Cal commented as he ignored Sir Kenneth's question and knelt in front of him.

"Did you not hear me? Why have my Captains not come?" Sir Kenneth demanded.

"They're most folk," Halden quipped.

"I will have you whipped, *Dwarf*!" Sir Kenneth snarled as he attempted to rise. The gesture was a futile effort. A trickle of blood ebbed through his bandages, his head grew light, his vision blackened, and he collapsed again. However, he was caught this time by the young man in front of him.

"That'll be the last time you call me dwarf, commander!" Halden threatened as he pointed his halberd at Sir Kenneth. "If another obscenity of my people happens upon your tongue, no laws of gods and men shall keep me from killing you."

Yslanna held Halden back. "Calm yourself, my friend," she soothed. "I will not let you soil your hand with his death. Besides, you should not have provoked him. Leave me to tend to this man while you calm yourself."

Halden kept his eyes fixed on the knight for a moment, but Yslanna's words removed his gaze. He lowered his weapon and turned away from him.

Yslanna knelt to examine Sir Kenneth further. She pressed at his wound and held him for a time. "You must not let your emotions control you, commander." Yslanna asserted as she and Cal lowered him to the cool ground. "If you quicken the blood, all you will do is freshen the wound. You must rest." She retrieved the waterskin from the knight's hands, a cloth from behind her, and wetted the cloth before resting it on his head. After a time, his heartbeat lessened, his vision solidified, and his breathing slowed.

"Most of the vanguard at the head of the attack were killed," Cal commented to Sir Kenneth as he drank water. "We began collecting the dead at sunrise and found most of your captains killed. There are two injured who've yet to awaken. What other questions..."

"Gods, you're alive!" Master Wendall proclaimed from beyond the brush. He panted in excess as he trudged with heavy boots and mud-covered trousers to where Sir Kenneth lay under a great oak tree. He survived the battle unscathed, apart from the forehead wound, which trickled blood down his left cheek. Even his absurd new chest plate still retained a reflective glow under the sun.

Sir Kenneth sighed heavily as his successor meandered into view. He blamed himself for the vanguard's state of affairs.

"Master Wendall, let me see to your wound," Yslanna offered.

Master Wendall welcomed her assistance as he plopped onto a boulder and began gulping water. "We will have you up and fighting quickly, I assure you, Sir Kenneth," Master Wendall pronounced after guzzling the last of the water. "No need to worry. I will set aside a healer like this one and will have you mended before the next sun rises. Furthermore, we will continue the pursuit and finish these buggers! Now, what remains of our forces? We look light but fit to carry on, yes?"

Sir Kenneth was baffled. Master Wendall was far more unprepared than Sir Kenneth realized and the condition of the cavalry was very much in question.

"You are supposed to have those answers, Master Wendall," Sir Kenneth spelled out. "How many men have we lost? Who commanded the pyres? Where are we planning to take the injured? Where has the enemy gone? How can you come before me and know nothing of our situation?"

Master Wendall peered over the grounds in bewilderment.

Sir Kenneth gritted his teeth as he wiped his brow with the rag. The wrong people of no status had risen to stations where they did not belong. It was an epidemic of the Mid and thousands of folk would suffer.

The merchant recoiled slightly, realizing his error. "We will make those assessments shortly and send out the scouts to determine the whereabouts of the enemy. I assure you I will thoroughly inspect our condition, and we will finish this task," he stammered.

"We've lost more than half," Cal interjected. "I told them to burn the bodies. We haven't the strength or the means to bury the dead. It was this or the crows. Our injured have been provided for, but they need much rest and protection."

"They do," Halden added. "And that complicates things further. If we are to continue this chase with little regard for the injured, we will be attacked piecemeal and routed. A decision was reached."

"By whom?" Sir Kenneth snapped.

"I made the decision with the counsel of my party," Cal replied. "There are villages nearby the river that are abandoned and could provide us shelter. They are well within a half-day's ride, even with the injured."

"I appreciate your enthusiasm and initiative, but we shouldn't be deterred from our efforts so easily," Master Wendall countered as if Cal jested. "My instincts were correct to utilize you and your companion's knowledge of the area. I think resting at the village is a superb notion. However, we should continue our efforts on the field. The persistent man reaps the reward."

"We haven't a man to spare for that!" Cal retorted, waving Master Wendall aside. "Yesterday, we rode to our limits, assuming the enemy was just as exhausted, and good men died!" The young man strained his voice and all but scolded the merchant.

Sir Kenneth knew very well what he meant. The sergeant had known someone among the dead; maybe a friend. He even made the difficult choice to burn their body. Few understood the burden of leadership.

"We survived the night but only just," Yslanna chimed. "They have outridden us and outmaneuvered us. No man here can say for sure that they are defeated, and some folk suspect we rode directly into a trap. Of what I am certain, Master Wendall, you are greatly overestimating our skill or miscalculating that of the enemy."

"Besides, if it weren't for us, you'd all be dead men," Jacoby added. "Granted, the old man gave us an edge, but he's unconscious, and I wouldn't want to fight them again without evening the odds."

Sir Kenneth fell speechless. *Had these commonfolk been truly leading his forces for the last few hours? And what farce happened upon Master Wendall that left him behind?*

"What do you mean?" Sir Kenneth questioned. "What happened?"

"Do you not remember?" Yslanna asked.

Sir Kenneth's memories continued to elude him. "I cannot recall all the details at the moment," he grudgingly admitted.

"We were set upon in the forest at dusk," Cal began. "Alec saved us. I don't understand how, but he conjured a powerful magic of light that revitalized us, repelled the darkness, and revealed the enemy. We were fortunate to have him. We charged them from behind, encircled them, and in the end, we drove into the midst of the battle and forced them back!"

Cal knelt beside Sir Kenneth and stared him in the eyes. "This was not luck or grace from the gods which snatched the vanguard from defeat. Without Alec and his magic, we would have all died. I fear without him, we cannot continue this fight."

Only the wind stirred among their silence.

"You were the ones in the night!" Master Wendall gasped.

Cal turned his head to the merchant and only nodded.

Sir Kenneth wanted to doubt the young man and dismiss the fable outright. He didn't altogether understand what he meant about conjuring or magic, but he had trouble doubting the sergeant's description of the battle. In no way had Sir Kenneth ever believed in the outlandish stories of magic; those were for children. And regarding Alec, the misanthrope, he was nothing more than a vagrant and a known degenerate. Any recount of that man selflessly helping others, much less the Mid, or possessing some form of power was farfetched, to say the least. Yet, Master Wendall corroborated the young man's story and his own obscure reminiscence gave Sir Kenneth pause. An image persisted in his mind of an orb of light plummeting through the field of battle; when the young sergeant mentioned this, the memory came without difficulty above all the others. He wanted to deny it, but he could not.

"I understand your passion. I even admire your guile," Master Wendall continued, his voice calm. "Let me make myself plain: the commander has been wounded and the responsibility falls to me to decide our course of action. There are many courses to consider…"

"We make for the villages as soon as we are able. I wish to have formed a defense before nightfall," Sir Kenneth interrupted.

Master Wendall was taken aback. "Commander, we cannot simply abandon our charge."

"I am well aware of our purpose and what is required of me. We are the vanguard. We travel first, gather what we can of the enemy, engage them if necessary, and then Lord Malcolm will follow. We have done this and much more. Now we must salvage what we can and report to the Lord of the Mid."

"I fear your wounds have clouded your judgment," replied Master Wendall.

"My judgment? I am wounded, not senile," Sir Kenneth countered. "We have not been defeated. However, this is far from the victory you and I seek. I will be judged equally on my persistence of the pursuit as well as the consequences. I am as eager to continue as you are, but we have been outmatched. What of your judgment, Master Wendall? Whatever madness compels you forward, I am declining for the moment. I also must question your competence!"

The accusation stunned Master Wendall. "Commander?"

"You were to be my second. Your responsibilities were to take command if I fell, and in the hour of need, I am to understand you had no part to play. You are without the grasp of the situation, and I am without captains. These four Crestfolk of a scouting party have managed to succeed our positions, corral our folk, and assess the condition of our situation. We've all been supplanted. What have you to say in your defense?"

Master Wendall shoved Yslanna to the side as he rose in a huff, red-faced and glaring down at Sir Kenneth.

"Commander, I will not be demeaned in front of our soldiers like a cur. Nor will I have my capability questioned! I will not have it, sir!" Master Wendall spat, pointing his finger at Sir Kenneth. "Have I not come to assume my post? Not that anyone inquired, but I fought the same fight as you. I charged into that chaos and I was thrown from my horse and knocked unconscious near that stream just within those trees. I will not be judged so quickly because of your actions, sir! I came the moment I awoke. Now, I have come to lead as I have been charged. Is that sufficient for you, commander?"

Master Wendall turned hastily from the group and stamped off.

Sir Kenneth may have judged him too harshly. He was more frustrated with himself than the Crestfolk or Master Wendall. He had pushed his force hard, been set upon by the enemy, lost many folk, and been injured in the process. It was not the result he desired.

"Which villages are close to us?" he asked.

"The Trouthavens," Cal replied.

Kenneth knew of them. There were no castles, but they could find shelter from the night, fish the White, and shore up against the enemy if needed. Under the circumstances, it was the necessary choice.

"So be it. Make way to the villages. And sergeant," Sir Kenneth said, pointing a finger to gain Cal's attention.

The sergeant had led well and made the difficult choices. Yet, despite Wendall's shortcomings, the chain of command was clear.

"Master Wendall is to take charge if I grow unconscious and am unable to command. You will assist him in this. I will not have this vanguard fall into a rabble."

Chapter XIII
The Betrayal

The dawn rose over the hills and flooded the fields as Gregory emerged from the city walls ready to dispel the rumors. He was taken aback by the trampled earth and the dead strewn throughout the field. The enemy indeed possessed a formidable mounted force.

He brought his mount alongside one of their dead. To Gregory's surprise, the mounts were not horses at all. They were monstrous rams from the deep mountains, trained by the enemy for war.

Gregory dismounted his horse to inspect the dead man. The enemy had a ghastly look about them and it was no wonder they struck such terror among the Crestfolk. The dead man wore dark leather skins and furs with various animal bones woven throughout his clothes. Four large shoulder-blade bones were fitted to shield his back and several ribcage bones wrapped around his torso. They crafted gauntlets and greaves by stringing together several bones. The enemy's helm was a large animal skull hollowed out to fit his head. Atop the helm, two curled horns emerged, and Gregory understood why the two-headed demon rumors had taken root so well among the stories.

He knelt beside the dead body and rolled him over. The black soot and dirt obscured his face, but it was clear enough what he was. However unnatural their depiction and supernatural their presence, he was no dark spirit or vaettir. He wasn't any form of golem or goblinoid. He was a wildman from beyond the north mountains.

Finally, Gregory had one answer to the great mystery, but there was so much more to uncover. *Why did they attack their realm? And more importantly, what was their connection to the traitor within the Mid?*

After inspecting the dead, Gregory and the council turned their attention to mustering the army and following Sir Kenneth. The Mid awoke and prepared a mighty sendoff. The carts were loaded and the men assembled in an illustrious manner befitting a state on the verge of greatness. A sea of burgundy and auburn banners danced in the wind as the crowds of Midfolk gleamed with fervor and cheered their soldiers onward to the Crestwood. As the army departed, the drums faithfully carried them one step in front of the other. Gregory, stoked with ambition, had driven every monger at his disposal to this point; there was no going back.

Once the army departed, the city was a different animal. The remaining citizens consisted of the old, the young, the cowards, the crippled, and the criminals. This was the moment the thieves and common thuggery stepped unafraid onto the main thoroughfares. They were only interested in preying upon the helpless during such times. This was Lady Alma's chief concern, and Gregory knew mastering the remaining lawless would be key to order in the city.

This task was left to Master Hector and Master Gregory as it was decided Sir Pavel, the old warhorse, would ultimately depart with Lord Malcolm. The remaining Midguard were bolstered by several hundred volunteers, and they prepared to keep the peace. Gregory sought out the leaders among those volunteers and persuaded them to serve in this capacity.

After coins passed hands, they became the new volunteer Midguardmen. They patrolled the vacant streets, the run-down taverns, and the lowly whoremongers daily. And with their service secured, Gregory was privately notified of any misgivings and who the offenders were. He positioned himself well.

Within the hour of the departure of the army, the gates were barred, the city was firmly secured, and much of the criminality was under watch. There were still minor squabbles among the Midfolk and the Crestfolk, but the majority of Crestfolk headed south and fewer folk in the city meant fewer disruptions. The peace was relatively well kept.

With order in hand, Gregory turned his attention to the matter at the forefront of his mind: there were rumored traitors among the council who intended to undermine the Mid in its great venture. *Who would want the Mid to fail in the defense of the Crest?* The council members accused of this conspiracy were greedy men who wanted for nothing except more coin and more power. At least, Gregory considered himself that kind of man, and the other merchants on the council were not far from that description either. So, he altered the question entirely.

What person would gain position from such an undertaking as the fall of the Mid? That, Gregory noted, may be worth a traitorous act.

Gregory knew he would need more information to uncover this mystery, and he was prepared to hire the best-skilled men for the job, whatever the cost. Cleverly, he had just bribed the new volunteer Midguardmen to keep him well informed of the remaining shadowmen lurking in the back alleys of the Mid. After all, he needed disreputable folk for disreputable tasking.

He gathered all reports and reviewed the characteristics of dozens of lowly folk of questionable behavior. He was a merchant, after all; one must shop around for the best wares. After the first two days of reports, he gathered the information he needed, and he invited seven men to a private gathering at Elena's.

Gregory had considered another venue; however, the prying eyes of the city were under his control, and he opted for convenience. Besides the wealth of customers, even the inquisitive ones had all but left. Elena's was as quiet as anywhere. The unscrupulous folk Gregory invited were primarily knifemen, informants, and one man who was a sell-sword. They all possessed the necessary characteristics he sought. All these folk knew how to pursue a person unseen, make a thorough report, and keep Master Gregory's discretion for a price. Gregory was all but happy to enlist their aid.

One after another, they arrived as requested. Gregory knew how to prepare potential associates and he passionately believed pampering clients led to successful trade. They were warmly welcomed and gathered in a private room. They were plied with wine and food, beautiful companions who caressed their laps, and the bards plucked harmonious strings as the evening wore on.

Each one was briefly pulled from the festivities and seated before Gregory in a quiet booth out of sight. He poured them a fresh goblet of wine and inquired about them. This was merely small talk to keep them at ease. However, Gregory also wanted to verify his reports. Each story was similar in a way. They preyed upon a place for a time, for a house or a lord. Then, once that time had ended or the authorities were after them, they would move on.

Gregory took his time assessing each candidate. He noted what they would divulge, what they would not, or if they were clever enough to get directly to the business at hand; the latter candidates piqued his interest.

In particular, there was a thin and nimble woman with sallow eyes named Gretchen, who kept numerous short blades around her waist and a suspicious cloaked man named Duncan whose only visible feature was his bearded chin. Both kept their wits about them as the revelry took place and during each of their negotiations. These were the professionals he had sought.

Out of the seven, five were chosen to observe the remaining council members: Corbus, Wex, Tessia, Gretchen, and Duncan. The other two, Ferdinand and Simon, were tasked specifically to protect Gregory and watch his back; he also wanted to know if he was under observation. If that were the case, Ferdinand and Simon were to acquire and compel the spy to reveal his master before disposing of them. A few haggled over the price; however, all were satisfied at the end of their meeting.

Gregory's new conscripts separated and each progressed toward the homes of the remaining masters of the city. They were to shadow the councilmen continuously from their homes to their daily routines among the inns, taverns, and castle. And every day, they would report all manner of insights to Gregory. Even if there were guards and other obstacles, Gregory was assured by each informant that they would be able to gain or bypass any access; this was vital to Gregory. He needed the traitor to be quickly identified before their plans to undermine the Mid were irreversible.

Gregory began his assessment with Master Tammany. He was the eldest of the councilmen, the least threatening, and a senior curmudgeon of the first order. Councilmen were advanced or discharged as needed by the masters of the city. At times there were as many as thirteen on the council and as few as five. If a council member was no longer capable of standing as such, he would be removed. Reasons for discharge included old age or serious illness. Some councilmen were sabotaged or their reputations were ruined by their peers. Master Tammany was not above that and was considered a force to be reckoned with during his midlife.

However, Master Tammany was now an elderly man who only kept his position because he could be counted as a reliable vote. As long as he was supportive in the majority's endeavors, he was allowed to maintain his position.

Altogether, Tammany was least suspected. The senior councilman had long ago let power slip from his hands and was either unable or unmotivated to grab ahold of the reins again.

Gregory then considered Lady Alma. She was the Lady of the Mid and well respected throughout the city and the council. Not all ladies of the Mid took part in the policy of the Mid; however, Lady Alma was not among them. She was opinionated and involved in numerous facets of the city. She was a valued advisor to Lord Malcolm, and as they had yet to make heirs, next in line to inherit the responsibility of the Mid.

Gregory considered Lady Alma's motive to undermine the current Lord, but he found no plausible reason. It was his opinion that Lord Malcolm and Lady Alma appeared quite happy within their relationship, and he understood them as holding each other in mutual respect. Additionally, it was a rarity if they disagreed publicly upon the council. If Lady Alma wanted to change the status quo, there was more for Gregory to uncover.

The real suspects among the Councilmen were Master Hector, Master Rhoades, and Master Liam. They were Gregory's peers, first among the citizens, and ambitious men. Their families were well established and had passed their inheritance to the next generation, ensuring their prosperity and elevation.

Master Hector was the first among them. Every member dabbled in a variety of trade, but they all had their own primary revenue. Master Hector owned a vast portion of lands around the Mid. Far more than the other councilmen. His family harvested grain and provided the very supplement to feed the entire region. He also associated himself with the exotic Vymas Isles, where he facilitated the exchange of sugars for grains from the basket of the west.

His family was invited to the council long before the others, and that would likely continue. Some families fall out of favor, and some find their way onto the council like Gregory. However, Hector's family was as old as Lord Malcolm's and they could have just as easily been the Lords of the Mid. It was an old rivalry that perhaps Master Hector wished to enliven. This was Hector's most obvious motivation. Perhaps he orchestrated the attack and this was Hector's elaborate means for his rise to power. Gregory snorted. An attempt like that was a bold gamble... even admirable. He would seriously consider it.

Master Liam and Master Rhoades were next to consider and had equal position to gain in this complex equation. Every generation played the game in order to gain further position. If Master Liam or Master Rhoades chose now to ascend, Gregory did not understand how that would come to pass.

Master Rhoades was the second largest landowner among the council members, and his position was secured by his supply of cattle, sheep, and other livestock. He was also the largest fishmonger among all the others. He possessed the key to feed the many peoples among the region and directly shared that power with Hector. Despite their friction with one another, the Mid always prospered from their competition; to outshine the other councilman meant providing food for the people. If Rhoades were to supplant Hector, he would all but command the distribution of food across the region. That power may allow him to control the Mid outright. Gregory considered the possibility.

Master Liam, comparatively, had the most to gain of all the others. He traded in the finer wares, silks, clothes, spices, and jewels. His family had provided these for generations once the Mid was established as a center of trade. Once the wealth accumulated, the rich would want for the exotic things that only served to elevate their status. The brighter their colors and more vibrant their jewels meant they were prospering far more than their peers. When they could no longer outshine each other, they outmaneuvered each other in other ways. They became patrons of the arts and music all in the attempt to surpass each other on the rungs of power to the council.

Master Liam's family, for generations, had provided the tools for elevation and was compensated with a mountain of coins. He had every position to gain by overcoming anyone on the council.

Yet, the questions still rang in Gregory's mind. *How could undermining the whole enterprise here and now catapult them to rise among the others?*

No one could unless they were to survive the chaos and rise from the ashes. And they could only survive such an event if it were agreed upon by the enemy; one of these councilmen had to have made a pact with the enemy. Gregory knew of all manner of transactions, and every agreement came with parchment signed by both parties. He would have his new associates look for such evidence. Perhaps the conspirators were clever enough to rid themselves of such correspondence, but Gregory would have every parchment or scroll reviewed nonetheless.

The only other means he possibly had to catch these conspirators was to follow up on the meeting Master Wendall revealed.

After three days of constant surveillance, Gregory had learned much. His recruits had uncovered many habits and a few quirks, but truly little notorious behavior was found. And of the actions that were disreputable, Gregory found them to be more dishonest than traitorous. Each merchantman profiteered well from the war. However, this was hardly unexpected. It was an infamous arrangement and these were the kind that made empires.

So, the results of all the inquiries and reports were disappointing. The informants were more than equal to the job and Gregory spent all his available moments poring over every detail. He was giddy with anticipation in hopes of stumbling upon some piece of wicked information, but no reports offered any concrete evidence.

Gregory decided it was time to partake in the subterfuge. There was a meeting to uncover, he had access to the castle, and if he were to be discovered, the guardsman would consider his presence routine. And besides all of that, he could not resist the urge to uncover the clue left by Master Wendall.

The next Sunday morning, Gregory set off. He altered his usual routine and went to a warehouse he owned. If there were men following him, this change would be of note. However, Gregory planned for this. Where he entered one door as a wealthy merchantman, he exited the other door on the far side of the warehouse, robed in the people's usual colors and blended into the morning crowd. He disguised himself as a lowly trader, donned his hood, and wore a false beard. He walked casually among the mongers, perused their wares, and eased his way toward the castle in great anticipation. No one recognized him.

His plan was simple and achievable. Many common folk sought out the castle and the Lord of the Mid to arbitrate disputes between the folk; Master Hector performed these duties in his absence. Commoners gathered as usual before the castle gates and they were allowed entry as necessary by the gatekeepers. Gregory joined the common folk. He did this primarily to conceal his presence within the castle. There would be no announcement of his title and the conspirators would have no cause to cancel a meeting because of his unusual visit. Once he reached the gatekeepers, he fabricated a dispute between two neighboring businesses and was granted passage. He swelled with pride when the guards waved him through.

He arrived two hours early for the prescribed time and proceeded to the stable across the open court to begin reviewing the current occupants. There, his vantage was unobscured, and he blended among the stable boys. To Gregory's knowledge, no one occupied the tower. Maids passed through the tower and the guards routinely patrolled. So, he patiently waited for the scene to unfold as he brushed a majestic dark-haired thoroughbred from beyond the mountains.

Gregory almost lost himself in the care of the animal when Lady Alma arrived unattended just before the appointed hour. Gregory was both shocked and delighted at such an outcome. His gaze almost lingered in surprise as she made her way to the tower. She opted to utilize the shadow of the walkway where the second floor extended over the first level rather than in the openness of the courtyard. This detail all but led Gregory to believe he had found one conspirator in the plot. However, she arrived early. Her affiliates would not be far behind and would reveal themselves in time.

The midday hour came as the bells rang across the city. And when they did, a cloaked man approached. He walked under the shadow of the castle as well. Although the man raised his hood, he took little care in hiding himself. Master Hector wore the same embroidered cloak he had always worn in the colors of his house and practically strutted into the tower.

Gregory's chest seized. This pair was unexpected, but more had to be revealed. He now understood Master Wendall's concern. If he were to bring up accusations against Lord Malcolm's most trusted advisors, one of them being his Lady, he would need to be sure-footed and in possession of substantial evidence. Master Wendall would have been out of his depth in the matter.

He lingered in the stable for a time, risking losing some valuable information. The risk was worth a moment of patience if another collaborator happened in the vicinity of the tower, but minutes passed and no one came. He darted across the courtyard and ascended the staircase like a shadow, his footsteps silent as he entered the tower. Floor by floor, he found rooms empty until he came almost to the top of the tower. The moment he heard the two panting through the door into the dark staircase, he recognized the activity. Gregory hadn't even conceived that notion, but it was arguably one of the oldest betrayals known to men. However, this was traitorous to a husband, not so much to a city. A salacious scandal, to be sure, but far from disloyal to the state.

Gregory was saddened at the betrayal; Lord Malcolm and his wife were such a united couple in public. Yet, it reminded him that no one was truly known among the council members.

They engaged passionately for a moment's time and came to a crescendo. Gregory remained in the hope that other discussions would emerge post the coupling, but nothing of note was discussed. Lady Alma praised Hector for his performance and urged them to return to their duties.

Gregory moved away quickly when he heard them stirring behind the door. He made it to the second floor just as their door on the floor above him opened. His pulse raced as he dashed into the second floor room and hid behind a dresser. He lingered too long, but it was worth the risk to uncover the depths of their plans. Although they had not discussed anything of note, he had to assume they planned to displace the current Lord of the Mid. It was the most reasonable conclusion, but he would set his new informants to gather the details. Today's divulgence was enough to satisfy his need to know.

They left separately just as they came. She departed the staircase first, hurrying to her next commitment. Hector left a moment later, recovering his breath from the previous activity. Once he left the tower, Gregory moved to the window to ensure both parties were well out of sight. And with that, the meeting concluded.

It was a grand start toward deciphering Wendall's enigma. He assured himself that everything worth knowing and all the sensational details of Lady Alma's and Master Hector's pact would soon be discovered. He also considered their ambition. *Should they desire to rule the Mid, would that hinder his own ambitions? More importantly, would their plans keep the Mid from rising to its full potential?* He did not know, but he would consider every possible outcome. He eagerly descended out of the tower in haste to return to his home and reassign his informants to focus on these two.

He did not see the club as he stepped out of the tower until it was too late. He was struck in the cheek and brought down to the stone floor. Blood splattered from his mouth, and his fake beard flew off. The hot white pain throbbed like nothing he had felt before as he clutched at his face. He did not see the second strike as his assailant attacked his ribs, and he collapsed to his side, crying out.

"What have we here, Harold? A thief or pickpocket?"

"I don't think so, Cobb!" Harold replied grimly. His laughter turned immediately to silence and suspicion as he picked up the blood-covered faux hairpiece.

"You are mistaken! I'm Master Greg…"

"Shut your mouth!" Cobb threatened as he struck Gregory again across the head. This time, he was rendered unconscious. He had remained unrecognized, just as he intended. Unfortunately, he was also beaten and bloodied.

"Fuck, Cobb! Is he dead?" Harold asked.

"Nah, he'll live for the moment. What's that?"

"That's the thing, my stupid friend. Thieves is one thing, but Cobb, my boy, this man's another thing entirely." He held the bloodied beard up so Cobb could inspect it. "No man disguises himself and isn't a spy."

Chapter XIV
The Reinforcements

The vanguard finished tending the dead and left the bright pyres burning behind them. They collected every injured soldier and paired them with capable riders for the journey. It was an uncomfortable trip for most, but all were delivered to the villages without further injury.

The Trouthavens were just as Cal had described. The villages were abandoned all along the River White, and there was sufficient room to house all the cavalry. The chosen village rested deep in the forest along the river and had a modest river rock wall at its entrance. A single road to the village was narrow and wound through steep hills. This made the village very defensible; a hidden gem among the others.

Although his injuries still plagued him, Sir Kenneth made the journey under the watchful eye of the healers, Master Wendall, and Cal. He kept firmly attentive during the ride but collapsed at the end with many of the other injured folk.

With Sir Kenneth bedridden, the command fell to Master Wendall. However, all the vanguard sought out the party who saved them from defeat for leadership and direction. Upon arrival at the village, Wendall's commands fell on deaf ears. The situation did not bode well; Master Wendall remained sour from Sir Kenneth's accusations of his incompetence. Pressured by the remaining cavalrymen, Master Wendall begrudgingly allowed these new heroes to oversee the defenses under his authority. With that established, the remaining cavalrymen fell in line and followed orders.

There were several tasks to be accomplished before the evening came. The bulk of the work was divided between erecting a proper defense and the much-coveted task of fishing for a thousand mouths. Many claimed to be expert fishermen and volunteered, but the honor of the best fisherman came to a blonde man named Vander who won many thanks with a trusted net he stowed in his saddle.

After the fishermen were set to the task, Halden and Jacoby took it upon themselves to ensure a proper defense. Jacoby ingeniously utilized the surplus of spears from the previous battle and affixed them outward and around the gate of the village. When they had finished, the entrance resembled a stone porcupine and Jacoby swelled with pride.

Eris and a few other healers tended to all the injured after several wounds had reopened from the journey. Although the road strained many, not one was lost. This was far more a victory to Cal than any other achievement.

With the defense in hand, fresh fish cooking at the fires, and the injured tended, Cal, Yslanna, and Clydes turned to patrolling the roads outside the villages for the enemy. This was imperative to their survival. Too many mistakes had led to their pyrrhic victory; they needed to learn from them.

The sentries were posted outside the villages, hidden in small groups among the trees. All their hope hinged on masking their presence at the Trouthavens, but there was no guarantee. If the enemy appeared, the sentries would loosen arrows from one hidden post to the next until the message had arrived at the village. The plan was well received by all, and even Master Wendall thought the tactic was brilliant.

When the evening came, Yslanna took charge of a few new scouts and monitored the northern road while Cal and Clydes monitored the eastern. Despite the danger outside the village, Cal was the first to agree to the post. Many cavalry thought him brave and volunteered to join him, but he wasn't looking to be their leader. He offered to take the watch to keep his mind from drifting to Bill, but it was difficult. Bill was a welcomed friend who always offered folksy wisdom in Cal's time of need. Now, forever silenced.

He was grateful when Clydes joined him, and the silent giant made for a perfect companion. This was a task for stealth, and although Clydes was a massive hulk of a man, he masterfully concealed himself in the forest. He also proved to be a vigilant observer where the other men struggled to stay awake.

By dusk, all had settled in the village, and they were ready for the enemy. The rest of the dismounted cavalry positioned themselves behind the walls, readied their bows, and sealed the injured in the huts of the village. However, the enemy did not come.

It was a blessing to the remaining few. Most folk had slept poorly, if at all, in anticipation. When the morning came without incident, those who believed in the gods took it as a good sign.

With this success, Master Wendall pressed for the folk heroes to act. He urged Cal to seize any advantage and uncover their whereabouts, but Cal was not enthusiastic about the bold assignment. There was only one remaining scouting party, much of the cavalry was recovering, and Alec had yet to wake. Cal tried to argue to remain hidden, but Wendall would not be dissuaded. Their orders were to once again find the enemy.

The party prepared as best they could with the many lessons they had learned from their encounter. Cal first formed new scouting parties from volunteers within the cavalry. The new parties were few and always led by one of the famed party members. Over the next three days, they practiced caution and silence at every patrol and they hid among the dense foliage, but it was a futile effort. The enemy was elusive. After a thorough review of the roads, they found the trails led in every direction. It was also likely why the enemy had not found them.

What made them successful was Yslanna's ingenuity. On the second evening, she swiftly ascended the tallest tree on a hill in hopes of spotting the darkness form just as dusk fell upon the Crestwood. There, on the horizon, she found it, but the details were far more informative than Cal would have thought.

She had spotted separate smaller forms of the darkness moving over the treetops across the horizon. The smaller forms separately wandered around the landscape like predators in the forest. Several soldiers had wondered if the enemy had survived the battle at all, but when Yslanna reported what she saw, the naysayers were silenced. When she described their movements, Cal knew two things: the enemy was far from defeated and they patrolled as well. It was now a matter of time before they found one another. The only question was what to do next.

The cavalry remained hidden over the next three days and waited for an attack or for dawn to come. Every dusk, they would find the darkness, and every evening, they would lose the trail within the night. On the fourth day of the unusual balance, they found banners on the southern road heading north.

Lord Malcolm had arrived, leading a host of eight thousand men marching in unison. It was an invigorating sight of steady marching with shield and spear. The scouts intercepted the new infantry and led them to the Whiteroad, concealed in the forest. When they arrived, the remaining villages suddenly became cramped and lively. The reunion was met with awe, shock, and cheer. The fresh infantrymen found grimy and weathered kin who had already tasted battle. They were intimidated and impressed by the cavalry. Conversely, the vanguard was grateful and relieved to see their reinforcements; a soldierly embrace could not be helped among all.

The camps became abuzz with stories as the fresh troops settled into their new surroundings. They were captivated as the reports shifted into unbelievable fables told over the campfires. Everyone enjoyed the mythical ending where a band of heroes had turned the night into day, blinded the enemy, and saved the cavalry. Their legends grew out of hand.

Upon Lord Malcolm's arrival, the pressures of leadership lifted from Cal's shoulders as the injured captains awakened and reassumed their positions. The folk among the cavalry still regarded him with gratitude and awe, but it was overwhelming at times. Now, the new troops passed him by as if he were just another soldier among the many, and those who began hearing the rumors could only speculate who the scouting party members were. That suited Cal better.

The infantry had settled and prepared a vast defense among the remaining villages. The new men welcomed the fight to come while the veterans prepared for an evening strike among the darkness due to the infantry's arrival. When the night came, even the most rambunctious infantrymen settled, and tension formed around the camps.

Lord Malcolm gathered his war council at the cusp of the evening. Sir Kenneth, who had regained much of his strength over the last few days, answered the Lord's call and left under his own power with Master Wendall in tow.

Cal and his party fell into their evening routine with supper and sharpening of their blades for the anticipated fight to come. However, Yslanna came from her perch atop the trees and revealed the enemy hadn't altered their movements. The darkness was scattered in the distance, and they continued to search aimlessly. It was another stroke of luck.

Just as her news came, another soldier arrived at the party's fire, but he was no cavalryman. The fresh infantryman's armor was in pristine condition and his tunic still shone vibrant colors under the firelight. He called for the famed scouts to report to the Lord of the Mid, and the discussions around the fire halted.

Cal, Halden, Jacoby, and Yslanna had begun to place their suppers aside and make themselves presentable while Clydes led the watch outside the encampment and Eris continued to tend to a still unconscious Alec. Under Cal's direction, the famed scouting party watched the enemy under the moonlight and protected the man who could turn the tide of battle.

They mounted up after Halden and Jacoby tidied themselves into more presentable soldiers and left. The road skirted the shoreline of the river to the village that housed the Lord's command post, where he resided in the largest hut available. The colors of the Mid draped the outside of the hut with flags and banners, and the entrance was extended with a long tent. Guards surrounded the command center and remained vigilant as patrols of soldiers marched in succession back and forth across the village lanes. The roads trafficked with men and supply wagons from all over the encampment as the village had transformed into an energetic epicenter of the army.

Cal entered the transformed hut with the remaining party members. The spacious size led Cal to believe it had once been the chieftain's home or at least a place where the elders gathered. It was lit with hundreds of candles in addition to the stone fireplace at its center. They had laid out a feast for the officers along the table where plates were emptied moments before.

Lord Malcolm and Sir Pavel sat at one side of the fireplace while Sir Kenneth and Master Wendall sat opposite of them as they discussed the events of the previous days.

"The scouts, my lord," the guard interrupted as Cal entered with his friends.

Lord Malcolm immediately shifted his attention to him while Master Wendall continued elaborating his story. The Lord of the Mid was a lean man of dark features whose trim black beard came to a point. The emblem of the Mid was stitched over his heart on his maroon tunic. His armor was hung on a model on a far table where it was ready to be donned at any moment. Lord Malcolm's piercing yellow eyes assessed the company who had entered his encampment.

"As I was saying, my lord…" Master Wendall continued. "… the wildmen were thwarted, and we could have continued the rout, I estimate."

Cal ignored Master Wendall's comments. It was better to let the nobles argue over what could have been while he was confident in his and his fellow party members' actions over the last few days. They had convinced Sir Kenneth to regroup and recoup. The remainder of the cavalry had survived because of that decision, and Cal could live with that. Now, with the arrival of the army, he knew they had greater opportunities to fight on their terms. It was the best outcome in Cal's estimation.

The party stood beside each other as the debate continued between the leaders Cal knew and the men he did not. The unknown men were fresh and clean, unlike the cavalryman in the hut. The only part of Lord Malcolm's attire not clean was his boots and they were still far more polished than Cal had ever seen on any man.

The new headmen hadn't really fought this enemy yet. They hadn't been set upon in the wood against ferocious wildmen or crossed swords with them man to man. If they had, they might not have questioned every decision point.

Lord Malcolm listened intently to the debate, but his eyes remained fixed on the party. As he listened to his councilors one after the other, he carefully weighed out each man's account. Of what he heard, he had not appeared intimidated by the retelling. The older knight was far more critical as he questioned the choices of the commander and Master Wendall while the pair of them defended each inquiry.

Sir Kenneth and Master Wendall were openly cross with one another as Master Wendall continued to make snide remarks and disagree with most of Sir Kenneth's reasons.

If Cal had not known Master Wendall, he would have easily guessed him a politician of some form.

"Thank you, gentlemen," Lord Malcolm interrupted, and the debate fell silent. "I wish to hear the retelling from another perspective unhindered by pride."

"My lord, the rumors surrounding these scouts have been embellished," Sir Kenneth protested.

"You can only speculate because you were made unconscious, Sir Kenneth. I, however, can validate their comments," Master Wendall jeered.

Sir Kenneth had no rebuttal, but he clearly stiffened in anger.

"I have heard enough from either of you. These young folk will be able to clear up the elaborations we've been hearing about," Lord Malcolm interjected. He removed his gaze from the party only for a moment to make his point to Sir Kenneth and Master Wendall.

They both chose not to argue any further, and Cal smirked at Sir Kenneth's recoil.

"Sergeant Cal? Is that short for Caleb?"

"Callum, son of Paulis," Cal corrected.

Lord Malcolm grinned at the response. "Callum is a strong name. Tell me your story, Sergeant Cal. How have you arrived here? I wish to know how you came under my service, how you met the infamous and cantankerous Alec, and I especially want to understand how you managed to turn the tide of the battle. I have heard the rumors, but as Sir Kenneth has said, they are quite illustrious, and they have become affixed into the hearts of many of the folk."

It was a long retelling and not unlike any other story told by a displaced son or daughter of the Crest. However, that was only the beginning of his story. He spoke of meeting a man who could conjure magic, of a pact with one between them, joining the cavalry, forming an unusual scouting party made up of folk from across the continent, and how they had beaten the enemy. Other stories didn't sound like that.

Their story ended in a hard-won triumph over a foe they hadn't fully understood, and their deeds thus far had captivated many folk in the encampment. It wasn't an overwhelming victory, but no one else had earned any measurement of a claim. Cal's only omission was Bill's death. His chest tightened as he left out Bill's death, but Cal still grieved deeply for his friend and clung onto the anger that now filled his heart.

"Well fought!" Sir Pavel approved at the end of the retelling. He was a beast of a man with a long-curled mane of salt and pepper hair that matched his full beard. His face bore the resemblance of a great cat more than that of a man.

"Indeed, you are due many praises from Crestfolk and Midfolk alike," Lord Malcolm agreed. "How is Alec now?"

"He hasn't woken since the night of the battle. Eris, our other companion, stays at his side day and night in case he wakes, my lord," Halden interjected.

"There are many who can tend over Alec. It seems to me, and many of the common folk, that your party would be underutilized if they are not leading in the front as my eyes and ears in this endeavor," Lord Malcolm responded.

Sir Kenneth's face scowled at the statement but said nothing.

Cal, on the other hand, appreciated the small recognition. Lord Malcolm was vastly different in his approach than Sir Kenneth or Master Wendall. It was no wonder why folk spoke of him with such reverence.

"Alec is not well received among many, my lord. He deserves a friend near when he wakes. He's also our best man to fight the darkness. I do not know how or why, but he has abilities other men do not possess. That is worth having one of our own look after him and ensuring our counter to the darkness," Cal responded.

The headmen weren't convinced as they grimaced uneasily in their chairs.

Lord Malcolm was the only one who did not wince or waver, but the concern was apparent as he furrowed his brow. "Perhaps. However, I do not fully understand how he has done such a thing. Nor am I sure I trust him to be able to do such a thing again," Lord Malcolm replied. "If he is unable to wake, we are left to carry on this fight, and we will do that."

Cal did not like the notion, but the Lord may have been right. They would have to somehow navigate a way if Alec could not wake. Cal hadn't considered that. "Alec can summon a force of light, I promise you. We can count on him despite the past character of the man," Cal pleaded.

Lord Malcolm raised his hand, and Cal held his tongue.

"I am not discounting Alec. I hope he regains his strength, and I welcome his support. I welcome all in this fight, but we cannot rely on the skill of one man alone. As of this moment, we are without him, and it is up to the good folk here to throw off evil."

"My lord, I'm not sure how we can succeed without him. They are out there as we speak, hunting for us. We are tracking the darkness through the sky as best we can see it, but there are nights where the skylight is hidden, and we see nothing at all. These are the nights that I fear the most."

Lord Malcolm gazed at Cal with interest. "How can you know they hunt for us?" he asked.

"At every dusk for three days, we've seen the enemy form the darkness, my lord. They scour the Crestwood from one end of the horizon to the other," Yslanna answered.

"They dart about the wood in much smaller forms. They're like separate fog banks who ignore the wind and only travel on the roads, my lord," Jacoby added. "Compared to the darkness we've encountered before, we gathered they must be patrolling."

"And they haven't altered their search since your arrival. We have managed to conceal ourselves and the army," Cal concluded.

"This is good news indeed. These reports may very well alter the scales in our favor. It is important we do not heedlessly move forward," Lord Malcolm stressed.

The scowl on Sir Kenneth's face transformed into a red grimace. "My lord, I did as commanded and took the fight to the enemy! No one could have foreseen their numbers or endurance," Sir Kenneth insisted.

"And without the aid of these scouts, I would be searching for survivors, if any. Worse still, the infantry would have likely fallen into the same ambush. We are fortunate the cavalry survived, Sir Kenneth," Lord Malcolm countered.

The knight grumbled at Lord Malcolm's words. The notion gnawed at him as he shook his head and shifted in his seat. "I took a risk, yes. However, it was not without consideration. I rode hard, pushed the enemy, and wagered on the discipline of the trained Midguardmen. That should have carried the day against any raiders."

"Enough," Lord Malcolm commanded.

Although Sir Kenneth suppressed his rebuttal, the disagreement festered inside him. He was like a tea kettle without a spout, boiling on the inside and blackening on the outside.

"I have heard enough of these arguments. What deeds have been done are now over, and we must learn from them. All of us. Yes, we do not know what we could have anticipated from the enemy, and the failure is as much mine as it is yours. Yet, if we do not set aside our pride and learn from these lessons, then we may repeat the same results. That is what I demand of us all," he continued.

"You are right, of course, my lord," Master Wendall agreed. "We cannot let carelessness of the past foul up our next course of action."

Sir Kenneth erupted from his seat with a dagger drawn from his belt, ready to strike a startled and cowering Master Wendall.

Sir Pavel, the guards within the tent, and the scouts instinctively countered with spears and swords drawn at the ready when Lord Malcolm rose to keep things from escalating further.

"Stay your hand!" Lord Malcolm shouted as he rose from his seat.

The knife shook with rage in Sir Kenneth's hand as he paused, still ready to strike.

"Remove yourself, Sir! If you refuse me this command, you will force me to make another," Lord Malcolm threatened as he pointed toward the exit.

Sir Kenneth took his attention away from Master Wendall for a moment to meet Malcolm's eyes. The Lord of the Mid stood firm.

Sir Kenneth lowered his dagger, sheathed it, and stormed from the hut while brushing through Cal and Halden. Everyone eased and sheathed their own weapons.

Lord Malcolm stopped the guards from following. "Leave him," Lord Malcolm commanded. "Let him cool on the bank of the White, and we will finish our plans without him. And I think you should choose your words more carefully and remain clear of him for a few days, Master Wendall."

Master Wendall grasped at his chest and exhaled deeply after the knight departed. "Forgive me, my lord. I meant only to acknowledge our past errors," he commented.

Cal didn't believe it. After receiving his own small berating three days past, Wendall meant to discredit Sir Kenneth in front of their lord. However, he was unprepared for the consequences. Sir Kenneth was a hard man whose honor meant a great deal to him, and Wendall was fortunate he was under Lord Malcolm's protection. If they had still been on the road, he may have been killed.

"I believe I will keep my distance," Master Wendall murmured, voice trembling.

"How shall we continue?" Sir Pavel asked, resuming the discussion.

Lord Malcolm sat back in his chair and refilled his goblet. "They have yet to attack this evening, and that concurs with the reports," Lord Malcolm emphasized. "The darkness is prowling the Crestwood, and yet they are separated. This makes them vulnerable and susceptible to our own counterattack."

"Very good, my lord. Are we to proceed with a full march in force?" Master Wendall inquired, regaining his composure.

"No," Lord Malcolm dismissed. "At least not yet. We have an opportunity to strike a blow against their reconnaissance. If we strike wisely, we may be able to rid ourselves of their current patrols and hopefully gain some insight to their power."

"How do you mean, my lord?" Sir Pavel inquired.

"The reports," Lord Malcolm recalled.

Sir Pavel mulled over the scout's reports, but the bemusement on his face was still present.

"If what these scouts have told me is accurate, and I believe that it is, the enemy is able to produce the darkness in a variety of sizes, and their size may very well be dependent on how many men they need to conceal. How can they do such a thing? We still know very little of their power, and if they are isolated in small patrols..."

"...we could catch them unawares and maybe even learn how they're able to wield such a power!" Cal blurted.

"You are clever, Sergeant Cal!" Lord Malcolm remarked.

"Why does it matter how these raiders can conjure the dark magic?" Master Wendall countered. "My lord, if we set the whole army to the task, we could take to these lesser forms like a hammer to the nail, and each will be crushed. Is that not the right action? These scouts report they are divided. Let us not be heedless, but we should be accurate. Let us strike boldly once again, and we will seize a victory that will ripple across the realms."

"What of their remaining force?" Lord Malcolm asked.

This time, Master Wendall was without an answer. "There is no such report, my lord. There are only these small groups of darkness," Wendall answered.

"They boldly prowl the countryside without any hesitation. They are a force who fears nothing. I'd wager because there are more of them to be found over that horizon, which bolsters their courage," Lord Malcolm concluded. And with that, Master Wendall was without rebuttal, and Sir Pavel nodded in agreement.

"It would be a dangerous strike," Sir Pavel commented.

"It would," Lord Malcolm replied. "However, the risk may well be worth the reward. Tell me, Sergeant Cal, how would you conduct such a maneuver?"

Cal was taken aback, but he took a moment to consider. "If possible, I would set up our own trap," Cal began. "We've hidden ourselves well in the Crestwood, but if we were to lure them in with a few good men and a campfire…"

"…We'd get no more than one of those patrols, and the surprise would be ours!" Halden completed.

"Very manageable indeed," Yslanna nodded in agreement while Jacoby chuckled to himself.

Lord Malcolm grinned at their confidence. "It's a bold plan. Can you see it through? Can you find out how they conjure this darkness?"

"The scouts are ready, my lord," Cal replied.

"Are we ready to risk our concealment for one patrol? Forgive me, my lord, but the reward is wanting compared to the risk," Master Wendall protested.

Cal almost couldn't believe Wendall. He pestered him daily to search farther into the Crestwood only to hesitate now.

Lord Malcolm stroked his beard in contemplation. "You are correct, Master Wendall. We should capitalize on our advantage. How many forms of darkness have you counted at dusk?" Lord Malcolm asked Yslanna.

"Five."

"Very good. Five traps for five patrols."

Chapter XV
The Chief

Su'ca rose with the sun, eager to continue their war. The campfire embers cooled as the crisp wind blew across the great grass-sea, and most of the horde continued their slumber after celebrating their victory well into the night. Yet, this was an auspicious day.

Tradition dictated a new Partho'sha must be chosen to lead the horde. They needed a head chief whose word was final and whose vision saw the path clearly. Without a Partho'sha, division among the clans was inevitable.

Su'ca's clan, the mighty Par'a'tu, also needed to choose a leader among them: their Chief Crato'sha. She was all but expected to be chosen. She had the experience, skill, and wisdom to lead them. She was the primary ambassador on behalf of her father, she led warriors into battle on countless occasions, and her father had groomed her to one day take his place. The clan had seen her path.

If she were selected, she would take her position. However, if she were challenged, she would send her brother or sister to the eternal plains without remorse.

The clan gathered around the smoldering fires. They shared the first meal of the day made of dried meats, nuts, and berries. Often, they would share words over their meal, but this morning, all were silent; only the wind spoke as it blew across the bloodied plain.

They knew what decision must be made, and the silence indicated her people had nothing left to discuss. They had already chosen the new chief among the warriors, and all that was left was to cast their vote. The meal concluded, and Tahop'ka broke the silence when he rose.

"We must have a new chief. One who will lead us wisely, who will speak on behalf of our people, and who the other clans will respect or fear. There are many who could lead us, but there are few who truly place the clan before themselves. I speak of Su'ca. She is her father's daughter. She would see the Par'a'tu flourish for a thousand generations or until the last days of the sun. Her spear drinks deeply upon the westmen and no warrior here is her equal. She is the only choice," Tahop'ka exclaimed.

Nothing was said in opposition. The clan heard Tahop'ka and clanged spears against their shields when he finished. They overwhelmingly approved of her nomination, and all celebrated their new chief when D'pa, an elder Crato'sha, came forward and raised his hands to be heard. He had neared his fortieth summer and was well respected among the clan.

"The young warriors have never elected a new chief, and because of this, they do not know the etiquette. I was a boy when Craa'su was nominated and another warrior came forward to submit his name. The clans chose Craa'su between them. When Bar'ra disagreed, he challenged as was his right. Bar'ra fought, and Bar'ra died, but we had a proven Chief. Are there no other nominations to be heard?" D'pa called. The clan respected what D'pa had said, and a moment was granted on behalf of his request, but no warrior stepped forward to nominate a clansman or themselves.

"So be it then," D'pa agreed. "Those who select Su'ca as the first among the Crato'sha and chief of the Par'a'tu, raise your fist with me." He bent his arm and raised it above his head with his fist clenched in strength. The clan followed as instructed. Once D'pa saw the clan vote, he cried out the warrior cry, and so did the rest.

She was elected unanimously.

She rose only after she was nominated chief. When the clan had concluded the vote, she rose, and Tahop'ka greeted her with a familiar pelt. He carried in his arms the fur of a white, long-toothed cat, which belonged to her father. Tahop'ka beamed with pride to present it to her.

The scent of her father still clung to the fur as if he were here beside her, and she battled to hold back her tears.

"This belongs to you. It is your right to wear it," Tahop'ka emphasized.

A single tear escaped her as the clan howled before the morning. She removed the black pelt her father had bestowed on her when she became a Crato'sha, handed it to D'pa, and turned around.

Tahop'ka placed the larger pelt on her shoulders and began readjusting the straps for his new chief. It was heavier than her previous pelt. The small plated armor woven underneath was flexible and would soon form to her.

With the straps tightened, the coronation was done. The Par'a'tu once again had its Chief of the Clan. They would not be lost among the grass-sea, but have a direction on the path of fate.

The clan shouted and sang in celebration, "Par'a'tu hmm, Par'a'tu hmm, Par'a'tu hmm!" They shook the ground as they stomped and clapped to the rhythm. Su'ca began her chiefdom by greeting every warrior one after the other and pressing her forehead to theirs in an embrace until all had a moment with the chief. The hundreds of warriors who had come from her clan surrounded her and rejoiced.

The news spread throughout the horde as other Par'sha clans were preparing for the even more important selection: a new Partho'sha would be chosen. Many chiefs would put themselves forward for the position, and some would be nominated. The honor would bring many tributes from all the clans. The clan of the chief selected would also rise in stature, and the order of the horde would shift, sometimes very dramatically. It was an important moment.

A correct selection of the Partho'sha would stabilize the horde; an incorrect selection would see more bloodshed across the plains. And much the same as selecting a chief, a challenge could be issued for position and then bloodshed was guaranteed.

Two chiefs came before the Par'a'tu once Su'ca was elected. Su'ca was still greeting her clan when Tahop'ka retrieved her. She hoped to conclude the greeting, but the horde waits for no one.

We'qeda and U'sabe's clans had long since been close allies to the Par'a'tu. They had come to gather Su'ca for the selection of the Partho'sha. They also might have considered Su'ca for the selection now that she was elevated, but she did not know. She was prepared to take her father's place as the chief but was indifferent to stepping into the role as the Partho'sha. Her concern was vengeance on behalf of her people; their honor demanded such a path. However, now that she had assumed the role of chief, there were many considerations she would need to reflect upon.

Su'ca would now need to consider what her clan and what her allies needed; it was almost certain why We'qeda and U'sabe had come to speak with her. If they continued to honor their bond, their combined influence and vote could certainly shift the selection of the

Partho'sha in their favor. The strong bond between their clans would see her people prosper among the Par'sha.

We'qeda and U'sabe greeted her as equals, touching foreheads together in respect and embrace.

"Su'ca, daughter of Craa'su, leader of the Par'a'tu people, we greet you in friendship. May our peoples continue to walk together in peace and in war," We'qeda declared as he embraced her.

"We'qeda, it would be an honor to my people to share the journey with your clan. And U'sabe, I wish for you to join us on our journey over the great grass-sea. Let our clans be united in friendship, and our enemies fear our strength," Su'ca replied, touching foreheads to one followed by the other.

"The Muun'kii embrace your friendship and are glad to be received by the daughter of Craa'su. It warms my heart to see you so honored, Su'ca. However, we wish to discuss the decision before us. Would you walk with us to the great meeting? There is little time," U'sabe requested as he motioned to the assembly.

She bowed her head in respect, and they began a slow stride toward the center of the Par'sha camp. There, at the base of several hills, the clans formed row upon row around a great circle, and at its center, the other chiefs began to take their seats in the clearing. As Su'ca and her allies approached, their clansmen filled in the path behind them and sat down.

"You will do well as the chief of the Par'a'tu, but now the clans gather to select the Partho'sha. There will be several nominated to serve, and some will nominate themselves. There are those who may certainly nominate you," We'qeda revealed. "You are a great warrior. Last night, you fought with the strength of the bear, the speed of the antelope, and the cunning of the desert cats. The horde was in disarray, and you led us to a great victory. Many chiefs will remember this."

"We wish to know if you would receive such an honor?" U'sabe continued.

The proposal surprised Su'ca, but she was prepared for their directness.

"I knew one day my clan would call on me to lead them, and I would not hesitate; I consider it a great honor. However, I do not know if my fate is to lead the Par'sha as my father did. That honor should go to a wise chief like you, U'sabe. You see the war path in your mind's eye and are well respected among the clans," Su'ca replied.

"You honor me, young chief. However, there are other young chiefs who seek nothing but power, and the power of the Partho'sha is within their grasp," U'sabe responded.

"They always lead with their spears, and that is good when you are a warrior. However, a good chief knows when to temper a warrior's passion," We'qeda added.

Su'ca took these words to heart. She had always been the first to lead to battle, and she often led without fear straight into the fight because that was expected of her as a Crato'sha. However, she was expected to lead in other ways now and prioritize the needs of the clan.

"With the horde crying for blood of the westmen, some chiefs will nominate themselves or another under the pretext of strength. And they will prove their strength by challenging any contender; blood will be shed. I do not know if I can defeat these challengers, and I do not know what would come of our clans if I were to fail," U'sabe appealed. "I wish you to consider accepting the nomination."

"You are modest, U'sabe. I have seen your skill upon the plains, and you have slain many enemies. Any Par'sha would think twice before challenging you."

"Ah, but you have also seen Fa'ru and Koa'bo. They are great warriors, but they are not wise like U'sabe. They do not think ahead, they are driven by anger and pride. This will not do as the Partho'sha. This will not do well for the horde," We'qeda interjected.

"I can also be driven by anger. Perhaps I am not the best choice," Su'ca cautioned.

We'qeda laughed at this. "We were all impatient warriors, young chief, but you blossom in the heart of battle. You know when to unleash your anger, and I know your heart beats to the rhythm of the horde. You will see vengeance taken upon the demon-westmen, but you also know to wisely choose our ground for battle. A great warrior and chief does these things. These other young chiefs do not consider before they launch their darts. They will attack boldly, and many Par'sha will die. If you worry about your impatience, then employ your friends and allies. I know U'sabe will make a fine councilor if you should wish it," We'qeda reassured.

This complicated her alliance, and she could not see the outcome of it. If she did not accept the nomination, an inferior Partho'sha could be selected. If she opposed the new Partho'sha, their clans would likely suffer under the new chief of chiefs.

"You are right about Fa'ru and Koa'bo. They should not be the Partho'sha. If they come forward and there is no other strong and wise chief nominated, then I will accept the nomination. If they choose to challenge me, I will accept that as well. But know that I wish for you, U'sabe, to be our Partho'sha," Su'ca replied.

U'sabe and We'qeda sighed but accepted her answer.

Su'ca was even relieved her allies had not been shunned from her stipulation, but now the great meeting was before them, and fate would decide again what role she would play.

The remaining chiefs moved to the great empty circle and the center of the assembly. As they approached the clearing, the path would fill in behind them with the many Par'sha people taking seats upon the burned and bloodied plain.

The chiefs sat at the edges of the great circle. They spaced themselves apart from one another so they might best be seen by their clans.

Su'ca knelt along the rim as well with twenty-two other chiefs. There were old chiefs and young chiefs. All had proven themselves in battle and had led their peoples, but only one would be the Partho'sha.

Ja'bu, one of the eldest chiefs, stood and raised his hand for the clan's attention. He looked as weathered as the leather that covered him, and the lines of his face were now permanent. He wore numerous tokens from many years of war that decorated his shoulder pelt, including braids, feathers, and teeth that caught in the wind with his long silver hair. Once the people were called to attention by him, they quieted.

"We gather here to elect a Partho'sha. Without the Chief of Chiefs, we are left headless; we cannot see, hear, or speak as one horde. The Partho'sha gives the horde direction and whose word is final. It is tradition that one of the chiefs of the many clans leads the horde. So, the chiefs have all gathered under the blue sky and great plain to elect one who is worthy of such an honor among them. Let us begin," Ja'bu declared.

A long moment passed before anyone came forward. The silence was broken by a respected chief named Im'tu.

"Warriors, you know me. I will speak quickly. There is one chief among us who understands the responsibility of the Partho'sha because he has seen many wars. Ja'bu is the eldest and wisest among us. He would lead the horde well and should be considered for the honored position."

Most of the chiefs nodded in approval, as did the Par'sha peoples as the crowd murmured. We'qeda raised his hand for silence, and he was granted it.

"Does Ja'bu accept such an honor?" We'qeda asked. Ja'bu stood from his seated position.

"I accept this nomination," Ja'bu declared. The clans favored him again in agreement as they clapped their hands upon their chests.

"Good. Ja'bu would make for an excellent Partho'sha. However, there is another who is worthy of the position," We'qeda began as he shifted his eyes to Su'ca, but instead, he hesitated for a moment. "U'sabe is a strong and worthy chief. He has led his clan through countless wars, and he has negotiated with the westmen. His wisdom and strength as a warrior will be an asset in the war. We can ask for no better Partho'sha."

Most of the clans praised U'sabe's nomination, and their excitement was exceptionally louder. U'sabe stood from his seat to accept the nomination when another intruded on his acceptance.

"Bah!" Fa'ru interrupted loudly, and his clan began hooting openly at U'sabe. All the clans were sent into a frenzy when Fa'ru spoke out against the older chief. Most of the other chiefs fervently called for Fa'ru's impudence to cease, but he did not care. He smirked at every chief, letting his clan's shouts stir the horde.

As was unique to his tribe, he shaved both sides of his head. Unlike many Par'sha, he stood taller and broader than most. His war-club dangled from his hip, and it bore many notches from the hundreds of foes he had slain. He was a dangerous warrior; even his own clansmen avoided their eyes.

"You know better than to disrespect the tradition, Fa'ru!" U'sabe warned, and all fell silent. "Are you so impatient, you do not understand the ways of the Par'sha?"

The young chief rolled his eyes at his elder but U'sabe did not cower. "Go then U'sabe! Say what you stood to say!" Fa'ru commanded.

The two glowered at one another, while Fa'ru goaded the elder chief before the clans and the gods.

"I, U'sabe, accept the nomination!" he shouted as he stared back at Fa'ru. The old chief showed he would not be intimidated, and the clans erupted in approval.

Fa'ru smirked at his rival. Multiple chiefs raised their hands for silence, but the crowd did not relent until U'sabe returned to his seat after remaining for a time. Su'ca knew he was the choice among the chiefs, and she showed favoritism as well. If the Par'sha approved of him with such ferocity, then fate was meant to have him as the Partho'sha. The clans quieted when U'sabe sat, and many turned to Fa'ru to see his reply.

"Is this the best of us?" Fa'ru spat. "These old men?" The crowds murmured once again, the point struck many of them. The Par'sha respected strength and courage and the old could be discounted for becoming weak and hesitant.

"Do you have another nomination?" Koa'bo demanded. Su'ca knew that he, too, may desire to be the Par'sha. He was a bulbous warrior compared to Fa'ru, but he was still powerful.

"Not you!" Fa'ru quipped, and the clans broke out in laughter.

Koa'bo dismissed the comment, but his name was tarnished, and he would not rebound from it, Su'ca thought.

"We need a Partho'sha who strikes fear into the westmen! These chiefs who have been named will not do this. Will they fear Ja'bu? Has U'sabe come to negotiate with them? Does the horde negotiate?" Fa'ru questioned, pointing to the crowd of warriors. The many clans rallied behind him.

"The horde has been called, and they seek the blood of the westmen! We demand a worthy Partho'sha!" Fa'ru continued as the clans clapped and rose on his behalf.

As Su'ca's allies forewarned, Fa'ru spurned the Par'sha into anger, and they responded in favor, but he did not inspire them. That was the difference between U'sabe and Fa'ru. The chiefs again called for silence among their peoples.

"Do you have a nomination, young chief?" Ja'bu questioned. Fa'ru stood to reply and stared squarely at U'sabe.

"Fa'ru nominates Fa'ru!" he shouted, and his clan hooted behind him in support. He received a large reception from several clans, but it was not the majority. He took a moment to soak in his admiration before sitting back down, but Su'ca, among many, was unimpressed.

"Is there another nomination?" Ja'bu called. The remaining chiefs said nothing else. It was a relief to Su'ca that she had not been nominated, but she understood the risk U'sabe now placed on himself.

"Good. Then, before we vote, I wish to withdraw my name for Partho'sha," Ja'bu insisted, bowing before all the Par'sha. "It is clear to me that these two are favored more than I. So, it is fitting for me to withdraw myself from this contest. However, these two have made fine arguments. It is important for our new Partho'sha to be wise, and U'sabe is far more experienced than Fa'ru. It is also important that the Partho'sha command fear from the westmen and Fa'ru is feared by many. However, I know of another chief. One who is strong and the westmen fear. I know this because I have seen this. She is courageous, focused, and battle tested. She personally commanded the horde into a victory, fended off our attackers, and drove them back across the mountains. There are no chiefs who can make that claim. I nominate Su'ca as the Partho'sha."

The clans erupted into a fervor. They beat their chests and shouted warrior cries. They would not be silenced again: "Su'ca! Su'ca! Su'ca!"

Su'ca looked at We'qeda and U'sabe. Each nodded and clapped as well with a smile. She could be the Partho'sha if she would only accept. Yet, she hesitated.

That path was muddled. In her mind's eye, she still saw herself as a warrior among her clan, just now elected to lead it. As for the Partho'sha, no chief so young had ever risen to the station, not in any of the songs, no matter how skilled a warrior. A doubt lingered in her mind, and from it, the answer became clear. Su'ca rose from her seat and the Par'sha quieted to a whisper.

"Thank you, Ja'bu, for your nomination. We have said many words about what a Partho'sha should be. It is clear to me a chief does embody these qualities, and it is not Fa'ru," Su'ca emphasized. Fa'ru's eyes nearly bulged out of his head as the Par'sha bellowed. Su'ca raised her hand again and all fell silent.

"There is one who is worthy of the title Partho'sha, and the clans know this as well. He is more than strong, feared, or wise. He is respected. I respect U'sabe, the clans respect him, and the westmen respect him. This has always been what makes a great Partho'sha. I respect your nomination, but I decline it. If you should favor me, then you should favor U'sabe as I do," she remarked.

The clans received her well and shouted for U'sabe. She turned to him and bowed her head; he returned the gesture. The clans clapped and sang his name and they called for him to assume the honor by an overwhelming majority. The chiefs called for silence, and after a time the horde finally consented. Ja'bu stood once again to address the horde.

"If there are no more nominations to be heard, then a vote must be had. Let those chiefs who select Fa'ru as the Partho'sha, raise their fists," Ja'bu declared. Two chiefs raised their fists above their heads, and little cheer was had.

"Very well. Those chiefs who select U'sabe as the Partho'sha. Raise your fists."

Twenty-one fists were thrust into the air. The clan once again erupted in favor, and Fa'ru had lost the vote. The horde had a Partho'sha again.

Fa'ru was furious. Not only had he been soundly defeated, but he had also lost the support of two chiefs. They had abandoned him and secured favor among the new Partho'sha. It was a reasonable course of action, but Fa'ru would not forgive or accept. He shouted beneath the deafening roar for an audience, but no words could be heard from him.

It would take time until order could be restored, but Su'ca saw through Fa'ru. He would not have the new Partho'sha; if he did not submit, then he would challenge U'sabe.

Su'ca feared what would become of the horde if Fa'ru won the challenge. U'sabe was a fine warrior and had defeated many enemies, but most warriors would pale in comparison to a savage fighter like Fa'ru. He was a bear of a man who shattered shields. If Fa'ru were to win, the horde would undoubtedly splinter, and the two factions would more than likely fight among themselves. There would be no vengeance after that. It would drift away like a weed caught by the wind.

The inevitable future loomed like mountains in the west. It was a path without clarity or purpose for the horde and Su'ca. However, it was Fa'ru's right to challenge U'sabe. She continued to wrestle the idea over in her mind until she became fixated on it. Any warrior reserved the right to challenge the chief, and any chief could challenge to become the Partho'sha.

The chiefs fought to subdue their clans' celebration. Others recognized Fa'ru's discontent; he would be allowed the floor to issue his challenge. When the clans finally subsided, Fa'ru took the center of the field.

"The Raf'a'nos do not recognize this weak imposter of a Partho'sha!" Fa'ru sneered.

"Then you have two paths, Fa'ru! Go and leave this horde or say what you have come to say!" U'sabe demanded.

"I invoke challenge!" Fa'ru roared. His remaining supporting clans echoed his sentiment and raised their arms behind him in unison. The other warrior clans were equally aroused and prepared to fight as well. All the Par'sha erupted in thunderous shouts, and the remaining chiefs desperately called for peace among the people.

Su'ca, for the first time, rose from her seated position and raised her hand for silence. It was not immediate, but the crowd took notice and, after a time, submitted to her. She took to the center of the assembly, stood in front of Fa'ru, and did the only thing that was her right.

"I invoke challenge!"

Chapter XVI
The Innocent

It was a foolhardy plan. Each scouting party would ride from the Trouthavens in five directions: north, northeast, east, southeast, and south. They would camp overnight and, while most of the scouts hid in the forest, let the campfire draw the darkness in. When the enemy committed, all the scouts would pounce from behind the would-be attackers where there would be good light and a fairer fight.

Every position carried risk. The scouts hidden within the forest could be found and killed. Also, the men at the campfire were bait in the scheme, and all knew it. They would have to hold on long enough for the trap to be sprung, and during that time they would be targets for the enemy bowmen.

Despite the peril, the plan was bold enough to succeed. It was Jacoby's creativity that made the plan feasible. He suggested making a real camp among the forest using tents, cookware, even a lute for ambience, and decoy soldiers to bolster their appeal to the enemy. The real men at the campfire would conceal themselves among the decoys and minimize the chances of being peppered with arrows from beyond the darkness. Yslanna suggested no one should wait around the fire at all, but Jacoby insisted real folk had to be there. When the party inquired further about Jacoby's brilliant tactic, he alluded to having spent time with pirates along the coast of the southern sea.

The plan gained the approval of Lord Malcolm's man, Sir Pavel. He specifically said the party was "clever and deft to use the enemy's tactics against them."

Master Wendall argued the opposite and thought it was reckless. Cal understood his doubt but also his responsibility; they needed to uncover the power of the enemy.

With permission granted, the party next sought out men to assist in the scheme. They turned to the cavalry to provide the remaining men for all five traps, and the cavalry didn't disappoint.

They asked one hundred good men of the cavalry to come forward and four hundred and twenty-two volunteered. Among those men, four other captains were chosen to gather twenty men, and Cal served as the fifth.

Cal met privately with each captain and explained the priority. They needed to uncover the power of the enemy at any cost. If they were able to discover how the enemy wielded the darkness, then the army would have a real chance to defeat them.

The morning of the following day, Cal and his party set off in a northeasterly direction into the Crestwood with sixteen other volunteer cavalrymen. The other parties followed suit in the other four directions. Each received their orders and all the equipment necessary to set their trap. They were eager to finally take the fight to the enemy.

They traveled past the main road and set out into the deep Crestwood. The damp air smelled of needles and pine; Cal almost felt at home again. Yslanna estimated a few hours' ride would take them to where the enemy usually gathered. Even in the daylight, Cal wagered they might come across an enemy unaided by the darkness. It was a silent and vigilant ride.

It was an hour past midday when the party found the perfect spot: a hill surrounded by giant fir trees. The trees provided cover for soldiers hidden in the wood and it was clear around the base so they could have a proper fight. The best advantage was the center of the camp itself. Three great red oaks huddled together at the top of the hill made for a well-protected campfire and large enough to host a dozen decoys. When the party saw the layout of the grove, everyone nodded in approval, dismounted, and began making their preparations.

The folk prepared the camp much like any other. They collected firewood, set a pot in place for stew, and pitched tents around the campfire. They corralled the horses far from their encampment and under the cover of a tree whose branches shaded their presence. They centered the campfire between the three huddled trees and placed logs in the gaps between the trees for seating; the decoys were fixed upright with stakes on the logs. At first glance, they looked stiff and unconvincing, but Jacoby assured everyone that they'd look more realistic as light flickered around them in the evening. To complete the trap, they dug out several holes for men to emerge and surprise the enemy. Once Cal saw the preparations, his confidence grew. They would give the enemy a good fight.

The last task was to decide who would ultimately stay within the camp. Although the men were eager for the fight to come, no cavalrymen stood forward for the duty. Cal understood the hesitation. He didn't prefer the exposure either.

"Well, my friends, if the task must be done, then I will see it through. However, I need at least two more volunteers," Cal announced. With his offer, another found their courage as well and came forward.

Halden took a deep breath, placed his hand on Cal's shoulder, looked up, and smiled at him. He didn't need to say anything further, but that wouldn't be like Halden.

"I can't let you go alone. If we lose you, there'd be no one else around here with the head to lead us through," Halden teased, and the other folk gathered grinned. "I'm with you."

Following Halden, another imposing figure came forward and said nothing at all. Clydes stepped forward and patted his chest. From what Cal could tell, this meant he just volunteered for the position, but Cal had one significant doubt.

"Thank you, Halden, but I expected you to be here. You're half a foot shorter than the rest of us, and the arrows always sail over your head. You're never in any danger," Cal joked back. Everyone, including the Darwishman, laughed.

"Clydes, I appreciate you volunteering, but if you sit there tonight with us, I'm afraid every arrow that goes over Halden would then hit you."

Everyone tittered again, but Cal was almost serious. Clydes was a huge man and a huge target. Yet, he did not waver. He lifted his hand once more, firmly patted his heart, and pointed to the camp. Cal grinned; no one could ever doubt the measure of the silent giant.

"Very well, Clydes," Cal agreed.

"I guess we'll give you the biggest tree," Halden jested to Clydes.

Everyone laughed, shoving the fear of what was about to come aside. Even the giant's chest heaved in a kind of muted laugh.

Jacoby, Yslanna, and the remaining folk finished digging the hiding spots at the base of the surrounding oaks and camouflaged the holes with bushes over top of them. They were ready.

The only thing left to do was imitate a group of scouts who had finished a day patrolling, and that was by far the easiest part. They prepared a stew over the fire, its scent hanging in the air while everyone ate heartily and conversed. Some folk napped in their tents while others spoke of home, loved ones, or what they would do after the war. Their spirits were high, and with that, a few songs came with it.

They patrolled around their encampment until dusk came over the horizon. When it did, the remaining cavalrymen finished their meals, collected their weapons, and concealed themselves in their holes, ready to strike.

When the others hid, Cal, Halden, and Clydes took their seats at the base of the camp and waited. It was a cool night, and tiny moonbeams penetrated the thick cover of the wood. It was a thoughtful reminder of his other encounter with the darkness and what the foe did. Cal knew the darkness would obscure all light and he made a mental note to take warning if he should see the moonlight vanish.

Halden, however, interrupted his thoughts. "At least we're warm," he reassured.

The fire was welcome, but Cal was gladdened by Halden's companionship more; his spirit never dampened in any condition.

"And we get to have all the stew that's left," Cal laughed. The two chuckled in the dark. Cal couldn't contain his amusement until it dawned on him the other soldiers had the opposite situation. He hoped they'd dressed appropriately and had eaten enough prior to hiding. However, no soldier showed any signs of discomfort. They were focused on the task at hand. So, Cal did as well.

Cal readied his bow and placed two quivers on each side of him just in case the enemy preferred to come from either side of their camp. He also prepared himself for a close engagement and sharpened his sword. His confidence swelled as his swordplay improved day after day since the party formed.

Clydes sat ready with his war hammer; it was the first time he would wield a shield, and Cal was glad of it. Clydes would be the unyielding force holding them off while the trap sprang into action. Clydes had placed a spear with every decoy earlier and he motioned to Halden that he would throw them into the wood. Cal pitied the unknown receiver who would intercept it.

Halden set aside his halberd and chose his ax and his shield that evening. He would stand ready beside Clydes to receive any enemy who would come.

They were prepared and alert, but it did not feel like a camp. The evening continued with little conversation; it was the opposite of what Cal hoped to portray. There was nothing left to say while they waited for an enemy to find them in the dark, and Cal forgot that Clydes would be of no help in that regard anyway.

"Let us have a song," Cal insisted.

Halden responded with a quizzical look upon his face. "What? Now?" Halden asked.

"Yeah, play us a tune! We're supposed to look like a patrol resting in the evening," Jacoby called out from the wood.

"And we won't if hidden voices are shouting from somewhere other than the campfire," Cal griped.

Jacoby did not reply.

"But he's right. Go on, then. Let's serenade the enemy and Jacoby. Perhaps it's just the thing to make this work."

Halden set aside his ax and shield. He picked up the lute, plucked a few notes, and then proceeded to tune it until he was satisfied. He took a moment to think of a good song as he strummed one chord and then another.

"I've been thinking of this one ever since we left," Halden voiced. He began playing a lovely song like the ones Cal had heard a dozen times at the tavern. It was the kind of song all young folk yearned for when the taverns held summer recitals and the Crestfolk would dance into the late evenings.

"There's a mountain in the south of Jhull,

Where I tend to toil.
There's a home of carved stone,
That's deep within the soil.

The old men brew a tasty stew,
And rabbits do a broil.
They fill the pot with carrot tops,
Salt, and seasoned oil.

And when the winds come roaring through,
It does not bother me.
The halls are warm, the hearths doth burn,
And keep us merry.

I found her at a summer dance,
Her skin was pearl and fair.
She wore a festive glimmered dress,
With flowers in her hair.

Her lips were colored ruby red;
Her eyes an emerald shine.
She flashed a grin that done me in;
I swore that she'd be mine.

The Oath

Although I dig amongst the roots

Of stone and rocks and earth,

There is no jewel within the ground

That equals what she's worth.

I chased her to the stony top

Where mountains meet the clouds.

I chased her down to willowed grounds

Through forest, hills, and mounds.

I chased her down the sandy coast

Where soil meets the sea.

And when I finally took her hand,

I asked if she'd marry me.

Now, we live within a stony hall

And I no longer work.

I have the rarest jewel that's found

beneath the ancient earth."

When Halden finished, Cal beamed from ear to ear. He and
Clydes gave him a warm applause. There were even a few claps heard

in the dark of the Crestwood, but Cal didn't feel like chastising anyone for disobeying. He felt too good to do so.

It was like before the raids when Bill and he traveled the roads and mingled with folk around the modest halls of the Crestwood. The halls were bright with life and song and the ale kept them merry. They were always met with kind folk who appreciated Bill, the shopkeeper, because he'd go out of his way to obtain the goods the folk needed. They loved him for that.

Cal missed his friend. For the previous few days, he had avoided thinking of him, but now, as he sprang to mind, he couldn't stop. He was the closest person to family he had left in this world after his folks passed. And now, there were no folk left who knew him at all. There were new friends who kept him company, all good folk, but none who knew him or his life prior to this. The only person who knew him for longer was Alec, another good soul who welcomed Cal, and that wasn't much.

His grief twisted inside into anger. Everyone else had been killed by these wildmen. He wiped the single tear that ran down his face and swore he would return the hospitality he had been shown. He would find out their power and would use it against them if he could.

Halden continued to pluck on the lute and hum while Clydes bobbed along with his head and hand; they were good folk indeed.

They cared and looked after each other like Bill had. It was the closest thing to family Cal had left. He was grateful they were with him.

The lute filled the camp with pleasant sounds, but as the cool air breezed into the camp, Cal looked for the moonbeam. The moonlight had vanished. He rose to his knee to peer over Halden and Clydes into the Crestwood. There was no distinction between the blackness of night and the darkness, but he knew. He gazed through the trees, and a pair of bushes became obscure followed by a tree trunk. They had arrived.

Cal's heart quickened, and he looked to Halden and Clydes. They were still preoccupied by their own amusement when a stone fell between them. They both looked back at the origin of the thrown pebble and found Cal's grim face in return. Their smiles vanished, and Halden stopped playing.

"No," Cal whispered. "Keep playing!"

Although uncomfortable, Halden picked the lute back up and nervously strummed for a moment. Then an idea struck him and he confidently sang once more.

> *"Can you hear me laddies*
> *From below the ground?*
> *The party is a-coming;*
> *Can you hear the sound?*

I've asked you here to welcome.
So, let them come on in.
Uncork the wine, we're set to dine;
Fill the glasses to the brim.

And when the fire's fading
Prepare to meet them out.
But if we're true and lucky
They'll stay below the ground."

The darkness came from the gap between Clydes and Halden. It enveloped trees and bushes and neared closer to their fire. Just as Halden finished his verse, arrows whistled through the air and toppled a few decoys in front of Cal. However, none hit the three men at the fire. After the initial volley of arrows, men came from within the darkness, scattering around like roaches in the presence of light. They were covered in bones and fur, with curled helms and green eyes.

Cal drew and loosened an arrow. It sailed in between the gap and found its target, and the man immediately fell. However, the enemy did not quiver or react. The heartless marauders disregarded their companions and continued forward.

Clydes and Halden rose to join the fight, each launching spears in the dark as Cal continued loosening arrows. Their shadows were cast over the wood like a pair of colossi in the light of the fire. The wildmen charged the pair but were battered back with shields, axes, and hammers. The pair blocked, feinted, and attacked over and over again at the men in front of them. They made an impressive duo; most of the enemy who had charged rolled back down the hill dead. That was until two dozen foes emerged from the darkness and raced up the hill.

"NOW!!!" Cal shouted, tearing at his own throat.

The cavalrymen sprang from the ground in all directions like giant rabbits. They roared in the dark as they rushed the unsuspecting enemy and initially struck numerous fatal blows.

Steel clanged in every direction, but most of the enemy were still in front of Cal and his two companions, and the two men desperately needed the aid of the other soldiers. Cal abandoned his bow, drew his sword, and joined them. Fueled by courage, he charged two of the four wildmen Clydes was holding back.

Cal hacked as fast as his arm could swing on their left while Clydes walloped them from their right until their defenses were overpowered. One by one, they succumbed to several blows and fell back on each other. When Cal looked for another to fight, he found

Yslanna leading their horses around the camp as she wielded her spear with deadly accuracy. The wildmen were cut off and falling.

The three companions leapt over the log and pressured the enemy at the center; they were surrounded this time and they could not recover. As the last of the attackers fell, the darkness lifted around them. The campfire again shed its light into the forest and the moonlight beamed from up above.

Cal did not understand. There was nothing that indicated how they conjured the darkness or how it disappeared. It was maddening to have succeeded in battle but to have failed in the one objective Lord Malcolm entrusted to him. Cal had nothing to show for what they had done, and he became overwhelmed with anger.

As the last of the darkness faded and the wood came back into sight, Cal found there was work still to be done. The last of the remaining wildmen appeared dazed and ran back into the Crestwood like frightened deer; once the darkness lifted all courage was lost. Cal made a mental note to remember that when another thought struck him.

If one wildman returned, they would alert the enemy of the cavalry's presence. Cal could not let that happen. He also had another purpose; the vengeance for Bill's death was at hand.

"After them!" he yelled. "I have this one!"

The other cavalrymen scattered into the Crest after the other wildmen while Cal set off behind the third. The forest air rushed past as Cal raced through the dark.

The wildman fled with purpose. He dodged around trees and bushes, he stumbled onto the ground, and he kept getting up. It reminded Cal of how he was chased from his own home while it was afire, and he grew angrier. With his remaining strength, he bolted after his agile foe, who was determined to get away. Cal would not have it. He reached back with his sword and flung it at the wildman. The sword flew from his hand, twirled through the air, struck the wildman, and he fell.

Cal cautiously came from behind the wildman, picked up his sword, and stopped to catch his breath as the exhilaration coursed over his body. For a moment the wildman didn't move. Cal had thought his sword throw might have been fatal, but he was wrong; he exhaled a breath into the crisp night air and then tried to get back on his feet. He survived and yet Cal could not let him live. Cal couldn't let him get away with alerting the rest of the raiders. Cal let the rage take over as he prepared for the killing blow. He raised his sword with both arms, and a voice cried out.

"Cal, don't!" Alec urged.

Shocked, Cal looked behind him and found Alec and Eris riding on two steeds that came to a halt. Cal doubted his eyes. *How could he be here?* He was almost dead since he last saw him; the life drained from his face, and he was a chill to the touch. Yet, he was there, as lively as the day he met him, shedding a small light into the forest, and great concern was etched upon his face. It was for Cal.

"Cal, look at his eyes! Look at the man," Alec urged, pointing with his staff.

Cal looked back at the wildman and found a young man not unlike himself. His eyes were green no more, and whiskers on his chin barely formed. He was hurt and trembling before him. Then it dawned on Cal who the young man feared so much.

He did not know why, but Bill came to mind. He didn't want them to kill needlessly when they joined the cavalry; he didn't want Cal to become that kind of man. And when Bill passed, he didn't blame the enemy at all. Bill was strong enough to let bygones be. So, Cal looked over the wildman one last time, lowered his sword, and collapsed back to the ground. Alec had dismounted and came to his side as Eris turned to the young wildman.

"I'm sorry," Cal lamented.

"There is nothing to be sorry for," Alec calmly replied.

"I was just so angry, and I couldn't let him warn them."

"I know, son. It's alright now."

"And I don't know how they do it. I have nothing to give Lord Malcolm."

"Perhaps and perhaps not. We have a guest now. Perhaps he can answer our many questions. That should appease Lord Malcolm."

"How are you even here right now?"

"It is not as interesting as why you are here, my young friend, and it is far less interesting than what you've done right now. Why don't you calm yourself and rest for a moment?" Alec suggested. The old man turned to the young wildman, but he was more of an adolescent nomad.

Cal looked closer, and he recognized some of the furs he wore. They were coarse furs from northern territories, and they were made of mountain goats, bears, and elk. The people there were a hardy mountainous people who kept to themselves and their country except to trade. However, that was a rare occurrence. Their country was harsh and most considered it barren, but their tribes somehow thrived despite the conditions.

Eris looked over the young wildman and tended his wounds. As she attended his right shoulder blade, the boy yelped in pain. *This was no wild raider who killed for sport. This was a pup among the wolves.* It was unlike any of the enemies they had encountered. They were always vicious and persistent. This boy appeared without these qualities ever since the darkness lifted.

"He will survive, but I must seal the wound and quickly," Eris cautioned.

Cal felt terrible for the first time in a long time. A moment ago, the boy was the enemy, but here he was crying from pain. Eris helped the boy up and led him back to the encampment.

"Let us follow suit," Alec replied, helping Cal to his feet. "And with haste, just in case there are further patrols among the wood."

"How are you here, Alec? I must know," Cal insisted.

The old man flashed the rebellious grin. "It is hard to say, but I awoke when I needed to, and when Eris told me of your task, I came to aid you," Alec responded.

"But why?"

"Because I felt you needed me, my young friend. You needed a voice of reason in your weakest moment. I saw it in my dream," Alec replied.

Cal avoided the old man's gaze in shame. He almost let himself become someone he never thought… a killer. "I didn't know he was a boy. I wish you hadn't seen that."

Alec pulled Cal to a halt. His old eyes peered through him. "You have nothing to be ashamed about. In fact, you should be proud. You attacked him when you thought he was an enemy, and you spared him when you found him defenseless. Perhaps you had a moment of weakness, but you made the decision, Cal. All that remains is to learn the lesson and better yourself. That is all any of us can do," Alec assured.

Cal was almost able to breathe again as Alec kindled some joyous magic into his soul. "What do we do now?" he asked.

"Let's uncover the mystery of this plot," Alec replied.

Chapter XVII
The Challenge

The horde was astonished, and most did not understand the declaration. Su'ca strode to the center of the gathering, looked Fa'ru in the eyes, and issued her challenge to become the Partho'sha immediately after Fa'ru declared his own.

Fa'ru stood confounded by her as was most of the clans. His gaping mouth showed he had not calculated past declaring his own challenge, fighting U'sabe, and assuming the position of Partho'sha.

Su'ca had briefly considered the conundrum after Fa'ru issued his challenge. There was no precedent, but she could see the paths. There would be a fight between the challengers, between all three opponents, or the Partho'sha would accept one challenge after the other.

Su'ca gambled on the first path. It was the most honorable path between warriors, and it was a path the clans would respect. If Fa'ru proved his strength in two open combats, his authority would be unequal among the horde; even the opposition would respect his ascendance to the position.

The second path was dishonorable. Fa'ru would be greatly disadvantaged if he were to face a unified Su'ca and U'sabe in open combat. Once he was dispatched, Su'ca would then also have to kill an ally and friend in honorable combat. She would do so, if necessary.

The third path was possible but unlikely. Fa'ru would challenge first, and then Su'ca would challenge the victor. However, Fa'ru would now have to calculate if he could beat U'sabe, and then Su'ca in order to claim the title of Partho'sha. He could withdraw his challenge and Su'ca could as well, but their reputations would suffer. That meant little to Su'ca.

Despite the unknown future, Su'ca accepted those paths. In every outcome, the clans would unite under a proven Partho'sha and they would continue the war; even if Fa'ru succeeded and the eternal plains waited for her. However, Su'ca did not think that would be her fate.

After several moments, the clans began to murmur again and discuss the conclusions Su'ca had already followed. Even the chiefs gathered in small huddles to confer.

"She cannot do this!" Fa'ru demanded.

"I reserve the right to challenge, Fa'ru. If you deny me this, you have no right to issue a challenge yourself," Su'ca replied.

All the chiefs nodded in agreement with Su'ca. They believed in the spirit of the warrior; a necessary characteristic of all their chiefs. If a chief was unworthy, then they could be challenged in honorable combat. Fate would decide which warrior merited leadership among the clan.

"But you declined the nomination!" Fa'ru urged. Su'ca smirked at his utter confusion. Fa'ru looked as if he was pandering to the chiefs and his position grew weaker by the moment.

"It does not matter, Fa'ru. Any chief may challenge for the right to lead the clans. There are no stipulations. I have invoked my right as you have," Su'ca reinforced.

The debate continued among the clans, but the conclusion stood. She was allowed to challenge just as Fa'ru was. Without support from the clans, the situation would be allowed to continue and elude Fa'ru's understanding.

Only one chief, Ja'bu, stood to speak. "Two worthy challengers appear before us. However, I am unsure of the challenges, and I wish to ask Su'ca a question. You have the right to challenge U'sabe for the Partho'sha, but you do not have the right to challenge Fa'ru. Have you come to challenge Fa'ru or U'sabe?" Ja'bu asked and the horde eagerly awaited her answer.

Su'ca reflected. Ultimately, Fa'ru could not be the Partho'sha. Some feared him because of his strength, but it was not enough. What good is the bear-sloth's strength if it cannot be tamed? If not, then it is just a wild beast, and you do not let loose wild beasts among the horde. Nor do you let mindless barbarians lead the horde. She took the necessary steps that prevented the danger.

"I challenge for the right to be Partho'sha," Su'ca replied. Ja'bu skeptically nodded, but accepted her answer, as did all the chiefs, while Fa'ru's hope of dismissal vanished.

"Very well. Then a way forward must be discussed," Ja'bu commented. There were no immediate suggestions, and the chiefs paused to reflect upon the way forward.

Once the chiefs had accepted her challenge, Su'ca returned to her seated position and waited patiently for their decision. As she returned to her spot, a spear and shield were delivered to her as if the gods had retrieved them. She looked to her clan and found Tahop'ka nodding; she returned the gesture. She set aside the shield, took her short-spear in her hand, and picked a rock from the ground. Her immediate path was clear; she began sharpening the blade's edge as the debate continued.

The other chiefs had not uttered any suggestions. The only chief who appeared to know what to do was Su'ca, and she said nothing. They gathered together and contemplated the situation while the only noise heard was the *shink* of Su'ca's short-spear as she ran the rock along the edge of the spear over and over again. U'sabe broke the silence.

"This is a different path and one no chief here has encountered before. The chiefs will confer and we will discuss the path forward," U'sabe said aloud. "I ask Fa'ru to also take his seat once again and wait for the remaining chiefs to come to a decision."

Fa'ru had little to say in return. His attention was divided by the chiefs who gathered around U'sabe and the one chief who prepared for combat, but he returned to his seating area.

The chiefs sat in a small circle, each as concerned as the next. The way forward was unfamiliar to even the most senior chief who had seen many challenges, but no one had anything to suggest.

We'qeda was the first to share his thoughts. "U'sabe, would you accept Fa'ru's challenge?" We'qeda asked.

"I would," U'sabe replied.

"Would you accept Su'ca's challenge?"

"How can he?" Ja'bu interrupted. "If Fa'ru defeats U'sabe, then the Partho'sha would be his title. U'sabe has no right to accept Su'ca's challenge at this time."

Some nodded, others pondered the conundrum. It would not be a simple matter.

"Ja'bu is correct," U'sabe concurred. "It would not be proper for me to do so."

"Then perhaps the correct etiquette is to proceed with the first challenge followed by the second," Ja'bu interjected.

"I do not see why Fa'ru's challenge must be allowed first or Su'ca's challenge second," Im'tu remarked. "Is one challenge more important than the other because one spoke it first? Neither has been accepted, but both rights have been invoked. They are equal in my eyes. And if they are equal, why should either be allowed the first opportunity?"

Half the chiefs disagreed with Im'tu, but several chiefs considered his point.

"What do you suggest, Im'tu?" U'sabe inquired.

"There are two challengers and only one Partho'sha. Let the challengers combat each other and we would know then whose contest is blessed by the gods."

"Im'tu, you forget. They have not challenged each other," Ja'bu rebutted.

"That is true. However, now that there are two challengers, a question persists in my mind. Is it more important for the Partho'sha to prove he is worthy, or is it the challenger who must be proven?" Im'tu asked.

Each chief contemplated the question, and those who had disagreed began to listen.

"Both must prove they are worthy, and one emerges worthy to lead the people. The victor is blessed by the gods during combat," U'sabe replied after much thought.

"I would agree with that. However, I think the Chief has already proven their worthiness, and thus, the Chief has less to prove."

"Why would a chief have less to prove? A chief who is challenged must prove he is still worthy of the position or he forfeits it," Ja'bu insisted. "There is much he must prove." The chiefs nodded in agreement.

"You misunderstand me. I agree that a contest between the two determines who is worthy. I also agree a challenger is an obstacle for the chief to overcome, but I asked which proof is more important. Let me share my thoughts. The warriors have elected their chiefs, and the chiefs have elected the Partho'sha. Those that have emerged from our peoples to lead are honored and elevated to these positions. They have been chosen because the clan believes they should lead them; they are worthy. Does anyone think the elected chief is not worthy of the position? If so, step down from their elevated position," Im'tu replied.

It was a very good point and each knew it. Their worthiness was implicit if they were chosen by their clans.

"I understand you. However, if every chief was worthy, there would be no challenges. Yet, challenges arise because some chiefs are believed to be unworthy. I am here because of the right to challenge. The gods deemed me worthy," Koa'bo rebutted.

"You speak truth from the heart, Koa'bo. Chiefs, at some point, are not worthy. Sometimes, they grow arrogant, they become corrupt, or their minds grow old. There are many ways that a chief may become unworthy and a warrior should challenge them. Eventually, we will all become unworthy, we are replaced, or we will be blessed with a glorious death in battle. However, I think the elected chief has proven his worthiness the moment the clan selects their chief among their warriors, and most here agree with that.

"Fine!" Koa'bo relented. "What is your point?"

"Only this. You, Koa'bo, proved your worthiness when you defeated your rival. You changed the minds of the gods and your people. You convinced them you were worthy. The elected chief's worth is proved because the clan has chosen them. So, in the contest between a chief and his rival, the challenger has much more to prove than the chief. That is what a challenge does in the eyes of the clans and the gods. We have two challengers, and both must prove they are worthy to become the Partho'sha. Why not a challenge between them to determine the worthiest between them? To determine a first challenger?"

Even the naysayers understood and supported Im'tu's reasoning. It was appealing because the Par'sha had many firsts. The chief was the first among Crato'sha; the Partho'sha was the first among Crato'sha. This challenge would establish another first.

"You are wise, Im'tu, and you see an honorable path for all concerned. However, I believe the two contenders must agree to the contest between them. We cannot force a challenge upon any Par'sha. If they do not agree, then we must provide another path. Their invocation has been for the Partho'sha, and it could be dishonorable to request they challenge one another," Ja'bu suggested.

"I would agree to your condition, Ja'bu, and I'm confident at least one of the challengers would consent as well," Im'tu said, pausing to look upon Su'ca as she sharpened her blade. "However, I disagree that it would be dishonorable. There is great honor in defeating all other challengers. Any chief knows this as well. If either Fa'ru or Su'ca emerges from these challenges, they will have brought much honor upon themselves."

"I will agree to the consensus of this council," U'sabe added. "I am prepared to accept the first challenge and, if the gods will it, the second challenge. I also see the wisdom and honor in consolidating the challengers. However, all of us must agree on the path. Does each chief concur?"

They had deliberated and reflected on all that was said, and nothing more was said in opposition. The chiefs saw a clear path where honor could be had in these contests. One by one, they nodded their agreement to the proposal. With the path selected, the day would end with the matter of the Partho'sha settled.

"Then let us proceed," U'sabe commanded.

The chiefs rose and returned to their positions in front of their clans. The gathered clans perked up in anticipation of their announcement. They commanded the attention of all except the chief, who sat calmly sharpening her blade. She looked focused on nothing else.

"The chiefs and I have heard both challengers. However, this event is unprecedented. In our discussion, we have found the purpose of the challenge is to measure the worthiness of both contestants. However, the Partho'sha has been elected and thus been deemed worthy by the clans. It is the challengers who must prove they are worthy and the Partho'sha unworthy. As there are two challengers, both of them chiefs, they have proven they are worthy to lead their clans, but they must prove they are worthy to lead the horde. Therefore, both challengers must agree to combat between them and prove who is the more worthy challenger," U'sabe decreed.

U'sabe's words echoed throughout the horde and they hung on to every word. It would be spoken again across fires all over their realm and regarded as Par'sha law. Many nodded in agreement, some disagreed entirely. Overall, the people favored their judgment.

"What is this? I have come to challenge U'sabe for the leadership of this horde! Now, I am unworthy, and I must fight another?" Fa'ru demanded, pointing in Su'ca's direction. "How is this the honorable path? Su'ca has sullied my invocation! She is the one who walks over our traditions. It should not be allowed!" His clan once again stood, howled like warriors, and shook their spears in the air in support.

Su'ca had listened to all that was said while she prepared. She agreed with the decision; it was what she had hoped for. She even thought the condition agreeable as well, but it was now up to her to lure Fa'ru to fight her. She finished sharpening her blade and set it aside, and stood once again.

"You are not worthy, Fa'ru!" Su'ca taunted.

All the clans stopped their debating and disagreement and were drawn to her.

"You are not worthy to become Partho'sha. I know it, the gods know it, and the clans know it as well. They have chosen another, but you insist you must become the Partho'sha."

"I am unworthy?" Fa'ru cried. "You dishonor yourself and our horde! You will not allow the gods to judge my contest, so you take it upon yourself to interfere!"

"I believe you dishonor the will of our people, and you believe I dishonor our gods. Let us settle the matter then, Fa'ru. There is no law preventing us from challenging each other for honor. Let us cross spear and war-club and let the gods decide!"

"There is no honor in defeating you. There is every honor defeating this weak Partho'sha," Fa'ru insisted, pointing to U'sabe.

"Are you afraid of me, Fa'ru?" Su'ca goaded. "I have no such fears of you. You can choose to disagree with the chiefs' decision but know this. There is no path where you do not face me. If you challenge U'sabe and win, you will face me. If you decline my challenge, you will be a coward among our people and prove to our people your unworthiness!" Fa'ru's eyes bulged and his entire body tightened. She had publicly called the warrior's bravery into question; he could not back down.

"I fear no one!" he asserted, beating his own chest.

"Then I challenge you, Fa'ru! I challenge you for the right to be the first challenger!" she shouted.

He was enraged like a mad bison on the plain as he paced back and forth before Su'ca.

She had taunted the bull as best she could in front of the horde. He had to accept or lose all credibility as chief and as a challenger.

"I accept!" he yelled hoarsely.

The clans roared in response. Thousands of Par'sha stood, clanged their spears against shields, and cried like warriors. They called for sport now, and nothing short of blood would appease them.

Even Su'ca rejoiced with them because the gamble had been played and won in her favor. Fa'ru would meet her here and now upon the open country and under the blue sky. All would bear witness, from the Par'sha on the field to the hawks high up among the clouds.

Su'ca looked toward her rival. Fa'ru was a formidable figure to be respected in a fight, and he had likely fought dozens of quick warriors like herself. Fa'ru strove to crush his opponents like all powerful warriors, but every swing was a windmill of a motion... always long and predictable. The more often he swung his club, the more tired he would become. Any attempt to withstand a single strike from his club would be foolish, if not deadly.

Su'ca would need to keep her wits if he had any surprising moves. She had insulted and instigated the beast. If he did not charge at the commencement, she would be disappointed. Her strategy demanded she dodge away from every swing or deflect his blows if necessary. She would let him try as he may to strike her, but she would be just out of reach. And when the opportunity arose, she would counter with a multitude of pierces or slashes, whichever was available to her.

Enough strikes and he would become sluggish and desperate. This would be the path to Fa'ru's defeat.

The circle cleared until there were only the two challengers. The chiefs pushed the clans back in order to give the competitors room. Once adequate space was made, they joined the audience on the fringes.

Now, Su'ca stood in an arena where honor could be found. She was ready; fate had already decided the conflict. There was nothing to fear or hold her back from unleashing her own fury.

She gazed at Fa'ru, and he stared back. He was a beast. She could see the fire blazing behind his eyes. He would come swiftly. So, she prepared to meet him with shield and spear.

U'sabe came forward from the edge of the crowd to give the word, but Su'ca kept her focus on Fa'ru.

"Begin!" U'sabe shouted.

The clans thundered in bloodlust and Fa'ru with them. With every fiber of his soul, he unleashed the barbarian. His right arm stretched behind him with club in hand, and he charged her as she anticipated; it was his first mistake.

It was up to her to control the fight now. She raced toward him and cut the distance between them in half. He did not expect her swiftness to attack him as he tried to slow himself. The ground between them evaporated as he tried to strike her with his club, but she was too quick, and he miscalculated. He was wrong-footed when the blow came down; Su'ca pivoted like a great cat and deflected the weak swing with her shield, leaving his whole right side exposed. Her spear darted out from behind her shield, slashed at his shoulder blade and arm, and then back across.

Her first strike was protected by his pelt and armor he had recovered from the westmen; the second upward strike drew blood. It was not enough to end the fight, but every cut would count.

He countered with his awesome strength as his club swung back around toward her. It made solid contact with the shield, but as the strike came, she leapt away from him. Her leather shield splintered along the bottom rim; it could only take so many of those blows. She landed, resumed her posture, and he came again.

However, the space between them was very much within his reach. This time, he swung swiftly as he traded power for speed. He thrust his club forward like a ram but feinted as he used Su'ca's deflection to rear his club around again. Back and forth, he swung wildly while frothing at the mouth.

Su'ca deflected one swing after the other, but with every swing his strides brought him closer until he was almost close enough to grapple her. She would be no match if he were able to pummel her with his fists; she would certainly die if he were able. She was now too close to deflect but not to evade. The club was coming around and falling when she ducked and rolled away from him, but that was the danger. He would come after her, and her back was turned to him. She rolled and leapt to her feet, pivoting toward him. And as she rose, her shield came around to deflect whatever blow was coming for her. She caught the end of the club as he stretched to finish her. It was his second mistake.

His stretch left him exposed, and her spear followed her shield. With all her strength, she sent her spear straight up at him. However, he managed to deflect. Her impatience was her mistake; now she was exposed and much too close.

He dropped his shield and backhanded her. She flew back but kept her wits. She knew he would follow the backhand with the club, and she had to keep him from reaching her!

As she fell, she managed to barrel roll and push herself from the ground onto her feet. She raised her shield and spear to block the blow to come, but he was not there to meet her.

He was slow to attack, and she saw why. Her deflected spear had found a mark. As the thrust glanced upward, the blade barely sliced his chest, and the same strike practically severed his eyebrow in two. She almost removed his eye, but then she had an epiphany. As he grasped at his head, desperate to keep the blood from pouring down his face, he could not open his left eye. He was injured, half-blind, and the eternal plains called for him. He should have continued his attack. It was his last mistake.

Su'ca took no time and pressed him. She savagely charged, slashed back and forth, and upward and downward with her short-spear. They shared a multitude of strikes, and he held well, but he was wearing and now without his shield. Even half-blind, he was impressive. However, the time had come.

She slashed for the last time and let the spear and club connect, but she did not follow through. Her spear deflected off her opponent's club, twirled in her grip until the blade faced inward. This he saw because he focused his remaining eyesight on Su'ca's blade-hand. He did little to stop her shield from bashing into him on his blindside. He was stunned and backed away from her blow.

Su'ca had to finish this now; the beast had to be killed. She tossed away her shield, took two steps, and leapt with both hands clasped around her spear. The spear came down on his head, pinning him beneath her.

She found herself with a knee on his chest, a foot on the ground, and her spear buried in his skull. She had not paid the clans any attention while she fought, but once she stood and removed her spear, there was no warrior who did not scream the warrior's cry. It was like the boom of lightning that struck the open plain. Su'ca wondered if any of the enemy had heard the horde from within the wood of the Crest. If they had, fear would have struck straight at their hearts. She joined the warrior cry.

U'sabe came forward during the thunder. He had removed the fur from his shoulders and carried his spear and shield.

The people silenced themselves as they prepared to witness the next challenge.

"Come then, young warrior. I am prepared for our challenge," U'sabe called. He was an honorable man and would meet her because it was demanded of him.

However, she did not want it. In her eyes, her path was correct, and now the path of the people was also where it should be. This fight was not.

"No," Su'ca replied.

Few murmured, most watched in awe. The eldest chief, however, was not amused. Ja'bu came forward with all haste to question her.

"You invoked challenge, Su'ca! To rescind your challenge would bring great dishonor..." Ja'bu began.

"I challenged for the right to be Partho'sha, Ja'bu!" Su'ca interrupted, pointing a bloody spear at him. "The council deemed it necessary I fight for the right to be first challenger. I have fought; I have won. I maintain the right as first challenger to challenge the Partho'sha; I choose not to."

The murmurs grew louder among the clans.

"So, you play tricks with our laws and play with our traditions?"

"I did not dictate the terms of the challenges, Ja'bu! It was you and the other chiefs. You could have mandated the other challenge come first, but you did not. I was prepared for that path. I have obeyed all the laws of the Par'sha and my right has been observed. My right to challenge is upheld and I bring no dishonor among my people!"

Although angered, Ja'bu could not argue further. The clans, too, accepted her answer. She had followed the rules as outlined by the chiefs. U'sabe sheathed his short-spear and approached Su'ca. His face was grim.

"I understand what you have done, but you must consider all the positions," U'sabe warned. "Because of this, many will question my leadership as Partho'sha."

"I have done what is right, U'sabe," Su'ca replied.

"What of my honor, Su'ca? I must be strong and defend myself. That is the way of the Par'sha as well. Some will believe you challenged just to protect me."

He was right. She had considered many things today but could not see past the withdrawal of her challenge. U'sabe would need to be strengthened, and the people would need to be reminded why they wished him to be the Partho'sha. So, an idea came to her that served both of those needs. She drew her blade across the palm of her hand and raised her bloodied palm to the clans; they silenced as blood dripped from her hand.

"I will make no challenge to U'sabe. He is the choice for Partho'sha and our decision should be honored. Fa'ru could not see it. So, he is now riding toward the eternal plains with honor. Now, we must look forward. There is the Crest," she said, pointing her spear to the mountains. "There are people who think they can strike at us and run. They may try, but the horde will follow, and we must be a united people. Not divided, but whole. So, I will make you a blood-oath. I will follow U'sabe into the Crestwood. We will find those responsible, and we will take vengeance upon them. Then all the world will remember what happens when you attack the Par'sha!"

She offered her bloodied hand to U'sabe. He unsheathed his spear and cut his own palm, and they shook. Thousands of warriors made blood-oaths as they raised their bloodied palms to the sky.

Chapter XVIII
The Discovery

Cal and Alec returned to the encampment where the remaining scouts had re-formed. After they counted the dead, they exchanged three lives for thirty-one of the enemies; the trap sprang true. For the first time, the scouts saw themselves able to overcome this evil and a jubilant spirit spread through the camp.

Spirits rose even higher after being reunited with Alec and Eris. Alec was welcomed as a friend. The other soldiers, who knew little about him other than he could conjure magic, revered him. Upon sight, Clydes pulled the old man in for a bear-like hug and the admiration among all was replaced with delight. Alec, unprepared for the gesture, welcomed it.

Eris and Yslanna, on the other hand, shared a quiet embrace where a few tears were shed between them. All the survivors embraced in moments as the campfire flickered beneath the foliage and the remaining stew filled the night air. Cal wanted the moment to continue for a lifetime, but the danger was ever present; the enemy was far from defeat.

After all greetings were passed, the scouts were warmed by the fire and they returned to the task at hand. A single captive was recovered, and the dangers of the night were still before them.

The prisoner was the easiest of Cal's concerns to address. The boy's wound was tended with fire. Although the searing pain caused him to cry out into the woods, it was sealed immediately, and Eris plied him with ointment and a tonic to lessen the pain. Within half an hour, the boy passed out from exhaustion. The only remaining concern was if he were to try to escape. Cal would not have it; the boy held answers to their questions. So, his wrists and ankles were tied as he slept.

With their captive well attended, the scouts turned their attention back to the forest where the enemy might be lurking. Yslanna, being accustomed to the task, once again scaled the tallest tree and reported on the enemy. The moonlight shone brightly over the canopy of the forest; the darkness was still far from them. It was a favorable sign. As a precaution, the scouts once again took positions in their holes and reset their trap. Throughout the night, several soldiers stood watch while the others slept. They did not regroup again until morning.

They rose with the sun, tired but grateful to see another day arrive. Cal hardly slept at all; he was eager to uncover the many questions gnawing at his mind. *Why did they attack the Crestwood?*

Were they just a tribe of northern wildmen who had decided to make war with their southern borders? And what was the source of their power?

Where Cal was anxious to get started, Alec was the opposite; this struck him as odd. After all, Alec had formed their pact under the sole condition to uncover the mystery of the darkness. This bound them together, and now they were on the verge of uncovering the mystery. Yet, Alec was as calm as the early morning breeze over the treetops.

He prepared tea, bread, meat, and cheese for breakfast. When he finished, to Cal's surprise, he placed the meal in front of their captive boy. It was the smell of cooked sausages that woke the young man, disbelieving the small meal that was prepared. He devoured his food as Alec chuckled to himself.

"I thought as much," Alec said, gushing. As the boy looked up, he found himself surrounded by Crestfolk scouts sharing their own morning meal; he recoiled with his plate.

"It's alright, my boy. We mean you no harm," Alec assured.

The cool words landed on the boy like a fresh morning mist. Even Cal was comforted by them. The boy refocused on Alec, composed himself, and ravenously finished his food.

Cal was not surprised after seeing the boy's gaunt face in the morning light. He hadn't noticed before, but the dark furs covering the boy gave him more bulk than he had. As Cal looked over the fallen enemy, he noticed all looked as malnourished as the young man. *Were they so desperate for food that they had no other choice than to pillage their southern neighbors for sustenance?* Perhaps this was why Cal's farm was untouched by the raid as was much of the countryside.

"Thank you," the boy said. "I can't remember the last time I enjoyed the taste of a meal."

"Why is that?" Alec asked.

The boy winced at the question as if it was painful to recall. "It is hard to say. I know I have eaten, but I can't remember what it was or the last time I ate. I don't even know where I am."

Alec began stroking his thin, scraggly beard and contemplating the boy's explanation. "Let us then start with something simpler. What is your name?"

The question strained the boy as he closed his eyes and furrowed his brow, attempting to recall it. "Lorcan! My name is Lorcan!" he declared once he retrieved it from the depths of his mind.

"You appear to struggle with your memory, my young friend," Alec commented. "What is the last thing you remember, Lorcan?"

The boy, once again, closed his eyes to focus his thoughts, but he continued to struggle. "I don't know," he whimpered.

"Augh, what good is he to us if he can't tell us anything?" Jacoby exclaimed. "I say we give him over to Lord Malcolm's men. Let them jog his memory."

"Are you suggesting we hand over a boy so that he can be beaten for information?" Alec demanded.

"I cannot abide by that course of action," Eris interjected.

"Neither can I," Yslanna concurred.

"Have you forgotten this boy is the enemy? He would have run any one of you through if the skirmish had gone another way," Jacoby said, exasperated. "His youth does not make him immune. He was caught fleeing from a fight he could not win, and now he is our captive. What else would any of you have us do with him?"

Cal found it hard to argue with Jacoby. Lorcan had fought them, lost, and was their captive. He may have raided along the countryside or ambushed the cavalry along the main road, although Cal did not know.

A part of Cal believed this boy should be held responsible for his actions. Yet, something gave him pause. He no longer looked like a killer with fiery green eyes; somehow he was different.

The boy reminded Cal a little of himself once upon a time... rudderless and needing help. Cal found guidance from Bill. He helped raise him in a way and, from time to time, got him into a little trouble. Bill and he both should have been jailed any number of times because of the spirits they sold throughout the Crestwood; they avoided the taxes across many villages. Bill always believed folk had the right to trade freely with one another without interference or compensation to anyone else. It was the life Cal knew and he had never suffered the consequences. Lorcan, on the other hand, would.

"It would be a mistake to waste this opportunity. Besides, I prefer the carrot to the stick," Alec responded.

The party looked on in bewilderment as the old man cupped Lorcan's face in his left hand and extended his staff in the air with his right. Alec closed his eyes and lightly hummed when the deep crevice between the stones on his staff began to glow.

Lorcan's eyes, along with the rest of the scouts, were immediately drawn to the fractured light emanating from his staff. The blue light pulsed into the woods and the air around them grew warm. Lorcan's eyes shut, and he let the magic pass through him.

Cal took in the moment. It had been days since Alec had last wielded the magic, and every time, it revitalized him. It was there, surrounded by the breeze that rushed over his body and passed deep within him, leaving him with a resonating calm.

A few moments passed as the darkness poured out of the young man and evaporated into the morning sun the moment it left his body. Several scouts gasped and stepped back from the boy; others covered their mouths in fear they might inhale the evil of it.

Lorcan gasped for fresh air like a whale breaching the surface of the ocean and he clung to Alec's arm as the glow from Alec's staff faded.

Even Cal was startled by the effect but felt refreshed and clear-headed by the end of the ritual.

"The darkness was very much embedded deep into the recesses of your mind. It will take some time to be totally driven from you, but you should begin to elicit your memories," Alec said, bracing Lorcan as he regained his breath. "Let us try to piece together your journey, shall we?"

There was an awareness to Lorcan; the darkness no longer hindered him. He was like a hare among the wood who heard the cracking of twigs underfoot. It was apparent he regained something of his mind.

"The darkness?" Lorcan questioned. "What is the darkness?"

"It is the name of the evil shroud of fog that surrounds your people when they come in the night," Eris replied.

"Evil fog?" Lorcan queried. He needed only a moment to understand Eris when the realization came to him. It appeared that Alec's mending was a success.

"No, the blessed mist is Dhula. She keeps and protects our people. She brings the rains in the spring and fills the valleys with sunlight in the summer. She is not evil. And neither are my people," Lorcan replied, firmly waving his hand.

Cal could not question his conviction, but a doubt remained. *If their people were not bad men and their gods not evil, then how could they have conducted these atrocities upon the Crestfolk?*

"I suppose it may be harsh to call one's people evil. However, your people have attacked ours unprovoked and laid waste to villages across this realm. Many have fallen under your swords, and there are those of us who wish to know why," Alec insisted.

"My people did not attack you," Lorcan pleaded.

Alec was not swayed. He merely waved his hand across the camp to show the remnants of his people lying on the ground.

"No, you misunderstand!" Lorcan urged, clenching his fists in frustration. "I know it looks as if we've attacked you. All of you! But just now, I have awoken from a nightmare, an endless dream, where I could not wake! I could not stop myself from doing what I was made to do!"

Cal looked to Alec who returned his gaze.

"Now that I am awake, I can once again choose for myself," Lorcan continued, straining his voice. "Now that I'm awake, my mind floods with memories that terrify me! My people are living this nightmare; we are not in our right minds. We did not choose to attack you, and I know we want nothing except peace."

The air grew stale with doubt; it was hard to believe. How could thousands of people become bewitched beyond their control? Cal hadn't heard of those fables. And if it were true, could he really hold these people accountable for their actions?

Alec received the news far worse than the rest. "If that is the case, how have your people become so captivated?" he asked.

Lorcan sighed with frustration, clenched his jaw, and shut his eyes. He strained to concentrate on the long-forgotten memories. "We gave ourselves to Dhula," he soberly replied as his eyes opened wide.

"It seems to me your people should rid themselves of this Dhula. She leads you to ruin my young friend," Alec said, grimacing. "Perhaps we can help you throw the shackles off your folk, and you can be free once again from her control."

"No!" Lorcan shouted. "You don't understand. Dhula has been corrupted! It's not her fault."

Alec's brow wrinkled at the young boy's responses; Cal sighed with frustration as did many. "First, you tell me your people are outside their control. Next, you tell me you submitted yourselves to your god and she commanded you. Now you tell me, she has been corrupted. The responsibility must lie on someone's shoulders, Lorcan. Tell us then who controls your people. Tell us how Dhula's power can be wielded. We wish for peace, but we must come to know these answers! We can help you; I swear it," he replied.

Lorcan thrashed his head back and forth at everything Alec said as if the answer in his mind fought from being revealed. The veins of his head looked ready to burst when he finally stopped shaking. His eyes ceased darting and became fixed on Alec like lightning had struck him. "The sorcerer!" he whispered.

Everyone froze. Alec matched the boy's gaze and intensity. The surrounding scouts said nothing in response, but all were equally disturbed by the young man's revelation.

"Tell me of him! Everything! From the beginning!" Alec demanded.

Lorcan took a few breaths as the color faded from his face; he finally had command of his mind. "My people are the Vechians. We live throughout the valleys within the northern mountains and our homes span all the way to the frigid northern sea. It can be a harsh place, but Dhula provides for us."

"How many are you?" Yslanna interjected.

"There is no number I can give you, but when we gather, we are tens of thousands," he replied.

"I don't believe it," Jacoby contested. "The northern mountains are a desolate place; there's not sustenance enough for tens of thousands. The peaks seldom shed their white caps, even in the best of summers. Even the Darwish have not carved out halls there. We would be fools to believe such falsehoods, and I say again, we should turn him over to the Midguardmen."

Several nodded in agreement. However, Alec was not dissuaded.

"That is true of my folk," Halden added. "We have only just begun settling in the soft rock of the Crescent range. Beyond that, the northern mountains are still untamed by my folk. I cannot speak to who else might dwell there or how many."

"You listen poorly," Lorcan rebutted. "We do not live within the mountains like some peoples. We live along the deep valleys where few outsiders have been; green places, sheltered from the harshest winters."

Jacoby waved him aside, shaking his head.

"We owe everything to Dhula. She shields our very existence with a simple cloud; there are other times she opens the sky, and lets the sunbeams into our homes. Rain falls from her when we have the most need of it, and there are narrow fields of crops that keep our villages fed. Even the slightest shard of Dhula can do such a thing. The smallest Vechian child knows this," Lorcan explained.

Jacoby was not persuaded, but several scouts had their interest piqued, including Cal. *Could such a place exist beyond the peaks of the Crest?* Cal had seen the darkness easily encompass the

Crestwood; it wasn't hard to envision a valley among the northern mountains hidden by the very same power. While he questioned the possibility, Alec was focused on an entirely different detail.

"How do you mean shard?" Alec repeated.

With a furrowed brow and squinted eyes, Lorcan's bemusement was obvious. "A shard. A small piece of Dhula. The villages keep her at the temples and the priests protect her."

"So, you are saying Dhula can be a small piece," Alec emphasized, glancing at Cal.

The point struck Cal immediately. Dhula was a piece of something and somehow, they could manipulate this power. It was like no god Cal had ever heard of throughout the many realms.

"Can it be held in the palm of my hand?" Cal asked.

"You should never touch Dhula!" Lorcan warned. "It is sacred among our people. Only the priests can handle her power."

Cal knew the concern continued to weigh on Alec as Lorcan revealed the details.

"Very well then. Are there large pieces of Dhula? Can they form a whole?" Alec inquired.

"There are seventeen pieces of Dhula among the Vechians; one for each of the brightest stars in our sky. They shine through the dancing blue and green lights of the night; it is a spectacle for my people. We take in great celebration when the dancing lights appear.

It is said Dhula was cracked long ago under the magic of that sky; she was fractured and broken, but her power was not lost," Lorcan explained, often pointing to the sky.

"Dhula was delivered to the Vechians to keep her safe; that is our great purpose. Only our priests watch over her, keep her, or make requests of her. We thrived with her; our people grew and moved from one valley to the next. As we moved, a piece was taken with the settlers so they may also flourish. However, she faded over time. So, we returned home to Vechi to bring Dhula back together, and we found that she rejuvenated. The people return every year to hold a festival of unity and rejuvenation. There, the largest piece of Dhula is kept in the great temple. There, she never fades. That is her home, but I think she is there no longer. In my dreams, Dhula was taken away by the sorcerer and his disciples. None of the temples keep her now."

It was a riddle within a riddle that left Cal perplexed. The dancing lights were familiar; travelers from the north would speak of the sky lit up in colors of the day. However, their god was a curious thing. *How can this god be in pieces?* She was broken and yet one of the most powerful gods Cal had ever heard.

"Do you know how the sorcerer convinced the priests to give Dhula to him?" Alec insisted.

Lorcan again reached deep within his mind, but he no longer struggled. He stared into the abyss of the forest but returned promptly with the answer plucked from his concentration. "It is hard to say why the priests allowed him to take Dhula, but I think it was because he was much like you," Lorcan emphasized to Alec.

"How do you mean?" Alec insisted.

"I was a small boy when he first came. Few had ever been to our home, and those who had were always those lost in the mountains. We rescued and cared for them. He was not one of those; he came on purpose. He was an explorer who came from beyond our farthest western valley, but he was like you. He could do impossible things no one had ever seen a man do. He could wield a staff like yours, and light would spurt through the air. He would do this, and mesmerize the people. The children would always ask him to create the sparks from nothing, and he would always grant their request."

Alec froze at Lorcan's comments and Cal saw the fear behind his eyes.

Cal understood why. A man who possessed magic gifts like Alec had convinced a people to give him the powers of a god. So far, he had used his powers to subdue a people under his control and use them to make war on another realm. It was terrifying to consider.

Alec then let out a sigh from his contemplation and continued his questions. "Please, continue. Tell me how he came to be among your people and how these events came to pass?"

"He came to know our people. He became fascinated with Dhula, then he became obsessed. How could you not be? She gives our people life among the mountains. He attended the temple and shared in our prayer. He studied Dhula among the priests until the day he left."

"Left?" Alec questioned.

"Yes, he left for many years. I had become a man when he returned, but he was not alone. Sixteen disciples followed him, and he counted as the seventeenth; just as many as there were pieces of Dhula. We were fools to think of him as our friend," Lorcan said, clenching his fist.

"He was our guest for a time, and he respected our people. The sorcerer and his disciples all worshipped her and then one day he emerged from the temple with Dhula in his hand. I do not know why the priests had allowed him to do this, but ultimately he was worthy. His eyes shone as Dhula shined. He held out his hand, the sky shifted, and commanded the powers of Dhula. Even the priests could not influence Dhula with such ease. The disciples bowed before him, the priests bowed, and then the people. They asked the people to come and join them in worship, one by one, and received our blessing from

Dhula. Once blessed, each Vechian's eyes would reflect the light of Dhula; they were closer than ever. This was the last time I was awake... my last true memory. After that, I have only nightmares."

It all made sense somehow. Cal knew it wasn't a difficult thing to manipulate folk with their own beliefs. Cal had seen a dozen convents pass through the Fork, attempting to spread their own gospel throughout the realms. Monks peddled the sea gods of the coastal cities, High Priests touted the twin gods Illum and Shade, a frequent group spread the gospel of forest Nymphs that were coveted by many Crestfolk, and dozens more like them. Those who genuinely believed would follow their chosen god to the end of this life and whatever lies after. Lorcan's people were no different. This sorcerer had only needed to show them he could wield this Dhula and they would follow him.

It was clear that the eyes were the sign of his control, but it was unclear how the sorcerer accomplished that feat. Perhaps Dhula had this ability as well, and the sorcerer found it, but it was only Cal's speculation.

The last comment intrigued Cal. Even his memories could be useful to them, and it was important to try now that his thoughts were flowing freely.

"I know they are nightmares, but can you tell us of them?" Cal asked.

Lorcan cupped his head and tried to recall his memories, but it was a struggle. "They're more like vague images, but I have a strong feeling they are true in a way," he sighed.

"Then tell us what you feel is true," Alec assured.

"I have the image of so many people gathered like they would during the festival, but we were not celebrating. We were amassed but lifeless. The disciples herded us from one valley to the next until all were gathered. Then we worked," Lorcan stressed as he opened his hands in front of him. "We dug for weeks."

"Mining!" Halden interjected. "Ore for weapons, no doubt."

"Yes!" Lorcan agreed as if he recalled once more. "We mined and forged. We made a chasm within the mountain that stretched into the deep bedrock and brought from it the seeds of steel. We put these seeds to fire and forged for months. We brought everything we could carry, armed ourselves, and then we rode the Shappas to a great shelf overlooking this realm."

"Shappas?" Yslanna asked.

"The blessed rams of the north," Lorcan replied as he caressed the bones of armor on his chest. "They've always carried my people through the mountains; they are sacred." It was another piece of the mystery that fit.

"Why this shelf?" Alec continued.

"That is the pass into this realm," Lorcan exclaimed. "I remember passing atop the perch overlooking the great forest below. That is where the sorcerer now resides with the largest piece of Dhula. I know that with every feeling I have!"

Alec turned to the party and nodded.

Cal finally knew who was responsible for the deaths of so many and where he was. He needed no more clues. The face of the northern Crescent range was called the Slopes. It was the long ridge that connected the east and the west ranges, and its face was so steep that no man could ascend it. However, somehow, the Vechians found a passage that thousands passed through. Cal had seen it many times and always wondered what it would look like from the top of the shelf. Now more than ever, he was determined to see for himself and bring as many men as he could.

Cal considered everything, but he only had Lorcan's word as his proof. "You mentioned Dhula is not at any of your temples. Do you think this is from your dreams? I mean, do you feel this is true?" Cal asked.

"Yes," Lorcan insisted as he looked around him. "She was among us last night."

The realization came swiftly. Not only had they brought Dhula to the realm of the Crescent and on top of the Slopes, but she had to have been here the night prior; she may be among the dead!

Cal leapt up immediately and left the group. He rushed frantically from one body to the next. The idea caught on like wildfire as the remaining scouts scoured the field and the ground for some kind of shard. Cal passed one corpse over the next until he came upon a body that looked like no other Vechian, and he had something clutched in his hand.

Chapter XIX
The Torture

Gregory awoke upon a cold, stony floor in a dark, round room. It wasn't a room he recognized, and he knew most of the spaces in the castle. The only faint light available streamed through a barred window high up in the wall, but little reached where he lay. He ached beyond measure, and although he desired to be plied with ointment and his wounds bandaged, he yearned for nothing more than to climb from the dark depths back into the light.

This room was fit only for the discarded and forgotten. He stared desperately at the window and heard the faintest sounds of folk conversing at length. They were completely unaware of the window and of anyone who might be below. Gregory tried to call out and bid them to come to his aid, but when his voice broke, it was weak and carried little sound. Even the echo of the room could not bring his plea to their ears. The folk outside carried on as if he said nothing at all. Gregory feared he would never be heard from again.

He planted his hand on the cold floor, attempting to rise, and found his arms chained. He stared in disbelief as the clinking of the chains rang in his cell. *How had this come to pass? How could the Midguardmen have been so unaware of their captive's identity?*

He was one of the councilmen of the Mid and one of the first citizens. Gregory was not a particularly violent man, but he desired to have those responsible flayed in the open courtyard where he was set upon.

His body ached with pain as he attempted to stand himself up, but every effort caused him discomfort. As he used the stones embedded in the wall to pull himself up, his chest burned with agony. He wasn't certain, but he believed some ribs on his left side were broken. He pushed through the sharp pain, but when he finally managed to stand, he found his leg wobbly, and he couldn't support himself. He braced himself against the wall, but it was like touching ice everywhere. The only warmth was far above him.

He slowly shuffled to the window, stretched toward the light, and tried to call out again. This time, he managed to put some power behind his voice, and it echoed throughout his chamber, but no one answered his call from above. However, someone had heard him from behind the chamber door. The gears of the lock clinked, and he feared who was turning the key. As he circled to meet the intruder, the door swung open, and the guardsman entered.

"There has been some mistake, sir! I am Master Greg…"

The guardsman responded to his plea with a backhand, and Gregory collapsed to the floor. Fresh blood poured from his mouth, but he could do nothing. He was so weak he was unable to caress his own face and a pool of blood formed where he lay.

"Leave him be! They want him questioned, so don't kill him, Trent!" A man's voice echoed down the hall. Trent turned away from Gregory with a sigh as Gregory whimpered on the cold floor.

Trent turned back to Gregory with contempt raging in his eyes. "I don't care what the masters want. If you don't shut the fuck up, I will shut you up!" Trent sneered in a low tone.

Gregory lowered his gaze; this man would keep his word. He had no voice to answer, so he nodded in terror as tears of pain ran down his cheeks.

Trent left the councilman motionless on the ground, allowing the pool of blood, tears, and snot to soak into his clothes. The door slammed and the key clicked in the lock once again.

After a time, Gregory eventually rolled himself into a position where he could free his arms enough to stop the bleeding. He tenderly pressed his fingertips to assess the bruising around his cheekbone. The fresh lump on his left jaw was sore but it was nothing compared to the sizable and inflamed mass upon the right side of his face.

The guards had struck him severely at the tower. His probing tongue found sensitive holes where his upper molars should have been, and the recent assault to the left of his face caused his other wounds to pulsate. Altogether, he was woefully unprepared for such brutality.

As time passed, the pain eased, and his mind was freer to assess his predicament. The guards had no care for him or his position, and he held no influence over them.

He grappled with the reality of the situation: he was powerless. He wanted to approach the guardsmen, he wanted himself identified as the councilman he was, but the risk against receiving further assault held back his tongue.

The guards also revealed another valuable clue. He was to be questioned. However, by whom?

If Hector were to come, he would certainly question him, and Hector could be a rigorous opponent. He would know to connect the location of Gregory's capture to his own transgressions against the Mid.

The real question came to Gregory's mind. *What would Hector do with him? Would Hector trust him to keep this affair a secret, or would he simply have him put to death?* Gregory had not known him to be a cold man, but under the circumstances was there any other choice than the latter?

On an entirely different note, one of the captains might come strolling through the door. Perhaps they might recognize the councilman, and he could still talk his way out of his dilemma. It was the slimmest of chances, but he may be able to convince someone like Captain Olfred to release him. Gregory was confident the entire arrest could be explained as merely a misunderstanding. The guards carried out their duties, and after all, it was Gregory's fault for having been dressed so commonly. It was an error he would soon not forget.

The latter scenario could conceivably unfold only if one of the captains were to see him immediately. Yet, he risked another battering by his current guardsman, Trent. That was the dilemma. Gregory couldn't believe what he was about to do, but he rose and readied himself for further physical abuse.

He shuffled to the door and braced himself for the beating to come. With every breath, he gathered the necessary courage to call out to the guards beyond his door. He also used the moment to form the right words.

"Gentlemen! I wish to confess to your captain!" Gregory pleaded. "Please, sirs, I want no more of this abuse."

The footsteps echoed briskly down the corridor toward his cell. They halted outside the door, and Gregory quickly backed away with a speed he did not realize he still possessed, considering the pain he was in. He gritted his teeth to kneel slowly by the wall furthest from the door. He covered his head with his arms to protect against the inevitable assault.

Slowly, the key slid into the lock and turned, but two men entered instead of one. The first man approached but before he landed another step, Gregory winced and shouted, "I yield, sirs! I yield!"

"What did I tell you, scum!" Trent raised his club.

"I wish to be questioned by your captain, sirs!" Gregory shouted, bracing himself with every remaining fiber.

The blow never landed. Trent's arm was held in place by the other guard. It was a small victory; he had wagered well and might come through this nightmare.

"You want to confess?" the other guard asked. He sounded like the reasonable one, the ear that Gregory needed for his message to be heard.

"Yes, sir. Send for your captain, and I will answer all questions required of me," Gregory insisted. "You have me, gentlemen."

Trent lowered his club, slapping it into the palm of his hand with a smirk. "Well then, I suppose we'll get answers from this slime quicker than expected. No backbone in this one."

"Enough, we've got orders," the other guardsmen commanded. "We'll return soon and have this out." They departed without further belittlement.

Gregory gulped; he may have done it. He may have ensured his own freedom. The window drew his eyes again, and a sliver of hope revived him. This time, it was a joyous tear that came. He would wait patiently, prepare his excuses for the misunderstandings surrounding his arrest, and then he would press for his release. This dreadful event was almost over. He considered how he might turn this story to his advantage. Perhaps he would blame the lawlessness of the streets as a robbery attempt on his person.

The time passed and the guards came. When they entered, Gregory knelt and raised his hands in an effort to plead no resistance.

"Up with you!" The other guard commanded as each lifted him from under his arms.

He tried to move quickly as they pushed him forward, but his injuries prevented any speed.

Without warning, the guards lifted and carried him as his feet dragged across the ground, causing further cuts and scrapes to form. He would remember their carelessness, but he would not resist now.

He was hauled down the hallway and into a dark and windowless room. The only light that crept in came from the torches along the walls, and that was little still. Gregory was dragged to the middle of the room and thrown down. He let out a whimper in the silence; this he would remember, too. He had already yielded, and this inexcusable treatment was unwarranted.

He was so consumed by pain, he did not notice when they exchanged different chains on his wrists for those that hung from the ceiling. The guards completed their preparations of him in silence and left him at the center of the room. He was relieved no further beating came. Before they left the room, they brought a chair out and placed it several paces before him. He stared at the empty chair, mentally preparing for his opponent, but his thoughts were broken when a sound of a mechanism beyond his room clicked into place, and his chains above him retracted.

He grew with alarm once his arms were pulled apart. The chains strung him upward and he cried out as the searing pain shot through his ribs. He forced himself to stand to relieve the pain.

This was unnecessary. This was cruel. Who had come to speak with him? This was not how he planned to speak with Captain Olfred or any other Midguardmen. He prepared for the worst.

A door opened on the other side of the room, and a figure entered, obscured in the blackness. As she drew closer, Lady Alma's unmistakable figure emerged into the light and sat before him. Gregory took hold of his pain, his fear, and focused his senses.

He noticed she was wearing the very same gown when last he saw her. Gregory had not thought until that moment, but he surmised it was still the same day he was set upon; maybe the evening had just begun.

Her expression bore him no kind concern for his situation but rather looked determined to have answers. She folded her hands in her lap and stared at him.

He had seen her single-minded before on the council, among many matters, and was unsure if she would accept his excuses. Regardless, he would make every effort to plead to her known tenderness in hopes of sparing him. That was the key.

"My lady, please, I beg you! I have suffered a grave wound to my chest and this outreaching does it no good. I beg you, let them lower me," Gregory requested.

"Why should I spare you discomfort, Gregory?" Lady Alma demanded. "Why would you deserve such hospitality?"

Gregory weighed the question carefully. "My lady, I have been ever faithful to the realm, to you, and your husband. Please…"

She raised a finger, and a crack echoed a thousand times within the chamber as the whip struck him from behind.

He writhed in pain as the whip struck his back, which caused further uncontrollable contortion of his chest and further pain to his ribs. He thrashed in every direction to relieve the agony, but it did not relent. He was barely able to hear her call him over his own screams as he tried to gather his remaining strength and control the pain.

"Master Gregory. Master Gregory!" she repeated, waiting until his wails ceased. "I will not hear your excuses or lies this evening. I will have the truth from you. So, please refrain from manipulating the conversation as you so often do. Now, why were you at the tower?"

He was confused by the lady in front of him. She was without sympathy as he had known her to be. She was cold and far more direct than he had ever seen her. Furthermore, he had never thought her so capable of enacting violence on another. He would have to tread carefully.

"My lady, this is a misunderstanding," Gregory pleaded. "I assure you."

She nodded, and the whip cracked a second and a third time.

He cried out in agony, knotted, twisted, and thrashed about the open chamber but ultimately fell under his weight. The pain surged through his back to his legs as he was forced to endure it.

"I wonder what flesh can be stripped from you before you understand, Master Gregory. You are a man of comfort, and I gather you will be unable to endure long but know this..." Lady Alma sneered, pointing her finger. "... I will have the truth. If your tongue should flounder, then you will receive the lash. If you dance about the facts, you will receive the lash. Any obfuscation will be responded to with the lash. I will keep you under my house until you submit, and the truth is plainly laid out before me. I am the rock which you will break upon like the sea. Now, why were you at the tower?"

He writhed, but he managed to get his knees under him. The pain was ever present. His mind was without options for the situation at hand. All rested on his honesty, and he possessed no other alternative to present to her. He was unprepared for such a resolute lady. If he wasn't so consumed with pain, he would have also been thoroughly impressed. He regained what focus he could, and he confessed.

"I was informed there was a meeting." No whip came after he spoke. He was relieved.

The room was silent as Lady Alma examined Gregory and his answer. "What were you told of the meeting?" she demanded.

"I was informed of a meeting but was unaware of its contents," Gregory whimpered.

"A lie!" Lady Alma claimed. The whip lashed three times, and he flailed in front of her.

"I swear! I swear, Alma," he cried aloud, contorted by the lash.

She pursed her lips, thinking about his words while he recovered what he could. "I do not believe you were made unaware of the contents of the meeting. You are a man who loves gossip. You inquired! You were told something! You were informed! And you were paid, Master Gregory!" She poured the contents of his pouch onto the floor and the rubies he had been given scattered everywhere.

He should have stored them with his other valuables, but he didn't. He needed to keep these gems near, and now he regretted it.

"I was told there were traitors," he sobbed.

"Traitors!" she retorted as her fists clenched in anger.

"I was told someone was undermining the Mid's efforts."

He attempted to gauge her reaction, but the mere effort to raise his head taxed him. So, he waited while she answered.

"I'm to believe that you sought out a meeting of conspirators and their purpose was to somehow undermine the Mid. If that were the case, I should have you beheaded as a co-conspirator and a sympathizer."

"No, my lady! I was there to confirm what I was informed. I swear it by all the gods!" he earnestly begged.

She scoffed at the notion and held up her hand to keep the strike from falling. "You are without a spiritual bone in your weak body; spare the gods and me your prayers," she sneered as she waved him off. "I could find it reasonable you would investigate such a claim. However, I find it highly unlikely the details were as vague as you would have me believe."

"It was, my lady! It was!" Gregory interrupted her in hopes of sparing himself. "It was without merit, but I was asked to verify the meeting."

"By whom?" Lady Alma insisted.

Gregory had come to the one detail he hoped to conceal from her. He hadn't decided whether he would aid Master Wendall yet. There was much more of this mystery to uncover and, given his circumstance, he doubted if he would ever get the chance; the current conversation undeniably dictated the course of his future. He also considered himself a supreme confidante, but as the test presented itself, he could not hide the truth. He sighed as he took the moment to prepare his disclosure.

"Master Wendall, my lady," he shamefully admitted.

"Master Wendall?" Alma questioned. "He doesn't seem the type to be involved with such conspiracy. Nor is he conveniently available for cross-examination."

Now that he had breached Wendall's trust, he chose to reveal the entirety of it. It was far easier than the lash. "No, my lady. He spoke of traitors who were undermining the Mid. I did not know in what way, and he would not divulge it. He said he was eavesdropping and found out some plot but was forced to retreat. I swear it."

Moments passed without further question as Lady Alma paced the room. The chains jangled around Gregory as he strained to lift his head to look for her reaction, but he only found Alma deep in calculation of his words. By the look of her disposition, something he said irked her, but he had no idea what it was. So, he graciously waited. He considered her moments of reflection a blessing and relief from further torment.

"Why would he not divulge it?" she muttered.

Gregory briefly held his tongue to her remark, but he did not wish for more lashings. So, he chose to answer. "He said he was being followed, my lady. He said his life was in danger. He wished me to investigate the matter, and then wanted my corroboration."

"Corroboration?" she hissed accusingly as she turned back to him. "You were going to align yourself with Master Wendall in this?"

"No. NO!" he insisted. "He asked it of me, but I had not decided."

"Why?" she demanded.

"I didn't know if I wanted to aid him. I didn't believe him."

"No?" She questioned as she narrowed her eyes at him.

"No," he confirmed.

She scoffed as she waved him away like a pestering gnat. "You merchants are all the same kind of greedy men. You are probably more selfish than the rest, Master Gregory. I can always count on you looking out for your best interest. However, you've just revealed your indifference and disloyalty to my lord husband and to the Mid," Alma accused.

"No, my lady! I would not!"

"A lie!"

The whip struck four times, and Gregory cried and squirmed under each lash as the pain surged through him with every strike. He tried to assure himself he was revealing all the details, but the pain took all his concentration.

She waited patiently for him to recover himself. "You have told me that Wendall spoke of a treasonous meeting, and you had not decided if you would assist him and corroborate the treason of another. That means you put your self-interest above a colleague and, subsequently, that of the Mid," Alma accused.

"Yes!" he cried. He could take no more of the whipping. "I admit it." He had nothing now. He would likely be beheaded for being a traitor to the Mid. His property would be claimed by the state, and everything his family had built would be consumed by his competitors. Those were nothing compared to the loss of his family's name to history. All their accomplishments would be forgotten except only to be regarded as traitors.

"That is an honest answer. Sometimes I wonder how you could disregard your home and people so easily," she replied.

As she began to turn away to leave the room, he grew furious. He knew he was selfish. He admitted as much to himself. However, to be accused of disloyalty churned his stomach, and he became infuriated at such a claim.

"No!" he rebuked. He had not realized he could, but the pain subsided as he managed to defy his own punishment. He raised his head up and looked her squarely in the eyes. "I would have used him if I could, but I was not disloyal! I have never been disloyal! I set us to task! I mustered the common-folk! I sacrificed to push us farther! I did not betray the Mid!" he declared.

"To what purpose did you press? What toils have you endured on the realm's behalf? What would you have of the Mid?" she countered as she turned back toward him.

"I would have us rise!" Gregory stood in defiance of every pain, the blood-soaked and shredded clothes, and of the mysterious guard behind him. "I would have us step upon the world stage as a power among the realms! That is why I have fought. It is more than time that the Crest be unified and observed as it should be! So, when these raiders came, I saw an opportunity for us and steered us with all the devotion I commanded. I make no apology for it!"

"That I believe!" she replied as she pointed a finger at him with the same enthusiasm. "Gods, even your patriotism is perverted by your selfishness. The only way you could wave our colors is in pursuit of wealth and position and only if such devotion benefited you. You are a vain man, Master Gregory."

"Yes, I do what I must for the realm. On that account, I have no regrets," he maintained.

As he looked upon Lady Alma, he could see her interest. She was invigorated by his position; even captivated. And now she truly understood the depths of his aspiration.

"Leave us," she commanded as she slowly approached back into the light.

Gregory had no idea who had commanded the whip, but a moment later, the door behind him opened and closed. Gregory kept his attention firmly on Lady Alma. He had not expected this trajectory, but there was an inkling of hope her interest could be attended as she sat back down and stared at him.

"In the quiet moments between Lord Malcolm and myself, we have spoken about such an outcome. We've argued the merits and even the necessity of such a thing," she said.

Gregory held his breath. Lady Alma, nor her husband, had never spoken openly about ascendance. It was such a fragile notion.

"If all the folk under the shadow of the Crest were to unite, we would unbalance the scale. All the Crescent, with the Mid at the helm, would shake the power from across the realms. And if the Harbors were to come into the fold, we would claim the center of the world. However, this is still a dangerous proposal. We would be pinned between the horde and the bickering realms of the west. The different ideologies of the world already clash in our land, and if we were to seize the reins, we would become a border to a thousand disputes. Would we ever know peace?"

"We could," Gregory insisted. "We could command respect. That could guarantee our peace. And our diversity is not our crutch, but our advantage! Who could've assembled what we have? This war is uncertain, but the achievement we have mustered has been astounding. All the folks have responded to us like moths to the flame because one man commanded it and the respect of all. Lord Malcolm could emerge from these events as our King."

"Perhaps," she remarked.

She remained the stoic figure, but behind her indifference, her eyes widened slightly, and Gregory could see she contemplated the idea. And if she was interested, she had to know the depths of Gregory's allegiance and his purpose. "Who else could impact all the folk? Who else commands the respect of so many different peoples as well as all the states bordering our lands and beyond? It has always been Lord Malcolm. This is what I have toiled for."

She returned her eyes to him as cold as ever. "This is all very academic, though. It is a convenient thing to preach loyalty while chained underfoot. What other path lies available to regain the realm's trust and, in turn, your freedom?" she challenged.

"About this, I would never lie."

"You would not?"

"Never!"

"Then who did you find when you arrived at the meeting of the tower?" she asked.

He contemplated lying for the briefest moment, but he gained a greater understanding of Lady Alma as well. She was as firm a figure as her husband. Perhaps even more so, and he was intimidated by it. Her will was as much of a match as the stoutest man, and she commanded a ruthlessness about her. Even Gregory struggled to look upon her when his turn came. The blood and gore of it did not sit well with him.

She, on the other hand, did not look away. She faced him boldly regardless of how damaged he was and demanded the truth.

"You," he whispered as he lowered his eyes.

"And who else?" she demanded.

"Hector."

"Yes, you did," she responded. There it was... the truth.

He was unsure what it had gained him, but he had divulged it as she commanded. He would have spared her if he could, but she was more than adequately prepared to hear it.

"Where does that leave us, Master Gregory?"

"I don't know, my lady," he gasped. How could she let him go free now? They may have shared an understanding that night, but her trust was breached. It was easier for Gregory to traverse a desert, barefooted and without water than to repair this confidence.

"Do you know why I've met with Hector?" Lady Alma inquired.

It was an odd question. He did not want to divulge any further assumptions and thus tighten the noose. Yet, it delayed the inevitable sentencing that was to come.

"I had many notions, but I dare not share them," he admitted.

"I imagine you would contemplate. You're a clever man, Master Gregory. My patriotism is not unlike yours, distorted from the truth of things. It is no secret Malcolm and I have wanted a child for some time. However, we've been denied. I do not know if the gods have cursed us, but I would give all that I have to give my husband a child. I would sacrifice everything I hold dear for that purpose. I would even suffer Hector to do so," Alma admitted as a single tear escaped her eyes and ran down her cheek.

Gregory, shocked, held his breath. He had assumed wrongly about her. Her devotion could span an ocean; his own loyalty paled in comparison. It shamed him. He had been wrong about many inferences upon this grand conspiracy, and he wondered what other false assumptions he had made.

"That is why you have found me," Lady Alma continued. "You understand me, and I understand you, but I do not understand Master Wendall."

Gregory's ears perked up. The wheels of his mind turned over every morsel of information Wendall had exposed to Gregory. He thought he understood him, but perhaps there was more to uncover.

"I had no man follow Wendall and I know for certain Hector had not as well."

"How could you know that?" Gregory contested.

"Hector has as much to lose as I, and he would have told me he suspected our secret was exposed. However, he did not, and I did not either until your capture was revealed to me this day. That is why I know we did not follow him. In fact, Hector knows nothing of this meeting. The ones who do are unaware of the identity of the man in this cell. Your face has been thoroughly mangled."

"If he was not followed..."

"It was a lie," Alma calmly reported. "Not yours, but a lie. So, why would he lie, Gregory? I do not understand Master Wendall in this. Or would you consider him a paranoid man?"

Gregory had no answer. Wendall came before him, practically pleading for his aid. Gregory suspected everything as it was divulged, and the conclusion led to him here and now. *Was this planned?* He grew furious.

"Why would the man enlist your help under false context, Master Gregory? Very little has ever stopped any of the councilmen from ousting another regardless of the collateral damage, but does he believe I had committed treason?" She scoffed at the notion. "Perhaps, but tell me this. How has my infidelity truly kept the Mid from her duties or subverted her purpose? It has not. This is also a lie. In fact, I swear to you that I have used Hector for one purpose alone and that is to help me produce an heir. We have neither spoken nor do I intend to supplant my beloved husband. So, I do not understand this false pretense and why you've been sent to inquire about it. However, I am resolved to find out." She stood again with her mind fixed on the task but stopped a moment to assess Gregory in his chains. He recoiled.

"I imagine you would want answers as well. I imagine the most pressing question you have is about your death," Alma mused. "A betrayal has occurred, Gregory! Was it against Malcolm, the Mid, or was it you? You should think long about this because justice demands balance upon the scales."

He had much to consider being chained below the keep, Wendall had much to answer, and Lady Alma had almost hinted that he might somehow get those answers. Hope rose in him. *Was the impossible about to happen? Would he be set free to ascertain the truth of it?*

"My lady, I would scour the earth to get you answers!" Gregory declared.

"I know you would. You would do anything under the circumstances to retain your freedom, your position, and your business. I am counting on it."

"I would."

"The price for your freedom is loyalty, Master Gregory! Unwavering and unfettered loyalty! It must be selfless. That is my price!"

He was taken by her. Even he was subject to the patriotic fervor, and she expertly wielded it as he had on the podium in the square. It didn't matter how it was managed, this was the route back to his freedom and, possibly, status. She had been cruel and brutal. She extorted his weakness. Yet, he had chosen her side.

"I swear it!" he declared. "I will find Master Wendall, my lady. You will have your answers."

"No," she maintained. "You will remain here until he returns. I will arrange the meeting, and you will get his confession here!"

Every hope he had about his prospects sank. He should have expected this. *Had he just been condemned?*

"My lady, what if he dies in battle?"

"Then we will never know the depths of his motivation, and I will be forced to dispose of you," Alma disclosed. "Understand me fully, Gregory. Your salvation lies with his admission. If he survives, I will arrange the meeting, and you must make his intentions known. You should think of your words wisely. You are good at that."

She turned away from him and strolled into the shadows. She looked as if she contemplated every course and action as she faded from the firelight.

Lady Alma of the Mid had outmaneuvered him magnificently, and Gregory understood the conditions of his release. This would be his only means back to the light; he even considered it fair under the circumstances.

Moments after she left, the tension of his chains was released. He would remain a prisoner but would be granted some small comfort after all. It was a mercy to Gregory that he was grateful for it. She was right. He could do only one thing now. So, he began planning the interrogation in his mind while a notion of his impending death was ever present.

Chapter XX
The War Plan

The corpse looked nothing like Lorcan's people. This unfortunate man wore a black robe over a fine set of light armor that was smithed from the western cities. A black mask covered his face and a red emblem of a fractured triangle upon his chest clearly marked the order of his sorcerous circle. This man was a disciple, and he lost his life to a deep slash from his chest up to his neck.

Cal had seen Yslanna deal this same cut to many enemies during the battle at the main road; it was fatal to every one of them. The dead man's sword had dropped on the ground near his body, but he had another item clutched in his hand.

It was a twisted rod of black steel and leather. At the head was a fragmented shard of serrated glass and stone. They had forged Dhula into a scepter, and the disciples wielded her power. Cal gasped as realization struck him... there were fifteen other scepters somewhere among the Crestwood!

Alec shouted, but Cal wasn't listening. He removed the scepter from the grasp of the dead man. The shard shimmered in the sunlight from the dark jade glass to the black stony outer shell. Cal had his proof.

The sorcerer was the key to this mystery. Cal suspected Alec knew as well. They knew where the sorcerer was roughly located, and he had in his possession the largest shard... the stone that never fades. If they could find the sorcerer and destroy the stone, they could end this war once and for all! As Cal pondered, Alec came running toward him with haste and anger.

"Are you mad?" he yelled.

Cal tore his attention from the scepter to Alec. He had never seen his friend so livid.

"Did you not listen? It could be dangerous to touch! The power within it might be unstable!"

"I didn't touch it, they made a scepter out of it. This is how they're able to bring about the darkness! This is the evidence we need," Cal urged.

Alec sighed in relief as Cal produced the scepter by the handle. Most of the scouts soon gathered around Cal to look at the source of power. Some feared it; others looked upon it in awe.

"You frightened me, my young friend! The extent of this magical item is unknown, and I feared the worst for a moment," Alec admitted, panting from his sprint.

Alec examined the evil-looking scepter; its design was ingenious and terrifying. Any man could carry the shard now, but he did not know if anyone could summon Dhula's power. "Give it a wave," Alec directed.

Cal's enthusiasm over the recovery of the shard quickly turned to unease. Eris arrived with their young captive and Lorcan's eyes immediately darted to the shard. He collapsed to his knees in prayer as he cupped his hands to his head.

Cal almost forgot the stone was a god to his folk. It was strange to hold such a thing in his hands.

"Are you sure?" Cal questioned.

Alec's fascination had turned into determination. "Yes, I must know the limits of this magic," Alec exclaimed.

Cal didn't exactly know what he meant, but a knot in his stomach formed. He mustered his courage and held the scepter above him; with a wave of his hand, several scouts gasped. However, to his eyes, nothing came from the shard.

The wind blew as it did and the branches swayed in the breeze, but nothing else happened around them.

Alec looked back and forth between the rod and Cal, unsure of the results.

"Would you relinquish the scepter to Halden?" Alec asked.

Cal hesitantly held out the scepter to Halden, who nervously accepted it.

"Now you, my friend," Alec directed.

Halden's eyes widened at Alec's request. "You must be joking."

"I must be sure," Alec urged.

Halden took a deep breath and jerked the rod into the air.

Several scouts jumped behind bushes and trees, including the giant Clydes. However, that was the extent of the commotion. The shard remained the same, and there was no difference in the forest.

Alec was bemused, but not undeterred. "May I?" Alec asked, holding his hand out to Halden, who immediately surrendered the scepter.

Alec examined it like the most studious apprentice. He studied the reflection of the glass, the edge of the shard, and the leather wrapping around the stone. With a deep concentration and a flick of his wrist, the shard beamed into life, and a cloud formed all around them, not dark and ominous, but gray and thick.

A moment later, a fat raindrop landed on Cal's forehead as he looked upward in awe. It was Dhula. It was real! The cool beads of water ran down his face as he closed his eyes and embraced the magic surrounding him. Those who doubted could no longer. Even Jacoby stood confounded.

When Cal looked down, he found Lorcan with his cupped hands full of water; the young man was beaming with pride. This was the god the boy spoke of with such reverence. He drank deeply from his hands and smiled. At that moment, Cal believed everything he had told him.

Alec brought the scepter down, and the clouds receded. Sunlight once again penetrated through the forest and landed on the forest floor.

"Interesting!" Alec exclaimed, peering at the scepter. "Perhaps only those who possess the gift can manipulate the shard. I also believe no harm could come from touching it, but that is a test for another day."

"Only the worthy are able to hold and influence Dhula," Lorcan maintained to Alec.

"Your inference is flattering; I know of priests who have argued the opposite of me," Alec stated as a matter of fact.

"Perhaps you're a little of both, Alec," Cal joked.

A smile returned to Alec for the first time since the night he had met him. "This stone is unlike anything I've come across. An ancient and powerful magic is embedded in the core of this shard despite being separated from the whole. This magic is also augmented by the one who wields it."

"How do you mean?" Halden asked.

Alec removed a worn knife from under his cloak. "This is a knife. I use it to cut mutton, among other things. However, a bandit might use it to threaten or worse. Yet, this blade cannot become sharper or deadlier based on the intentions of the wielder," Alec explained, then bringing the scepter forward. "On the other hand, the shard is enhanced by the user and reflects my will or my essence. I ask for Dhula to show herself to us and the result is a cool cloud and rain upon a warm midmorning. If an evil man with my gifts stood in my place, I could only guess what powers might be twisted; it would be terrible to behold. It is a strange kind of magic."

Cal understood what Alec meant. The disciples took their power, manipulated the Vechians, and attacked the Crescent realm. And behind all of them was a sorcerer who held the final piece of Dhula somewhere atop the long slopes. *Why wouldn't he be among his disciples?* Cal wagered the sorcerer was there for a purpose.

"Pack everything," Cal ordered. "We ride to report what we've found." No more words needed to be given, and the scouts began tearing their camp down.

However, Alec remained by Cal's side as the others quickly got to work. "And what direction would you have us travel, my young friend?" Alec whispered outside of earshot.

"You're right about this scepter, but I think we should go after this sorcerer, Alec," Cal confessed. "In the wrong hands, some men are capable of awful things with this kind of power, but I think there is more to what Lorcan told us."

Alec nodded in agreement as he stood in thought. "Go on!" he urged.

"We have one scepter and there are fifteen other shards. We must assume they've made scepters out of all of them. Except the last piece!" Cal explained. "Why isn't the sorcerer here? Why does he sit on top of the Slopes like a vulture? I don't know why, but he has in his possession the last shard and it never fades in power. If he covets and protects the last shard, then it is vitally more important than all the others put together. He must be confronted, Alec."

A satisfied smile spread across Alec's face. "You know, you are a bright young man and, of course, correct," Alec said, beaming with pride. "This sorcerer is the fulcrum of this quest. But it must be reiterated, with the base-stone and his other gifts, I cannot begin to guess what powers he possesses."

Cal understood; this course was more dangerous than any other and taking it was likely trudging toward their death. "I won't make anyone go... volunteers only," Cal gravely stated.

"Oh, I have no doubts about our companions' resolve," Alec reassured. "They will follow you, my friend. As will I. I am only sorry that we led them to such a foe."

Cal was still apprehensive to ask. He didn't want to see his friends die.

"I am glad you are with us, Alec. I don't know if this quest of ours could be accomplished without you. You have been my guide on this endeavor, and regardless of the outcome, I am glad we are sharing this road," Cal said, placing a hand on the old man's shoulder.

"You flatter me too much, my friend. It is more than my abilities alone. I can feel it in my bones," Alec replied, waving at their party. "There is a bond between us that I cannot explain. It is like a magic aura pulsating among us; it binds our path and strengthens our skills. It is like threads woven together to make a tapestry. I sensed something special when I met you and when the party gathered, the feeling multiplied. This ember within my soul feeds my courage to press on toward this challenge. So, let us be off then."

As Cal listened, he almost knew what the old man meant. It was like several creeks merging into a raging river; they were all made better together.

It was decided, at least between the two of them. Somehow, they would travel north and locate the sorcerer among the Slopes. Alec patted Cal on the back, handed him the scepter, and helped break the camp.

They left before the midday sun reached its height; there was enough time to return to the Trouthavens without fear of sunset.

During their travel, many spoke openly about the morning's revelations. Of what Cal overheard, many couldn't deny what Lorcan had disclosed and what they saw from the scepter. And the question everyone asked was: what will the Midguard do?

They arrived at the Trouthavens and were met by thankful soldiers that the famed party had returned. As the scouts passed through the gates, they received word of the other scouting parties; two of the five groups had not yet returned.

Of the returning groups, one group returned with only ten of the twenty men; they had faced similar enemy patrols and had won. The other group had defeated their enemy as well. However, only four of the volunteers survived their own fight. Neither of those groups had discovered anything of the enemy or their power.

Where a hundred men had left the day before, a little over thirty returned. Cal's heart sank upon hearing the news of the other parties. He had sent all those men to the forest, and a handful returned. He understood why his fellow soldiers rejoiced upon seeing their return; everyone needed a little hope.

The party split upon returning to the encampment. Cal, Alec, Halden, and Jacoby rode to meet with Lord Malcolm. Jacoby insisted he go to meet the Lord with them. Perhaps he wanted the chance to give his opinion on the report, but Cal wasn't concerned. Jacoby would find it difficult to argue against the facts with what he had seen.

Yslanna and Eris returned to the cavalry with their captive. As the party split, Cal's thoughts turned to Lorcan. He didn't know what would become of him, but he knew they had brought Lorcan to a dangerous place. Hundreds of soldiers gazed at him with contempt.

Those prejudiced soldiers didn't know the facts; Lorcan's people were bewitched and misled. Cal could no longer blame the Vechians for the raids no matter how much anger he carried. There was only one thing to do; he had to let Lord Malcolm know what they discovered.

The real enemy was someone else altogether; someone secreted along the long ridge, perhaps orchestrating this invasion from a distance and Lorcan had an idea where.

An entirely different thought struck Cal. *What if Lorcan could lead them to the sorcerer? Wouldn't that assistance help clear the tainted Vechian name?* Cal knew what to do. For now, Lorcan was safe with Yslanna and Eris, away from anyone who would do him harm.

Cal, Alec, Halden, and Jacoby arrived and entered Lord Malcolm's hut. There, he presided over his war council. Lord Malcolm, Sir Pavel, Sir Kenneth, and Master Wendall surrounded the long table of the hut. They stared at an unraveled map of the Crestwood and shuffled tokens across the map as if their tactics would win this conflict, but they didn't understand the reality.

This was an entirely different war. Their enemy wasn't commanded like that of Lord Malcolm's army; the Vechians wouldn't travel, set up camp, or strategize their movements. They were manipulated by the disciples who would wait for the opportune moment to unleash waves of possessed men under the cover of darkness. All they needed was a sign.

Then Cal realized their predicament. Despite his efforts to keep Vechians from getting away when they were attacked, the other scouting parties had failed in their traps. The enemy knew the cavalry was somewhere near. They would be back in the area in force and ready to strike. Soon they would have to battle. Cal needed to convince Lord Malcolm to end the sorcerer; it was the only way to stop him.

Malcolm looked up as the party entered the hut and smirked upon their arrival as if he had known they would succeed. Cal took a deep breath at the remaining men surrounding the table. He needed rational minds to prevail, and Sir Kenneth tended to act irrationally at Alec's instigations as well as Master Wendall's. Cal hoped since his time away, the old knight had come to his senses and some sense of civility could be had.

"What news arrives from the Crestwood?" Sir Pavel said, gushing as he greeted and shook all the hands of the party.

Sir Kenneth remained stone-faced but was not unhappy with their return.

"A messenger just informed us of your arrival! I am incredibly pleased you survived your evening among the woods," Lord Malcolm said, greeting each party member behind Sir Pavel.

"As are we, my lord," Cal replied.

"Well then, do not keep us waiting. Tell us of your success!"

Cal tried to keep it brief, but there was much to tell. Alec provided much-needed details upon the retelling. Their story was met with skepticism from the beginning. There were tens of thousands of people who lived among the northern mountains, and they possessed an unknown power in the realm. They became enslaved to it by way of the sorcerer and his disciples; then they had laid waste to Crescent realm.

Most were receptive except Sir Kenneth. Even Master Wendall requested more specifics from them, and Cal answered. Yet, when Sir Kenneth outright refuted them, Cal removed the scepter from beneath his cloak, handed it to Alec, and Sir Kenneth froze.

With some hesitation, the old man took the scepter and showed them. He took a breath, held the scepter out, and in an instant the shard came to life. Clouds formed around them in a massive bank in and outside the hut during the waning daylight. Rain pelted against the roof of the hut as everything became hidden in obscurity.

The darkness had just formed at the center of their camp. Outside the hut, chaos erupted in the encampment as soldiers raised the alarm and frantically armed themselves. Everyone from within the hut rushed outside to see it around the camp; it was everywhere. The noble men were astonished.

The party had done it. They had recovered the power of the darkness and brought it back to the Lord of the Mid. A moment later, Alec lowered the scepter and the cloud dissipated.

"Calm yourselves!" Sir Pavel shouted as the cloud dissolved around them. Once again, everyone could see each other, and hundreds of nearby soldiers had haphazardly surrounded the headquarters prepared to rescue their lord.

Sir Pavel left the council to regain order in the encampment. "It is not here! Calm yourselves! Go back to your supper," he commanded. They were all befuddled.

"That is what I was hoping to avoid," Alec murmured.

Cal grinned. "They needed to see," Cal reassured.

Lord Malcolm, Sir Kenneth, and Master Wendall returned inside. Lord Malcolm and Sir Kenneth were without words, and Master Wendall looked deep in thought.

"This is how the disciples were able to create the darkness," Cal declared as he took the scepter from Alec. "We think there are fifteen other scepters in the Crestwood, but the last shard, the base of this shattered stone, is atop the Slopes! That is the source of the power, where the sorcerer is and where we must go!"

Malcolm crossed the hut and sat in his chair. He rested his chin on his clasped fingertips and dwelled in thought. The silence was so deafening that Sir Kenneth broke away from his own mental calculation to gauge what direction Lord Malcolm was considering.

"We cannot give chase across fifty leagues without incurring thousands of losses," Sir Kenneth chimed.

Cal knew he would disagree with any recommendation Cal or Alec made.

"I wholeheartedly agree," Master Wendall added as Sir Kenneth looked uneasy at having his concurrence.

"I know it is a difficult request," Alec interjected. "We recognize the dangers, but to attack solely against the forces now with their advantage has repeatedly proven to be costly. We must attack the source. Any other course prolongs our engagement; in the end, it will cost many lives."

"It is not simply a matter of attacking them here. Nor am I advocating for such a thing. We cannot risk marching our forces over that distance without being set upon repeatedly until our forces are decimated into remnants of nothing," Sir Kenneth rebutted as he positioned himself back to the long table.

"If you do not think we can take the fight to this sorcerer and we should not attack, then what do you advise, Sir Kenneth?" Lord Malcolm queried as he raised his head from his contemplations. Sir Kenneth reviewed the map of the Crestwood.

"This position is very defensible. These hills are formidable, and their numbers coming through the narrow roads will mean little if we can keep them funneled," Sir Kenneth insisted.

"How will you encourage them to commit to such a frontal assault?" Alec asked.

"You said it yourself. These folk are under some enchantment by these disciples. These aren't military men, I take it, and they have committed themselves without mercy against us. We have already tipped them off that we are somewhere here. I'll wager they will commit themselves to wiping us out if we lead them to within these hills. And then, their power will be useless against a long wall of shields and spears."

Cal's stomach dropped. "You would lure ten thousand folks to their deaths?" he demanded.

"We recovered a boy among fighting women and men. They're just plain folk," Halden pleaded.

"It would be genocide against their people," Alec stressed.

"I do not make my recommendation lightly," Sir Kenneth maintained. "And I grieve with you. Thousands will die but look at the alternative. The scouts lost more than half their number the night prior. We cannot sustain these losses! The possessed enemy will continue to fight until we have disposed of every scepter in their possession or until we've all been killed."

Silence took hold within the hut. Cal hated to admit it, but Sir Kenneth spoke truth. There was no right course; Cal wanted the Crestfolk to see peace again, but not at the expense of massacring another.

"I understand your concerns, gentlemen, but Sir Kenneth makes a good argument," Lord Malcolm added. "I take no pleasure in this course of action against folk who are outside their minds. However, as you and Sir Kenneth have both stated, we cannot march boldly north without heavy losses. That would play into their hands, and we've already seen it on the main road and as you have described in the traps," Lord Malcolm said, concurring with Sir Kenneth.

"We would be fools to not use that to our advantage and draw them into an impenetrable defense. Once we have whittled their numbers down and we have removed these scepters from these disciples, then we can go after this sorcerer. It will be a bloody day, but it will not be the Midfolk's or the Crestfolk's blood."

There was almost nothing to refute. Cal also wanted his people to come through this struggle as unharmed as possible. Yet, he could not stand by and let the Vechians be slaughtered. He wasn't afraid to fight, nor was he afraid to defend himself against a swarm of enemies. He just couldn't be a part of a massacre.

"Perhaps it would be beneficial to venture into the hills and survey every point of access to us. We will want to prepare for every possible attacking point if we are to succeed. I would be happy to make the assessments myself," Master Wendall offered.

"Our maps are sufficient, Master Wendall. I would not seek to waste your time," Lord Malcolm said, shaking his head.

"May I have your leave to pursue the sorcerer myself? I will also need the captive Lorcan as my guide," Cal insisted.

The hut fell silent, and they stared at Cal in disbelief... everyone except Lord Malcolm. He looked at him with admiration. He rose from his chair, walked over to Cal, and put his hand on his shoulder. Cal felt little comfort staring back at the Lord of the Mid with want in his eyes, hoping his request would be granted.

"Sergeant Cal, you are an honorable man. You have assisted me and both our folks more than I can repay. In fact, I am convinced the gods have blessed you on your journey; I would be remiss to go against their will," Lord Malcolm emphasized. "However, I have no doubt the enemy are gathering around us; I would grieve if you were to succumb to your death by my allowing such a passage. I cannot grant it. I could use you and your companions here."

"But you would grant the deaths of thousands of these Vechians?" Cal bluntly countered.

"Steady, Sergeant!" Sir Kenneth ordered.

Lord Malcolm raised his hand to Sir Kenneth, and he fell silent. Malcolm turned back to Cal, and the two men stared at each other; neither submitted.

"It is a fair question," Lord Malcolm admitted. "Yes. If it were a choice between our folk and theirs, I choose ours, Cal," Lord Malcolm said, squeezing Cal's shoulder lightly. He turned from him to return to the table where Sir Kenneth stood.

"That will be all, Sergeant. See yourself back to the cavalry," Sir Kenneth spat.

As Cal turned away to exit, he found Sir Pavel behind him, nodding as Cal and the other party members left the headquarters. They mounted their horses and continued to the other village where the remaining cavalry were camped.

As they rode, Cal's mind dwelled on the discussion. He understood their reasons, and he even accepted them. Yet, Bill's words echoed in his mind: he didn't want Cal to kill anyone unnecessarily, and Cal didn't want that either. Bill wanted Cal to do what was right, and there was only one way to save these people. Cal knew what he needed to do.

They arrived at their camp within a half hour. All around the camp, the cavalry was hard at work. Campfires were roaring, stews were boiling in pots filling the air with delicious aromas, and the fish sizzled in pans above the flames. They unmounted and assembled around their own campfire where his party had gathered for the evening. Lorcan was there, unharmed, and happy to see them return.

Cal stood and looked over them as they attended their supper and rested. This was his family now, bound together by this war. He dreaded what he was about to ask them. He needed to travel across hostile terrain, evade the enemy without being killed or seen, and then fight a sorcerer with abilities he couldn't comprehend and who would doubtless kill him. And he wanted them to help him.

Alec came beside Cal, placed a hand on his shoulders, and smiled. He was there beside him now, and he was going to be beside him when he faced the sorcerer. It gave Cal all the courage he needed.

"I have something to say," Cal declared. The party quieted themselves and gave him their attention. "The army will barricade themselves in these hills and lure the enemy into spear and shield alike until the Vechians no longer come or until they can't."

There was no reply except for Lorcan, who cried for his people.

"I cannot participate in the slaughter of an entire people. So, I won't," Cal said.

"You'd be going against your oath," Jacoby pressed.

"Maybe. Maybe not. I'm going north," Cal admitted. "I can only see one way to save their people and stop the bloodshed... or at least as much as possible."

"Talk sense into him, Alec! It's suicide," Jacoby urged. "You heard Lord Malcolm. You're talking about getting past a thousand possessed killers."

"It's much worse, I'm afraid," Alec replied. "Yes, we'd have to go against Lord Malcolm's wishes, but we would also face a foe who is powerful beyond our perception. Yet it is a necessary path to take."

"You mean to tell me you're with him? You're both mad as hatters!" Jacoby remarked.

"No one is obliged to come, but everyone here would be gladly welcomed," Cal said, turning to face Lorcan. "Lorcan, I ask that you join us."

Lorcan was taken aback, even concerned about what they were proposing. "What do you mean?" he asked.

"I need you to guide us to the sorcerer, and maybe we can rid your people of Dhula's corruption," Cal replied.

Lorcan needed little time to reflect. He nodded to Cal's request with tears in his eyes.

"What say the rest of you?"

"I'm with you," Halden responded without hesitation.

"When do we leave?" Yslanna said as she and Eris stood.

Clydes stood and swatted his massive hands against his chest twice. Cal needed no interpretation to know the giant would come with them.

Jacoby, however, stood alone. "I can't do this, mates," he admitted. "I'm glad to serve alongside you, but this is too much."

Cal wasn't upset. He was pleased just to have the others come with him. "Can I ask a favor of you then?" he asked.

"Anything except to come," Jacoby stipulated.

"Don't tell them we've gone until morning."

Chapter XXI
The Deserters

By night's end, the war council agreed on a plan. Sir Kenneth and the cavalry would engage the possessed Vechians until the enemy pursued them down the five narrow roads leading to an impregnable defense. The enemy forces would be severely crippled.

Lord Malcolm pored over the map and considered the strategy long after the young Sergeant Cal had left for the evening; this approach outweighed every other course. With their magic and scepters, simply attacking the enemy was out of the question; their numbers were too great, and they inflicted far too many casualties. They also considered targeting the disciples to break the enchantment. However, it was impossible. They were among the darkness and no doubt well protected. A single decisive battle was the only option to end the hostilities quickly and preserve the lives of their own folk.

After the council had finished, Sir Kenneth returned to the northern village. At dawn, the army would be put to work digging trenches, cutting down trees, blocking gaps, and funneling village entrances into a barricade of walls and pikes.

Sir Kenneth, pleased with himself, eased into his sleep. This would be the beginning of the end of the entire debacle. Enough good Midguardmen had died, and this sorcery was getting out of hand. It needed to be snuffed out and never reignited. First, they would dispose of the disciples, and then the sorcerer would be hunted and killed.

The whole thing would be wrapped up apart from the vagrant, Alec. He was an irritation even before he could wield these new abilities. Now, there was no conceivable future where Alec did not become a danger. *What would stop him from using it against the Midguardmen, Sir Kenneth, or the Lord of the Mid himself?* Sir Kenneth wouldn't allow it; he would see Alec jailed or killed before he threatened the Mid. The scepter in Sergeant Cal's possession would also need to be removed.

Yet, it could wait. The evening was late and no one suspected anything. Sir Kenneth would bring order to this chaos once and for all.

***

Sir Kenneth woke early and sent for his captains and sergeants. There were few left among the entire cavalry. None felt the loss more than he. He had trained his Midguardmen for years, and in a single night many were snuffed from this world. Unfortunately, now was not the time to mourn them. A battle loomed; he needed to replace the fallen and get to work.

Within minutes, Captains Willem and Dietrich arrived, as well as Sergeants Foust, Roache, Nedry, Devon, and Ellaine. Sergeant Cal was absent; this was the last straw. The young sergeant had some promise when Sir Kenneth met him, but he was as defiant as his companion Alec. It was time to remove him. Sir Kenneth would strip him of his rank, make him hand over the scepter, and order his party to guard duty. He had no more patience for rebels, vagrants, and scouting parties.

"Captain Willem, send for Sergeant Cal and have him come here immediately!" Sir Kenneth ordered.

Willem scratched his head and shuffled his feet. "I can send riders after them, but I don't think they'll find them until midafternoon, sir," he replied.

Sir Kenneth gaped in confusion, and then he sprang from his seat. "When did they leave?" he demanded.

"Right after supper, sir."

"You let them leave in the dead of night?"

"They said you ordered them to scout north for the missing parties, sir. I had no reason to hold them!"

"You idiot!" Sir Kenneth snapped. He stomped to his horse, mounted, and spurred the beast into a gallop toward his lordship's camp. He'd had it with Sergeant Cal and the rest of that treacherous party. They had gone too far and defied Lord Malcolm. The party would answer for the crime of desertion; one of them might even hang. Sergeant Cal was the obvious choice, but he preferred Alec; he'd poisoned the young man's mind from the very start. Alec would not escape justice this time. Lord Malcolm would finally see the mutiny of it all.

"It was very convincing, sir!" he heard Captain Willem yell as he galloped away.

Sir Kenneth arrived at Lord Malcolm's village and found the defenses well in hand. He grew angrier, knowing he should be attending to the defenses of his own village. The mutinous behavior was costing him precious time, which made the offense even more grievous.

He arrived at his Lord's headquarters, exhausted. His pulse throbbed and his vision blurred. He had not ridden so vigorously since the battle along the main road; it was clear he was not fully recovered from his wounds.

"Are you alright, Commander?" Master Wendall inquired. "You look flushed, sir. Shall I retrieve a healer for you?"

"No! I must report to Lord Malcolm," Sir Kenneth grumbled, trying to hide his condition. He grew frustrated that his wounds weren't recovering as quickly as he desired. It would not do for a knight and a commander of the cavalry to collapse or faint. He drank slowly from his waterskin and let the cool water quench him. The moment of pause helped. He dismounted slowly, always keeping one hand firmly on his saddle. He took a deep breath and walked into the hut with Master Wendall following eagerly behind.

"My lord, Sir Kenneth and Master Wendall," Sir Pavel announced as Lord Malcolm turned to greet him.

"Sir Kenneth, Master Wendall, good day to you both. What news brings you to me this morning?" Lord Malcolm asked.

"Sergeant Cal and his party have deserted us!" Sir Kenneth announced.

Lord Malcolm froze and stared. His unrelenting gaze fell on Sir Kenneth as if the blame was his.

"I know the man was passionate, but I didn't think he would desert us now," Sir Pavel commented. "How could this have happened?"

"How, indeed?" Malcolm repeated coldly.

"He convinced our guards I had sent him to look for the missing scouting parties," Sir Kenneth explained.

"Oh, I understand how he could have ridden past our gates! I mean, how could you not take extra precautions after last evening?" Lord Malcolm fumed as Sir Kenneth fell silent. "I thought at the very least you would have had someone watch over him, or the guards should have alerted you if anyone was to leave your village!"

"My lord..." Sir Kenneth began.

"No! I will not have excuses. We have lost good men this evening. And for what? A disagreement?" Lord Malcolm shouted. "Furthermore, Alec, whom I know we've had misgivings about, can fend off the darkness! We need his skill, gentlemen! And they have abandoned us?" Lord Malcolm slammed his goblet on the table, toppling several tokens on the map. The hut fell silent as he looked to each one of his advisers.

As his gaze landed on Sir Pavel, an epiphany struck him. "I think you are correct," Lord Malcolm uttered.

"My lord?" replied the grizzled Sir Pavel.

"What direction did they travel?" Malcolm asked, disregarding Sir Pavel's confusion.

"North, my lord," Sir Kenneth said, gritting his teeth.

Lord Malcolm grinned, looking back to Sir Pavel. "It appears they have not abandoned us after all."

"Gods, they could be dead already!" Sir Pavel commented as the realization came to him.

"My lord, they have deserted their posts!" Sir Kenneth emphasized. "Regardless of their intentions!"

"They ride against a vast enemy to kill a sorcerer and save a people. Some would call that valiant, sir," Lord Malcolm responded, turning back to Sir Kenneth.

"Valiant and seditious!" Sir Kenneth countered, pointing his finger. "This act of defiance could undermine all our efforts! What if half our soldiers were to decide they should join him? Could we stop them? They'd be lambs to the slaughter on the road, and our plan would be put into serious jeopardy, my lord."

Lord Malcolm was without words. He sighed and slumped into his seat.

Finally, Sir Kenneth had been able to make him see Cal and his party for what they were... reckless and now a liability.

"What do you advise then, sir?" Lord Malcolm demanded.

"I will ride out, retrieve them, and bring them back to receive due justice."

"I do not think it wise to send Sir Kenneth, my lord," Master Wendall interrupted.

"I don't think so either. Sir Pavel could very well be correct; they may already be dead. Besides, if they've survived getting through the enemy forces, their quest may very well be plausible. Furthermore, I don't want to endanger any more men if I can avoid it," Lord Malcolm replied bluntly.

"My lord, you misunderstand me. I should be the one to retrieve them," Master Wendall insisted.

Lord Malcolm was surprised, and Sir Kenneth was caught off guard.

"And why is that, Master Wendall?"

"Forgive me, Sir Kenneth. I by no means wish to wound you," Master Wendall prefaced, hoping to avoid any further conflict between them. "I wholeheartedly concur. Sergeant Cal's defiance against you may lead to mutiny. The soldiers must see him returned and subjugated to your commands, my lord."

"Gods, do both of you really think the army is so fragile they would rebel against us on the eve of our victory... their victory?"

"He is very popular, my lord," Sir Pavel agreed.

"Popular is one thing! However, the rumors surrounding them are almost mythical, my lord," Master Wendall emphasized, waving his hand in the air. "Their actions saved the cavalry along the main road; they survived the evening trap nearly intact and recovered the source of the darkness's power. Do you recall what you said to the young Sergeant the evening prior, my lord? Blessed by the Gods? The small folk often take these omens as reality. They will follow him!"

Lord Malcolm stood, walked to the hut entrance, and peered out at their camp and thousands of soldiers toiling at the siegeworks. He shook his head and turned back to his advisors as they followed behind. "You have little faith in our men. Sir Pavel's drills have been essential in forming this ragtag of men into soldiers. They march on command, raise their shields on command, and are eager to take back their homeland. And still, you haven't answered my question, Master Wendall. Why you and not Sir Kenneth?" Lord Malcolm pressed.

Master Wendall took a deep breath. "I mean no disrespect. However, Sir Kenneth has not fully recovered from his wounds," Master Wendall stressed.

Sir Kenneth grew angry, but not at Master Wendall. He grew angry because it was true. He had spent days resting where he could, but every great expenditure of energy took its toll on him, and Master Wendall had noticed.

"I admit my energy has been reduced. However, I have recovered enough and feel I am up to the task," Sir Kenneth countered.

"I wish not to press the matter, but I disagree, sir. You are still flushed from your ride," Master Wendall argued. "And if I may further add, I do not think you are the best candidate for this assignment at any rate."

Sir Kenneth's temper flared. It wasn't enough that the scouting party argued with him about every course of action, but Master Wendall, who often criticized his tactics, now attacked his person.

"I am his superior! How in the world does that disqualify me?" Sir Kenneth spat.

"I mean not to offend, sir!" Master Wendall urged. "Sergeant Cal must be convinced to come back! His own defiance suggests he will take no further orders. A persuasive voice should go and convince him to return. I can be that voice, my lord."

"And if Sergeant Cal should refuse to come back? What then?" asked Lord Malcolm.

"If it comes to that, then we should take him and his party into custody as Sir Kenneth has so eloquently proposed, my lord," Master Wendall replied.

Lord Malcolm hung his head in thought as he rubbed his temples and walked back to his chair. "Why not let him make the attempt at the sorcerer? He risks the lives of half a dozen men. To retrieve his party, I should think at least double would be necessary, and we waste valuable time and resources, gentlemen," Lord Malcolm reasoned.

"To allow his quest to continue, noble as it is, is to welcome open defiance against you, my lord," Master Wendall countered bluntly.

Lord Malcolm exhaled a deep groan. It was the point that struck the truest. Lord Malcolm could not allow them to defy him now; it would weaken his power and authority among the realm and the world. Sergeant Cal's submission was as necessary to his rule as to the laws of his realm. Either Lord Malcolm had authority, or he did not, and Master Wendall was holding him to it.

"Sir Kenneth, I need you to continue to recover here and assist with our defenses," Lord Malcolm commanded.

"My lord?" Sir Kenneth replied, but Lord Malcolm waved a hand, and his next argument was silenced. He would not go.

"Master Wendall, take fifteen good men, ride out, and retrieve Sergeant Cal as expeditiously as possible. If you find him dead, report back to us swiftly."

"It will be done, my lord."

"And if you should come across the Vechians, do not engage with them!" Lord Malcolm stressed. "Return to us at best speed. I wish to preserve our men for the fight to come."

"As you say, my lord."

"And what of the men? Who knows the scouting party has ridden north?" Lord Malcolm inquired.

Sir Kenneth did not have a firm answer. Captain Willem had the watch the evening prior and another notion came to mind. No one knew their departure was irregular except the young Captain; it was a stroke of luck. Captain Willem was good, but at times he was a slow man. There was time to still ride out and curb misconceptions among the soldiers.

"Very few, my lord," Sir Kenneth assured.

"A few is enough that the men will undoubtedly think something is suspicious about their leaving," Lord Malcolm maintained.

"I know the men who let Sergeant Cal ride through the gates, my lord. They will accompany Master Wendall to retrieve them," Sir Kenneth insisted. "This will keep wagging tongues from spreading rumors, and I will assure the cavalry that their leaving was as ordered."

"Yes, that is very good," Master Wendall agreed. "They left; it was authorized. That should sufficiently keep this from unraveling. And you may even emphasize our miscommunication. Their lives may be in danger, and we need to retrieve our heroes. That sort of thing."

Lord Malcolm stared, unamused, at Master Wendall. "I don't like lying to our soldiers. This kind of thing breeds mistrust," Lord Malcolm insisted as Master Wendall looked uneasy about amplifying the falsehoods.

"However, I understand the need for the situation at hand. See it done," Lord Malcolm commanded and waved them away.

Sir Kenneth and Master Wendall left the hut immediately for the cavalry camp. The old knight took his time on his return trip, and Master Wendall trotted along, matching his speed.

The council had not gone exactly to plan, but the result would be the same; the party would be retrieved and justice would be done.

There would be no more defiance against Sir Kenneth and certainly none to be had against Lord Malcolm. The folk of this army would come to order.

However, it was evident Lord Malcolm favored the young sergeant. Only a small few would be punished, and the others would be spared. Lord Malcolm would show mercy; his sparing the few would, in turn, earn further respect among the small folk. If Sir Kenneth had his preference, he would see both the young sergeant and the old vagrant receive their due justice; a lashing for one and a noose for the other.

Sir Kenneth found the captains and sergeants still around his tent when he and Master Wendall arrived. It was the kind of behavior Sir Kenneth expected... good soldierly discipline. They were gossiping, but it wasn't too late to curb the rumors.

"My apologies, sir! I will retrieve the party at once," Captain Willem stammered as Sir Kenneth dismounted.

"That can wait a moment, Captain," Sir Kenneth commanded. He took a moment to form his words. Lord Malcolm was right; lying was an uneasy task for the unpracticed. He ground his teeth. "They are a clever party; I'm sure they have survived another night in the wild."

"No doubt at all," Master Wendall chimed as the tension broke among the remaining men. "To think that they spent another night in the cold and dangerous Crestwood when, in fact, a morning investigation was desired. I shall never forgive myself."

The men didn't hesitate to believe Master Wendall. He was as practiced as any man upon the council to speak all kinds of falsehoods.

Captain Willem hung his head. "My apologies, Master Wendall. I should have known better to let them go."

"Not to worry, Captain," Master Wendall assured. "You and I will collect them in a moment's time, and you will see no harm has been done to them."

It was done. All the soldiers could suspect was a minor miscommunication. There might be a few rumors, but there would be no one to corroborate the story.

"Now then! There is much to do and little time to waste. Captain Dietrich, you will oversee the breadth of the work while Captain Willem is off," Sir Kenneth commanded.

"As you command, sir."

"Sergeant Nedry, you and your men will see to the hills connecting our village to the southern Trouthavens. No man or beast should get past them. Cut down trees and create a barricade so it forces the enemy to attack our gates or those of the southern villages."

"It will be done, sir."

"Sergeant Foust, you have the hills east of this village. I see a gap along that ridge that must be closed."

"Yes, sir."

"Sergeants Devon and Ellaine are to attend to the roads leading to the gates. They should be riddled with as many stakes and spears as can be affixed. There will be no escape!"

The pair of sergeants nodded.

"Roache, your men have the guard today. Have your men stationed at the gates and patrolling the immediate area."

"Sir."

"We have already lost too much daylight. You have your orders. Get to work," Sir Kenneth reiterated. "Captain Willem, stay behind a moment longer."

The soldiers were set to task and departed; they understood the commands and followed them without a debate. That's how all who served were expected to respond.

Captain Willem did as well, but he looked frustrated; a minor byproduct of the whole unfortunate event. It was nothing that some small victory would cure and boost his own confidence.

"Captain Willem, I have further orders for you," Sir Kenneth began. "You will take the guards who let the scouting party pass last night and ten other loyal men and find Sergeant Cal and his party. If you find them dead, report back to us immediately."

"Dead, sir?" Captain Willem lamented.

"Do not think on it, Captain!" Sir Kenneth assured.

"And if that is the case, it is best not to worry the rest of the soldiers," Master Wendall added.

"I understand, sir. Mum's the word."

"Very good, Captain," Sir Kenneth continued. "You will follow Master Wendall's order to the letter, Captain."

"Of course, sir. Wouldn't dream otherwise," he exclaimed.

"I know, Captain, but I must be clear. If Master Wendall should order you to seize Sergeant Cal's party, you will obey," Sir Kenneth emphasized.

"Take them captive, sir?"

"Yes, do you understand, Captain?"

"Of course, sir."

"Not to worry, lad," Master Wendall assured as he patted the captain on his back. "It's only a precaution."

Captain Willem nodded as he left the pair of them.

Sir Kenneth knew he was a good lad who would follow his instructions implicitly and in a moment's time, the risk of discovery would be almost nonexistent. Sir Kenneth sighed with relief.

"And what task would you have of me, gentlemen?" A man called from behind Sir Kenneth and Master Wendall. He grinned as he leaned next to a wagon.

Sir Kenneth turned, and his stomach dropped. The man was one of the famous scouts. If he opened his mouth to anyone, it would ruin all their plans and risk further mutiny. Furthermore, he looked like a talker, and he grinned like a moneylender.

"Jacoby!" Wendall exclaimed. "This is a surprise, I must say. We were informed all the scouts left last evening. Any ideas as to where they may have gone?"

"I think you know where, Master Wendall," he replied, tilting his head.

Sir Kenneth wasn't amused. Jacoby would be the first to receive a thorough punishment if his flippant attitude continued. "You would do well to cooperate, soldier! Or you will find how unpleasant a lashing can be," Sir Kenneth threatened, pointing a finger.

Master Wendall turned to the old knight with a cautious look. "If you flog one of the famed scouts, then the game is up," Master Wendall whispered.

"Beg your pardon, sirs," Jacoby said, grinning as he interrupted them. "All I know is what direction they have traveled."

"How do you know which direction they traveled?" Master Wendall inquired as he turned back to Jacoby.

"Sergeant Cal was determined to go you know where and fight you know who. I didn't think he'd leave, much less without so much as a goodbye, but when I woke this morning, all my friends had gone off," Jacoby explained.

"And why did you not go, Master Jacoby?"

"I have my reasons, but the foremost is that it's a death sentence. Eight men against the possessed and some kind of sorcerer. No thanks, I said. I thought a good night's rest would do us all good, but Cal had other ideas, I suppose."

"A reasonable man. Perhaps you could assist me in retrieving them?" Master Wendall offered.

Sir Kenneth immediately guessed what Master Wendall was thinking.

"Perhaps I could, but is that the best use of my talents?" Jacoby asked.

Master Wendall was intrigued. "What other purpose would we have of a scout who clearly could be used for a scouting mission?" Master Wendall argued.

"Yeah, I could do that, but have you seen the entrance to this village?" Jacoby countered. The entrance had already been well fortified by Jacoby and Halden days earlier; it was extremely formidable.

"I have. It is a very robust defense."

"Well, I helped make that defense a reality. I helped set up the whole damn village when we arrived here, and you can vouch for me,

Master Wendall," Jacoby flattered. "I happen to like the plan, and I can help make it work."

"I see," Master Wendall uttered.

"You see, I'm the one you should have made into the sergeant. None of this business would have happened, and we would have been here, finishing this enemy off." Jacoby said, eyeing Sir Kenneth.

Master Wendall smirked at Jacoby. "Well, that is a simple matter. I'm sure Sir Kenneth could use a man of your leadership around the camp." Master Wendall smiled as he looked at Sir Kenneth.

Sir Kenneth remained stony-faced, but with a raise of his brow even he showed the slightest interest. Perhaps Jacoby was the kind of man he needed.

"I see you're short of quite a few Captains, and one of them is riding off to find Cal and them," Jacoby insinuated.

Sir Kenneth grimaced. "I could use a man of your talents, but I require commitment and loyalty!" he demanded.

"I can be counted on to follow orders. I mean... I'm here, unlike some other folk."

"Then you will assist in making these fortifications sound and you will say nothing as to why the other folk in your scouting party have left to anyone who asks, Sergeant Jacoby," Sir Kenneth commanded.

Master Wendall said nothing, but his brief nod showed he thoroughly approved of the maneuver.

"You know, Captain Jacoby has such a good ring to it," he mused. "He would be able to accomplish all that you require."

Sir Kenneth pursed his lips. "I think Sergeant Jacoby will have earned the title Captain once the enemy is broken," Sir Kenneth maintained as he held his hand out.

Jacoby's grin stretched from ear to ear. "So be it then," Jacoby said, shaking the knight's hand.

Chapter XXII
The Capture

The party rode furiously into the Crestwood. Once dusk came, they moved cautiously throughout the night. It was a careful pace; there was no room for error against the enemy. Yet, they had to risk it. In the morning, the Midguard would follow right behind them.

This was the only course of action Cal could see. If they stopped the sorcerer, the war would be over. If he failed, thousands of innocents would die. It was a difficult quest, an impossible quest, but it was the right one.

Cal didn't know how much time he had left to reach the Slopes and find the passage that led to the sorcerer. Lord Malcolm would need four or five days to fortify the villages... a week at the most.

Fortunately, Lorcan was with them, and his memories were returning to him. Cal, Halden, and Clydes knew the Slopes well enough that even a meager description might narrow the area to within a day's ride from the Fork.

They also possessed one of the scepters. Cal knew only what Alec had told him of magic, but he had a strange feeling it would be useful when they came across the possessed Vechians or even the sorcerer himself.

Their vigilance and patience paid off the first night. They found no presence of the darkness as they progressed north through the Crestwood. The moon lit the sky, and they climbed several trees to scan the canopy of the forest, but no darkness was sighted.

It was an eerie response to the scouting traps they had set the evening prior and the enemy losing one of their disciples. Cal took this as a good omen, and the party continued riding cautiously through the night.

At first light, they rested briefly, and Lorcan recalled more from the nightmarish memories that plagued him. As he stared at the rising sun, he revealed the possessed Vechians did not travel by day; they rested deep within the darkest recesses of the forest before every dawn.

It was a welcome revelation. The main northern road was theirs to use as they pleased during the day, and the Slopes could be reached in three days.

After their morning meal and a light doze by a few, they made for the main road and drove north. They were unhindered for the rest of the day by the enemy ahead of them and the Midguard who might be following behind. Cal knew the Midguardmen would be slow to track their party if they tried.

As they traveled north, Cal found himself in a familiar area. There was still a hard day's ride on the main road to get to the Fork, but Cal had visited this area on occasion; there used to be families along the road... families with homes. As they looked for lodging for the evening, they found one burned cabin followed by another; the enemy had done a thorough job. Cal avoided looking at the charcoal and ash. He suppressed his remaining anger and turned his thoughts to Bill. If he were still alive, he would believe in what Cal was doing. Even among the death, he would try to save the Vechians too.

There was little choice but to search deeper in the Crestwood for lodging. They came upon a stable an hour before sunset. It had been neglected for some time; it leaned slightly to the left and vines climbed along the walls. Yet, compared to sleeping on the cold ground, it was a luxurious estate.

The party forced the door open and settled for the night. After the horses were stabled, one stall remained for the party. The air was stale, and it was slightly cramped for horse and folk alike, but they were concealed. They ate their provisions and took to their bedrolls while Cal and Clydes stood the first watch.

Two hours after the last light of the day had faded and the group of friends were peacefully asleep, the air grew heavy with the black fog as it trickled across the grounds outside the stable. They had come across the enemy.

Cal knew the meeting was inevitable, but he hoped to postpone it until they arrived at the Slopes. As the darkness crept slowly across the yard, he wondered if the enemy even knew the party was present. There was no sign the stable was occupied. All were still and soundless, with only the slight wheeze of the old man as he slept. *What if they had passed by this stable already a dozen times in their patrols? Why not one more?*

Cal shook his head. It was too risky; the party needed to be ready in the event the evening turned sour. He turned to wake up the others, and he found Clydes, still as a gargoyle, hovering at the door, ready to strike with his war hammer. Cal held a finger to his mouth in response, and let a light "shush" pass his lips. The giant nodded but held his position. Cal hurried to the stable where the others slept and shook them awake one by one.

"What is it?" Halden asked. Cal lightly shushed him with a serious gaze that everyone understood. Without a sound, each person began creeping toward the entrance, windows, and the broken slats along the walls to watch the darkness spread around them.

"What is the plan?" Eris whispered across the stable as Cal gazed out the window. "If we run, we'll have to fight our way out. If we hide and we're discovered, we'll still have to fight."

Cal cursed under his breath. He looked around the dark stable at his companions, but he could barely see any of them. Immediately, he knew what to do.

"Everyone hold! Do not loose any arrows!" Cal whispered urgently. He could barely make out the grimaces upon their faces, but no one argued. They drew their weapons and watched as the darkness enveloped the grounds around their stable.

They were in the thick of it now. Moments passed as the blackness seeped in, but nothing came to the doors. No one held torches to the roof or screeched in the night. There was only the darkness. Then Cal heard them. It was the slow trudge of marching by mount and by foot. As he listened to the march, the black fog slithered past them and cleared his sight, and the force behind the darkness was revealed. Cal was right, but he didn't know how right he was. Hundreds of Vechians with blazing green eyes lumbered through the Crestwood toward the main road. They were mounted on their Shappas, and the rest extended in a line that stretched further than he could see.

This was their response to the traps: the disciples were amassing all the possessed soldiers at their disposal and moving slowly and surely toward the army of the Mid. The bewitched forces were heavily armed with all manner of pikes, clubs, shields, and swords. They were covered in leather, fur, and bones from head to toe. This was the force that Lorcan had warned them about. The march carried on for an hour, and the force was at least two thousand strong, but as they neared the end of their column, they were more sluggish and staggered. The last of the Vechians were injured.

It was a cruelty to their people. Arrows jutted from their limbs, and slashed wounds across their fur and armor bled openly, but they slogged forward. Their injuries did not matter to the possessors, nor did they matter to the bewitched. There was no aid for these folk; they would obey until they succumbed to their wounds and died. It was an awful fate. The last of the enemy hobbled out of sight, and the party breathed a sigh of relief.

"Gods, did you see how many there were?" Halden whispered, breaking the silence. "Do you think each disciple has that many now?"

"I think that is an assumption we must make," Yslanna replied.

"The enemy must outnumber the Midguard three to one," Alec surmised.

"Did anyone see the Disciple?" Halden asked.

Cal cursed himself for not thinking of it earlier. If they had taken even the smallest risk and put an arrow through the heart of the disciple, perhaps the Vechians could have been freed.

"I think I may have seen them," Eris replied. "But they were on the other side of the column."

"A missed opportunity," Cal muttered.

"I would have advised against it," Alec warned. "There were too many under his power and if Eris had missed, many of us would have been cut down at the attempt."

To Cal's relief, Alec's words soothed him. Yet, he still wondered if one loosed arrow in the dark would have been worth it.

"Where do you think they were injured?" Yslanna asked.

Cal had no answer for her. They hadn't seen significant enemy forces since the battle, and every indication led them to believe the cavalry were elsewhere.

"Maybe the battle?" Cal replied.

"Gods, to have those wounds for so many days! How are they still standing?" Halden marveled.

Cal had no answer. "Do you think the shard gives them strength to continue forward?" he asked Alec.

The old man shivered upon reflection. "I think it compels the Vechians to do as commanded. The hold on them is powerful; it took a great deal of concentration and magic to release Lorcan. It stands to reason the Vechians are deeply bewitched and would follow their Dhula to death. I cannot stress how persistent they will be in the fight to come with their substantial numbers," Alec exclaimed.

Cal's heart seized. He wagered even Lord Malcolm couldn't defend against an enemy so desensitized to pain or fear. The corpses would pile up, but the possessed would press forward; the gates of the villages would be pried open by sheer force. If the party failed to kill the sorcerer, thousands of the Vechians, the Midfolk, and Crestfolk would die, killing each other. No one would win except for the disciples and their master.

"We've killed them before, and none continued once we struck them down. How can those folk still be walking?" Eris asked.

"Yes, I have seen you strike many foes from afar, but your aim is superb. We've all defended ourselves and struck fatal blows. The reason why the fighting has been so relentless is because the enemy's bewitchment releases only upon death," Alec replied. "Besides, who here can honestly say if every blow they dealt ended the life of a man?"

Clydes patted his chest in retort.

"Yes, well, you're the exception, my large friend," Alec admitted, and the tension among the party reduced a little. "But I think it's clear the ones we saw this evening, although injured, none were fatal. They do call it dark magic for a reason," Alec said with a sigh.

"This isn't just about saving these folk anymore," Cal said, steadying his voice. "The Vechians won't stop. There are probably thirty thousand of them and Lord Malcolm thinks the army's defenses will hold. If even one gate falls and the Vechians lose ten thousand, they'll swarm and cut all of them down. This is about saving all the folk now, ours and theirs."

The party received the news well, given the scope of what was at stake.

"Cal is correct," Alec confirmed. "There is no other alternative. We must stop the sorcerer."

"Then let us move with purpose," Halden urged as he began grabbing his things, but Cal stopped him.

"I know it's counterintuitive, but we must wait until the morning comes," Cal insisted. "The roads will be ours at dawn, and we will ride hard from daybreak to dusk until we reach the Fork. If anything should happen, we'll be well rested to fight."

"But the enemy is driving them now!" Halden exclaimed.

"I know they are heading there, but they are slow, like a caravan. Their trudge gives us time, my friend," Cal reassured.

Halden frowned. He didn't like the idea of waiting, but he put his pack down and nodded. "I don't know if I can get back to sleep after this," he remarked.

"Then you and I will take the next watch for a time," Alec interjected. "Let us talk quietly while the others rest."

The Darwishman smiled and agreed while the others took to the empty stable and back to bed.

They woke early with the sun and rode hard through the heart of the Crestwood. They approached the Slopes as quickly as their mounts would allow. The sun fought through the forest canopy to reach the ground. The woods were always cool, dark, and thick with vegetation. For the first time, his home felt eerie to him. Each twig breaking among the trees reminded him that a great danger still lurked in the wood waiting to be unleashed. The Crestwood scared him.

Ever vigilant, they watched the forest with caution. As they rode past a grove, he glanced over his shoulder to verify they were alone and a flock of birds sprang up from within the wood. Something had disturbed them.

Cal gripped his reins and drove the party into a gallop for as long as the horses could manage. At each rest, the party looked behind them and heard the rumble of hooves trailing behind them. They were being followed.

"This is unfortunate," Alec muttered.

"Do you think it's the Midguard?" Cal asked.

"I've seen no tunics among them," Eris replied.

"Nor the reflection of bones," Yslanna added. "But there is too much overgrowth."

"We cannot outrun them all day," Halden insisted. "We'll have to turn and meet them."

"No," Cal snapped. He hated the idea of having to fight against the Midguardmen or any more Vechians, but he had little choice. As he looked around him and recognized the area, an idea occurred.

"We can make the Fork!" he said. "We may be a few hours away, but night will fall before they catch up to us. If they're Midguardmen, they'll be forced to find their own shelter. If they're more Vechians, it's a good place to set an ambush."

"A good plan if we can make it before the night ends," Halden maintained.

"Then there is no time to waste," Alec interrupted as he kicked his steed hard and bolted along the road. It was a race to beat the setting sun and keep their pursuers at bay.

The forest whizzed by as Cal neared his home, but after hours on Alice's back, the Fork finally came into view in the distance. The twin pillars at the entrance of the Fork stood tall just as the colors of the dusk painted over the sky. They beckoned him home.

Cal's relief rapidly subsided as he passed through the pillars and found himself facing a giant, short-snouted bear-like creature on his hind legs, unleashing a terrifying roar.

Cal pulled back on his reins to stop himself as the creature swatted at empty air instead of clawing him. A man covered in body paint was atop the beast. He was dressed in the leathers of a nomad, and he screamed like an eagle screeching overhead. He drew his arm back and launched a spear with a speed Cal didn't know was possible. Without thinking, Cal raised his shield, and at the last moment, the spear pierced the shield, narrowly missing his arm. The shield was useless. He threw it to the ground, drew his sword, and looked around the village. Everywhere, hundreds of folk were running from their fires, grabbing shields and spears, all heading straight for him. They weren't wildmen.

These were people from far over the mountains from a land of open sky and deep canyons who basked in the sun. These were the Par'sha, and Cal had no idea why they were here.

His companions followed him, weapons drawn. But there were too many in front and too many behind. They were trapped in a fight they could not win, and as Cal's thoughts turned to his friends, he regretted taking this road and leading them there. However, before the rest of the spears were sent sailing at them, a light blazed around him. It was a warm light that touched his soul and gave him courage. All his guilt fell from his mind as the magic poured around him. It illuminated the entire village entrance. Every man and beast cowered before Alec and his staff. The party had seen this effect before and knew these folk were hindered.

"STOP!" Alec shouted at the top of his lungs. "Do not attack!"

Cal was confused. His sword arm was raised; his party was primed to charge their foes. They were helpless, but he hesitated because his friend asked it of him.

"What do we do then?" Cal yelled back.

"Do nothing! This is not the enemy!" Alec urged. "We are not your enemy!" he shouted into the village. A moment later, the light receded, back to the head of his staff.

A dark woman walked forward from the rest of her folk. She was petite and athletic, her bushy hair bounced with each step, and a white pelt covered her shoulders. By her confident walk alone, she appeared intimidating.

As the torchlight came over her face, Cal found a beautiful woman who was unafraid of them or Alec's powers. She cautiously lowered her shield and spear, but Cal could see she was ready to draw them up at a moment's notice.

She did not speak but raised her spear back and signaled her mystified people. This alone relaxed the warriors, as they peered from behind their leather shields.

No one moved except the woman. She approached each horse and the rider it carried. She stopped at a trembling Lorcan and pointed her spear at him. Without warning, the entire Par'sha raised their arms and spears once again.

"Please, I beg of you! Do him no harm!" Cal shouted as he put his horse and himself between all the spears of these nomads and Lorcan.

"Why do you ride with this demon?" she demanded. "Why are the crows not feasting on his eyes?"

The Par'sha shouted as her people thumped their chests as if echoing the woman's questions.

"Because he isn't my enemy either! Look at his eyes! He is a demon no more!" Cal shouted for all these folk to hear. It seemed to help.

With a wave of her spear, she motioned for Cal to move aside and cocked her head to better examine him. Many of the other Par'sha looked out from behind their shields to see Lorcan as well.

"Lorcan, lower your hood and show them!" Cal said as he backed Alice and himself out of the way. "You need to show them."

The young man was terrified but somehow found the courage he needed. He threw his hood back and looked directly at the warrior woman as she gazed back at him in interest.

"You see, he is not possessed," Alec called out.

"This man is under my protection," Cal added. "He is not our enemy!"

They did not attack, but they did not lower their weapons either. The warrior continued to look over the entire party and stopped once again, but this time, she halted beside the giant Clydes. She motioned for the giant to remove his own helm and hood.

Cal never questioned or asked the man to remove his garments. He respected the giant's wishes not to be seen. However, the issue was being forced.

"Clydes, would you remove your helm?" Cal asked kindly.

The giant looked at the Par'sha, back to him, and hesitated.

For the first time, Cal thought the giant was afraid. He did not know what it could be, but Cal would not judge him. He nodded and smiled at the giant, hoping the gesture would bring him confidence.

Clydes received the message well enough, laid his hammer across his lap, threw back his hood, and began unfastening the straps of his helm. He lifted the back of the helm on a hinge, and it came off his face in his massive, gloved hands. When he revealed himself, all the Par'sha gasped in fear, and the whole party stared in shock.

Chapter XXIII
The Condemned

His black hair fell from underneath his mask, but once the mask was removed, his olive skin showed. He had a pronounced jaw, and his canines protruded from his lips. He was not a man at all. He was an Orc, and the creature's revelation surprised everyone.

"That's going to be hard to explain," the Darwishman muttered.

"Put down your weapons or be killed," Su'ca insisted.

The man who spoke for the party broke away from his own stunned silence and looked back at her. He lowered his sword slowly as Su'ca demanded, but then he did something unexpected. He rode forward and positioned himself between his warriors and her spear. She was a lunge away from killing him then and there.

He was either incredibly brave or extremely naive. Regardless, she was prepared to take every precaution with this odd group of strangers. So, she laid her spear along his neck, ready to take his life. Surprisingly, he did not deflect it, and he did not back away. He halted his horse and stared back at her as he froze... he was brave, after all.

"Cal?" the old man stammered.

"Do nothing!" Cal shouted back.

"Swear to me you will do them no harm, and we will submit," Cal said calmly.

Su'ca gazed deep into his eyes. This man cared for his warriors' lives and that was something to be respected. She nodded to his request.

"Lay down your weapons!" Cal ordered as he handed Su'ca his sword. The others followed his lead.

The Par'sha surrounded them, pulled them from their horses, and bound their hands to poles laid across their backs. It was a far better way to keep captives because allowing their hands to be tied together only encouraged them to escape. The Par'sha seldom kept prisoners. It was not their way.

Their way was to conquer or be conquered. Those conquered would submit to the clans that had defeated them, or they would scatter to the wind. The clan Raf'a'nos had accepted their chief's death and U'sabe as Partho'sha. With the matter settled, they had made blood-oaths like all the other Par'sha people. The clans moved forward, and the horde chased the elusive demon-westmen across the infested realm of the Crest. However, the enemy continued to remain just out of reach as they charged deep into this country.

They only found the enemy at night, but they would not engage. They simply stared at them through the dark night with their flaming green eyes and beckoned them to continue the pursuit. After a week's travel through the realm, the horde had killed very few of the enemy and had crossed half of the Crestwood. The only thing the horde had caught was this odd group of westmen, but their intentions were not clear.

They separated the westmen into three groups. The women were carried to one tent; the men were further divided and brought to their own tents. The old man who could change night into day was paired with the short Darwishman, while their leader was paired with the young raider and the vile creature they kept. If the leader wished his fate to be tied to the demon-boy and an evil creature, she would not deny him. However, his words and actions rang in her mind.

She expected him to speak falsely and tell her words that would attempt to dissuade her or lead her elsewhere, but he did no such thing and denied her nothing. In fact, he honorably stood between her blade and his men. That earned him a momentary mercy.

He claimed the boy was no enemy of the Par'sha and this young raider was very much clear-eyed. The only time their eyes were other than a brilliant green was after they were forever shut by her blade. She considered it a curious thing, but it did not excuse him or his people. This boy was one of the demons, and he would answer for their crimes.

The other matter that concerned her was the creature. When the creature revealed himself, she could not believe this group of westmen, who affiliated themselves with such a dark beast, were far from innocent. Considering the nature of the enemy, the makeup of this small party, and the fact one of them could wield magic, it was clear they needed to be taken captive.

It was a bizarre group during a dangerous time, and questions flooded her mind. *Why did they ride with a raider if they weren't in league with the enemy? Why did the young warrior stand up for the beast? How did the old man make the colors of the day appear? What was their purpose?* The truth would have to be found among them.

After the groups were removed to their tents for holding, Tahop'ka entered the burnt village with his riders. They were exhausted from their scouting throughout the country. Like her father had done before him, U'sabe continued to send the scouts to hunt for the enemy and gain knowledge of their whereabouts, but they were as unsuccessful as before. Something kept them from finding the enemy, and she did not know how that could be.

She also scouted and found little except the remnants of camps, trails that led nowhere, or the occasional dead raider who had succumbed to the arrows of the Par'sha. It was infuriating to be so close and to lead the horde to nothing. Perhaps this group could answer those questions as well.

"Did you find the westmen?" Tahop'ka asked as he dismounted.

"Yes, we have captured them," Su'ca replied.

"We found them on the road much earlier today, and once they discovered us, they rode hard north. These are the only people we have found. There are thousands of tracks continuing south, but no one at the end of the trail. It was peculiar to find these westmen going the other way."

Su'ca thought about what he had told her. *Why would this group be going north?*

"It remains to be seen," Su'ca replied.

"What?"

"There is something odd about these westmen, but I cannot say for sure," Su'ca stated. "They have a young boy who is one of the raiders. The others wear the colors of the Mid, including... an Orc."

Tahop'ka, revolted, spat on the ground. "Truly? Why would they keep such a beast?"

"I do not know, but we will discover the answers to our questions," Su'ca reassured. "Rest now, Tahop'ka. The chiefs will gather soon and discuss these westmen."

Tahop'ka nodded and departed with the rest of his warriors.

The horde was abuzz with curiosity about the strange captives. They looked over their weapons and held in awe the staff that brought light into the world. However, it was another object altogether that piqued her interest. It was a twisted black wooden rod with a dark green stone affixed at the head of it. The stone was sharp enough to cut, but considering the forged weapons they kept, this was no spear or dagger. She examined the stone and found the color reminiscent of the enemy's eye color; the fury inside her stirred.

"Su'ca," We'qeda called.

She turned to find We'qeda beckoning her to join him. The chiefs were assembling immediately to consider this odd group, and she would have answers as well.

They gathered around the remnants of an old building whose blackened stone fireplace still stood from the raid the village had endured. They had cleared the debris from the floor and found it spacious. So, the Par'sha set a large tent over the remaining structure for the Crato'sha to gather. All were present, including two captives brought before them. They were the women of the group, Elvians. They were similar in many ways, but Su'ca could see the difference. Where one was calm and patient, the other was all passion and anger. She preferred the latter Elvian.

Su'ca took her seat alongside the other Chief Crato'sha and listened to the Partho'sha interrogate the westmen.

"Who are you, and why have your people come?" U'sabe asked.

"I am Eris, and this is my sister Yslanna. Cal is the sergeant who leads us, Alec is the conjurer, Halden is the Darwishman, Clydes is the Orc, and Lorcan is the boy. We have come to find an evil man and stop him," the calm Elvian answered.

"There are many evil men in this realm; you ride with one of the raiders and another wicked creature. Perhaps you lie to us about your purpose," U'sabe replied.

The wooden stave across Yslanna's back flexed in her anger. This one was a warrior like Su'ca and would fight if pushed.

"I have told you no lie. Our errand is to stop the same plague that you are fighting. We liberated a young boy from his bewitchment, and he has the courage to help us. He is no longer a raider to your people or mine," Eris continued.

"And that foulness you keep as a pet?" U'sabe interrupted.

"That creature has fought nobly against the darkness like a paladin of the stoutest faith!" Yslanna snapped, standing up while the guards readied their spears and Eris tried to console her. "I have seen his boundless loyalty and goodness firsthand and will not stand for any further insult against him!"

U'sabe waved a hand, and in a moment, several warriors took Yslanna by the arms and began dragging her from the council.

"Where do you take my sister?!" Eris demanded.

"Away," U'sabe replied.

"I have nothing to say to you as long as my sister is kept from me."

"And if you hold your tongue from us, I will command your sister's death," U'sabe threatened, but the Elvian did not flinch or recoil. She remained stoic, turned to Su'ca, and stared.

Su'ca gritted her teeth. A promise was made that no harm would be done to them, and Su'ca was a proud warrior who kept her honored word. At least, she would keep it until she discovered without a doubt that these people were in league with the demon-westmen. Perhaps this Elvian knew this about the Par'sha. Regardless, Su'ca remained collected and showed no change to the Elvian's gaze.

"I will not be separated from her," Eris insisted. "We will share in the fate if it is deemed to be so."

U'sabe was not one to be challenged, and Su'ca knew it. He raised his hand once more.

"U'sabe!" Su'ca called. "I swore to their leader no harm would come to his people, and in exchange, he surrendered them."

U'sabe stilled his hand, but he was clearly displeased to do so as he lowered his hand and nodded to the remaining Par'sha guard.

They lifted the Elvian up and walked away from the tent.

"You should not have made such a promise, Su'ca," Ja'bu insisted.

"If you had seen the courage of their leader, you would have granted such a request," Su'ca replied. "Besides, there are answers among these westmen I wish to know. Why does the enemy not fight us? Why do they lead us further into this infestation? The horde has scoured this realm and found no answers. Maybe these westmen know. Maybe they do not, but they are the only ones we have found that we can ask. That is worth sparing."

Even Ja'bu nodded among the other chiefs in understanding. It was a different war than previous conflicts. Su'ca knew she was right to try and comprehend this deceptive enemy.

"What if they are found to be in collusion with these demons?" Im'tu asked. "There is strong evidence to suggest that is the truth of things."

She listened intently as she held the mysterious rod in her hands. "Then they are my enemy, and I am not bound to keep such a promise. Honor demands that they should die, and I will take these westmen to the knife myself if that were the case," Su'ca declared.

Im'tu nodded in agreement as well as the others. The captives would not be harmed for now. It was another moment until two new captives were brought before them and made to kneel. They were bearded men. One was tall, dirty, old, and lively, and the other was a short, clean, young, stern Darwishman.

They also brought the old man's staff and passed it among the Crato'sha. It was an odd thing. It was not a weapon to be wielded against another like a spear. It would shatter if struck with a real blade, but somehow, the old man could make such a spectacle from it.

Su'ca began wondering what else the old man could do.

"Quite a horde you've assembled!" Alec exclaimed. "How goes the war, great chief of chiefs?" He was the oddest of these westmen, and far more exuberant than a man of his age ought to have been. There were chiefs who were bewildered by him, but U'sabe was not among them. He was indifferent to the old man's quirkiness.

"It goes," U'sabe replied briskly. "You are the one who makes light against my people?"

"I do not wish to cross words with you, great chief. I used the light to prevent a fight between our folk, but I do not use my gifts against your people. You are no enemy of mine," Alec maintained.

"What else can you do?" Su'ca interrupted.

U'sabe turned his head to Su'ca but allowed her question. It was an important one.

"It is not so much a question of what I can do, rather than the folk around me. I believe I am a rod, and the magic surrounding me is lightning; given the right environment, I can help energize the senses and focus the soul of a man," he babbled.

The chiefs sat befuddled by Alec's reply, but Su'ca was not dissuaded by his eccentricities. In fact, she was interested in his choice of words as she looked down at the black rod in her hands.

"Can you make the day turn into night as well?" she asked coldly. "Can you make blackness form instead?"

He hesitated at her suggestion and took a moment to reply. "It is possible that I could. However, that is not the kind of wizard I wish to be."

She hurled the rod to the ground before him, and he stared at it with contempt.

"What is that?" she demanded.

"This is a tool of the enemy."

"Maybe, but it is little different than your other staff. It has powers, and you can make them come to life," Su'ca accused. "What does this tool do?"

"This scepter can do wondrous things or terrible things," he lamented. "However, that is not the answer you seek. This is one of sixteen scepters that can make the darkness you have seen, and it commands the soldiers that we both fight."

All the chiefs shuffled to look more closely at the scepter. They feared it, and they began to fear the old man. All except Su'ca.

"This was found in your company's possession. Doesn't that make you our enemy?" she alleged.

He looked Su'ca over with a strange interest like a Shaman might, but she remained firm.

"I know it is difficult for some to accept what you cannot understand, but I am not the conjurer you seek," the old man insisted. "We recovered this tool when we found the boy."

"So, the young raider possessed this scepter, and he is our enemy."

"No!" the old man declared. "We took this from another, one of the real enemies. That disciple died in a skirmish, and we learned of this weapon from the boy. Without Lorcan, we would have no knowledge of their power or how to defeat them. Lorcan has earned our mercy. Besides, his people are bewitched; they know not what they do!"

The chiefs began muttering to each other about his claim. It was hard for the Par'sha to believe that a people could be outside their own control. They followed the path; if it was deemed so, the warrior could will it to change.

Su'ca saw herself becoming chief, and she saw herself defeating Fa'ru because, for her, the path was clear, even if others could not see it.

"This makes no sense! What purpose would any of this sorcery serve?" U'sabe refuted.

"Ah, yes! Why indeed?" Alec repeated, gazing back at U'sabe with fervor. "I have been asking myself that since before we departed the Mid. Why have all his folk come under this dark spell? Is it simply because an evil man wanted a few to do his bidding? Furthermore, what is the bidding of such a man? Some say he wishes to see the world turned into ash, but this is folly, I say. Humph! No, he has another purpose that lies beyond my grasp. The fire and death visited upon my folk, and yours is merely the means to the end."

There were those who nodded and those who did not follow at all. There was something strangely deceptive about the enemy, and Alec's answers were mired in riddles to confuse her fellow chiefs, but she was not. Su'ca understood what he had said, but she did not know if she believed him. This old man knew much of their enemy, these scepters, why their eyes had burned with a green fire, and the power of the black fog. She wagered he was misleading them and he could do it himself.

"Can you show us this power?" Su'ca began.

Alec's smile faded as his eyes dashed between Su'ca and the scepter.

"Show me the power of this scepter! Show me how it can make the black fog and possess a man!"

"I cannot, mighty chief. I am bound and cannot do such a thing."

"Untie him!" she demanded.

U'sabe held out a hand, and the other Par'sha stopped.

"What are you trying to prove, Su'ca?" Im'tu asked.

"This old man attempts to deceive us, and he tries to hide his powers behind another. What if these westmen are not possessed at all? What if they are enhanced?" Su'ca claimed. "That is what he can do; he said it. And I know he could make the black fog if he wished. Maybe there are more like him, and he was the fool who was caught by us."

The other chiefs glared at the old man with clenched fists.

"And what if he tries to bewitch us?" U'sabe demanded.

"He would be a fool to try," Su'ca replied. "And I would end his life if he attempted to do so." Su'ca removed a dagger from her belt and held it out for all to see.

U'sabe thought for several seconds, then waved the guards forward. They cut the rope from the old man's wrists, and every warrior under the large tent positioned themselves to strike their would-be enemy if he truly showed himself.

The old man dropped his arms but did nothing more. The tent remained silent.

"Show us," U'sabe demanded, but the old man just sat.

"I cannot show you what you seek," Alec stammered. "The scepter will not react with me like it would an evil man. Furthermore,

I refuse to try. I will not have my friends and myself condemned because of your misunderstanding of how the magic works."

"Bah!" Koa'bo yelled, rising with a club in hand. "He does not because he is guilty!"

"That's enough!" Halden shouted. "Have you taken into consideration what he has done? He chose not to attack your people when we arrived here!"

The chiefs broke their gaze from the old man to the short Darwishman. Su'ca's anger fractured with doubt.

"He stopped us from charging, and believe me, we could've. We could've charged the lot of you when you were blinded and probably still died in the process, but I tell you now, a hundred of your warriors would be lying dead beside us. Does that make sense if we're the enemy?" Halden yelled.

All the chiefs paused, including Su'ca. The Darwishman spoke the truth, and no one could deny it. *Why hadn't they just attacked? Why didn't they try to escape capture?* She didn't have the answer. Perhaps it was a mistake. However, she also knew the enemy was deceptive. This could all be a trick.

"If you will not show us the power of the scepter, then I have nothing further to ask you," U'sabe declared. "Bind the old man and take them away."

The Par'sha guards did as commanded, and the two men were removed. They brought only one other man forward; he was the young warrior, leader of the small group, but old enough to have led a war party if he were a Par'sha. Perhaps he possessed the warrior spirit. He was brave enough to stand before her blade and protect his people. That was something of note.

As the guards brought him to his knees and he found the scepter on the ground, he did not waver. He stared back at the gathered chiefs and was not afraid.

"Your people have told us much," U'sabe stated. "But I do not know if the truth is among what they have said."

"What reason have you been given to mistrust what you have been told?" Cal countered.

"The enemy is devious!" Su'ca replied. "They do not fight with honor. They fight among the shadows and attack in the dead of night, and when they could not beat the warriors of the open sky, they fled. Ever since they have stayed afar and yet close enough to give chase."

"Maybe you are the deception this time, and they hide among the forest now, waiting to strike while we are distracted here," U'sabe added, pointing to the Crestwood.

"The enemy is deceptive, but that does not prove we are in league with them," Cal refuted.

"Yes, but there is one among you who at least was a raider. He was in league with them. Do you deny this?"

"He is no longer a raider," Cal maintained.

"Does that excuse his trespasses against you or us?" U'sabe countered while the young man shook his head.

"Can you condemn the boy either?" Cal demanded. "I can't say if he burnt down my farm, your land, or he was the one who killed the last family I had in the world. I could blame him, but without proof, I'd be condemning an innocent, and I won't do that."

U'sabe stroked his chin and squinted his eyes as Cal spoke; many chiefs could not believe to spare this boy who was clearly a raider.

"I can say he's no longer under the spell. He chooses not to do those awful things. That is who he is, and no longer my enemy. Anything else that he did while possessed, he'll have to learn to live. All the Vechians will, and I will have to learn to forgive those who wronged me."

Su'ca snorted. She could not understand this or forgive so easily. Her father was killed by them, and because of that, she would ride to the world's end to fulfill her vengeance. That is what the blood-oath demanded of her and her people by those who wronged them; that boy was one of them. They didn't deny it.

"And what of the dark creature you ride with? What kind of people keeps company with monsters?" U'sabe insisted.

"Have you seen any of his kind among the enemy? Because I haven't. I've found only men disguised as terrors of the forest."

Su'ca's anger flared; there was truth to what he said and it frustrated her. None of the enemy they had killed were Orcs, and she had never seen or fought an Orc before this day. They were myths to scare children, and as she looked around the chiefs, they were afraid.

"We have not, but you could be disguised too. All of you haphazardly drape the colors of the Mid except the young boy. They do not fit you."

Cal laughed at U'sabe's comments aloud to much confusion. "I know an ornery knight who'd agree with you," he laughed. "These tunics are ours, and they were given to us by the Mid. We swore oaths to fight for her and all the Crestwood. We swore to fight until the enemy was vanquished."

"Why are you not fighting alongside them now?" U'sabe queried. He let out a heavy sigh at the question, and Su'ca knew they were onto something.

"Because the real enemy is somewhere north of here."

"No!" Su'ca replied. "If that were true, then the Midguard would be here with you, but they are not! So, why are you not with them?"

"It is true! The enemy is here!" Cal insisted. "Lord Malcolm disagreed on what we should do, and we left because of it," he admitted.

"So, you dishonored your word to fight with the Mid?"

"No, I choose to find the sorcerer and end this war once and for all!" he exclaimed. "I stand by the oath that I have sworn, and I don't need to justify it to you!"

The chiefs were silent and thought about what he had said. It was hard to believe the enemy was bewitched, that they were blameless, and another was responsible for the transgressions of so many, but this group believed it, and they would not claim otherwise.

U'sabe had little further to ask. He waved the young warrior away, and two guards left with him as the council of chiefs began weighing what they had heard.

After Cal had spoken, Su'ca was unsure of the truth of things. She respected him for standing his ground. Yet, there was considerable evidence against this party. They carried a scepter of the enemy, and they had a man who she believed could make it work. They traveled with a monster, and they did not deny the boy was once a raider. All of this seemed to show their connection to the demon-westmen, but something caused her to doubt this. Su'ca did not know why, but she believed Cal. He was a fool to believe in such things, but he was an honest westman.

"I cannot say for certain that these people are our enemy," Im'tu stated as he broke their contemplations.

"They have the demon's weapon!" Koa'bo argued. "They would not give this up easily! This must be a trick to deceive us. Let us remove their heads and be done with it."

"If this is a trick, I don't understand it. Why come to us and take their weapon with them? Why bring a raider that could mistake them as the enemy?" Im'tu asked.

"They were caught, and now they must lie to us to be released! You cannot believe them," Koa'bo countered.

"It is hard to accept anything the westmen says, but I cannot say for sure that they tell lies," Im'tu maintained. "What do you think, U'sabe?"

The Partho'sha did not waver from his thoughts and continued to doubt the intentions of the group.

"We know something aids the demons. We know because we can see it in their eyes. We have caught a man who can give them the strength and power, and a man with such gifts disturbs me. I do not believe this is some coincidence. Furthermore, I cannot believe why they would keep such a creature among them. It is unclear what path we must take, but another question rings within my mind. Can we risk letting them go?"

Most of the chiefs immediately pounded their chests and cried out in disagreement. They wouldn't allow that. And if they could not release their captives, there was only one alternative. The Par'sha did not keep captives like that. It was not their way.

Su'ca was not among those who disagreed, but she did not know if even that was the correct path. She did know she wanted more time to consider it. She raised her open hand to the council to be heard and was granted it.

"There is much evidence to support their affiliation with the demons. However, their actions speak as well. They chose not to attack us; they surrendered willingly where no other demon has, and no one can deny they are different from what we have seen. I cannot say if the demons are possessed or not, but I can say this group has no green eyes among them. These are hard considerations to overcome. So, I wish to have the evening to think about it further," Su'ca requested.

Many chiefs hesitated over her words and lost their fervor to ask for blood, but all chiefs respected her request.

"Su'ca is a wise chief," Im'tu added. "We can spare an evening to decide the fate of the group."

They nodded in succession at the request and U'sabe stood.

"Very good. We'll decide their fate before the noonday sun, but no longer. The war must continue."

Chapter XXIV
The Warrior's Heart

The Par'sha took Cal back to the tent where his other two companions, Clydes and Lorcan, were kept. They tied him to a post opposite the giant Orc. Clydes sat motionless and stared at the ground; he remained silent even after the guards had left them.

Cal knew nothing of Orcs except the fables, but Clydes was nothing like that. He wasn't a vicious brute bent on killing folk. He was like all the other folk Cal knew, and if he had to guess, right now, the giant looked sad.

Cal found Clydes remarkable. He joined the Mid, just like many folks, knowing if he would be discovered, he'd be killed out of fear. Yet, he chose to risk his life and share in the defense of the Crestfolk. He likely had, somewhere among their vast realm, a home, maybe even a clan of people.

"How are you holding up, Clydes?" Cal asked.

The giant raised his head and met Cal's eyes.

They were kind eyes, without a shred of wickedness. If Cal did not know him, he would need no more evidence to know he was a kind soul, much like other folk of the realm.

"I'm fine," he said in a low, raspy voice.

Cal grinned. "I thought you might be able to talk."

The giant smiled and looked down. "I'm sorry I lied to you."

"You have nothing to be sorry for," Cal insisted. "In fact, I'm glad you're here."

The Orc smiled again, but as he looked away from Cal, it faded.

"I have condemned us," he sighed.

"No! There's nothing you have done here that has sealed our fate," Cal insisted, but it did little good to make the giant feel better.

"Folk fear my people; they would outright destroy us if they could. I should not have removed my mask. It only made things worse!" he maintained.

"You can't control other men's fears, Clydes. All you can do is temper their fear with your actions. And you, my friend, have shown me that you are not what they think you are. I will defend that to the end," Cal countered and that was the truth.

The Par'sha doubted every word because the relationship between the western folk and the territory of the nomads was built on a shaky trust. For hundreds of years, the realms found a way to bribe the lords of the plain into allowing the caravan's passage. Some words were kept, and others were abandoned along the road. Every so often, a war would erupt from their disagreements, and distrust between the Par'sha and the city-folk grew. Cal couldn't repair their mistrust in an evening.

He considered the other option. Escape wasn't impossible, but it was unlikely. He didn't know where his companions were held, how many Par'sha there were, and death couldn't be avoided in the attempt. He might hope for stealth, but it would be a fool's attempt. There was no good answer in this situation, but he wouldn't let his friends succumb to death. They had to press on.

With few options left, the answer came to him immediately. He had to persuade his captors to release them.

"That's not my name," the giant said.

"What?" Cal replied, pulled from his thoughts.

"Clydes isn't my name," he maintained.

Cal thought about it and realized it was an odd name, and maybe he should have questioned it earlier.

"Well, what's your name then?" Lorcan asked.

"Rahuum."

"How did you get the name Clydes?" Lorcan asked.

"Everyone called my horse 'Clydesdale' when I arrived at the Mid, and I liked it. When I signed on the parchment that Alec made, that is what I wrote... at least, I think that's what I wrote," the giant replied, and Cal laughed to himself.

"It's good to meet you, Rahuum," Cal said, chuckling aloud and hoping their laughter would last. However, he needed to share the reality of their situation.

"You know, I've been thinking about what we should do," Cal said more seriously.

"There's little we can do," Rahuum replied, raising his head.

"It doesn't look good," Cal admitted.

Rahuum's brow furrowed, and a heavy sigh emptied his chest.

"What causes them to doubt your word?" Rahuum asked.

"It's hard for them to trust anything we say. They know the enemy deceives them, we have a scepter, and they're skeptical of our words."

"Is there anything else that causes them to doubt us?" Rahuum pressed.

Cal had hoped not to discuss it further, but the Orc was persistent. "It is hard for them to understand why Lorcan and you ride with us," he admitted.

"So, they do not trust your word, which is good, and they captured us once they saw my face. They do not trust me either; they fear me," Rahuum replied.

"They have many concerns, Rahuum," Cal stressed. "I will speak with them again, and we will continue to make our case."

"They will never let me go alive, Cal," Rahuum asserted.

"I will not let that happen!" Cal snapped, clenching his bound fist.

"What if it were for a purpose?" Rahuum asked. "What if my death secured your release?"

Cal's heart skipped a beat. He couldn't lose another friend, not like that. "I will not barter our lives for yours, Rahuum!"

"Do you have another way out of here?"

Cal did not. He would beg, plead, or do anything to see them released. The Par'sha had to see their innocence.

"I'll talk with them again."

"And if you can't convince them?" Rahuum said, cocking his head to the side.

"I liked you better when you were a mute."

"... Then you must make an agreement. If they agreed to let the rest of you go in exchange for my life, would you continue the journey?"

"You're asking me something I can't do, Rahuum!"

"I'm asking you to continue the quest... I believe in it! You've led us so close to the end, and I would have us finish it... whatever the cost."

Cal let out a long sigh and looked back to the Orc. It was a fair trade and Cal hated it: one life in exchange for the chance to save ten thousand. He shouldn't have to make that trade, but he struggled to think of another option. His friend was honorable to sacrifice his life for the realm.

Cal would as well. He'd joined the Mid, fought for them, and defied Lord Malcolm's wishes because it was the right thing to do.

"I'm not prepared to do that." Cal maintained. "Even if I tried, they already have us, and I'm not sure they would see the benefit of that proposal."

Rahuum shrugged his massive shoulders. "Maybe they would, and maybe they would not. I think my death may alleviate their fears about us, but I don't know. Just the same, I'm prepared to suggest it with or without your blessing," he replied.

"Promise me you'll refrain from proposing that until I have spoken with them again," Cal insisted as Rahuum looked away. "Promise me!"

For a moment, neither said anything. Rahuum finally met Cal's eyes and his jaw tightened before he reluctantly nodded.

It was a massive relief to Cal. They spoke no more of the subject. Instead, they talked of their lives, their work, and their folk. They were practically neighbors and maybe even the last two folk who used to live in the far northern Crestwood. And as he got to know his friend better, Cal worried about the approaching morning. He hoped to keep his new friend alive for as long as possible.

For the first time in weeks, Cal didn't fear the evening. A thousand warriors stood between them and the possessed Vechians. So, despite being tied to a post, he nodded off and slept.

The morning abruptly started when the Par'sha came and untied him, but only him. They removed Cal from the tent and dragged him away, leaving both his companions tied up. He didn't know why he was being taken, but he would likely see the chiefs one last time. He had little time to get his wits about him for the discussion ahead. He needed to stick to the facts to save his friends' lives; if he were lucky, maybe he could make them understand.

He was taken through the large tent the Par'sha had erected the previous night and thrown down upon a wooden floor. This used to be the tavern of the Fork. There was little left of the building, apart from memories. Cal recalled that hearings among the lawbreakers of the Fork were held in this very room. He shook his head, wondering how many times he had avoided such a trial only now to be brought before a council of Par'sha chiefs to face justice.

"Yes, this is the Sergeant I've been after."

Cal frowned. The voice was familiar and surprising; a voice of the city. He looked up and found Master Wendall standing over him with an expression of smug satisfaction.

"I assume the others have been killed?" Master Wendall asked.

"No," U'sabe corrected. "These people gave us pause to do so."

Cal couldn't tell if Master Wendall was happy or displeased about the news.

"How kind of you," he murmured.

"If you say these men are yours and they have deserted you, then I will accept this. We will not pass judgment upon them on this day and I will return them to your lord."

A sour relief washed over Cal. His friends and their deaths had been inadvertently delayed, only to be handed back to the Mid. If they were returned south, they would never find the sorcerer, and they would be killed in the inevitable battle to come.

"Alas, I cannot accept these captives. I have been separated from my men, and these misguided folk would only attempt to abandon us once again," Master Wendall replied.

Cal gritted his teeth with frustration. He was already thinking of dashing off at the first chance he was given.

"Then I will spare warriors to escort you and your people back to Lord Malcolm as a gesture of friendship," U'sabe insisted.

Master Wendall was taken aback at him. "My lord, your generosity is boundless, and I'm sure Lord Malcolm would be honored to accept such a noble gift."

Cal held his breath in hope. Maybe there was still a chance of escape; it was a long ride to the Trouthavens.

"Then it will be…"

"My lord, you have inspired me with a wonderful alternative. My Lord Malcolm would indeed be overjoyed at such a gift of friendship. However, I believe a more binding gesture can be had," Master Wendall emphasized. "Would you consider joining in with Lord Malcolm against these dark forces?"

U'sabe's attention was gained, as were the other chieftains. Many nodded among each other.

"The Par'sha have heard these words before."

"And we have not rescinded these words, my lord," Master Wendall exclaimed. "Think of it. We would do well with such a heavy cavalry, and you possess such a powerful force. Between our army of ruffians and your noble warriors, we will gain all the advantage we need against the enemy. I implore you! Come to the Trouthavens, bring these deserters, and form a friendship between the Mid and the Par'sha. We could share in an alliance that spans a thousand years, and it is but a gesture away, my lord!"

Wendall opened his arms and bowed his head, winning the bulk of approval from the chiefs.

A pit formed in Cal's stomach. If U'sabe accepted, he and his friends would travel with the Par'sha horde. There would be no chance of escape.

On the other hand, the odds against the Vechians in the coming battle had shrunk significantly. With the Par'sha as their ally, the Mid might survive.

U'sabe turned to his fellow chiefs and found nods among all of them.

"Lord Malcolm has now extended his friendship and trust to us twice. He is a noble lord. Trust like this can be achieved by sharing the battlefield. We will accept this proposal, and the Par'sha will leave immediately to rendezvous with your Lord," U'sabe declared.

The council of chiefs pounded their chests and whooped aloud. The fever spread through the camp.

"Wonderful!" Master Wendall exclaimed as the chiefs enthusiastically applauded U'sabe. "I will ride out in advance and bring the news to my lord."

"The road is dangerous for a single rider," U'sabe replied. "It would be safer and more comfortable to journey with us. We will take the first step in honoring our friendship by providing you safe passage."

"My lord, your gesture is well received! But I assure you, I will be safe enough. I traveled the roads these past two days without incident and we've found the enemy does not travel by day. I'm confident my comrades will be found expeditiously and we will quickly return to the Trouthavens. Besides, my lord will want to hear this joyous unification pressingly," Master Wendall insisted.

U'sabe reluctantly nodded. "Then please take with you a fresh horse to aid you on your journey."

"Thank you, my lord. I wholeheartedly accept," Master Wendall bowed. He turned to Cal and smiled. "Sergeant, do be on your best behavior. I would be cross with you if you waste this opportunity."

Master Wendall sneered as he left the tent.

After Wendall left, Cal turned his attention back to the chiefs. They no longer looked at him with suspicion; they looked at him with interest.

"You are not my enemy," U'sabe stated.

"No. I am not."

"And the young boy? The Orc?"

"As I have said, the boy is helping us, and the Orc has stood alongside the Mid since the army was assembled. He remained hidden because he feared he would not be accepted. No one knows what he is, but he has been faithful and he is my friend."

U'sabe and the other chiefs exchanged cynical glances. As hard as it was to accept, even the Orc had been vouched as a soldier of the Mid by Master Wendall, and Cal would press this if their doubt resumed.

"Before, you spoke of a disagreement with your lord. Tell me why you disagreed?" U'sabe inquired.

"We spent many days trying to understand the enemy's power and how to defeat them. We discovered the scepters, the Vechian people who were bewitched, and we found out about the sorcerer who controls everything. Without Lorcan, we would know none of these things. Lord Malcolm intends to lure the Vechians into a trap where he believes they will be destroyed."

"Lord Malcolm is a deft man. What is wrong with this plan?"

"As I have said, there is a sorcerer who controls everything, and I'd rather fight him than kill scores of his lackeys," Cal explained.

U'sabe nodded at his reasons but still looked unconvinced.

Perhaps it was too much to believe, but Cal didn't care. It was the right thing for him. "Also, I have reason to believe the Mid will not succeed," he added.

"Why?"

"Because as we hid in a stable the evening before last, we saw at least two thousand of the enemy, and only one scepter controlled them," Cal stated as the chiefs looked amongst each other in concern. "There are fourteen other scepters that likely control just as many, if not more."

"Why haven't you mentioned this before?" Su'ca asked. It was the same woman who held a spear to Cal's throat the evening prior.

"I answered truthfully what you asked of me and if you had asked me about the Vechians, I would have answered that as well."

She seemed content with the answer but still desired more detail.

"This is a large number of demon-westmen, but all men fall against the horde," U'sabe maintained.

"These men won't fall so easily," Cal urged.

"Why is that?"

"Because we saw the injured Vechians with arrows still plunged into their arms and legs, trudging through the mud without care. Do you know what that means?"

Su'ca exchanged glances with the U'sabe; both were extremely concerned. "We have found the enemy dead scattered along the wood for many days; they were struck by our arrows and cut from our blades. We did not know why they were abandoned and trampled by their own people," she revealed.

Now the injured Vechians Cal witnessed the other night made sense; the Par'sha were the ones who fought them. "It's because the Vechians are possessed! They don't feel pain and they won't stop. The spell compels them forward until they are killed outright or the spell is broken!" Cal gravely said, looking to all the chiefs to understand.

"The Mid is in a fight they cannot win! Killing this sorcerer and destroying his power is the only way to break their control over the Vechians. If my party doesn't stop him in time, the Mid will fall!"

U'sabe took a long pause considering what Cal said as the chiefs in the tent softly spoke between them.

"Perhaps, with our combined forces, victory will be ours," U'sabe countered.

"Maybe… maybe not. I do know we can find this madman and prevent a massacre because if we don't, that's what it'll become… a massacre! And I don't know if it will be the Vechians, the Mid, or yours if you ride to join the Mid, but I'd rather try and save those lives than take them if I can. So, I'm asking you to release us from these bonds and let us continue our quest."

The great chief sighed, weighing the request. "If I release you, I have no gift for the Lord of the Mid."

Cal's stomach knotted, but the high chief was considering it. Cal decided to keep pressing.

"Your strength is a gift, and Lord Malcolm knows it," Cal pleaded. "That's what he and his councilors desire; he would accept your friendship solely on its own merits."

"I also gave my word! That may mean little to the Western people, but not to the Par'sha," U'sabe said, waving his hand around the tent while his fellow chiefs pounded their chests.

Cal waited for them to finish. "I made an oath as well. We all did. I said I would defend the Mid and the Crest. I also said I would help defeat the enemy; this is how we defeat him! I know it! We ought to be given leave to try," Cal pleaded.

The great chief was stubborn, but when Cal finished speaking, he was silenced. As Cal gazed across the husk of a building into his eyes, he thought maybe the chief of chiefs understood him.

"I will accompany this man," Su'ca declared.

Every chief in the tent fell silent. Cal stared in astonishment as the tent billowed under the morning breeze.

"How can you do this?" Ja'bu shouted, pointing a finger as the other chiefs finally broke their silence and grumbled among each other.

"Master Wendall confirmed their allegiance; U'sabe has declared them no enemy of ours. Everything this man has told us is as straight as the dart flies. If he says there is a sorcerer responsible for the attack on my people, then that is where I will go, Ja'bu!"

Cal was speechless.

"What of your blood-oath? What of your honor?" Ja'bu insisted thumping his chest.

"Did I not swear to take vengeance? This man can take me to this sorcerer, and I will kill him. The honor and glory will be mine alone, and I keep both my oath and honor intact."

"And what if he is wrong, Su'ca? Would you risk your honor on a fool's errand?" Ja'bu asked.

She wasn't dissuaded by the old chief. She didn't even look at him. She stared at Cal, and he stared back. She believed him and Cal knew he had finally gotten through to one of them.

"Then the horde will be where the fight will be," she replied. "But you do not ask the right question. What if this man is right and the Par'sha did nothing to help him? Where would any of our honor be?"

Ja'bu was silenced; no other chief had an answer for her.

"I would not have it; I will see our vengeance done!" Su'ca declared.

The chiefs didn't like her reasoning, but no one spoke against her.

"You've said the horde should unite under this war, and we have. If you go off with these people, you could divide our people, Su'ca," U'sabe urged.

Su'ca nodded in agreement but waved her hand through the tent. "I would not have us divided. I will take only a handful of warriors with me, and the rest of my clan will go with you, U'sabe. I trust you will look after my clan as if they were yours," Su'ca said.

U'sabe thought for many moments, stroking his chin and looking between Cal and Su'ca. Reluctantly, he nodded at her request.

"You are determined to fulfill your blood-oath and perhaps this sorcerer is the one responsible for these attacks. I do not know, but you have the warrior's heart and you see the path. Possessed or not, I will fulfill our word and take this horde to fight this enemy. I, however, will not stop you from walking the path you see."

U'sabe lowered his head in respect to Su'ca. She returned the gesture.

U'sabe then turned to Cal. "Let it be known among our peoples that this man and his companions are no longer our captives. He is free to continue your journey. May the warrior spirit guide and keep you!" U'sabe declared.

Cal was shocked by what had unfolded. Not only would the party be allowed to leave, but they even gained some warriors to help with their quest.

His bonds were cut from the pole across his back, and he dropped his arms to his side. The Mid was no longer hunting them, and hopefully, all that was between the sorcerer and his party was a small contingent of possessed Vechians. If they hurried, they could prevent the great battle from happening.

The chief Su'ca walked over to him, offered her hand to him, and pulled him up from the ground. "Come, Sergeant Cal. Let's retrieve your people and be on our way."

Chapter XXV
The Ascent

Su'ca took Cal to Alec and Halden, then to Rahuum and Lorcan, and finally to Yslanna and Eris. Su'ca kept her word; all were unharmed from their capture. Although a few were still irritated about the ordeal, when Cal appeared free from bondage in front of them, all ill feelings were set aside and replaced by astonishment.

Cal reintroduced everyone to Rahuum, but the giant preferred to remain reclusive and avoid further eye contact. That was until the twins engaged him in a long embrace. After that, he became much more relaxed.

They were led back to their horses, who were watered and well attended to by the Par'sha. Along with their horses, the party had their weapons returned to them. They were also provided their first meal since the day before. Altogether, they had lost a little time and a comfortable night's sleep.

The party spent their morning meal inquiring how Cal managed their release. Cal shared everything that transpired, but the most surprising and unbelievable news was Master Wendall's involvement. He must have ridden to exhaustion to catch up with them, but no one doubted his ability to lose his Midguardmen escorts in the process. A good laugh was had at the councilman's expense.

While they ate, Chief Su'ca departed but swiftly returned with thirty fierce warriors at her side. Initially, both parties shared some hesitation and distrust; the Par'sha especially regarded Rahuum with fear. Yet, Cal didn't worry. Su'ca had honored her word to keep their party unharmed during their capture and she brought warriors with her like she told the council of chiefs. They would learn to build trust, and Cal knew how. He offered his hand in friendship and Su'ca took it.

The company of Crestfolk and Par'sha was nearly forty strong when they departed along the northern road while the Par'sha horde headed south. There were no farewells among the nomads when they departed; they simply wished each other strength in the fight to come.

The company came upon the Slopes in the late afternoon. Emerging from underneath the canopy of the forest, they found the steep cliff towering above them. It stretched from the east to the west. They had arrived.

In all his time, Cal had heard of no such route north through the Slopes; they were regarded as impassable and treacherous. All they needed to do was locate a hidden passage among a range of mountains that stretched for a hundred leagues. That was impossible with the time they had remaining, but it was why Cal brought Lorcan.

As they stopped before the Slopes, the young Vechian gazed upon the mountain with a great longing and sadness. Cal understood; the mountains beckoned him home, and yet there was a task to do before he could return.

"The passage my people entered through began at the top of the cliff overlooking the Crest. There, the dark red winding cave descends deep into the rock and opens onto a plateau before the Crestwood. We entered the forest between two creeks that washed down from the mountainside, past two hills, and into the river," Lorcan recalled.

Cal thought long about his description, as did Halden and Rahuum.

"I think I would know of such a place along the western hills, and I do not. Come to think of it, I have seen no soil with such a rich color among my home," Halden recalled.

"And you, Rahuum?" Cal asked.

"I can't say there is a plateau near the Slopes of my home, but I have seen the splashes of the red rock on the walls of the mountainside."

"That determines our direction," Cal stated.

"I think prudence demands we travel inside the Crestwood," Alec warned. "The way Lorcan describes the entrance, they may be able to see us long before we see them."

"Let us be on our way then," Su'ca added.

With all nodding, the company turned east and began their search for the entrance before nightfall. Several pairs of Crestfolk and Par'sha scouts were sent ahead to search. Only one cave was found along the mountainside that day, but it was not the passage they sought. There were no creeks or a plateau and the cave itself was shallow. Cal grew frustrated.

It was several days since they left the army, and Lord Malcolm had all the resources he needed to make all the preparations for their war. The Par'sha's arrival would only escalate their plans and Sir Kenneth would also jump at the first opportunity to unleash their trap and reclaim his own honor. Yet, Cal had at least one more full day until the Par'sha arrived at the Trouthavens. One day, to find and stop the sorcerer.

Night came quickly. The cave may not have been the passage they were looking for, but it made for a good shelter. All the horses and company fit within the damp cavern. There was little warmth outside of companions cuddling against each other for warmth as they were, once again, without fire.

Cal slept well until he was awoken by Su'ca and another Par'sha warrior to take the watch in the last hours before dawn. As he walked outside, he found the sky illuminated with the wondrous blue and green lights Lorcan had described. It ebbed and flowed in waves into the eastern sky.

"Do you often get these beautiful lights in your home?" Su'ca asked in awe.

"No," Cal replied as a thought struck him. "I have never seen such a sight among our evening skies, but I have heard of them. Lorcan spoke of them. The green shards broke from base-stone under a night like this."

"What does this mean then?" Su'ca asked.

Cal turned from the sky and gazed at Su'ca. "It means we are close," he replied.

Su'ca smiled for the first time since he'd met her as she turned away and returned to the cave.

"Where are you going? Don't you want to watch?"

"I am going to bed to rest. For tomorrow, I will complete my vengeance."

She left him to stand the remaining watch as the dawn rose over the trees in the east. The company broke their fast on dried meats of the great grass-sea and bread from the ovens of the Mid. At dawn, the word spread among them of what they had witnessed the prior evening and all prepared in anticipation.

They mounted their horses and rode hard. Some rode at the edge of the forest while others along the shadow of the mountain. All looked for the same signs... a plateau, signs of dark red soil, a pair of hills to the south, and a set of creeks. There was no sign in the morning or the early afternoon that matched the description, but the late day brought hope when blotches of red stone appeared on the surface of the mountainside.

As dusk approached, a Par'sha rider returned from ahead of the company with news of a great clearing of rock just above the tree line and a large number of men outside a cave. They had found it.

They dismounted far from the edge of the forest and crawled closer to better inspect their foes and the entrance. It was as expected, if not worse.

A hundred green-eyed Vechians stood like armed statues outside the opening of a well-lit cavern within the mountainside and gazed over the Crestwood. Cal assumed there were as many, if not more, inside the cavern. They needed to even the odds. The company could not take on the whole force of the enemy head on; a fight between forty mounted folk and one hundred foot soldiers could err either way. Yet, he wagered on his mounted company with the Par'sha on their side.

"I know what to do," he whispered as the details came to him. It was a foolish plan, yet bold enough to seize the victory they needed. Fortunately, foolish plans were the ones that had brought them most success so far, and this plan might be the only way to draw the possessed Vechians out from the passage… maybe even the sorcerer. Nevertheless, the party agreed to his daring idea, and Su'ca, along with her fellow Par'sha, approved wholeheartedly.

Apart from Cal, Yslanna, Rahuum, and Alec, the remaining company gathered their horses, quietly backed away, and faded into the early evening. Cal and his few companions remained at the forest's edge and gave the rest of the company time to position themselves. The night was their ally now, and they would be the ones to strike.

Cal had no more qualms or reservations about what he was going to do. A few Vechians would die tonight, but with the distraction he had planned, he would fool the possessed Vechians, reach the sorcerer, and end his bewitchment over them. It was the best plan he had to save them and the realm.

As night fell, the phenomenon of light burst into the sky above and around them once again. The colors were brighter than before, and Cal wondered if the sorcerer was now using the full measure of power; it scared him. The phenomenon lit up everything from the forest to the walls of the Slopes and the Vechian guards, but tonight, Cal was going to use this power against them.

An hour had passed since the company departed when a bright streak of light from an arrow darted through the night. The others were in position and ready.

Cal nodded to his companions. Alec drew forth the scepter from under his cloak and removed the leather cloth they had wrapped around the shard. It glowed with the deep green color as if the shard knew the source was near and desired to return to it.

"It's now or never," he muttered.

"It has been an honor, my young friend!" Alec replied.

"Enough of that! I plan to tell hundreds of my kin the deeds we did here upon the mountain!" Rahuum interrupted as he readied his war hammer.

Cal decided he liked Rahuum even better than before.

"Let's show this bastard how folk fight back!" Rahuum continued.

"Then stand aside, and you will see," Yslanna retorted as she smirked under the light of the sky.

With that, Alec waved the scepter into the sky. Dhula came to life all around them, and a blanket of clouds appeared throughout the wood. Alec stretched out the rod, and it glowed a vibrant jade brighter than ever as the fog stretched farther and farther. It extended from the wood to the wall of the mountain, enveloping every Vechian outside the cave entrance. The Vechians were in awe of it, but as Cal and his party appeared at the edge of the plateau, their wonder turned to alarm, and they approached the four with weapons at the ready.

Cal and his party held their ground as the thunder approached and the rain fell from the foggy clouds above. However, it was not a storm that Alec had conjured from their shard. Just as the Vechians began sprinting toward their company, almost three dozen horses broke through the mist and struck the enemy from the west. The Par'sha, Halden, Eris, and Lorcan arrived like a stampede. The company speared and slashed through the surprised Vechian ranks as easily as a knife through butter.

Just as the riders appeared from one side of the fog, they disappeared through the other side. They struck true as several dozen Vechians were killed by the company as they flew through them. Cal noticed the enemy's attention was divided between the four horsemen on the edge of the plateau and the thirty who rode through them.

The enemy had succumbed to the chaos of his plan; it was the best Cal could've hoped for. The remaining Vechians split apart as many charged Cal and his three companions and the few others looked for the company that had escaped beyond the veil of the fog.

They didn't get far when the thunder raged again. The Vechians turned at the last moment to find the company once again driving and slashing through their ranks. They were cut down in vast numbers.

As the company charged, Yslanna and Rahuum both edged closer and closer in hopes of being released upon the Vechians as well.

"Hold! We must stay here to protect Alec!" Cal shouted. Yslanna and Rahuum pulled back on their reins.

A deep horn bellowed from within the mountain as the remaining Vechians poured from the cavemouth. Cal didn't know how many joined, but he waited until no more Vechians left the mouth of the mountain. The odds against the company were dramatically altered.

The enemy flooded from the cave in scores, and their ranks were replenished as Su'ca continued to drive the thirty warriors back and forth across the plateau. The chaos was no longer serving as fresh Vechian soldiers appeared on the battlefield. They began organizing rows of spearmen against their company, and with Su'ca's remaining charge, they were prevented from going any further.

At that moment, Alec released the scepter's power, and the fog and rain dissipated around them, allowing the lights of the sky to reveal the ongoing fight. The company had only one more surprise, and there was no time to lose. Su'ca and her warriors were holding strong against the Vechians, but she could not hold them forever.

"Come on!" Cal yelled as they galloped to join the company. They followed him past the Vechian ranks, cutting down any foot soldier who crossed their path with sword, spear, and war hammer. After they passed, they wheeled around to the center of the battle to support the wavering company. And when they came from behind the tired Par'sha and westmen, a light burst from Alec's staff. It was a blinding light that made the Vechians recoil; but the company basked in its glow. The magic flowed around Cal like sunlight on a cool spring morning. The fear of failure evaporated, and in an instant, his senses piqued, his mind focused, and courage filled his soul.

With renewed strength, the company drove through the distracted Vechians one last time as they hacked with their swords and thrust spears against the Vechian foot soldiers. Cal kept his eye on the entrance of the cave; no more came from the cavern, and the sorcerer had not graced them with his presence.
He had ordered the possessed men down and thought they would dispose of the small company. That was his mistake.

The company held the line, and now the route leading back to the sorcerer was clear. It was time.

"Alec!" Cal yelled as he slashed through the head of one Vechian, followed by another.

Alec raised his staff with one arm, and with the other, he swung his old sword in long, lopsided slashes. He finished his downward slash and turned to Cal.

"The entrance is open!" he bellowed.

"I cannot abandon our friends and take away the light! It is up to you now! Go!" Alec shouted.

He was right. The company needed his magic to help them. It was up to Cal to see to the sorcerer's end.

"The scepter?" Cal called as he stretched out his hand.

In the heat of the battle, the old man smirked; he trusted Cal completely. With one motion, Alec clenched his sword underneath his armpit, drew the scepter from his side and threw it. Cal caught it with his free hand and rode through the trenches of bone-clad Vechians. He swung his sword from one side to the other, clearing anyone who stood against him as he cantered toward the entrance of the cave.

He entered a wide, torch-lit passage. There was no one in front of him, but several Vechians followed behind him. He kicked Alice and together they darted through the cavern. The path twisted upward as he trotted, ready to swing his sword at any unexpected adversary.

As the path twisted upward, it forked into separate tunnels and he pulled back his reins to stop. He suspected there might be several turns among the tunnels but that is why he asked for the scepter. He raised the scepter to one entrance and then to the other; the answer came immediately. It brightened at the first opening but dimmed at the second. The scepter was showing him the way to the source of its power.

Several injured Vechians were slowly gaining on him, but he had to leave a marker. There were dozens of torches attached to the walls. On the ground, the enemy had placed large metal cauldrons serving as fires with bedrolls surrounding them. He dismounted quickly, ran to the closest cauldron, turned it over with his sword, and blocked the wrong pathway with flames. The pelts and bedrolls caught on fire immediately. If his friends followed, there was only one path to take.

He remounted as the Vechians rounded the corner. They had caught up with him. Cal charged at them and at the last moment, swung Alice around, knocking four men to the ground.

As they toppled over, he gave Alice a firm kick, and she burst into a gallop up the corridor. The tunnel continued to rise as he traveled higher and higher toward the shelf of the Slopes and the scepter's glow grew brighter. He would be at the top at any moment.

Cal did not know what to expect when he found the sorcerer, but he trusted his bow rather than his sword. The sorcerer could be killed just like his disciple and he wasn't leaving anything to chance. No. At the first opportunity, Cal would let an arrow fly at his evil heart and be done with it. He sheathed his sword, retrieved his bow, and nocked a single arrow on the string as he snaked through the tunnel.

As he passed a pen of Shappas, he found what he was seeking. The colors of the sky illuminated the tunnel ahead of him; he was nearing the exit. As he galloped near the mouth of the cavern, he belted the scepter and then drew his bow.

He charged through the exit onto the shelf of the mountain and found himself racing through monumental pillars supporting a roof of red rock like a corridor to the sky. The room was lit with large cauldrons at the base of the pillars, and beyond that was the shelf itself. He kicked his mare hard, and Alice darted along the cavern only to find several possessed Vechians drawing bows and swords of their own. Without thinking, Cal loosened one arrow and then another as he slowed to avoid arrows whizzing by him.

He found his mark with all of them and the Vechians fell permanently as he emerged from underneath the roofed cavern and atop the cliff.

Before he could pull another arrow, a bolt of lightning thundered in front of him, narrowly missing him, and shattered one of the red pillars supporting the cavern ceiling behind him. Alice, terrified by the crack of the thunder, skidded to a halt.

Cal flew over Alice's neck and tumbled onto the stone floor as rock and debris burst around him. He fell head over heels, and the momentum carried him swiftly to the cliff's edge. Thinking quickly, he abandoned his bow and clung to the rocky floor.

He landed with a thud on his stomach and hands; his head was well over the edge, giving him a full view over the mountain, the

Crestwood, and the fighting still raging below. The light from Alec's staff beamed like the sun on the grounds below and it gave him hope they would win and they would come. Yet, he was still alive, and he could still try to finish their quest.

He looked up and found a pair of dark, sullen eyes underneath a tangled mess of black hair. It was him, the sorcerer.

There were streaks of silver in his matted hair, which matched his pointed beard. His outer robes were black, with a set of fine leather armor underneath. Embossed on his chest was the same red emblem of a fractured triangle that Cal saw on his dead disciple.

The sorcerer stood next to a single dark-marble pedestal that housed a broken dark-green orb at the top. A third of the sphere was fractured from the whole, but that was it. It was the remnants of the Vechian God they called Dhula; the source of their power. Cal needed to find a way to destroy it and stop the sorcerer. He had to continue the fight regardless of the odds against him. He elbowed himself from the ground but found that as hard as he tried to push up, he was unable to lift himself. He was sore from his fall, but that was not the reason. He was being forced to the ground.

The sorcerer approached, his hand outstretched and grasping a blackened staff with an odd-shaped ruby-red stone at its pinnacle.

The sorcerer's eyes pierced Cal as he pointed his staff and muttered incantations under his breath. It was useless to resist. Cal could neither stand nor roll over. The only power he had left was to watch, but the sorcerer did not strike.

He walked calmly over to Cal's bow that had flown from his hands, and with one swipe of his foot, he kicked it over the edge.

It fell through the air, but losing it did not concern him. He still had his sword, and he was lying on it.

The sorcerer looked over the edge of the cliff and then back at Cal. His eyes were wide and unfocused, darting from side to side.

Madman, Cal thought. He must know his guard was almost finished. Alec's light was as strong as ever. It burst from his staff and strengthened Cal's companions as they fought below. And as the light beamed onto Cal's face, he could feel the smallest fraction of the magic course through him. He reached out, clinging to the light so he could overcome the power pinning him to the floor.

"No, there will be no more of that." The sorcerer's cold voice cut through the air as if reading Cal's mind.

But Cal desperately needed to feel the rejuvenation of the magic. He needed it to focus him and let him gain control once again. Just as he reached out, the sorcerer conjured a series of sparks from his blackened hand and channeled it into the fractured orb.

The darkness formed like a torrent of water spewing from the orb upward into the sky. In moments, the green and blue colors of the heavenly phenomenon were blocked from view and were replaced by

a black cloud that thundered with occasional patches of light. It was a
dark thunderstorm. When the dark clouds became saturated with
energy, lightning exploded from it, down the mountainside, and
struck the battleground below, fracturing the massive plateau.
Everyone fell... all of them. In a single moment, the fighting ceased,
and the light that his company depended on vanished.

Chapter XXVI
The Rendezvous

The siege works began immediately and every soldier under Lord Malcolm's command toiled to complete it. The army cleared hilltops, tunneled the entrances with logged walls, furnished thousands of stakes, and barricaded the gaps in between the hills with walls of rock and earth. In doing so, they encircled the villages with steep mounds and elevated ramparts for a thousand bowmen to perch upon. The Trouthavens were forever transformed into the most fortified villages of the realm.

Lord Malcolm insisted on personally overseeing the seven leagues of siege works. The enemy would have to cross through a dense forest, around boulders, across sharpened stakes, and under a constant barrage of arrows just to reach their works. This time, their numbers and magic would be meaningless against the Mid's defenses.

If, by chance, they reached the village walls, several thousand soldiers would be awaiting them along the ramparts with swords and shields. It was an exhaustive defense, and Sir Kenneth had no doubt in his mind their victory was assured.

However important the works were, Sir Kenneth's recovery took precedence. He had to limit his expenditure of energy and rest as much as possible. So, he relied on folk like his newly appointed sergeant, and as the progress continued, he had to give Jacoby credit.

Jacoby understood the necessity and importance of what Sir Kenneth was trying to accomplish. The new sergeant toed the line, completed sections quickly, and continued the works without further direction. For a man of the eastern lands, he was more than competent to meet the demands.

After serious consideration, Sir Kenneth thought his elevation to Lieutenant was warranted. However, there was little time for such pomp and circumstance. The battle was before them.

In preparation for the battle, they continued to watch for the enemy at dusk and dawn. For days, all reports indicated increased patrols, and Lord Malcolm took this as an excellent sign the enemy were already returning to the area since the traps were set. All that remained was for the men to occupy the walls when the time came.

They completed the works at noon on the fourth day. Sir Kenneth didn't care for the celebration of it. He would only join in when it was done, the enemy buried, and this unfortunate business was behind them.

With the works completed and his health improved, he pressed Lord Malcolm to allow him to begin the campaign. All Sir

Kenneth needed to do was goad the Vechians into chasing him, and he would lead them right to the Mid's fortifications. There was no doubt in his mind that he could lure their darkness, their beasts, and all their forces into one final confrontation.

Lord Malcolm conceded, and Sir Kenneth prepared his cavalry to begin that evening. All the Midfolk and Crestfolk looked ready to take on the enemy who had scorned their homeland and finally rid themselves of the evil that surrounded them. The soldiers were even prepared to target hooded men carrying scepters should they come across them. If Sergeant Cal was right, killing them would release the possessed folk, and they would retreat in disarray. That would end the battle quickly, but Sir Kenneth doubted the disciples would put themselves in danger. So, it was left to the Midguard to weaken their forces the old-fashioned way through sword and shield. That's how they would seize victory.

Sir Kenneth, along with Sergeant Jacoby and fifty men, was mounted and ready to depart when he received the news. Thousands were spotted along the northern road, but it was not the enemy.

The Par'sha were assembled as they promised, but it was hard to believe. *Why was the horde coming from the north? Had they resisted the enemy throughout the Crestwood, or had they beaten them entirely? What if the Par'sha joined them? On the other hand, what if the barbarians came to fight the Mid?* Questions raced through his head without answers. Sir Kenneth had to confer with his lord. He took his fifty men and led them to Lord Malcolm's camp.

When he arrived, he found Lord Malcolm preparing to mount up with his personal guard of a hundred men and meet with them. Sir Kenneth disapproved of his eagerness. The barbarians were a lesser people, and they should be the ones to request an audience with the Lord of the Mid.

"My lord, do you think it wise to greet the Par'sha yourself?" Sir Kenneth cautioned. "I am already prepared to take to the road. I will retrieve their head chief and bring him before you."

Lord Malcolm smiled and disregarded the knight's comments as he slid his sword into place on his saddle. "Good afternoon, Sir Kenneth! Why so glum? This is a historic day for us! The Par'sha and the Mid side by side against a common enemy! Think of it?" Lord Malcolm argued enthusiastically.

"They could be seizing an opportunity against us, my lord!" Sir Kenneth maintained. "I beg you! Let me exchange words with them and uncover their intentions."

Lord Malcolm shook his head, smiled, and held up his hand. Sir Kenneth knew he would not be allowed. He would do anything to protect his lord, but sometimes he was damned foolish.

"I embrace your cautiousness and care for my life, my friend. However, sometimes one must risk much so that all the folk will benefit. I mean to meet them, greet them, and personally show them my hospitality. Perhaps that simple gesture will clasp our hands in friendship," Lord Malcolm exclaimed as he mounted his horse. "Besides, if they should try and kill me, I'll have you and a hundred and fifty men with me. Think of the songs they'll write."

Sir Kenneth wasn't amused. He was annoyed. He wanted to be on his way and in the wood just as the sun was setting. He wanted to make noise and grab the enemy's attention. He wanted to take some revenge on the enemy, but now he was trotting along with his lord toward the main road, about to exchange words with a host whose purpose was unknown. He gritted his teeth and let out a long sigh as he joined Lord Malcolm to meet the Par'sha host.

The Midguard escort emerged from the siege works, the hills, and turned onto the main road. As they approached, the long column of Par'sha halted along the road and formed a line of horsemen at the head of their column.

Sir Kenneth found himself surprised by their discipline. The caravan-men who crossed their lands often spoke of the barbarians stirring themselves into a frenzy just before they attacked. He remained vigilant for such signs.

The armed guard halted before the Par'sha and mirrored their line. The Par'sha column stretched far beyond Sir Kenneth's sight, and he felt naked in comparison to their host of men. If there were any miscommunication, they would fight valiantly but in vain.

Lord Malcolm came forward through the gap and presented himself; Sir Kenneth and his new Sergeant Jacoby followed close behind. They waited only moments before an opening formed in the Par'sha line.

A man on horseback came forward. He stood apart from the usual plain leather-clad warriors. He draped a black pelt over his shoulders, and his gold-plated gauntlets shimmered in the late afternoon sun. His long strands of hair were beaded and jeweled, and his chest was thoroughly covered in paint. Each accessory told a story of his extensive accomplishments. This was a grand chief. He nodded at Lord Malcolm and sheathed his spear.

Sir Kenneth was relieved to see the nomad's blade removed.

"I am U'sabe, chief of the Muun'kii, chosen Partho'sha among the clans. I greet the Lord of the Mid in friendship."

Lord Malcolm turned to Sir Kenneth and grinned. He then returned his attention to U'sabe, brought his horse alongside him, and offered his hand.

"I am Malcolm, son of Malakai, of the family Corraine, Lord of the Mid, and I gratefully welcome your friendship, U'sabe."

The chief took his hand, and they shook. As they embraced, the Par'sha let loose their cries of approval, and then the

Midguardmen followed. After several moments, the celebration came to an end. "Your help is most welcome and fortunately timed. We are on the eve of battle."

"I have been told, and we have come," U'sabe replied to Lord Malcolm's surprise.

"How have you come to know our plans?"

"Three days past, we came across an odd party that belonged to you and they told us of the enemy here and your plans to fight them."

Lord Malcolm turned to Sir Kenneth; both were astonished to hear Sergeant Cal had traversed the wood into Par'sha hands.

"Gods, they're alive!" muttered Jacoby.

"Where are they now? Are they still with you?" Lord Malcolm asked, tilting his head to see along the Par'sha ranks.

The great chief let out a long breath. "They were on a path no one could turn them from, and I allowed them to continue their journey," U'sabe replied. "I know I promised to bring them with me, but it is a warrior path and near to my own heart. I understand how compelling the call can be, and I had no right to remove them from it. So, I did not."

Lord Malcolm sighed and nodded.

"Then you did what I could not," Lord Malcolm admitted. "However, I am confused. Who did you promise to bring me these folk?"

"Master Wendall?" U'sabe replied. "Did he not return to you?"

"No!" Lord Malcolm responded, surprised. "I sent him with men to retrieve the other scouts days ago."

U'sabe hesitated to reply. "He was separated when he came to us, and unfortunately, I bring ill news as well," U'sabe began. "We came across your other scouts on our way here, and they were slaughtered on the road. We did not find Master Wendall among them. I had hoped he had returned to you. I should have insisted he ride with the horde."

Sir Kenneth boiled with anger. He should have gone instead. He should have fought harder against Master Wendall and Lord Malcolm, but now more of his men were dead, and he knew whose fault it was. Those men died because of Sergeant Cal's decision, and Sir Kenneth would do anything to see that he paid for it.

"That damned fool Wendall is either dead or lost somewhere along the Crest," Jacoby interrupted.

"Hold your tongue, Sergeant," Sir Kenneth seethed while Lord Malcolm ignored the comment.

"I will send warriors into the wood. Perhaps he is alive and near," U'sabe offered.

"It would be a great risk to your warriors to navigate through the woods this close to dusk," Lord Malcolm argued. "And I think the sergeant is right. He has likely fallen along with my other men. Let us journey to my camp, and together, we can include you in our strategy. Together, we can end these marauders once and for all."

A long bellow of a roar was let out from behind the Par'sha, and all discussion stopped. It was one of their giant, lumbering bear sloths.

Sir Kenneth clenched his jaw. He didn't even begin to know how to house the behemoth creatures along with all the rest of the Par'sha. However, before they could discuss it further, another one of the beasts roared out, followed by another.

U'sabe turned his horse from them and trotted along the long column of warriors to see the reason for the disturbance. The creature stood on its hind legs and roared; its snout pointed at the tree line. Something was wrong. All the Par'sha readied themselves and shifted their attention to the trees.

Then they appeared.

Thousands of figures emerged from within the wood. Their bright-green eyes blazed from the saddles of the curled-horned mounts. Their bone armor reflected brightly in the dusk light. The enemy was everywhere, on both sides of the road, in a line that extended well past the horde.

Sir Kenneth's stomach dropped. He turned his horse around, trying to find an end to them, but more stepped out from under the forest and continued to form along the road and behind the Midguard, cutting them off from the encampment.

Lord Malcolm, his men, and the Par'sha were surrounded.

The Par'sha began facing the tree line, raised their spears, and cried out again; this time, it was a warrior's cry.

Sir Kenneth turned to the rest of his men, who trembled at the sight of so many Vechians and their green eyes blazing all around them. He would not have it. He brought his horse around to face his men, placing himself between them and the Vechians.

"Turn around!" Sir Kenneth shouted. The Midguardmen wheeled around their horses and formed two lines with their backs to the Par'sha. "Courage, men! You will hold your ground and protect your lord at any cost!"

At that instant, Lord Malcolm came from behind his men to face the enemy as well.

"My lord, please return yourself behind your guard!" Sir Kenneth pleaded.

"Enough!" he shouted back at Sir Kenneth. "Men, there is no hiding from them anymore! You and I will fight together today! And if we should fall, then we will fall with swords in our hands! So, I say to you, fight with me!"

The Midguardmen found their courage as they unsheathed their swords, brought their shields to their chests, and cried out along with the Par'sha.

The enemy did not attack right away. Thousands waited as the combined forces screamed into the sky for all the gods to hear. The Par'sha beat their shields and let out hoarse shouts that usually shook the core of any foe.

But the enemy stood and did nothing. Out of exhaustion and confusion, the shouting finally ceased and an eerie silence followed.

Then the darkness came. It enveloped all the enemy like a raging black thunderstorm, billowing waves of smoke that rose in defiance of the setting sun. The dark fog grew upward like a wall and stopped short from the lines of the Par'sha and the Midfolk. Only silence remained as the enemy hid inside their darkness.

The silence did not last. It was replaced by a shrill whistle as thousands of arrows flew out from the dark. Hundreds of men fell immediately as the arrows rained down. It was clear the barrage would be the death of them if they did nothing.

"Charge!" Lord Malcolm yelled, and every man followed him into the dark mist.

They charged into darkness and were left blind to everything except for the faint light of the setting sun. Lord Malcolm led them straight to where the enemy had stood when the darkness came.

The Vechians appeared suddenly in the darkness with just enough time to begin hacking and swinging. Sir Kenneth spotted the enemy just as his horse barreled over them, and they were prepared. At the last moment, he dodged a pike that nearly removed his head as he swung his sword down upon his foe. They continued their charge and ended well beyond the ranks of possessed men. When they broke through the black fog on the other side, Lord Malcolm wheeled them back around.

"My Lord, the road is just there!" Sir Kenneth shouted. "We can regroup with the army!"

"No! We cannot abandon the Par'sha!" Lord Malcolm exclaimed. "To me, men! To me!"

The cavalry followed their lord back into the heart of the darkness. They galloped along the road and charged through the line of Vechians, drawing their bows. They trampled and cut down as many folk as they could see. Lord Malcolm continued to yell out, "To me! To me!"

It did not take long to come back upon the Par'sha along the road. The darkness had not totally enclosed the road where the many Par'sha fought. The sky appeared above them like a break among the clouds. As they appeared from the darkness, Sir Kenneth saw the evidence of the grueling fight. There were those Par'sha and beast alike who had fallen to arrows along the road and those who had lost their mounts and were forced to the ground, fighting whatever came from the darkness. However, thousands of them took to the shroud of mist like the Midfolk had, but they were still remarkably close among the edges of it. He could hear the fierceness of the fighting as the blades crossed and screams echoed all around him in the black obscurity.

Lord Malcolm dismounted and went to an injured warrior who was desperately fending off three Vechians with an arrow in his leg. Lord Malcolm came from behind and dispatched one while the others were cut down by Sir Kenneth and Sergeant Jacoby.

The warrior raised his arms to defend himself further, but he stopped short, realizing they were Midfolk.

"Where is U'sabe?" Lord Malcolm yelled as the battle raged. The warrior looked around, but it was useless. He had been turned around in the fight and did not know where his chief had charged.

More Vechians came from beyond the darkness and were struck down by the guard at the last moment, but it was getting increasingly difficult as the sun finally left the sky.

Sir Kenneth was at an impasse; he could not keep his Lord safe from harm under these conditions. He formed the guard around Lord Malcolm and dismounted as well.

"My lord, we must retreat!" Sir Kenneth pleaded as wave after wave came at them.

The guardsmen swatted at them, but a few Vechians managed to penetrate the circle. The Midguardmen were also falling.

Sir Kenneth raised his sword to deflect one blow and then another before he struck true at a possessed man. He was poised to bring his sword down on another foe coming from behind Lord Malcolm, and his lord quickly moved out of the way. The blade came down on his foe's head, but more continued to come. "We cannot hold here!" Sir Kenneth shouted.

The fight was wearing on the old knight. His head was fine, but his shoulder pained him. He had spent days with healers hoping to cure every injury, but he had ignored his sword practice. For that, he was a damned fool. He was growing sluggish among the battle, and it was increasingly difficult to deflect or raise his sword. He tried pacing himself among the chaos, but the enemy was relentless. He was no longer able to protect the man next to him. A small fear planted in his mind; he was failing to do his duty.

"We have to leave!" Jacoby shouted as he swung at one Vechian, followed by another.

"I won't abandon them here without trying to get as many of them as we possibly can! I need to find U'sabe!" Lord Malcolm exclaimed.

"This is madness, my lord! He is lost with the rest of them! We must escape while we can!" Jacoby strained.

Lord Malcolm looked over and found Sir Kenneth speechless and straining at his shoulder. Lord Malcolm knew then he was hurt.

Sir Kenneth turned and struck at one Vechian, followed by another. They came repeatedly and what seemed impossible was that several continued to rise after they were struck. The work was sheer drudgery and his strikes were weaker with every swing.

"You are still injured, my old war horse!" he shouted as Lord Malcolm grabbed Sir Kenneth's steed and led the animal to the knight.

Sir Kenneth shook his head. He couldn't leave his lord. Not now. Not while all their men furiously fought against the waves of possessed Vechians and their lord remained behind.

"You are commanded to the rear, Sir Kenneth! Prepare to receive me and as many Par'sha as I can bring to the villages!" Lord Malcolm commanded, holding out the reins for Sir Kenneth to take.

He hesitated to take them.

"You waste our time and our men's lives! Go! Warn the camp!" Lord Malcolm said, shoving the reins into Sir Kenneth's hands.

Sir Kenneth reluctantly sheathed his sword while Lord Malcolm helped him into the saddle.

The old knight hated the orders and did not want to abandon his lord, but he had never in his life disobeyed the Lord of the Mid. He did as commanded and would always do so. However, to leave Lord Malcolm here among the battle went against everything he held true.

"You!" Lord Malcolm pointed at Sergeant Jacoby. "You will see him to the gates and find Sir Pavel! Sound the alarm! Everyone is to arm themselves! I will not be far behind."

"It will be done, my lord," Jacoby shouted back as he tugged on Sir Kenneth's horse.

Lord Malcolm once again mounted his horse and rallied his guard as they valiantly charged into the darkness.

Sir Kenneth turned to the road ahead, where Jacoby led with sword in hand. The mist was darker than ever with the sun gone, but they pushed through. The Midguard had punched through the line of the enemy, and the path remained clear. With no resistance, they galloped hard toward the villages but were forced to slow at the twisting spiked defenses of the entrance while Jacoby shouted, "We're Midfolk! Ease your bows!"

The gates opened to them as they galloped through and pulled hard on their reins. It was clear the folk inside knew of the battle. Thousands were armed and taking position along the hills, the walls, and the ramparts. Fire arrows were nocked in place, and swords were unsheathed among the men on the ground. They were ready.

As they dismounted, another group of riders stormed toward them in a hurry. It was Sir Pavel with an attachment of fifty men of his own.

"Where is Lord Malcolm?" he demanded.

"He is gathering what Par'sha he can and bringing them here," Sir Kenneth stammered.

The Midfolk collectively gasped.

"You abandoned him?!"

"I did no such thing!" Sir Kenneth rebuked. His stomach churned trying to justify why he was here instead of beside his Lord.

"He's injured, sir!" Jacoby interrupted. "Lord Malcolm ordered us back to see the army ready to open the gates! He said he'd be right behind us!"

Sir Pavel didn't like the answer at all as he shifted in his saddle. "Stand aside! We will retrieve him!" he called out as the gates swung open.

"They're coming!" shouted a bowman along the ramparts.

"Over here!" Another soldier yelled from across the wall. Sir Kenneth's hopes were raised that Lord Malcolm and the rest of them were on their way. He kept his word, and he was right behind them. However, the bowmen began loosening arrows over the walls. That meant something entirely different. Sir Kenneth shuffled with Jacoby up to the ramparts to see why the soldiers were shouting. His heart sank.

Their green eyes glowed through the approaching mist darting between the rocks and the forest. The bowmen loosed one arrow after another, hoping to hold them off, but hundreds of the green-eyed enemies emerged all around them.

"The enemy is here!" Sir Kenneth yelled. "To arms!"

Thousands of men rose and manned every section of wall that could be manned. Thousands of bowmen began sending arrows whistling through the air at the enemy.

"What of Lord Malcolm?" Sir Pavel bellowed at them. The enemy was coming from the forest, but the road was clear. Sir Kenneth knew that meant the battle continued, and under his breath, he praised the mighty Par'sha for withstanding such a force.

"No sign!" Jacoby called down.

"Then we will retrieve him! With me, men!" Sir Pavel charged toward the gate when something appeared on the road. To Sir Kenneth's relief, it was Midguardmen and Par'sha alike riding toward them. They were streaming out of the darkness, following the funneled path and dodging stakes as quickly as possible.

"Wait!" Sir Kenneth cried joyfully as he pointed at the road. "Here they come!" The line of men and beasts poured out from the darkness and onto the road. However, they were superbly constrained by the head of the siege works as they were engineered to do so. More unfortunately, it was their men who suffered. They stalled, and the horses whinnied at the restriction of their space as they attempted to avoid stakes and walls while arrows flew overhead, protecting the rear.

Sir Pavel turned his men back into the village as they approached. Finally, the worn soldiers and warriors alike started streaming through the gates like cattle into a pen. All folk who funneled into the villages were bloodied and worn.

As the Midguard and Par'sha forces came, thousands of Vechians now appeared behind the retreating men, firing arrows into them and attacking any who were running on the ground.

Sir Kenneth knew they were unable to ride out and help them, but the Par'sha weren't without aid. He hobbled along the ramparts as quickly as he could with Jacoby in tow until he reached the hilltop that extended furthest out. The bowmen were firing at anything with green eyes, but he reached them just in time and redirected their aim.

The company of bowmen unleashed one lit arrow after another over the heads of the amassed group of Par'sha warriors. Miraculously, the Par'sha saw the pileup, their protection from above, and formed a line of men and beasts as the last line of defense while the rest continued to make their way through the maze. Four giant bear-sloths and every rider along the edge of their cavalry turned around and held their ground as hundreds of darts sailed from the slings behind them.

The Vechians came in waves as arrows and darts alike cut them down. The giant bear-sloths were riddled with arrows but still managed to swat riders and foot soldiers down like flies. Any Vechian who managed to get through was met with a dozen pointed spears. The impromptu defense was somehow working, and they were managing to save their allies. The Par'sha slowly and surely funneled their way in as the mass of men collapsed at the head of the path, and the last thing that passed through their gates was the three enormous bear-sloths and their riders.

The gates closed behind them and the darkness rapidly enclosed the villages on all sides. Thousands of pairs of glowing green eyes approached every wall. It was up to their defenses now. They were behind thick walls of stone, earth, and wood. They had the high ground. They could make it!

Sir Kenneth only saw a heap of men and beasts along the road before the darkness loomed over their corpses. Many of the dead were Par'sha, and it only seemed like a handful had made it through to them. He moved as quickly as he could along the rampart to the gate and found a familiar face.

U'sabe was still mounted on his black steed, but even he suffered numerous injuries, as his right arm bled from various slashes and an arrow protruded from his thigh.

"Chief U'sabe!" Sir Kenneth called. "Did Lord Malcolm find you? Did you see him?" The chief looked up and realized who had asked.

"Yes! He found me," he gasped. "We held our ground, but there were too many, and we were forced back. He helped lead my people from the battle, but I lost him. I was following a Midguardman I thought was him."

Sir Kenneth's fears were realized as he yelled for anyone who had seen their Lord pass through the gate. None had, and no surviving Midguardmen from the battlefield knew where he was. Sir Kenneth was desperate. If something happened to his lord, if even one soldier believed he had left his post, he would know nothing but shame. However, that wasn't the case. He was entrusted to get the gates open, and he succeeded.

Sir Pavel joined him on the ramparts and looked over the walls. The field was infested with possessed men. The darkness encroached onto the walls, all but stopped, and then fire rained down on them from the sky.

"Shields!" Sir Pavel screamed as the arrows landed on everything, as dozens of men dropped and screamed in pain. The bowmen tried to return arrows, but they were blind now and couldn't target anything. They stood helplessly with drawn bows, squinting at nothing as more arrows came down on them. Scores of men either fell or managed to hide underneath the shadows of the walls.

"Swords to the walls!" Sir Pavel commanded, and thousands of folk took positions on the ramparts with shields above them as the bowmen departed. The bowmen re-formed on the ground below and loosened everything left. It was working. The arrows flying in were fewer and fewer, but all men trembled when the gates buckled under an enormous impact.

"Wham!"

"Wham!"

"Wham!"

Wood splintered off the gates with every strike.

"Brace the gates!" Sir Kenneth yelled to the men below while dozens of Midguardmen and Par'sha braced the wooden gate. The gates warped and bowed after each strike, and Sir Kenneth knew it would not be long. The gate was going to break, the encampment was catching on fire, the army was being peppered with arrows.

He did what he should have done on the battlefield. He unsheathed his sword, clasped it with two hands, and endured through the pain.

The Par'sha turned the few remaining bear-sloths around and stood ready at the gates. Behind them were hundreds of folk, spears at the ready. Some were men of the Crest, some were Midfolk, and the rest were nomads far from home. All were waiting for the gate to fall and the final charge of the possessed men.

The enemy swung steel from the shadows in every direction as they climbed over the walls. Thousands of men desperately clung to their shields as the blows came down while they wildly thrust their swords down in retaliation.

The walls held even under constant surprise, but there were sections of the wall where the enemy was infiltrating the village. Slowly, the enemy overwhelmed the men at the walls and pushed folk back. Hundreds of Midguardmen were forced to retreat from the ramparts.

Sir Kenneth saw Sir Pavel scramble what men he could to reinforce the crumbling defenses as he held his place along the wall. There were few folk left at Sir Kenneth's position, and as he looked to see Jacoby beside him, he was gone. He did not know if he had fallen or run. It didn't matter. Sir Kenneth stood with his sword and his aching shoulder, and he would stand there until they took his life.

Three came over the wall and madly swung their swords around. He dispatched one and shoved another off the ramparts, but he was not fast enough to block the third blow. He was lucky; it landed on his weak shoulder instead of his head. He fell backward, lost his sword, and dropped to the ground. The possessed man walked over to him to deliver the final thrust when an odd green light coursed across the sky. He was ready to strike, and he had Sir Kenneth dead to rights, but then another thing happened altogether. The Vechian did not.

Chapter XXVII
The Sorcerer

They looked lifeless upon the ground, and Cal's stomach gave out. Hundreds of folk littered the plateau below with their motionless bodies from the shock of the lightning. Cal stared over the edge, hoping someone would rise, someone would come and help him. No one moved.

"It is unlikely," the sorcerer said.

Cal felt like the sorcerer was reading his thoughts. It was uncanny. The sorcerer turned away, lowered his staff, and disregarded Cal altogether. The darkness faded as the energy surged back into the orb.

The sorcerer had begun some other ritual. He circled his hand around the orb, and it drew from the colored sky above like a funnel drawing water. The sky's energy poured into the orb as it pulsated with light and power.

Cal felt the force of the sorcerer's magic keeping him pinned to the ground, receding but not completely gone as he tried to raise himself. In an instant, the sorcerer caught him breaking free, and he was shoved back down.

Immediately, Cal knew his foe's crutch. Cal relaxed on the ground, giving the sorcerer no further reason to waste his attention on him. When the opportunity was right, he would rise with all possible speed, draw his sword, and strike the man down.

He exhaled a long breath and turned his gaze upon the battleground below. His heart all but stopped. A single figure in a red tunic managed to get up and head toward the mouth of the cavern. Whoever it was could help him.

"Who are you? Why have you come?" Cal asked.

The sorcerer ignored him and continued to draw in the powers of the sky. When the orb was saturated with light and power, he released it across and to the horizon like a wave trundling to the farthest edges of the sky and beyond. Cal then understood. The sorcerer was sending power or a signal to his disciples. Whatever it was, Cal had to stop the sorcerer now or destroy the orb.

"Answer my question, you bastard!" Cal shouted.

The sorcerer broke from his incantation and walked over to where Cal lay and peered through him.

"I am Qadir the Deimas," he finally replied. "And I have come because I must."

Cal frowned, but he was used to the riddles Alec often muttered. All he had to do was keep prodding him until the answer made sense.

"That's a lie. You've bewitched an entire people for a better reason than simply because you had to! What do you want?"

The sorcerer cackled in response and knelt beside Cal. "I have questions of my own, woodman. Who was the conjurer below who has been disrupting my progress?"

"I'll answer your questions if you answer mine," Cal said.

The smile faded from the sorcerer's face. "You are in no position to argue, my young foe!" he said as he unleashed a series of jolts across Cal's body.

Cal writhed in pain as the power surged through him.

After several moments, the sorcerer ceased his destructive jolts, and Cal took the break to recover. He hadn't experienced pain like the shock he received, and he didn't want to know more about it. However, he would do what he needed until help came. Even if it meant enduring several more shocks.

"I'm waiting. Who was that conjurer? How did he come into the service of Lord Malcolm? What are their plans against me?"

Cal clenched his whole body and took a deep breath. It was a long way to the shelf and he needed to give his friend as much time as he could spare.

"That's fair," Cal said, rocking his body from the pain of the shock. "You already answered one question, so it's my turn."

The sorcerer let out another long laugh. "You're a brave man but a foolish one," he jeered.

"His name was Alec. He was a nobody until you came... a vagrant of the Mid," Cal said, wheezing with every breath. His answer seemed to please the sorcerer and he was spared another jolt; it was a good sign.

"How odd? You wouldn't lie to me, would you?" the sorcerer threatened.

"No!" Cal said, shaking his head. "It's the truth. He was a vagabond who couldn't spark a flame when I met him, but his powers grew."

The sorcerer neared Cal, his face full of enthusiastic curiosity. "How do you know this?"

"I was his friend. He told me these things. He said to me once, 'Magic begets magic.'" Cal was fatigued from the jolt of lightning, but he had the sorcerer's attention. He would tell him all the truths if it satisfied his curiosity.

"Now, what is the real reason you've come?" Cal pressed, risking further shock; he wagered the sorcerer would entertain him with an answer. Cal also desperately wanted to understand.

The sorcerer smirked at him. "What do you know of the world?"

"I've seen my share," Cal responded, but Qadir waved his response away like a gnat.

"You've seen nothing except the Crest!" he scolded, standing once again to peer out over the edge. "The world is cruel, as you will find out by my hand as I have found out by another. Not all motivations are clear, and you will be forced to do another's bidding regardless of your desire."

Cal saw through his words. With all the powers this man possessed, he was still following someone else's orders. That also meant his master had a purpose, and Cal wagered the sorcerer knew what it was.

"If you are doing the bidding of another, who is this person, and why do they wish to see the death of my folk?"

The sorcerer looked down and glowered at him. "You cheat! You're not reciprocating the order of questions and answers. The next question is mine. Do you need reminding?" he threatened again, holding up his hand as a spark flickered from it.

"No!" Cal pleaded, holding up his hands in defense. "I am just eager to understand. What was your second question?"

"How did Alec the Vagrant come under Lord Malcolm's service if he was such a lowly commoner?"

The pain was easing, and Cal hung on to his wits. "Actually, a knight tried to have him removed from service, but Alec was lucky. He was allowed to sign along with me and several others because a councilman granted it," Cal answered as he regained the rest of his breath. "Now, who is your master?"

The smirk left the sorcerer's face.

The sorcerer didn't care to be referred to as someone's puppet, and Cal prepared himself for another jolt for his poor choice of words.

"No, I think not," Qadir refused, lowering his hand. "You will have to die without that knowledge, I'm afraid."

Even in pain, Cal grew frustrated. He was so close to uncovering everything only to be refused. Cal wouldn't let the answer slide so easily.

"What does it matter if I know something and then you kill me?" Cal argued, hoping to bait Qadir. "I'm a good listener. Besides, it would be good to unburden your mind."

The sorcerer revealed a crooked smile. "You are a clever man, but alas, you will be disappointed," Qadir maintained, eyeing Cal as he lay on the ground. "But I will reveal why they have asked me to do this. Just the same, you will not like that answer. I have done these things because there is a hunger that cannot be satiated by anything less than absolute power."

Of course, it had to be a riddle. Why couldn't any of these conjurers speak plainly? "So, someone attacked my people because it was a road to power?" Cal inferred.

"In a manner of speaking, yes," Qadir confirmed, tilting his head. "Now, what has the Lord of the Mid planned against my forces?"

Cal felt a lump in his throat; the last thing he wanted to speak of was the army and their plans. The sorcerer saw his reluctance.

"Come now, woodman. If you resist me now, there will be no end to your suffering. Your death will be prolonged over days. Or it can be swift, like going to sleep after a long day's work. Choose wisely!" The sorcerer raised his staff and pointed in Cal's direction.

He could feel it. Qadir possessed another kind of magic through the ruby stone. That's how the sorcerer knew his thoughts and how he kept him pinned to the ground. Any falsehoods would only result in further torture, and his hesitancy vanished. "He plans to lure the Vechians into a trap," Cal revealed.

The sorcerer maintained his cold gaze and continued to direct his staff at him, then stood and placed the stone on his chest.

Cal didn't know what magic Qadir planned to use, but it was clear he wasn't satisfied.

"Do not test me! Tell me all of it!"

"He has taken up at the Trouthavens, and he has ten thousand under his command. They have spent days fortifying the villages, and they didn't need all that time. He's advised by a man who's anxious to draw your forces in, and although I don't know, I doubt they've held off this long."

The sorcerer gazed long at Cal with narrowed eyes.

Cal could see the calculation behind his eyes, and then the sorcerer smiled back at him.

"It matters not. He is a fool for taking up arms against me, and that village will become his tomb. Once it has finished, my legions will continue through this realm and conquer any remaining resistance."

"Because the spell forces the Vechians ahead despite injury or pain?"

The sorcerer raised an eyebrow at Cal's reply.

"Lord Malcolm has prepared for that as well."

"How did you come to know these things?"

"We've learned many things about the Vechians," Cal revealed. "My scouting party spent several cold nights deep in the wood trying to understand them, and little by little, we did. Some thought they were demons, but we watched and discovered the disciples, the scepters, and you. We learned the truth."

The sorcerer didn't flinch at any of Cal's revelations.

Cal expected at least some concern to cross the sorcerer's face, but he stood there pleased with every detail. The sorcerer's indifference was unsettling.

"You failed to mention the Par'sha," he replied smugly at last.

"You didn't ask about them," Cal answered, confused.

"No, I didn't. However, I will save you the pleasure of informing me. The horde has ridden down to rendezvous with the lord of the Mid," Qadir added.

Something was amiss. The combined strength of the Mid and the Par'sha should have caused him concern. Yet, it didn't.

"You know many things, it seems. Can you answer me this? Why did my legions not wipe out the Par'sha? Or, for that matter, the Mid? Why did we lead the horde farther into this realm? Why did I allow them to meet with Malcolm?" he inquired.

Cal racked his mind to understand Qadir, but it made little sense to him. If all these moves were by design, then the trap wasn't Lord Malcolm's. It was Qadir's!

"You're planning to ambush Lord Malcolm and the Par'sha!" Cal answered.

"Yes, I am. I have them surrounded, and they will all be wiped out. There will be no power within two hundred leagues that could stop me once they've been crushed."

"Why didn't you destroy us one by one?" Cal asked.

Qadir combed through his messy beard before answering. "That was the intention. Lord Malcolm was lured away from his high walls, little by little, and I struck at his cavalrymen. Yet, our initial attack was repelled by some unknown entity; it would appear your party was responsible for the miraculous victory," Qadir said, pointing a blackened finger at Cal.

"So, I also took time to observe. I waited and let him gather his strength. While I waited, my forces in the east came across much resistance. Did you know some of the Par'sha clans rested along the border of this realm? I did not. They were drawn into this conflict and assembled their horde. They were formidable. So, I formed a new strategy... one that would ensnare both forces. I drew the Par'sha deep into this country where they would either merge with or even fight the Mid's forces. Neither outcome mattered because both forces are now surrounded by all my legions. This very evening, I stand on the cusp of victory. They are all cut off and do not possess the strength to oppose me, young woodman."

Cal's breath froze. Qadir had orchestrated everything and they played right into his hands. Yet, a small hope sprang in his heart like the light of Alec's magic. "You underestimate their chances," Cal spat, defiant to his fear.

The sorcerer chortled. "You and your wizard are far from the equation now. The day is mine," he declared as he rose to stare deep into the fractured orb. "I'm afraid I no longer have further use of you. You've confirmed what I need to know. I will say it is a shame your friend below had to die. He would have made a useful disciple."

"More than you know," Alec shouted from the shadows of the cavern's roof.

Qadir turned in surprise but was blinded by a searing light that burst into the night and illuminated everything.

The magic surged through Cal, but it came with something else. The light radiated with a heat that burned like a furnace that almost drove him back. Yet, there was no time to concern himself. Cal was released from his hold, and he sprang upward using every ounce of might he had left. He drew his sword and jumped into a sprint. But he was blasted backward.

The sorcerer had drawn the orb from its seat and the darkness erupted from it like the gust of a hurricane.

Cal was driven back by the force of the darkness, and he drove his sword into the rock to steady himself, but it did not pierce through. He slid farther and farther until he was pushed from the shelf. He dropped his sword and as it flung into the Crestwood, he clung to the ledge.

As he dangled, Cal found a small ledge to push with his feet and pull himself up enough to peer over the shelf. Cal's stomach sank.

The sorcerer had unleashed the full force of the orb, and the current was directed at Alec. The old man was holding firm with his staff planted like a tree. He forced every ounce of light and heat outward, but the darkness was focused solely on him now. It enveloped him and gushed over his light like a deluge of water over a glowing stone. Through the muddied ripples of conflicting magics, Alec held firm, but his light was waning. He could only hold this for so long; Qadir's stone held far more powerful magic.

Cal clambered up over the edge using every small ledge and crack he could grab ahold of. It was a struggle, but he made it back onto the shelf.

Once safe on the shelf, he looked at the pair of dueling wizards. The sorcerer was using the full force of his magic and empowering the orb with his staff.

Alec began to falter.

He needed aid now or never, and Cal knew how. He rose to his feet and sprinted toward the convergence of magic. He snatched an item from his belt... not his knife, but the scepter. He lunged toward Alec with the scepter outstretched in his hand. As he flew into the stream of darkness, he was blown aside and behind Alec. He rolled onto the stony floor as the darkness rushed past him like a cyclone, but the storm grew weaker. As he finally stopped and looked to Alec, the black fog sputtered around his friend.

To Cal's surprise, a light burst through the dark void. Alec held his staff in one hand and the scepter in the other, countering the rush of the darkness. The light grew brighter as the darkness funneled all the power of the orb directly into the shard of the scepter. The sorcerer cowered under the power of Alec's magic. Cal had done it; Alec had the upper hand.

The wizards exerted every ounce of magic against one another. Even with the scepter Alec received, the sorcerer was holding his ground, and Alec was bitterly fighting through gritted teeth. Cal doubted his friend could last much longer. Before they lost momentum, Cal darted around, looking for anything he could use against Qadir. Then he spotted it. A dead Vechian was lying on a bow at the base of a pillar. Cal grabbed the bow and ripped the arrow from the dead man's chest.

He stepped from the shadow of the pillar and raised his bow at the sorcerer. Just as Cal moved forward, the sorcerer cut the magical bond, directed the darkness toward the sky, and a torrential wave rippled through the shelf. Cal and Alec struggled to maintain their balance.

Qadir unleashed a powerful jolt of lightning directly into the orb. Cal saw it channel into the dark cloud above, and as he nocked the arrow, it struck. The bolt of lightning struck the pillar beside Cal and shattered it to the base. Rock and debris blew in every direction, and all of them were thrown to the floor.

Cal landed hard, and all breath left his body. He could see the sorcerer, too. He was exhausted from the energy he expended. Cal twisted around to check on Alec. To his surprise, his friend Alec, not a vagrant of the Mid, but a defiant conjurer of the realm, staggered to his feet and raised his worn staff.

The stones affixed to his staff were blackened with soot and all but destroyed, but he seemed unconcerned. Alec flexed his hand, waved his staff, and a bright-blue, engorged flame burst into life from the stones. He thrust the staff forward and a single ball of blue fire was hurled through the night air.

Qadir used his staff like a shield, and the fire ricocheted around him.

Alec fired another ball of flame, then a third and a fourth, as he paced toward his nemesis.

Cal struggled to rise and help his friend, but the explosion of the pillar left him in shock.

Alec unleashed waves of flames until he almost reached the sorcerer, and then he swung his staff overhead like an ax on fire. Explosions of fire and smoke magnified with every strike. Alec attacked from on high, from the left, from the right; he beat the sorcerer down while Qadir shielded against every blow. With every clash, Alec's blows grew weaker; his energy was waning until both staffs merely forced magic between them. Fire and sparks erupted from the contact of their staffs, and then, suddenly the magic stopped.

Qadir's bolts weren't accurate over great distances, but up close, he couldn't miss. The sorcerer directed his energy at Alec's staff, and it shattered in his hands.

The flame snuffed out, and Alec stood confounded and defenseless.

The sorcerer wasted no time and unleashed the full force of the darkness like a stream directed into Alec. Alec flew past Cal and into the shadows of the cavern.

A pit formed in Cal's stomach. His friend did not get back up.

The sorcerer ceased his dark magic and Cal found him panting from the exertion; he was completely drained by the expenditure of magic.

Cal saw it before with Alec after the battle along the main road.

The sorcerer would need rest. And that meant, now was the time to press him further. Cal needed to give everything… even if that meant his life. He rose slowly and painfully. The shock wore at him, and pain from the rocks that had pelted him all over his right side throbbed excruciatingly. He was scratched and bleeding, but he stood defiantly.

"Enough, woodman!" the sorcerer shouted.

Cal was right. He didn't demand Cal stop; he begged him.

"You've been beaten! Here and at the Trouthavens! Submit, and I will be merciful!" Qadir demanded.

Cal ignored him and looked around for the bow. It had blown thirty feet from him, and the arrow was in his hand. He stumbled toward it with no regard for the sorcerer, who was gasping for air.

"What are you doing?" he called out, but Cal didn't care.

It was up to him. He came to a knee to retrieve the bow, and as he knelt, a flash of lightning surged past and onto the walls behind him. The blast was far enough to push him forward, but he still had his balance. He lifted himself from the ground as more rocks flew at him; he tried to draw the bow. It was the hardest draw he had ever attempted. Another surge of lightning flew past him as the force pushed him down to his knees. He wiped the blood from his eyes and took a breath. He needed one good pull, but as he opened his eyes, the sorcerer crept forward with barely suppressed rage.

Cal couldn't stop now, even though his muscles ached, and he couldn't see. He would try with all his remaining strength to raise his bow and release.

The sorcerer looked down and pointed his burnt staff directly at him. It looked like the end.

A ferocious cry echoed throughout the cavern. It was deafening and startling to the heart, but as Cal turned to see what could make such a noise, a blur of a man stormed past him and sent the sorcerer back onto the shelf and beneath the open sky.

It was Rahuum, like an untethered berserker without fear or mercy. The Orc swung his hammer with the force of a giant, and just as it came down, Qadir shielded himself with an impenetrable force of magic from his staff. However, Rahuum's mighty strike forced the sorcerer backwards and he staggered onto the open shelf. The Orc raged as he swung his hammer repeatedly, but the sorcerer's staff was light and he was quick with it. Qadir conjured a block to every one of Rahuum's furious blows. The sorcerer was losing ground, and the edge of the mountain neared.

As the rapid blows came down, the orb was lost from his grasp and tumbled away from him.

Cal's heart leapt as he caught his breath. Rahuum could do it. He could destroy the orb with one swing of his war hammer. Cal tried to call out to him, but his voice was weak, and before he could get Rahuum's attention, the tide had turned.

With the orb free from his grasp, the sorcerer unleashed the last of his lightning directly into Rahuum's chest. The Orc brought his hammer and his blade up to protect himself, but it did little against the jolt. The metal of both weapons reddened with a molten glow. The Orc cried out, desperate to hold onto his weapons, but he could no longer. He opened his burning hands and dropped both weapons; there was nothing left to protect him. He took the full power of the lightning as he was brought down to his knees.

He defiantly roared as the lightning burned his chest. Exhausted, the sorcerer released his power, and the Orc fell onto his burnt hands. With a single motion, the sorcerer approached the mighty hammer, directed his staff at it, and it jumped into his other empty hand as if it were as light as a feather. Then he pivoted on his foot and swung both his staff and the enormous hammer at Rahuum. The sorcerer struck Rahuum like he was working at an anvil, and the Orc flew into the wall, leaving the rock fractured and broken.

The weary sorcerer dropped the hammer and turned from the Orc. Rahuum was twisting on the floor with pain; he was tired and bleeding but still alive. With all his strength, he lifted one leg but struggled to stand. Even then, he didn't give up.

Qadir bent over, retrieved the orb, and turned back toward the injured Orc. The sorcerer began swirling his staff around the orb, and it radiated waves of green light as if he was drawing more power from it. Then he approached the giant, and with another wave of his staff, he sent the energy directly into his eyes.

Cal's chest seized as the Orc's eyes lit up with the same color and intensity as he had seen of all the Vechian folk; the sorcerer was bewitching him right then and there.

Cal looked down and found his arrow. He nocked the arrow, and drew the bow. He trembled as he brought the arrow to his eye, but he steadied himself, exhaled his breath, and released.

The arrow sailed through the air and struck the sorcerer in the shoulder. He cried out and dropped his staff. The spell was broken and the green in Rahuum's eyes vanished as he awoke to a dazed and wounded man standing over him.

The Orc didn't waste time. As Qadir stumbled backward from the arrow, Rahuum reached for his hammer. He grabbed it and with his remaining strength swung the hammer overhead at the orb. The impact disintegrated the orb, Qadir's arm snapped downward, and all the magic was released in an explosion.

The last thing Cal saw before the wave hit him was the sorcerer's limp body flying off the edge of the cliff.

Chapter XXVIII
The Consequences

Cal found himself lying on a pelt of wool next to a warm fire with the cool breeze lightly blowing through the cavern. As he looked across the fire, he found two familiar faces sleeping peacefully.

Alec had scratches all along the right side of his face where the debris had struck him, and his fingers were blackened as if he had been handling coal from a mine.

Rahuum was snoring lightly, and Cal was glad of it. His chest and hands were bandaged from the charring jolts he had received, as well as the savage assault he took from his own hammer.

Cal sighed with relief; all of them survived.

He groaned as he sat up. He couldn't remember how many explosions happened around him, but every muscle ached from the pummeling his body had taken.

The cavern was empty but several voices echoed along the corridor. Despite the throbbing pain, he rose to his feet and hobbled toward the sounds, hoping to find the other familiar faces he cared about: Yslanna, Eris, Halden, Lorcan, Su'ca, and her Par'sha companions.

As he rounded the corner and saw the people talking, they were not who he expected to find. He almost dashed back into the dark corridor.

The Vechians were sitting peacefully around their own fire, conversing and even laughing. They were themselves again, and their eyes free from bewitchment. He had done it. These people were free. He grinned like a fool.

As Cal leaned against the cool wall and basked in their good fortune, Su'ca appeared in the firelight bearing food and ointment, but the change in her demeanor that was the most striking. For the first time, she wasn't the stern warrior. Her smile was warm and her kind eyes were welcoming.

"You should still be resting, Cal," she warmly advised.

"And miss the celebration? Not a chance!" he said, chuckling and then wincing as the soreness throbbed with every laugh. He doubled over in pain, amusement, and relief.

Su'ca caught him and escorted him back to his soft pelt near the warm fire. Even under the triumphant circumstances, the dried meat and stale bread she provided were divine. She generously applied a healing salve, but every dollop of ointment she smeared was icy to the touch; she seemed to relish his slight anguish. She applied the same care to Alec and Rahuum and once she had finished, Cal sat upright with little discomfort and devoured his meal.

"Where are the others?" he asked.

"Most everyone is tending to the wounded," she replied solemnly. As her cheery demeanor faded, he knew she had lost warriors whose efforts helped turn the tide and win the day. He grieved with her.

"I'm sorry if anyone close to you lost their life last night," he said.

She paused at his comments. "My warriors died good deaths in battle. They ride along the eternal plains now. They will hunt every day and celebrate every night until the end of time. The Par'sha do not weep for our dead like the men of the west. Death is much harder for the people of this land."

His heart seized as he looked around the cavern and saw only two of his companions.

"Did any of my party fall?" he asked.

"Eris," Su'ca replied.

His stomach sank and he grieved for her sister Yslanna. He had clung to the idea they might survive because they were all such skilled fighters. Deep down, that wasn't how it worked. They accepted the danger of their quest and the price was always going to be their lives.

Su'ca was right; it was hard not to shed a tear. Eris was a skilled archer, a healer, but more than that, she was one of the party.

And like Alec said, they shared a deep bond almost as if it were… well, magic. Cal nodded as he fought back the tears in front of her.

"Maybe she'll ride along with your warriors. I think she might enjoy that," he said, wiping a tear on his sleeve.

Su'ca smiled as she brushed back the hair from Cal's face. "My people did not know her, but they would gladly welcome a noble warrior who fought beside them to the eternal plains."

Like the sun, she lifted the grief from his heart. Her gentle touch pushed against all the ache he carried from the Fork to the top of the world. He smiled, knowing Eris was welcomed among the Par'sha in the next life.

"How are the Vechians?" Cal asked, hoping to change the subject.

"Shaken but recovering," Su'ca recalled. "The sorcery left them when the green power erupted across the sky. Most dropped their weapons and ran. There were few that cowered before us, but they did not meet their end. I could see they were no longer possessed by the green power. The victory was ours."

It was a good outcome. All that had been sacrificed had been to save folk because that was the right thing. Bill would have wanted it that way, but he couldn't have known the cost.

A few lives were given to save thousands, but they were Cal's friends, and he didn't care for the trade.

"I hope they won't forget what we did to get us here," he muttered.

"The songs will echo through the generations," she emphasized. "My people will not forget easily. I will spread the story so that all remember what we did here, especially you."

He chuckled and shook his head at his name being told in a song. "I don't know that I did all that much," he replied.

She gazed at him. "You convinced me, a foreigner of your lands, the honor of your path; you led a war party to the edge of the world to stop an evil man. I saw what was left of the man on the ground below. His body was mangled, but there was a broken arrow plunged into him. Only you are so skilled with the bow."

"It didn't even kill him. It just stunned him long enough for Rahuum to smash the orb into pieces. When the magic released, he flew from the shelf. It was the fall that killed him," he argued, shaking his head.

"Then the glory is still yours," she said, pointing a finger at him. "Without you, the blow could not have been struck. Without you, it may have been just you seven and yet I still think you would have found a way. Without you, there is no song."

His mouth opened to reply, but no words came out.

"I couldn't agree more," Alec injected from where he lay with his eyes closed and a smile across his face.

The following day, Rahuum woke, and Alec was more vigorous than he had been in weeks. The party re-formed, hugged, laughed, and grieved. They were mostly themselves again as they were before the darkness came. They were just Crestfolk without fear of war; all were eager to return to their homes.

Before they departed, they buried their dead. Over a hundred mounds between all the folk formed along the steep mountain face; all who passed between the realms would know how many were sacrificed for the greater good. There was one exception. The sorcerer was left to the crows and the wolves.

They journeyed south to the Trouthavens and left the passage in the care of Lorcan and the Vechians. Any of their kinsmen who sought out the cavern would be safely delivered to their realm.

The road south was frequented by many weary Vechians fleeing north. However, upon approach, they concealed themselves in the woods. Few were convinced to show themselves, but all were encouraged to return to the passage along the Slopes.
As the company approached the Trouthavens after a week's travel, Cal saw the reasons the Vechians avoided them. They passed several long burial mounds where the army laid to rest thousands of men and beasts. They also passed along an enormous, scorched field where the remains of blackened bone armor were found. They buried their

allies and burned their enemy. It was a sour reminder to Cal that he had not arrived in time.

"Who goes there?" shouted the guard of the village.

"I am Sergeant Cal, and these are my companions." Cal gestured to his party. "We have returned from the northern Crestwood with Su'ca, a chief of the Par'sha, and her folk to bring news and rest. What happened here?"

The gates opened and a stocky squat man, who could have only been a Darwishman, came forward. He was stunned to see them.

"Gods, you're alive!" he exclaimed.

"As are you! What keeps us from our passage?" Alec grumbled.

The guard fumbled to find his reply as the gate opened fully to the other two soldiers, who were equally dumbfounded.

"Yes, of course! Come in! Come in!" The Darwishman exclaimed.

The company entered what remained of the village. It had been trampled and emptied except for a few soldiers who remained, but most of the huts were still standing and would be a welcome sight to returning families.

"You are the famed scouts, aren't you?" he asked.

Cal never liked the prestige of any of their accomplishments, but fables tended to grow outside his control.

"Famed?" Su'ca questioned, glancing at Cal.

"Please, don't encourage him," Cal muttered.

"Yes, we are!" Halden acknowledged, ignoring Cal. "We have returned from our travels. And you are?"

"Micah, son of Ticah, my fellow kinsman. No one has heard from you since days before the battle, but we could only guess your party must have done the impossible!" Micah said, waving a hand around the camp.

"What do you mean?" Yslanna queried.

"The battle? The darkness? Those folk? One moment, they were flooding over the walls, and another moment, the aura from their eyes vanished and they ran. It was so unbelievable we didn't even go after them," Micah said, regaling the story in awe.

He told them everything that had happened. The Par'sha fought valiantly against impossible odds, the army recovered as many of the cavalry and horde as possible, and the Vechians who overwhelmed the defenses and were charging over the walls. They were outnumbered, and their defenses crumbled around them, but something saved them in the heat of the battle. The rumors spread like wildfire as to why the enemy had awoken; there was only one conclusion... The famed party had saved them.

The soldiery was enthralled by the fables, which grew with the telling after retelling. The party killed the enemy enchanters, they defeated the feared sorcerer, or the wizard, Alec, used his mighty powers and snuffed the bewitchment from the Vechians. It was seven against a hundred thousand, and no one could tell them differently.

Cal swelled with pride. All regrets and misgivings faded from memory. For the first time, he even liked the attention.

Lastly, Micah informed them of the news since the battle. To everyone's dismay, Lord Malcolm was killed on the battlefield. He took an arrow to the chest and fell while he arranged for the Par'sha retreat.

Chief U'sabe was so moved by his regard for the Par'sha lives that he commanded the rest of the horde to escort his remains to the Mid where everyone else was now. It became clear that's where their journey would end; Cal would pay his respects to the late Lord Malcolm.

"Why do the Mid's forces remain here?" Cal asked.

"Because it was our duty." A cold voice sneered. Cal looked up and found Sir Kenneth staring back at him. He looked worn from his slinged shoulder to his muddied boots, and his demeanor hadn't improved. "Follow me!" he commanded.

Cal gritted his teeth.

The party followed him to the headquarters of the abandoned villages. The once-proud epicenter of the camp had been ransacked of the drapery, the carpet, and the colors of the Mid. Now, it was just another hut apart from the scrolls of parchments and maps littered about the table.

Master Wendall slumped at the end of the long table. He looked as if he had succumbed to worse injuries than his counterpart. His left leg was braced, and his right arm bandaged, but that did not hinder his duties. He was deep in correspondence when the party entered the hut, and as he finished his letter, he looked up in disbelief at their return.

"Well, this is a surprise!" he exclaimed. "To the top of the world and back among the civilized with new friends as well!"

"Good day to you, Master Wendall. How do you fare?" Alec responded politely.

Wendall shifted his gaze and his demeanor to Alec. "All things considered, I'm recovering as well as can be expected, but not all were as lucky as I."

"Yes, we heard of Lord Malcolm and grieve the loss," Alec sighed.

"He was a good man," Cal added.

"He was indeed. They were all good folk. However, now that I think on it, there is further ill news to share," Master Wendall lamented. "I'm afraid your companion, Jacoby, fell as well."

Cal's breath froze. Another friend was taken from him.

"How did he die?" Cal asked.

"Well, that is the question!" Master Wendall mused. "I'm told it was very chaotic at the end. The men along the ramparts were being forced back, arrows were falling all around them, and, of course, the enemy mysteriously retreated."

"Were you not there?" Halden asked.

Wendall took a breath and cocked his head to the side. "I, unfortunately, was set upon by the enemy before my return. I dealt them what blows I could, but in the end, I did not give as good as I received," Wendall explained, showing his bandaged arm. "The enemy assumed me dead and left me. I managed to wrap my wounds with my torn cloak and hobble my way to the Trouthavens. I arrived days ago and have had to piece together all the events myself. Sir Kenneth was here. He witnessed the whole ordeal," he said, pointing a finger to Sir Kenneth.

"What about Jacoby?" Cal urged, trying to stay on topic.

"He abandoned his post!" Sir Kenneth griped.

Cal didn't believe it. Jacoby fought as bravely as any of them. He may have elected to stay behind, but Cal couldn't fault him for that. The odds of the party's success were long and Jacoby knew it; he saw the war plan as reasonable, but in no way was he a coward.

"Lies!" Halden shouted.

"Let us calm ourselves..." Master Wendall interjected, holding up a hand. "... before tempers begin flaring out of control! It was well reported. He was found just outside the most southern gate on the road."

It was a hard truth to accept by all the party. Halden had grown close to the easterner and clenched his fists, eager to deny them, but they weren't there. Perhaps, in the final moments when the enemy was coming over the wall, Jacoby had a moment of weakness. Cal knew he had his moments.

"Perhaps that was where he was needed, and he fought there," Cal suggested, hoping something would exonerate his late friend.

"No!" Sir Kenneth spat. "He was alongside me on the wall at the front of the battle, and then he wasn't."

"Yes, I'm afraid our good knight is correct, and others can corroborate the story. In fact, the south gate wasn't even attacked. The guards there abandoned it to help along the east and northern villages. I'm told it was a grueling affair," Wendall explained.

"Then what killed him?" Cal asked.

"That's the mystery!" Wendall exclaimed, shaking a finger. "He was neither pierced with an arrow nor sword. Yet, his eyes were blackened like two obsidian stones. As far as anyone could tell, the man collapsed to death, but there is something far more to it than that."

The party was speechless. Only Alec delved deep into the recesses of his mind for answers as he scratched at his chin.

"I just don't believe it," Halden murmured, finally breaking the silence.

"Understandable," Wendall agreed. "However, as interesting as that mystery is, it is not as interesting as your story. No?"

"We have succeeded, if that's what you're asking?" Cal somberly replied.

"Oh, I am," Master Wendall exclaimed. "I am at the edge of my seat to hear such a tale."

"Is this necessary?" Sir Kenneth spat.

Wendall glanced at him and looked away. "Come now, good sir. Where is your sense of curiosity? A band of soldiers set off to undertake an impossible deed and they have returned with news of its completion. I want to be the first to hear how they accomplished such a feat."

Cal began his tale from their last encounter in that very hut, all the way through their journey north. Alec ensured all the finer details were incorporated while the others listened. The only detail that was changed was Rahuum's identity. The Orc decided on their return south to don his mask once again and conceal himself. As the story unfolded, Master Wendall was fascinated with every escape and feat the party endured. On the other hand, Sir Kenneth stood annoyed.

"What an adventure!" Master Wendall exclaimed. "I am surprised Chief U'sabe could've been swayed to free you after our agreement."

"I persuaded him," Su'ca interjected.

"Without her, we would have been among the Par'sha when the enemy attacked, and the sorcerer Qadir would have succeeded," Cal added.

"Ah, so, you are the reason for our fortune," Master Wendall reiterated. "I must find a suitable reward for your services."

"Must we continue with these inconsequential pleasantries?" Sir Kenneth interrupted. "I have grievances that will be answered for." The old knight said, scrutinizing Cal and Alec with his gaze while Master Wendall let out a long sigh.

Cal did not waver from under the hate-filled glower but stood ready to receive whatever accusation Sir Kenneth had been boiling from and ready to charge.

"Ah yes, we must address those as well," Master Wendall conceded. "I appreciate your efforts and the deed you have done for the Mid and many Crestfolk. However, by your own admission, you have carried out trespasses against the Mid."

"What transgression have we committed?" Alec insisted.

"You disobeyed the Lord of the Mid, you deserted your post, and your abandonment caused the deaths of fourteen other soldiers!" Sir Kenneth snapped.

Cal gawked at him. *Was he blind?* Without their aid, the whole of the realm would have fallen; Every one of them would be dead. That was the truth Cal had finally realized upon reentering the village and hearing Micah.

"You can't be serious!" Cal hissed, but the old knight didn't flinch.

"You signed an oath! All of you! If you were citizens, I'd charge you for treason…"

"We saved your lives!" Cal interrupted. "The spell was broken because of us! Most folk would offer thanks, sir!"

"You could've fought here! You should have fought here! That man…" Sir Kenneth pointed to Alec. "… can blind the enemy at whim, and yet he chose to ride off with you! You should have been here!"

"Is that what this is truly about? Whether we fought here or a hundred leagues away? We fought them! We were outnumbered ten to one, and we fought. And we prevailed so that you and all the others could be standing here!"

"And my men?" Sir Kenneth inquired. "Those who were sent to retrieve you and died along the road because of your careless actions. What of them?"

Cal's fist tightened. Many had died, and some had died following them.

"You didn't have to send them either! That was your choice!" Cal replied, pointing a finger at Sir Kenneth.

"No, that was Lord Malcolm's!" Sir Kenneth scolded, dismissing him.

Cal fumed with anger, but he fell silent.

"And if we had been retrieved, we would have all been here, and we would have all died," Alec calmly replied.

"No!" Sir Kenneth spat, turning to Alec. "You have the abilities, old man! You could have been the pendulum that swung the battle in the other direction. So, no, I don't think so!"

"There is no way to know if we could have beaten them," Alec maintained. "We know for certain the bewitchment was broken because we left. Perhaps if we stayed, I could have helped a great deal, but against the tens of thousands they had amassed... it is unknowable."

"Enough!" Master Wendall chimed. "We cannot go back and forth. We must let an arbiter decide the fate of these folk."

"I must protest!" Yslanna shouted.

"Idiots!" Halden muttered alongside Su'ca as the Par'sha warriors began hooting and shouting further obscenities.

"Enough, I say," Master Wendall yelled, waving a hand for silence.

"What gives you the right?" Cal shouted.

"I have been authorized by the Lady of the Mid to conclude the Mid's business here. So, in fact, I *do* have the authority."

"The war is done! The Mid has no authority here among the Crestwood," Yslanna added, waving his claim aside.

"You five signed oaths with the Mid and gave your word to defend her! You've been accused of dishonoring your oath. So, we have every right to charge and try you!" Wendall said to all the party.

"I have no intention of handing myself or any of my men over to this insanity!" Cal retorted, resting his hand on the pommel of his sword.

The company followed as Sir Kenneth unsheathed a knife, and the uneasy guards inside the hut pointed their spears at them.

Alec stepped between Cal and Sir Kenneth. No one moved.

"Think this through, lad," Master Wendall replied softly, holding his palm up to Cal.

"I've made my choice," Cal maintained, staring back at Sir Kenneth. "This grudge has gone on long enough."

"No!" Alec urged. "We mustn't stoop to this, my friend. We know who we are, and we know what we've done is right."

"You would trust an arbiter with our lives?" Cal demanded, ready to once again defy Sir Kenneth and Master Wendall.

"No. However, I would trust one with mine," Alec said steadily.

Cal, poised to fight, shifted his gaze from Sir Kenneth to Alec.

"What do you mean?"

"My arrest for the exchange of charges against my companions," Alec declared for all to hear.

Cal wouldn't have; enough of his friends had been lost. He shook his head but kept his attention on Sir Kenneth and his knife.

Wendall stroked his pointy beard as he considered the exchange. "It could be accepted," Wendall remarked.

"No!" Sir Kenneth argued. "Cal was the Sergeant in charge! It was his responsibility!"

"Come now, Sir Kenneth. You blame me for the crimes, you think me reckless, and you know me as Cal's advisor. Surely, you can agree," Alec argued.

"No!" Sir Kenneth interrupted again. "He will stand for himself alongside you, and all of you will be held accountable!"

Cal's jaw tightened. He loathed Sir Kenneth. He hated his smug face, the arrogant superiority he wafted around, and his ridiculous accusations against them. Cal would do anything to protect his friends. Yet, he also trusted in something... Alec had something up his sleeve.

"The others go free!" Cal demanded.

"And the arbiter must be Lady Alma!" Alec added.

Even Cal was shocked. He was wagering Alec had some wild idea, but not the Lady who just lost her husband, and whose mercy might be out of reach.

"You would trust your fate to the widow of a man you might have saved?" Wendall inquired.

Cal held his breath, but Alec had no qualms; he was as cool as a stream from the mountain. The old man looked back at Cal and nodded warmly before turning to Wendall.

"I would," Alec replied.

Cal let out a long sigh and reluctantly nodded.

"Done. Gentlemen, you are under arrest."

Chapter XXIX
The Crown

The caravan from the Trouthavens was the last of the soldiers returning to the Mid. Cal sat alongside Alec in the middle of all the wagons with tied wrists and anxious guards. The guards were uneasy because they were unsure why the two were arrested. The story of their exploits swept throughout the remaining folk like the runoff of a spring thunderstorm, and the rain continued to fall was because of Cal's friends.

Before they departed, Halden and Yslanna traveled from hut to hut, retelling their adventure. Cal and Alec saved the realm and ended the evil sorcerer forever. They wanted the rumors to grow and everyone to question the farce of their apprehension while Cal and Alec stood before the Lady of the Mid and answered for their so-called "crimes." Every guard couldn't help themself from gazing at the heroic warrior, his mysterious companion, and ask about the fable.

Cal found the whole thing ridiculous, but Alec urged him to confirm every outlandish tale; he helplessly obliged the old man.

"They say you charged the sorcerer alone and pierced his heart with an enchanted blade you won from a Par'sha princess. Is that true?" a young Elvian girl asked.

Cal hadn't heard that one yet, but he had an idea who told it. The remaining party and their Par'sha companions always followed closely behind their wagon, letting Cal and Alec know they weren't alone.

Halden liked to watch the soldiers approach Cal and ask about their quest. The more eccentric the fable, the wider his smile expanded across his face.

"It was a bow I had stolen from a dead Vechian I had killed earlier. The sorcerer disarmed me of everything else," he corrected.

The Elvian girl nodded in understanding as she rode away and called out to her friends, "It was a bow from a Vechian princess!"

"No, that's not what I meant…" Cal said, trying to correct her, but it was too late. The Elvian heard nothing as she galloped down the line of the caravan while Alec chuckled to himself.

They arrived at midday on the third day. The outskirts of the city were flooded with tents and camps of thousands of different folk. All the realm had heard the crisis was finally over and had returned to the Mid to reunite with their kin and to stock up on supplies before returning home. The roads were crowded, the shops were industrious as ever, and the last of the fighting men had at last returned.

As they entered the city, the crowds cheered them like conquering heroes. Yet, to Cal's surprise, it was their names they shouted. Cal, Alec, Yslanna, Eris, Jacoby, Clydes, and Bill all had their names called out as they passed; the rumors had reached the gates long before they had.

Thousands swarmed around the wagon like moths to the flame, hoping for just the chance to see the famed scouts and the leaders of the party. The guards flanked both sides of the wagon to keep the crowds at bay.

"There he is!"

"... Slain a thousand, did he!"

"... With a wave of his hand, he broke the spell, and they fled!"

The folk called out their names as if they'd known them their entire life; the welcome was surreal. With shackled hands, he lightly waved while his companions basked in the admiration.

Under Sir Kenneth's orders, the caravan pushed through the mob; he had no interest in the jubilations. He had business with the Lady of the Mid; justice was all he sought.

The castle was abuzz with folk from all over the realm. It looked as though the elders, chiefs, and masters from every small village had assembled. Old Darwishmen stood next to stoic Elvians and other Crestfolk while colorful Par'sha chiefs told them of the battle between the darkness and all their folk. However, all stood aside as the column of Midguardmen marched through the hall.

Sir Kenneth led at the front while Master Wendall was carried in a litter by four men. Twenty Midguardmen followed behind surrounding Cal and Alec while his friends brought up the rear. It was an imposing spectacle that cleared the halls and silenced one group after another.

The large carved doors opened at their approach, and their arrival was announced. The hall was filled with everyone who wished to see the spectacle of the two men who were being escorted into the great hall. After further speculation, the answer was spread in hushed voices among the crowded hall. The two were Sergeant Cal and the vagabond, Alec. Heroes of the small folk, defenders of the Crest, and apparently prisoners.

Sir Kenneth halted at the bottom of three stone steps that led to a large semi-circular table where Lady Alma and the remaining council sat. As Cal and Alec were brought forward to face the long table, Cal looked upon the Lady. She wore a matching black mourning gown and veil that covered her face.

Cal's chest seized as his palms became clammy and a pit formed in his stomach. Even after all his trials, this court and facing Lady Alma terrified him more. *How could a grieving wife judge them impartially?*

He looked to Alec and found him calm as ever. He didn't understand why the old asked for this, but Cal found some courage in his friend's example and clung to a small hope he held in his heart. Cal took a deep breath and tried to remember Alec's words, "We know who we are and what we've done is right."

Sir Kenneth almost started when Master Wendall had his litter brought up the steps and positioned at the end of the table to join his fellow councilors.

"I hope your injuries do not impair you, Master Wendall. There are many matters of the realm to discuss and settle," Lady Alma broke the tension.

"Fear not, my lady. I'm told my wounds are healing well, and I serve at your pleasure," Master Wendall replied, bowing his head.

"I am glad to hear that because there are Masters and Chieftains all waiting to discuss further aid among the Crestwood. I also have correspondence from our neighboring realms questioning our authority to march our forces into the Crestwood as well as providing aid to these people. However, all of that must wait because Sir Kenneth and you insisted upon a pressing matter of a contract."

Master Wendall pursed his lips and shifted in his seat as Lady Alma's faceless veil focused on him. "My lady, it's a matter of duty, loyalty, and fidelity. The circumstances of which surround these two men who swore oaths to the Mid, the outcome of the battle of the

Trouthavens, and, as Sir Kenneth will argue, the death of Lord Malcolm," Master Wendall explained as voices among the crowd gasped and murmured. "So, I do believe it is a pressing matter."

Cal's heart raced. He could not tell how Lady Alma reacted behind the faceless veil, but the silence was palpable.

"State the charges, Sir Kenneth," Lady Alma commanded as she turned toward him.

"These two men signed an oath to join our forces and fight the enemy of the darkness. However, when the time came, they defied Lord Malcolm's wishes. I charge them with disobedience, desertion, and negligence that directly resulted in the deaths of fourteen men," Sir Kenneth claimed as the crowds gawked at the accusations.

"Those are serious offenses," Lady Alma said silencing the folk. "Are you claiming one of the resulting deaths was Lord Malcolm's?" The hall fell silent.

"I cannot accuse these men directly of Lord Malcolm's death," Sir Kenneth begrudgingly conceded. "However, one of these men has magical abilities unlike that of normal men. He has been credited with saving the cavalry..."

"Was this the first engagement when you overextended yourself?" she asked, interrupting Sir Kenneth.

"Yes," he admitted through gritted teeth. "If Alec, the *user*, had stayed as Lord Malcolm commanded, he would have been present to use his magic again at the battle of the Trouthavens. However, he abandoned his post as commanded by his Sergeant. Their treachery is a foul crime because they should have been there!"

The chatter flooded through the crowds. There were those who remained unconvinced, those who disbelieved, and some who had already begun to raise their voices in anger over the pair of them. After all the rumor and conjecture, Cal feared the folk with the loudest voices, but it was the quiet rasp of an old man who stilled his fear.

"May I speak?" Alec asked politely as he raised his chained hands. He was without fear or doubt. He almost glided as he paced without a care in the world.

The council turned their attention to the old man who waited patiently to be granted his request.

"What do you have to say in your defense, Alec?" Lady Alma granted.

"I would like to address each charge and answer for them, but first, there is an important detail that Sir Kenneth failed to mention. Without our party's aid from afar, the Trouthavens would have fallen..."

"That is speculation, my lady…" Sir Kenneth quickly retorted, dismissing Alec with a wave of his hand.

"It's a fact!" Cal added as all the folk debated around the hall.

The chatter became so loud Sir Pavel had to bang his empty mug against the long table to restore order.

"Silence!" Sir Pavel called throughout the hall. "We will have order here!"

"The event has been described to me, but there is still much speculation surrounding the mysterious victory of the Trouthavens," Lady Alma began. "How can I be assured that your party was responsible for the miraculous circumstances surrounding the… Vechians' retreat."

Cal was speechless, but he didn't need to talk. Chief Su'ca stepped forward among the Par'sha and stood alongside Cal.

"I will vouch for them," she called into the hall as all the folk quieted to hear the strange foreign woman. "I was along the foot of the mountain when the green magic exploded across the sky, and the sorcerer fell. And when he fell, the Vechians ran or submitted. I saw their eyes clear and knew they were no longer possessed by the green demon."

Many within the hall began to murmur quietly at the revelations, but Sir Pavel was ready with his mug to call the hall to order.

"I also saw the remains of the battered corpse that was this sorcerer and the arrow that struck him; Sergeant Cal had been the one to send the sorcerer to the afterlife. I scaled the mountain to find out if he had survived his confrontation, and I found him, Alec, and… that one just clinging to life," Su'ca said, pointing at Rahuum who was still concealed from all the folk.

The muffled voices stirred again, but to Cal's great relief, they quietly agreed with her story and nodded around the hall.

As Su'ca finished, another Par'sha came forward. He was a mighty warrior and known as the chief of all Par'sha chiefs.

"I trust Su'ca's words above all. If she says these men killed this sorcerer, then her words are beyond reproach," U'sabe added.

Lady Alma nodded to the mighty chief who stepped back among his warriors.

"And I can say with certainty that the enemy retreated when a fading green light flashed throughout the sky!" Sir Pavel added.

Lady Alma looked to her left and right and found nods among her other advisors. "Thank you, Su'ca, for speaking on behalf of these men," Lady Alma stated. "Sir Kenneth, do you still deny the connection between the retreat at the Trouthavens and this party's deed?"

"I do not," he reluctantly admitted.

"Then Alec, you may proceed," she directed.

"Thank you, my lady. We have been charged with disobedience, desertion, and negligence. To the first charge, I say this. Cal, Halden, Yslanna, Eris, Jacoby, Bill, Clydes, and myself, have been at the forefront of this conflict. We fought the enemy along the North Road, we scouted the enemy for days on end, and we discovered their power as commanded by Lord Malcolm. Cal saw the way forward to stop them forever and that was also a part of our oath. Cal asked Lord Malcolm for leave to fulfill that aspect, and his lordship did not grant it. However, he did not entirely forbid us from leaving either!" Alec declared, pointing a finger to the air.

The hall erupted in chatter among the many folk as Sir Pavel had to again call for order.

"Is that your defense of the first charge?" Lady Alma questioned. "You saw fit to take leave because of the difference between denying your leave and forbidding it?"

"No, my lady. My point is this: we swore to stop the sorcerer and Lord Malcolm placed us in an impossible position to uphold that oath and honor his wishes. We left without his blessing because our oath demanded it."

He was right. Cal was both encouraged by Alec's reasoning and impressed he remembered what was written on the oath.

"My lady, we cannot let a silver tongue dissuade reason. Lord Malcolm's disapproval of their leave is the same as his outright prohibition..." Sir Kenneth argued.

"I understand completely, sir. However, does the contract stipulate serving until the enemy has been thoroughly dispatched? Can anyone verify and, if it does, can we claim they did not uphold that clause?" Alma interrupted.

Sir Kenneth was silenced along with both Sir Pavel and Master Wendall.

"I cannot say for certain, my lady, but..." Master Wendall admitted.

"Then we must examine the oath to verify the terms of the agreement, but first, I wish to hear Alec's further responses to the charges," she stated.

"Of course, my lady. I will have my man retrieve it immediately," Wendall acknowledged as a young aide of the councilor nodded and then bolted through the crowd and out of the hall.

"To the second charge, we cannot be accused of desertion," Alec said flatly, pacing in front of the table as Sir Kenneth scoffed the remark. "We risked our lives to reach the sorcerer, through scores of the possessed enemies, and directly into the hands of the noble Par'sha horde. Cal convinced the honorable warriors the necessity of our quest and to release us. We traveled through infested wood and scaled a mountainside to fight the one responsible for so much death and destruction."

"We rode toward the danger. We stood our ground the same night as the army of the Mid, and we won! We deserted nothing!" Cal added, pointing toward the mountains beyond the walls.

The scores of folk cheered Cal on as he passionately joined Alec in the defense. The applause rang throughout the hall as Cal felt the relief of the support. When the folk were silenced from the gavel, Alec continued.

"As to the third charge, Sir Kenneth blames us for the indirect deaths of the cavalrymen who followed us into the fray. They were set upon the road in an attempt to retrieve our party," Alec began, but stumbled to continue further.

With a clenched jaw, Cal stepped forward again to continue their defense. "My biggest regret isn't losing my home, my folk, or my friends, but I do wonder if all the decisions I made were the right ones. I wanted… I needed to fight this evil, and I wanted my anger to be directed toward the ones responsible. That was my choice, and I asked if these folk would join me, and they did. Somewhere along the way, I found out the enemy… the Vechian folk themselves weren't that. They were puppets and under someone else's bidding. Once we understood who it was and where to find them, I knew where I had to go. I was willing to risk my life to stop him. I'm sorry Lord Malcolm sent folk to retrieve us. I wish he hadn't. But I don't regret my decision to leave. We fought them, won, and saved the lives of countless folk. Thousands of Crestfolk, Midfolk, Vechians, and Par'sha survived because we did the right thing. That doesn't sound like negligence to me."

The hall erupted in murmurs and chatter from all folk, including the remaining councilors and guards. Sir Pavel had to bang his mug until the handle broke off, and his hoarse voice echoed through the hall.

Lady Alma stood to be heard, and in response, the hall quieted. "I have one final question," she began. "Is it possible Lord Malcolm could have been saved if you would have heeded his will?"

There wasn't a sound left in the hall as they waited for a reply. Cal could not see her face but knew she was gazing at him for the truth.

He sighed and met her gaze. "I do not know if we could have saved his life. I know we would have tried. Alec would have followed me deep in the abyss that was the darkness if Lord Malcolm was there, and maybe we would have collected him..." Cal answered truthfully, shaking his head. "But it should also be asked if we could have then saved the Trouthavens as well because that's where we would have retreated. I was not there, but it is a fact they were overrun, and I don't know if we could have stopped that without stopping the source of their power."

Lady Alma moved little in response as the whole of the folk took in Cal's words. When she turned to Sir Pavel, Sir Kenneth, and the many warrior Par'sha among the hall, she found blank expressions.

The silence was interrupted as the doors swung open for a messenger. He made his way through the crowds of folk, exhausted from his retrieval but successful. He carried a scroll and personally delivered it to Master Wendall. The councilor broke the seal, unrolled the parchment, and read its contents. However, there was something unusual about the parchment.

Master Wendall was confused with what he read and saw. There were several distinctive markings that the scroll had received but he did not understand why or how the parchment could have received it.

"I apologize, but there seems to be some tampering… " Master Wendall muttered.

"What is it?" Lady Alma demanded.

"The parchment has been marked… rather, some of their names have been marked," he replied as he passed the oath down the table, and each councilor perused it before it was laid in front of

Lady Alma. She studied the oath thoroughly but found little answer to why marks appeared on the page.

"Whose names?" Alec insisted, grasping up for the document.

"It appears the names Eris and Bill have been marked through, and a sell-sword's name has been burnt out," Alma replied.

Cal was bewildered but as he looked to his old friend, he found Alec vindicated.

"I can offer nothing better than the proof you hold in your hand," Alec remarked, pointing at the document.

"The oath does, in fact, swear to defeat the enemy so they may never return..."

"No, you misunderstand me," Alec stammered. "I must explain in a different way." With a finger to his lips, he collected his thoughts and then affixed all his attention to the scroll.

"On with it!" Sir Kenneth ordered impatiently.

"Very well then," Alec declared, pointing a finger to Sir Kenneth. "Who quilled this parchment, Sir?"

The old knight was at his wits' end with Alec's ridiculous eccentricity, but he answered. "Sergeant Willem! A man who died retrieving these men..."

"No!" Alec cut him off, pacing back toward the long table. "He, in fact, did not write upon this parchment! I asked if I could put this oath into words and was granted by Master Gregory himself, if you remember. Willem wrote many oaths that evening, but it was my hand that scripted that document. There were witnesses and you will find my penmanship is vastly different from the late Sergeant Willem's."

"Fine, I vaguely recall you writing the oath. What of it?" Sir Kenneth demanded.

"I admit I have been a challenging citizen. I have always been critical of various policies publicly in the forum, and for that, I have not been popular among many here," Alec rambled. "I've also claimed for years that I've had abilities that would shock and awe the folk of this city, and those claims were met with skepticism, scorn, and altogether disregarded."

"Agreed," Sir Kenneth added.

His tone was silenced when Alec twisted his hand, and it became engulfed in a blue flame. It flickered light and warmth of the faces of everyone in the hall as the magic washed over them and left them in awe.

"However, when strange tidings of raiders with unknown powers reached our city, my impotent skills once more coursed through my soul like the rapids of the White. I could once again call upon my skills and be of use again. So, I took that opportunity when Cal arrived in this city and befriended me."

"What is your point, Alec?" Lady Alma insisted, staring at the flame.

"I enchanted the parchment, my lady. My hands wrote the oath, and like a lightning rod, the magic coursed through the quill onto the paper," Alec claimed as all the folk became transfixed with him. "This contract is not just legally binding… it's magically binding." He flexed his hand once more, and the flame vanished, leaving his withered hand unharmed and clean.

"This is madness!" Sir Kenneth shouted as everyone felt the magic leave. "He is attempting to warp our minds."

Before anyone could agree with him, Alec turned to him and smiled. "Then let the parchment speak for us," Alec exclaimed. "Three of our party have left this world. One died on the main road among hundreds of cavalrymen. He fulfilled his oath and reminded Sergeant Cal of the reasons to fight, to live, and let live. The second name fell on the foot of the mountain, holding back a dozen possessed men so he could have a chance to end this evil once and for all. She, too, fulfilled her obligation. The last died mysteriously at the Trouthavens and, up to this point, no one knows how. He was a brave man, a skilled fighter among thousands, but when the time came to stand against the darkness, he ran! That man, in a moment of weakness, but truly in his heart, ran from his duty, and the oath claimed his life for such disobedience."

"This is absurd!" Sir Kenneth shouted, but Alec disregarded him as he turned back to Lady Alma. Her hands trembled ever so slightly holding the parchment.

It was true; all of it. Alec wrote the oath, and the small parchment showed who had died, who had lived, and who had kept their word.

"My lady, Sir Kenneth and Master Wendall, told us of Jacoby's death. We were not there, but they said he had collapsed inexplicably paces outside the southern gate, and his eyes had been blackened like stones... or like his life was snuffed from this world... The oath holds us to our words," Alec explained as he raised his hands to her. "This was my doing. I charmed the parchment, and I must live with Jacoby's death. However, no man can say we did not uphold our oath."

The hall fell silent.

"My lady, if I may..." Master Wendall interrupted.

"No, you may not," Lady Alma snapped coldly. "The contract was in your possession; you broke the seal, and you discovered the truth."

Master Wendall held his tongue.

"These men have kept their vows to this realm and if I have read this correctly and understand the power of this contract, they have stopped this evil from ever returning. We owe them our gratitude, our thanks, and their freedom," Lady Alma declared.

Cal couldn't believe what he had heard as the cheers echoed throughout the hall. Alec had done it. They were exonerated from their charges, and his legs almost gave out under him as the relief flooded his chest, and his friends surrounded him in an embrace.

"My lady?!" Sir Kenneth shouted as the people celebrated the just ruling. "What of my men?! What of Lord Malcolm?!"

The folk did not quiet immediately, but all could see the old knight was far from conceding.

"I have made my decision, sir. We honor our contracts in the Mid, and I see this agreement fulfilled unless you insist upon some other reason…"

"I insist! I protest this hasty decision!" Sir Kenneth spat, but the Lady would not have it as she removed her veil and revealed her face. She was a beautiful, fair-skinned woman whose only distinguishable flaw was the puffy eyes that let a single tear escape her. Her blue-eyed gaze pierced Sir Kenneth as he recoiled back from his outburst.

"So be it! Let us discuss the fault of my husband's death!" she exclaimed. "Since you are so determined to see justice be done!"

"My lady?" Sir Pavel begged.

"Silence!" she scolded as the room fell silent. "I have been told a hundred and fifty riders guarded my husband when the darkness came! Men who swore to shield him and to protect him. Tell me, how many of them survived?" There was no answer from her many advisors as the hall suffered under her wrath, but it was finally Sir Pavel who braved reprisal to answer her.

"A few dozen Midguardmen… maybe," he uttered. "And, of course, the many fine Par'sha warriors."

"A few dozen Midguardmen," she repeated. "And who here among this hall was beside him when he fell?"

There were a handful of folk among the hall who raised their hands, but most of them were those of the Par'sha and a pair of Midguardmen who stood at the entrance of the hall. "I thank you for your honored words. You stood when he needed you the most, and it is a debt I can never repay."

She directed her gaze to Sir Kenneth, who could not acknowledge her questions. He wasn't with Lord Malcolm when he fell, and it gnawed at him.

"I do not understand, Sir Kenneth. I'm told you rode with him and his guard to meet the Par'sha," she said.

"I was, my lady…"

"Then why were you not with him, his loyal knight, to shield him in his final moments?"

He shook with fury as the realm heard his greatest regret. The councilors, merchantmen, and Midfolk would never let him forget because now the idea would be seared into their minds.

"It's not as simple as that, my lady. Before the end, he ordered me to ready the fort for the arrival of all…" he stressed.

"Why would he send an advisor and knight of this court as skilled as you to act as a mere messenger?" She pressed him, but he didn't want to answer it.

"I was injured, my lady…"

"Were you bleeding? Had you been struck and wounded?" she insisted.

"No, I was wounded days earlier," he said, head hanging.

"I have seen the wounded from that battle, and you are neither maimed nor clinging for dear life with a healer at your side! Why didn't you refuse him? Why didn't you send another?" she cried as the knight averted his eyes.

"It was my duty to obey…"

"Duty? *Duty*? It was your duty to put your life before my husband's, and you did not. That is the difference between your idea of duty and this man," Alma shouted, pointing to Cal.

"Two commands were given by my late husband. One command was defied at significant risk for a chance to save a thousand and the other command should have been refused so you could have had the opportunity to just save one."

Sir Kenneth was stunned by her assessment and there was no sound among the hall. He fumbled to find any word to reply, and when he mustered a sound, it was a mere stutter.

However, she would not have that sound either. "It is not enough to follow blindly, Sir Kenneth. And I cannot... I will not keep the services of a man who does not fully understand his duty and blames others for his failures," she declared. "You have honored this realm with many years of service, and for that, you have our appreciation. However, I cannot see past your most recent failing. You are hereby dismissed."

Sir Kenneth was shocked by her decision, but the final injury took him by complete surprise.

"You can't..." he muttered pitifully.

"I am the Lady of the Mid, the last of this family, and head of this city. I have every authority!"

His confusion subsided as the blood rushed to his furrowed brow and flaring nostrils.

"NO! I HAVE DONE EVERYTHING FOR THIS CITY!" he yelled.

"It was not enough," she replied as she calmly sat back down and ignored his outburst. "You may leave at once."

Sir Kenneth tried to find an ally among the council, but not one met his gaze. In a moment, she had stripped him of his position.

"You will regret this... this... slander! I will have retribution from this city! I swear it!" he threatened, shaking his fist before he finally turned and stormed out. As he approached the doors, the guards lowered their spears and pointed them directly at the knight.

"No!" Lady Alma rose again. "His words are hollow, and I command that he be left unharmed. He shall live today, tomorrow, and the next day with nothing but his regret, and you shall not harm him!"

The guards raised their spears and opened the door for the knight. He left without another word. The folk filling the hall resumed their commentary, and they showed their approval of both momentous decisions with thunderous applause.

Two men were freed and praised for their deeds, while another was removed for his inaction.

Lady Alma looked over the folk as they showed their favoritism. They admired her as they would any lord in her position. As they nodded in approval, she held out her hand to be heard once more.

"Many have come before this hall for justice. They came when there was no one else to stand up against the raiding of our realm, and now, many more have simply come to ask our assistance so they can proudly stand once more while they rebuild, but it is not enough..." she declared, pointing a finger to the table.

"Justice and fairness are nothing without wisdom, leadership, and security. We are all children under the shadow of the Crescent Mountains who have fought and died for an opportunity. Without each other, folk around our realm would have all perished under the oppression of evil and foreign power."

"What are you suggesting, my lady?" Master Wendall insisted.

"A unification," Lady Alma declared, waving her hand around the hall as all folk held a moment of silence and then broke into uncontrolled murmurs.

She stopped Sir Pavel from banging his broken gavel just so the folk could discuss it. However, another had to be heard.

"Are you suggesting we place a crown on your brow, my lady?" Master Wendall demanded. "Because consolidated power only leads to tyranny!"

"I do not ask for tyranny, nor do I wish it for our folk," she said, dismissing him. "Besides, look around you, Master Wendall. There are many seats at this table and the Mid has always welcomed wise councilors to sit and be heard. Masters and Chiefs could be made lords under a crown, and their voices could resonate into the crown's ears and throughout these halls. We could become a Kingdom of the Crescent, with laws, protection, justice, and fair trade for all. If you wise Masters consent to a crown and yield to the Mid as its capital, that dream could be a reality."

"My lady, you risk grievance against our neighboring city-states and further criticism…" Master Wendall added.

"So be it!" Lady Alma maintained as he was further silenced. "None of us should bow before the demands of these foreign powers! By our combined strength, we have sent a message to all who have had their eyes upon the Crescent… they have no say in our realm. Together, we can rebuild the Crest as so many of us need. And we should do it from the strength of a crown."

They were in awe of such an idea that the Masters and Chiefs of the smallest villages let the delight build until, at last, the triumphant cheer burst into the castle. Today, many would get far more than they had dreamed. They would leave with food, security, justice, and lordships, but above everything else… a crown.

Chapter XXX
The Confession

Weeks had passed since Master Gregory's last visitor. Once Lady Alma had left, he was taken back to his cell, where he had remained ever since. He saw little of the guards except through the tiny slot at the bottom of the door: once in the morning for his chamber pot, and once in the evening for his meager plate of slop. There was nothing else except the happenings outside his very high window. He could smell the freshness of the air and faintly hear the voices from the courtyard.

During the first week, he pored over all the discussions in his mind between Master Wendall, the Council, and Lady Alma. He ate everything he had been given, but for a man who lived a life of plenty, the last few weeks of insufficient sustenance weren't enough to heal his aching body and sustain his mind. The results left him tired, hungry, and unable to keep his thoughts clear.

Gregory dealt with the hunger over time, and his body regained some strength, but it was not knowing the unfolding events around the realm and his inability to participate that drove him mad. As the days lapsed, the mutterings of bystanders passed through his window, but little was understood; it was his jailors he eavesdropped on the most.

Wulfred and Trent were talkers, and Gregory hung on to every rumor. It took days, but news finally echoed into the bowels of the Mid's dungeon.

Gregory first learned of an ambush along the main road, but the cavalry had survived. At first, the news worried him. *What if Master Wendall had died?* Lady Alma would have no further use of him. However, the days had passed one by one, and no one came to end his life.

By week's end, as the pair of guards were divvying the evening rations, further news spread to his cell. Gregory had learned the army was encamped at the Trouthavens and had begun preparing for a siege. They also mentioned a small party had learned the secrets of the enemy, but the guards walked too far away before Gregory could learn more. He took the rumors as good news of progress on the front.

Then, on what he believed to be a Tuesday, the bells rang. They could be heard as clearly as the birds in the woods, and their signal was either incredibly good or horrifically bad. As the bells echoed into his chamber, Gregory heard folk rejoicing. For the first time in decades, he dropped to his knees and gave thanks to the gods. The Mid was victorious in some fashion. When his guards passed later that day, they confirmed his suspicions; the enemy retreated and the darkness was gone. The Midguard and the Crestfolk volunteers had won.

Their victory stirred life within him once again. All would be returning soon, including Master Wendall. Gregory refocused his energy with a newfound determinism. He reviewed the questions he wished to ask Master Wendall and how he intended to coax him into revealing something of value; he focused on nothing else.

When he heard further celebrations and Trent confirmed that soldiers had returned, Gregory grew anxious; Wendall had not yet appeared. His nemesis would surely be one of the first to return to the Mid. Master Wendall wouldn't dream of missing the opportunity to revel as a valiant hero among the small folk. The days continued to tick away, and Gregory remained in the cell without a visitor.

At the end of three weeks since his capture, he questioned if he would ever see beyond the chamber. Yet, he couldn't be sure. With every breath he drew, Lady Alma kept him alive. It felt like ages since he heard they were victorious on the battlefield and the soldiers had returned. *What kept Master Wendall away? Had Lady Alma not found a way to broach the subject? Was Wendall lost to a battlefield?* Gregory's hope faded as he slowly succumbed to madness.

As the evening air flooded into his chamber, he prepared himself for another night of restless pacing, but the ringing of the bells once again echoed through the window. Some other joyous news befell the city, and he listened carefully.

Gregory became familiar with most of the happenings among the dungeons. In fact, Wulfred and Trent were punctual men of habit who roved regularly through the dungeon halls. When heavy footsteps, the rattling of keys, and the opening of gates sounded through the dungeon halls at an odd hour, his attention was piqued. However, when the lock of his own door followed those sounds, his heart almost seized in his chest.

The door swung open and Wulfred entered first, followed by Trent. The last encounter with the guards, especially Trent, was unpleasant. Upon their entry, Gregory immediately held his hands up and lowered his head in obedience. This was far easier to swallow than cowering in a corner.

"Up with you!" Trent ordered, but Gregory had every trepidation as he rose slowly. Each man clamped a shackle onto his wrist, but he dared not look them in the eye.

"Can you walk, or do we have to carry you?" Wulfred asked. Gregory's pulse quickened, an encouraging sign to be asked to navigate under his own power.

"I can walk," he answered carefully.

"Good. I don't want any problems with you, so hear me. If you attempt to escape or if you so much as trip, Trent is going to beat you first and ask questions after. So, follow me and don't do anything stupid!" Wulfred ordered.

"You have my word, sirs," Gregory assured as Wulfred nodded. They traveled down the hallway and into the only other familiar room he had known beneath the castle. There, at the center of the room, another pair of shackles hung where he was strung up like a marionette and tortured. He took a deep breath, and followed Wulfred into the room.

Wulfred led him to the chains and he followed despite every hesitation. They removed his shackles, attached the chains, and left. The chains hung loose from the ceiling, and Gregory's mind began to wander. Perhaps Lady Alma granted him mercy for his injuries or she afforded him some measure of freedom. Whatever the reasons, it was unusual for sure. What he did know was that the game was changing, and he was ready for the next cue.

It started with the turning of gears as the chains recoiled upward into the ceiling. As his arms were slowly pulled apart, a persistent doubt formed in his mind; his heart raced, and he gritted his teeth. *Would Lady Alma keep her word? Or was he about to meet his end?* Just as his arms came overhead and a twinge of pain flashed through his ribs, the mechanism stopped.

As he stood tethered to the ceiling, he found the situation almost tolerable; this was Lady Alma's mercy. And if that were the case, he wagered the situation was drastically different. With purpose reinforced, he stared at the chamber door.

His heart quickened at the prospect of meeting his peer one more time, and when his impatience peaked after half an hour's time, he finally heard someone from down the hall. A cane echoed throughout the dungeon as it struck the ground from afar, and with every firm plant, it hit a nerve. When the door opened, the outline of a man shone in the hallway.

He hobbled into the room amidst his own audible confusion of why he was there and for what purpose. However, his endless questions ceased once he recognized the man at the center of the room.

"Master Gregory?" the man called out. "Is that really you?"

Gregory knew the high-pitched voice. "Come to the light. I cannot see you unless you come to the light," Gregory replied.

Wendall approached cautiously as he limped into the dimly lit chamber, but when his face emerged from the dark, Gregory found astonishment on his colleague's face. Wendall did not expect to find Gregory suspended by chains within the depths of the Mid's Keep.

Before a word passed Wendall's bemused face, the sound of a loud "crunch" underfoot grabbed his attention, and he glanced to see what unfortunate stones he had crushed. Yet, his gaze was immediately drawn to the faintest red shimmer. As he looked closer and recognized the stones, Wendall froze.

Gregory watched as Wendall apprehensively picked one of the rubies from the stony floor to examine it further. Gregory recognized them and, from Wendall's face, it appeared he had as well; it was Gregory's gift. Now, they were scattered onto a prison floor and Wendall looked baffled by it.

As torchlight glimmered off the ruby in Wendall's hand, Gregory fumed with rage. He regretted listening to Wendall's damned conspiracy and accepting the rubies; everything led to this cell. Gregory greedily kept the gems in a small sack on his belt. In a way, the gems were reassuring having the evidence of Wendall's payment on hand in the event things spiraled out of control... which they most certainly had. The blood rushed to his face; it was the first time in weeks he felt alive and he swore under his breath the situation would be rectified.

Gregory was surprised the gems had not been plucked up by the guards, but they hadn't. They remained hidden for weeks in the darkened chamber while he waited for Wendall to arrive. Now, Wendall brushed over the gems within a dank cell, and he appeared mystified.

Wendall turned his wary gaze back to Gregory. "Gods! What has happened to you?" Master Wendall asked as he moved toward the chair in the center of the room. Gregory distrusted his concern. Wendall had held back his knowledge of the raiders, he had exaggerated Lady Alma's treacherous plot against the Mid, and he had lied about his life being in danger. His concern was as meaningless as ever. Gregory decided to use it against him if he could.

"Oh, Wendall! The torture I have seen! I've been beaten and whipped like a cur. I am at your mercy, my dear friend! Have you any water? Please, sir," Gregory stammered as Master Wendall produced a waterskin and proceeded to feebly assist him with an injured arm.

Gregory drank from the waterskin, hoping his own meager acting would convince Wendall of his plight. However, it wasn't far from the truth of his current state. The cool water passed his lips, and he began to guzzle every drop.

"Gods, how did you come to this fate? Who did this?" Wendall inquired.

Gregory decided to take the dramatic performance even further as he pretended to check the doors for any eavesdropper. The ruse demanded Gregory's commitment and all but ensured Wendall's trust. In all actuality, he hoped Lady Alma was truly listening.

"Lady Alma!" Gregory whispered as her name sounded off the walls. "I've discovered what you asked of me, but it was a trap. She set the guards on me, Wendall! They took the club to me and I awoke in this cell where I've been ever since! You can't imagine the pain I've endured, my friend! Look at what she's done to me!" Gregory tried to produce tears, but it was difficult to command such a thing.

"It was Lady Alma who sent me here!" Wendall remarked as he took a pause at his own reflection and looked around the room as well. Gregory knew then his suspicion was raised and needed to continue to derive Wendall's trust.

"Why have you come, Wendall?" Gregory asked, hoping to steer his thoughts before he came to any conclusions.

"Lady Alma asked me to inquire on a treasonous situation in the dungeon and, forgive me Gregory, if necessary, make a recommendation on resolving it," Wendall admitted. Gregory didn't like the sound of the accusation, but he had to trust Lady Alma; she was the way to freedom.

"There is nothing to forgive, my old friend!" Gregory lied. He intended to hold Wendall accountable and, if possible, make him pay dearly for every lash.

"When you came to me, I thought the whole thing absurd, but you were right to fear for your safety! I've seen what you had intended, Wendall. They were there just as you said," he continued as Wendall raised his hand and let a series of "shushes" pass his lips.

"Quiet, you fool!" Wendall snapped as softly as possible. They both looked back at the cell door and found no one peering into the room.

"Gregory, be calm. What have you told them?" Wendall whispered, but Gregory did not recoil. He guessed this line of questioning would undoubtedly be asked, and he was ready. He prepared several lies, but ultimately, Gregory thought something closer to the truth was more convincing than anything else.

"She set the lashes on me! Oh, Wendall, I couldn't take it!" Gregory cried, tearing at the recollection and drawing Wendall in.

"Calm yourself, Gregory!" Wendall rose and again provided the waterskin. Gregory drank deeply and took a breath as if he was recovering his breath.

"It is important that I know everything that has been discussed. Now, tell me what you said to your captors," he pressed. Gregory almost smiled, but he resisted.

"I was questioned why I was in the vicinity of the south tower. Every perceived lie produced another lash, Wendall. I told them what I had found. I saw Lady Alma and Master Hector and still they let the whip fly!" Gregory said, babbling.

"What of me?! Did you mention my name?" Wendall demanded, grabbing Gregory by his shabby robes.

"Is that all you care about? I have endured lash after lash, and all you can ask me is about yourself?" Gregory accused, hoping to prolong Wendall's internal suffering. Wendall sighed in exasperation, released Gregory, and collapsed on the chair with his head in his hands.

"Forgive me, my friend. I'm just... I'm exhausted from the road. The journey has taxed me and I am weary from my toils. Please, Gregory, you know I will do what I can for you, but if this is a trap, then we are both securely in this cell now!" Wendall reasoned.

His suspicion did him justice, Gregory thought. This was indeed a trap.

"No, your name did not pass my lips. In fact, the whip stopped once I said Lord Malcolm sent me," Gregory lied as the relief washed over Master Wendall, although he did not deserve it. "That was the last of the punishment I sustained, and for some time, I have been kept locked in the bowels of the place without so much as a word from my captors. What has happened, my friend?"

"I'm afraid Lord Malcolm is dead!" Wendall revealed, looking back up at Gregory.

Gregory let out a long sigh of regret, a genuine emotion among his performance. Their former lord commanded respect and power among all folk of the realm and Gregory would mourn him.

Gregory shook off the thought and focused back to Wendall. The news of Lord Malcolm's death was highly coincidental given Wendall's other conduct; Wendall may have even been involved. If that were so, the treasonous culprit Master Gregory had been looking for would have been right in front of him the entire time.

"Gods! How… you must tell me!" Gregory demanded as Master Wendall sighed and took a seat.

"He was killed in battle at the Trouthavens. I'm afraid his hubris finally caught up with him," Wendall remarked, but Gregory questioned him immediately. Lord Malcolm never struck him as overtly prideful. He had to know more.

"How so?"

"He was ambushed outside the Trouthavens with a small contingent of soldiers parlaying with the Par'sha… oh, forgive me. I have forgotten. This is all news to you," Wendall apologized, gesturing to Gregory. "The Par'sha chased the enemy across the realm. When I happened upon them while trying to locate a rebellious scouting party, I had convinced them to join our forces, but alas, their meeting was ill-fated. They all fought valiantly, even those barbarians, but it was all in vain."

Gregory knew something was amiss, although he was unsure where he lied.

"I don't understand. I heard the bells and the celebrations. Did we not prevail?" he asked.

"We did, but only because the enemy's spell was broken," Wendall explained. "A powerful sorcerer possessed tens of thousands of folk who descended upon our realm. However, those rebellious scouts I spoke of learned of the sorcerer's power and killed him. When they did that, the enemy fled. Our realm is once again safe."

"… but Lord Malcolm?"

"He died at the beginning of the battle. They surrounded him with every warrior at their disposal," Wendall answered, but Gregory still felt in his gut that something was wrong.

"This is a blow," Gregory remarked. "Without him, Alma will no doubt see me killed, and I am not long of this world, Master Wendall! I am a small obstacle on her road to becoming the Mid's new master. You must disassociate yourself from me!" Gregory insisted.

"It is far more dire than you realize, my old friend," Master Wendall said, sighing as he rubbed his weary leg. "Lady Alma has all but declared herself Queen of the Crescent!"

Gregory was shocked. He had dreamt of such a momentous change among the realm, and his single regret was that he was not present to see her take such a significant step.

"Have the folks accepted the proposal?" Gregory genuinely inquired.

"She left the decisions in the hands of the Masters among the realm, but the proposition was celebrated not an hour ago! They will undoubtedly accept," Wendall declared.

That was the answer to the celebrations Gregory had heard earlier in the evening. She had done it. She stood to unite all the various folk within the Crescent Mountains. Gregory was at a loss for words.

"I know the feeling," Wendall remarked to Gregory's awe. "She has all but ousted any other potential rival to the position. However, there is the matter of what you and I know."

"The game is up for me, my friend," Gregory lamented. "A queen cannot allow my tongue to wag and hinder her ascension. Nor can Master Hector? What can we possibly do?"

Wendall let a maniacal smile stretch across his face. Now, Gregory would speak to the mastermind behind the plot.

"We are not so foiled, my old friend. Power is momentary, and those who have it can easily lose it. Even we can manipulate our fate," Wendall remarked as he produced a small dagger, but it looked very odd. The hilt was made of white bone, but the blade wasn't metal. It was a dark green crystal shimmering among the torches.

"What is that?" Gregory inquired as Wendall handled the blade with care.

"This was a piece of the enemy's power. With it, they were able to form the darkness that all men feared, but, in the end, that power was broken, and now there is truly little magic remaining in the precious stone."

"The power is gone because the scouts you mentioned killed this sorcerer?" Gregory inquired.

"Yes and no. They destroyed the source of this magic, but when they killed the sorcerer, they unintentionally stopped another power altogether."

"How do you mean?" Gregory inquired.

"The sorcerer possessed another stone, one with an unmistakable color and power," Wendall remarked as he sorted through the rubies he had given Gregory, and in turn, Lady Alma poured onto the ground. He tossed one valuable gem to the side, followed by another until he came upon the one that satisfied him. It was then, after further inspection, that Gregory found it slightly different than the rest. The color of the stone matched the rubies flawlessly, but the base of the stone possessed a rocky face.

"Here we are," Wendall exclaimed.

"I don't understand. These were the rubies you gave me."

"Yes, and I kept a secret from you as well." He admitted. "This tiny red stone is remarkably similar to the green shard. They both possess powers beyond what most men can see or control. The green shard possessed a power of the clouds, and the red does something vastly different... it influences the will. It can even control a body or mind."

The room fell silent. Gregory stared down at the red shard, and he became blind with rage.

"Are you saying this stone manipulated me?" Gregory demanded.

"In a manner of speaking," Wendall replied.

Gregory's chest seized and his stomach almost lurched. *What had he done? What did Wendall make him do?*

"You… you gave it to me to ensure I would investigate this scheme! You tricked me!" He snapped, pulling at his chains.

"You give me too much credit. I haven't the skill to truly manipulate this stone, but I know how to put it to use. I needed you to investigate the matter and you've always been one driven to climb the political ladder. With your natural intrigue with anything scandalous, this small stone merely encouraged you to follow your inclinations."

Wendall had thoroughly summed him up in an instant, and what made Gregory even more furious was that Wendall was right. He was obsessed with power and the game to keep it. He acted upon any means, including the disreputable ones, to forge ahead. Gregory was assessed and found as predictable as any other man by someone he underestimated. Gregory hated him for it.

"I will not be maneuvered like some pawn, Wendall!"

"And I couldn't chance you not assisting me…"

"You did this to me!" Gregory shouted.

"Enough!" Wendall shouted back. "Did I set the guards on you? Did I send you to be clubbed and whipped? No! This was Lady Alma! I may have influenced your aid, but it was she who set you to the lash and left you here to die! Think carefully about who you blame before you let your accusations carelessly fly!"

Gregory had to take a breath. His temper was getting away from him, and so was the discussion. He closed his eyes and tried to remember what he desired most... he wanted to leave. He wanted his position and power back. However, with his heart pounding and his fists clenched, he wanted revenge more.

"What can you possibly do with these stones?" Gregory asked.

"That depends on you," Wendall emphasized, holding the stone and the dagger with his outstretched hand. "I could imagine several uses of these stones. I think I could influence the guards just enough to visit their favorite whorehouse and see you escape, but how does that help me?"

It was laid before Gregory so easily, and he didn't even know it was available to him... another way out of the dungeon.

"What do you want in return?"

"I would need your assistance keeping Alma from the throne," Wendall stated bluntly, leaning forward.

Gregory had only a moment to respond. To accept this was to forgo Lady Alma's offer and very much her loyalty. Gregory thought of what he most desired and one was far above the rest.

"There is no offer I wouldn't accept to leave this place," Gregory admitted, staring at the red stone.

"Good! Let's see to these guards then." Wendall expressed as he awkwardly rose from his chair with his cane in hand.

"Would you first tell me how you came by this red stone?" Gregory asked.

"We haven't the time. We must see you from these chambers if we are to dissuade Alma's supporters."

"You tell me a sorcerer possessed a great power that commands the wills of others, and you somehow also possess a similar stone... that is far too coincidental, Wendall!"

"It is a story for another time! We must be off."

"I think it is precisely the time. By your own admission, you possessed a powerful artifact long before we even undertook the campaign against the enemy. How can I not conclude you were in league with him?" Gregory surmised.

"Do you wish to leave this place?" Wendall asked, irritated.

"More than anything," Gregory stated. "I would sacrifice much for the opportunity to walk through those doors."

"Then I warn you to desist this line of questioning!" Wendall threatened.

"How can I? You asked me to encourage war before we knew the scope of the enemy, you have the powers of the enemy clutched in your hands, and you asked me to inquire into matters treasonous to the Mid. So, I must ask. Are you the traitor I was looking for?"

Wendall had all but risen, turned his back, and hobbled a few paces, but after Gregory's last question, he stopped completely. He turned slowly with the shimmering dark green dagger clenched under his white knuckles.

"I am," Wendall replied.

Gregory was astonished.

"I asked for your aid because I wanted Malcolm to lead a host expeditiously outside his walls. He would have been surrounded, dispatched, and the city would have long been under our control. However, I was assigned to the cavalry. So, I worked within my new position to create havoc. I enlisted your aid to distract Lord Malcolm from the warfront, but you were unsuccessful in bringing Lady Alma's betrayal to light," Wendall said, pointing the blade at Gregory and slowly hobbling forward.

"I also, regrettably, assembled a scouting party of miscreants in hopes their combined shortfalls would slow the cavalry's efforts and irritate our commander. In fact, I countered Sir Kenneth at every opportunity at risk of my own life. I led the cavalry into their ambush, but they miraculously survived their encounter," Wendall remarked, stopping to shake his fists in frustration.

"Once Lord Malcolm arrived, I urged him to unwisely attack when thousands were awaiting to ambush him, but they had learned much of the enemy. So, I took any opportunity to abandon them, rendezvous with the enemy, and subvert Lord Malcolm's battle plan. That's when I learned of the Par'sha, and helped arrange one final confrontation among the Midguard, the Par'sha, and the Vechians. I was successful, you know. All the eggs were in one basket, and I had all but assured victory for my Master. However, it was not meant to be. Those barbarian scum robbed me of my victory when they let a single group of scouts free. I did not foresee it."

"Why have you done this? Why have you betrayed the Mid?" Gregory demanded.

"Because I was promised to become the Lord of the Mid. All I needed to do was see Malcolm dead and it would be under my control," Wendall answered. "My master trusted me… tested me, and I alone succeeded among my peers in the grand plan. However, the scheme itself failed, but I can still be of service."

Gregory couldn't have dreamed of what Wendall was divulging, but there were important details to uncover.

"Wait! You said Lord Malcolm was ambushed and died in battle. How did you succeed?" Gregory asked.

"I rendezvoused with the enemy, of course, and when all the soldiers had gathered, we were going to surround and kill them, but Lord Malcolm was out in the open for the taking. It was an opportunity I had been arranging for some time."

"Why didn't you murder him here at the Mid?" Gregory asked as Wendall hobbled closer and closer with the blade still firmly in his grip.

"Surrounded by his guards and knowing I would be a suspect? No, that wouldn't do. I arranged for forty thousand swords to have at him. What difference does it make if it's my knife or someone else's?"

Alma would have him flayed in the square, but question after question flooded Gregory's mind.

"You were one of the sorcerer's followers?" Gregory inquired.

"I am not. The sorcerer had a master as well... that is whom I serve," Wendall divulged. "However, I'm afraid you cannot know who they are... in fact, I have said too much as it is."

"Then where do we stand?" Gregory asked, eyeing the knife in his hands.

"I'm afraid I must rescind my offer." Wendall sneered.

Gregory's pulse pounded in his chest; Wendall was almost within striking distance now, and Gregory was defenseless.

"You pressed too hard, Gregory! That has always been your flaw. You must know everything, but you paid no price for it. However, I have a price in mind. In fact, I know how you can repay me, how I can win Lady Alma's favor… I will dispose of the traitor for her!"

Gregory's chest heaved as Wendall edged closer with the blade raised, ready to strike. As he neared, somewhere in the recesses of the dungeon, a lever shifted and a loud mechanism clicked into place. Both Gregory and Wendall recoiled at the sound as Gregory's chains fell from the ceiling, and his arms dropped. It was only Wendall who was left shocked.

"Kill him!" A voice boomed from beyond the shadows.

Gregory took no time and swung the only weapon he had available to him… his chains. With all his remaining strength, he swung his arm over and down like a smith at the forge, and the attached chain followed his arm toward Wendall's head. Wendall tried to deflect, but the chain merely wrapped around his arm and struck him from behind. He was stunned from the blow but not dispatched. Even injured, Gregory could not let Wendall recover. He swung his other arm with his remaining strength, and the chain rounded through the air and collided in full force with his head again. Wendall fell backward and Gregory followed after him, thrashing his chained wrists repeatedly onto his face until it was a pulped bloody mess, and Gregory was breathless.

With his heart racing and breath wheezing, Gregory stopped a moment and found Wendall still clung to life. Gregory wouldn't have it. Wendall lied to him, played him, and was the reason he was imprisoned. He had to die. There, on the ground, lay the green blade.

Gregory picked up the blade. In one swift motion, he thrust it into Wendall's throat and shouted like a sell-sword. The blood poured from Wendall, and for the first time in weeks, Gregory felt powerful again.

The door to the cell opened, and a woman emerged from the shadows. She was different from the last he had seen her; she had taken the step he had desired for the realm, and there was an air of royalty about her.

He knelt before her in a pool of blood. The chamber was silent.

"I have done what you asked of me," Gregory said as he regained his breath.

"You have, but I will require more," Lady Alma replied.

"What more can I do?" Gregory said, exasperated.

She walked through the puddle of blood and lifted his head with a single hand so that their eyes met. "You must remember every day for the rest of your life who gave you this opportunity and know the debt can only be repaid with your obedience."

He understood. He would serve her until his last day, but he didn't care. He would have his freedom, he would have position, and he would again have power.

"I swear it, my queen."

Chapter XXXI
The Bond

Cal and Alec were free to leave. The charges had been cleared, and they were seen as heroes of the realm. As the party and their new Par'sha companions departed the great hall, they all received thanks and congratulations from some of the wealthiest and most powerful folk the realm had to offer. They all knew Cal's name now, but more importantly, he had been proven right. The party had saved the realm, and Cal had honored his oath.

With his name cleared and the realm safe, it was time to return home with all the other Crestfolk. Many would need to rebuild, and more aid would be coming from the Mid. Yet, Cal knew no one remained of the Fork; he was returning to it because it was his home.

He planned to depart in the morning with the other Crestfolk who had started returning to the Crestwood, but they weren't the only ones. Every party member had been called home, and all looked forward to reuniting with their folk and rebuilding. As the celebrations of victory continued into the evening, Halden reconnected with his Darwishmen, Yslanna found solace in her fellow Elvians, and Su'ca raised goblets of wine with her Par'sha. All had remembered those who had gone, but they rejoiced for those who had remained, including their newfound friends. Theirs was a bond that couldn't easily be broken; their connection was forged through trials of magic.

Their last moments together came the next morning at breakfast. Halden was the first to depart with his folk to the western hills. Few words were spoken during their meal, but when the young Darwishman finally said goodbye, the sadness tugged at Cal's heart; they were finally going their separate ways.

Yslanna jumped from her chair, hugged him, and made him promise he would write. He swore he would, but asked her not to sign anything written by Alec, and the whole table broke into laughter. Halden said his farewells, hugged, and departed.

Soon after the Darwishmen departed, the Par'sha folk followed suit. Many Midfolk cheered them with a newfound respect as they did their own soldiers.

Su'ca spoke no words as she departed, but one by one, she came to each party member and pressed her forehead next to theirs. Cal had seen it only once, and, although the party were outsiders, they were honored like fellow clansmen. As she came to Cal, she promised to sing his song among the vast canyons of her people. Cal grinned, shaking his head, but Su'ca's warm gaze persisted. She pressed her forehead to his, and then she left.

With the Par'sha's departure, he knew it was time. There was no reason to delay; the party had separated. He gathered the strange belongings he had acquired during his adventure: a worn tunic of the Mid, a lifeless scepter, and a broken sorcerer's staff. In all his life, he never thought he'd obtain such things. The best idea for such odds and ends was to decorate the wall of his own tavern back home. All who'd pass through would stare up at them in wonder.

He gathered his bag and made his way down Nightingales, only to find his friends waiting to see him off. Yslanna hugged him as well, and before she could demand, he promised the letters would fly. There, she left him and reunited with her own folk while Alec and Rahuum followed him to Alice, where her saddlebags were filled with provisions for the road. Cal mounted Alice only to find both his friends had joined along.

"Thank you, my friends, but you do not need to see me to the gate," Cal remarked.

"I mean to see you safely home," Alec replied, waving to the far-off mountains. "All is well here. There is little trouble for me to instigate." He smiled like a fool, but Cal was grateful.

"And you?" Cal asked Rahuum.

The masked giant looked around slowly to see if anyone could hear them.

"I go where you go," Rahuum said, pointing at Cal.

"What do you mean?" he asked.

"You saved my life. Wherever you go, I shall follow until I can repay my debt," he maintained as Alec nodded at the gesture.

"What about our charges? What if we had been sentenced to death?" Alec inquired, but the giant shook his head.

"I had faith you'd debate the matter endlessly. I also trusted you. You would see Cal and yourself free, but if the charges went the other way, we had a plan for that as well," Rahuum admitted.

"We?" Cal asked.

"Do you think any of us would have let anything happen to either of you?" Rahuum asked.

"I guess not," Cal replied.

"You'd be right," Rahuum assured as Alec asked him the details of the escape that never was. Cal departed the Mid for a final time, and as he looked back at the mighty city, he wondered if he would ever return.

The road saw many folk returning north, but the farther north they traveled, the less often they crossed another's path. Cal continued to look for lone Vechians, but none appeared. He was grateful and knew many were directed north toward their home.

When they arrived at the Fork, it looked exactly as it had when they left. The buildings were hollow shells of what they'd been before, but as he looked over the tavern where he had met with the Par'sha Chiefs, he found the stone fireplace in decent shape and the floor salvageable. It was a good place to begin again.

Over the next few days, they salvaged what they could of the remains. Few had kept cellars beneath the ruins like Bill had, but those who did had stores to offer. There was wine in barrels, sacks of potatoes, furs ready to be traded, and tools lying on the ground ready to be put to work.

Cal's luck had risen; from the ashes of misfortune, he had the resources to build something new. The overgrowth of brush and vines might swallow the rest of the town, but he would rebuild this one piece of civilization among the northern wood.

Folk would come from the east and the west and find this single tavern and consider it salvation upon the road. It may have been a dream, but he was determined to see it become reality. So, he planted his homestead there in the ruins and lit a fire once again in the fireplace.

On the third night, they reminisced over their grand adventure and, in turn, Alma's proposal... a Kingdom of the Crescent. Cal could only imagine what shape the realm would take if all the Masters from the Crestwood accepted Lady Alma's proposal. All within the Crescent Mountains must have heard the news by now, and if the reaction from the great hall was any indication, the realm would likely have a Queen soon.

In addition to a Queen, there would be Masters quarreling for lordships throughout the realm and even for the Fork. He hoped it would be someone of worth. The best noble he met was Lord Malcolm; the worst was Sir Kenneth. There were so few good folk left in the Crestwood, he feared they might be poorly led, forgotten, or, worse, dismissed.

Cal wouldn't let that happen. Not to him, Rahuum, or anyone left. He would use his name on behalf of the Northern Crestwood to help his folk. Regardless of who the new Lord would be, they would still answer the Queen. Cal liked her. She commanded a respect like her former husband had and would do well reigning over her lords.

Like a cold breath on the back of his neck, his mind briefly thought of another who was commanded... the sorcerer Qadir. He answered to another; someone who was so powerful they controlled a sorcerer.

He gritted his teeth in his own frustration; he neglected everything Qadir revealed.

"With all the power he possessed, he was still a servant to another," he said aloud, recalling the battle on the mountain ledge.

"What did you say?" Alec asked.

"I was thinking of Qadir. When we spoke on the cliff, he revealed he had a master," Cal replied. Alec completely broke away from his conversation with Rahuum, rose to his feet and paced as he so often did.

"Why have you not mentioned this before?" Alec snapped.

"Honestly, I'd forgotten. I was just asking the sorcerer questions to buy time for someone to help me. Besides, the darkness was destroyed. Whatever plan his master had, it must have been foiled," Cal answered, pointing to the mountain where they had fought. Alec paced before the fire, letting several harrumphs pass his lips.

"Gods, what fools are we!" Alec said, rubbing his temples. "What exactly did Qadir say?"

Cal focused on that fateful evening. He remembered the caverns, the red stone roof, and the ledge where a pedestal held the fractured green orb. The sorcerer forced him down with magic, and his friends, Alec and Rahuum, came to help him.

"He spoke in riddles at first, but I pressed him to tell me something. He served someone else, but he wouldn't tell me who," Cal reflected.

"Nothing else?"

"Nothing that I recall," Cal replied while Alec let out a sigh. It was not the clue he hoped to receive as he slumped back into his seat.

"This bodes ill for our realm as well," Alec grimly replied.

"But we beat them?" Rahuum interrupted. "Their army has been scattered and their power broken."

"I wish it was that simple, my large friend," Alec professed.

"What more can this master do?" Cal argued. "We will have a Queen soon, and we have an army now as well."

"It may not be enough!" Alec maintained, shaking his head and pointing a finger in the air. "I have been concerned about why someone would invade our realm since the raids. As we uncovered more of the mystery, we found a people possessed, dark conjurers controlling them, and now an orchestrator behind the veil! There is a purpose behind these moves, and one grander than I can fathom. If someone is powerful enough to move these pawns, then they are most certainly determined enough to see the game through. I question if this war is truly over!"

Cal's heart sank. *What if this was the beginning? What if more forces would come and try to destroy their realm and people like the sorcerer had?* They would have controlled the entire realm if it hadn't been for the army and the party. It was then he was reminded of that last thing the sorcerer said about his master.

"Wait! He said one last riddle before you rescued me…" Cal shouted, closing his eyes and focusing on that evening. "Qadir would not tell me who was his master, but I had to know why they attacked us. He said, 'There is a hunger that cannot be satiated by anything less than absolute power.'"

Cal opened his eyes and found Alec frozen, reflecting on those words.

"Someone who must have total control… Who then?" Alec muttered to himself, pacing once again as Cal and Rahuum looked to each other. "They coerced an entire people to conquer another, they clearly desire the Mid for her wealth and position, and they've hidden their identity behind these elusive maneuvers. Who could've managed this feat?"

"An emperor!" Rahuum declared, pointing a finger to Alec.

"There are no emperors, and that would only solve the first part of the riddle," Cal pointed out.

Alec waved away both their thoughts, but then he stopped in his tracks and gazed back at his companions.

"No! Not an emperor... someone who desires to be an emperor!" Alec elaborated.

"I don't understand," Rahuum said as Alec gathered his thoughts.

"I'd like both of you to imagine being one of the lords of a faraway realm," Alec began. "How would you conquer another? How would you conquer them all?"

"You would gather an army and defeat the others!" Rahuum answered.

"Ah, but you have only so many soldiers. You could defeat some nations, but it would be nearly impossible to defeat all of them. Then what would you do?" Cal understood where Alec was going.

"You would use other means to conquer them? You'd threaten them, purchase them outright so they'd become your vassal, or even get another army to do your work for you," Cal answered, standing alongside Alec. "What if they didn't even know they were doing it?"

"Precisely!" Alec exclaimed, patting Cal on the shoulder. "Someone engineered this war, and they failed. Yet, why wouldn't they just use their own army against another realm?"

Rahuum scratched his large head and Cal was equally stumped.

"Maybe they couldn't use their own army…" Rahuum muttered as Alec nodded.

"But why?" Alec inquired further but the giant had no response. "Let me ask another question, then. Cal, would you let me attack our large friend here?"

"No, I would stop you…" Cal remarked as he considered Alec's reasoning. "They couldn't use their own forces because the other realms would have interfered!"

"Exactly! So, they tried another option as you have so eloquently listed. Someone manipulated a dark and powerful sorcerer to enslave an entire people and use them as an invading force, leaving them blameless if their scheme should fail. However, if they succeeded, then they would have become the new rulers of this land!"

Cal was speechless. He knew little of all the western realms and even less of the leaders there, but he had a feeling he would soon learn of them all.

"Who among the foreign lords could have manipulated Qadir?" Rahuum asked.

Cal thought about the mountain Lord of the Darwishmen, High Elvian princes, the Overlord of southern Berrenese Isles, the Croagan Kingdom, the Falhorn Kingdom, the Lords of Talon, and every other western province that sprang to mind, but then another thought persisted. Someone was powerful enough to control a sorcerer. *Who could have controlled Qadir?*

He retrieved his satchel and rummaged through the contents until he found the item. He pulled the head of the sorcerer's staff from his satchel and stared at the red crystal; the reflection pulled him in.

Qadir used this power along with the green orb to manipulate the Vechian people and almost Rahuum. Yet, it was only this stone that kept Cal under the sorcerer's control and wielded Rahuum's war hammer like a feather. This mysterious stone gave Qadir the power to control people and even things.

"What do you know of this?" Alec asked.

"We know that Qadir manipulated the Vechians, and he was controlled as well. He used this stone against Rahuum, and I wonder if his master used something similar. How else could someone so powerful become another's puppet?" Cal asked as Alec reviewed the stone.

"How did he use this red stone?" Alec inquired.

"He used his staff with this stone atop it to control me from getting up, but it was when he swirled it around the orb and sent the magic into Rahuum's eye, I knew he was trying to bewitch him just like the Vechians," Cal explained as Alec stared deep into stone.

"May I see it?" Alec asked, extending his hand. Cal nodded and handed him the red stone. Alec held it above the firelight. He weighed it and flicked at it. Every odd test perplexed him. Finally, he placed a firm hand on the red shard, the other on the head of the staff, and separated the two. As he dispensed with the staff head, he gasped.

"What is it?" Cal asked.

Alec tore away his gaze slowly.

"It has a round stone base like the green shards! It's but a piece of a larger whole... a shard!" Alec answered with trembling hands.

Neither spoke; only the fire crackled in the night.

"There is a base-stone!" Cal inferred.

"Yes," Alec confirmed.

Cal sank onto a log like someone had knocked the wind out of him. They had fought hard, lost many, and won, but it may as well have been for naught. There was another magic orb in the world, and under its control was a man who desired nothing more than total power over all the world.

"What do we do?" Rahuum asked, breaking the silence.

Cal exhaled a long breath. They had little clues left, but as he looked back at his loyal friends, he found hope. It was when the darkness came that he left to find others like himself… Good folk who stood against it. Thousands of them came together, and they had beaten back the enemy. They had accomplished remarkable things, and once again they sat under the night sky unafraid of the dark.

"First, we rebuild and live in peace. But if our home is threatened again by the enemy, then we will be there to stand against them."

They both smiled back at him under the starry sky.

Author Bio

This is the first book written by Henry Cantleberry. He is a husband, father, amateur guitar player, songwriter, avid gamer, and lover of fantasy. He has a Bachelors in Philosophy and resides in the Pacific Northwest.